Michelle Rawlins is an award-winning freelance journalist with over twenty-five years' experience working in print and digital media. After learning her trade, Michelle began her freelance career writing for national newspapers and women's magazines concentrating on real-life stories – living by the mantra: 'It's always the most ordinary people who have the most extraordinary stories.' Michelle currently teaches journalism at the University of Sheffield.

She is the author of *Women of Steel* and *The Steel Girls* was her debut novel. You can follow Michelle on Twitter @ Mrawlins1974 and on Facebook/MichelleRawlinsAuthor.

The Steel Girls series

The Steel Girls
Christmas Hope for the Steel Girls
Steel Girls on the Home Front
Steel Girls at War

Steel Girls
at War

Michelle Rawlins

ONE PLACE. MANY STORIES

HQ
An imprint of HarperCollins*Publishers* Ltd
1 London Bridge Street
London SE1 9GF

www.harpercollins.co.uk

HarperCollins*Publishers*
Macken House, 39/40 Mayor Street Upper,
Dublin 1, D01 C9W8, Ireland

This edition 2023

1
First published in Great Britain by
HQ, an imprint of HarperCollins*Publishers* Ltd 2023

ISBN: 978-0-00-859851-8

For my two wonderful children Archie & Tilly,
who bring me so much joy.

Chapter 1

Saturday, 1 June 1940

Nancy strolled down Prince Street towards her mid-terrace house spurred on by her plans for the following day, to cook up a big Sunday roast, then take the kids roller skating, before an evening curled up on the couch. Feeling buoyed from the night out with the girls, she was determined not to let her constant worries about Bert, whom she hadn't heard from in months, ruin the rest of the weekend with Billy and Linda. More than anything, with their daddy away and Nancy working all the hours God sent, her children deserved at least one quality day with their mum.

Her head full of ideas, Nancy hadn't noticed the uniformed man stood outside her front door.

It was only as she made to turn into the gennel between her house and her neighbour's that the arresting sight stopped Nancy in her tracks.

'Mrs Edwards?' Asked the solemn, older-looking man who was dressed in khaki with a matching beret.

'Yes,' Nancy croaked, the sound emanating from her suddenly dry throat barely audible. She looked at the officer, but her eyes fell to the sinister brown envelope he was holding. *It can't be. There's been no shooting stars*, she told herself. Wasn't that what the women in the canteen said? For every shooting star, another soldier had fallen. No. She would know, instinctively, if something had happened to her Bert. She might not have received a letter for weeks and weeks, but there could be any number of plausible explanations for that.

But as the man smiled at her weakly through his bushy, greying moustache, his eyes full of compassion and sympathy, an overwhelming feeling of dread consumed Nancy.

Then to confirm her worst fears, the man said gently, 'I'm afraid I have some bad news.'

Her mind began to whirl at a rate of knots and everything before her eyes began to get darker.

'No,' Nancy gasped, the word catching in her throat. The ground beneath her no longer felt solid and her legs started to give way.

'Easy does it,' the officer said, as he reached for Nancy's arm to support her. 'Why don't we get you inside?'

'Bad news. You said it was bad news,' Nancy whispered, her voice trembling.

Panic coursed through her as she desperately tried to steady herself, holding onto the man. *Bert, don't leave me now,* she silently pleaded. *We need you. We all need you. Billy and Linda, they need you. You're their daddy. Their everything.*

Nancy was only just coping as it was. She'd clung to the

hope; no, it was a cemented, non-negotiable fact, in her own mind at least, that Bert *was* coming home. It might not be today, or tomorrow, or even next month, but one day, he would be by her side again. The man of the house, Billy and Linda's daddy, her loving and attentive husband. This was what Nancy had clung to for the last eight months. It's what had got her through each day, enabled her to put one foot in front of the other, paint on a smile and tell her children with conviction that everything would be all right. Nancy couldn't, no, she wouldn't allow her determination for a brighter future to be broken by this officious stranger.

'Mrs Edwards.'

The words, once again, pierced Nancy's well-built defences. Her barriers, which had kept her upright for months, were crumbling. The reality of this godforsaken war drowning out her fragile threads of optimism.

'Is he okay? Please tell me he's okay,' was all she could manage, her stomach now churning, as she quietly prayed her husband, the man she loved with all her heart, was still alive. The alternative didn't bear thinking about. But here he was, the man with the brown envelope, holding her upright. Nancy wasn't daft. They didn't send sombre, official-looking senior officers, carrying a letter, for nothing.

'Why don't we go inside?' he suggested kindly. 'I think you need to sit down.'

No! This was it. The confirmation.

'Sit down?' Nancy asked, her voice no more than a murmur.

'I just think you might be more comfortable. I can get you a cup of tea.'

Tea. A balm to the soul. Restorative. Healing. Nancy didn't want any of it. She wanted Bert. She wanted him alive. She wanted him now.

'Come on. Let me take you inside, Mrs Edwards,' the officer urged.

Shaking her head, Nancy stood stock-still, her feet firmly cemented to the ground. If she moved, if she allowed herself to be ushered into the house, he would have to tell her. He would have to explain what was in that ominous brown envelope, the ones that never revealed anything happy. Maybe that's why they were brown, the shade of gloom; how clever of whoever thought of the colour to coordinate the two. Just like autumn leaves, indicating summer was over and winter was looming. Dark and long cold nights ahead. No, Nancy couldn't face that. She just couldn't. She wouldn't allow the end of a season, a chapter, the happiest years of her life to be brought to such an abrupt stop.

If she stayed rooted to the spot, frozen in time, nothing would change. Everything would be just how it was. Bert would still be doing the job he'd felt compelled to sign up for after war had been declared. She might have hated it, despised the fact he was hundreds of miles away from their little family, but he was alive. And yes, she worried about him, but he would still be out there, *doing the right thing*. A new letter would arrive soon. A letter from Bert. One hadn't come for weeks, but they were probably just held up

4

somewhere in transit. Nothing to worry about. They would all arrive in a cluster, tied with string, any day now. Isn't that what she had been telling herself? Isn't that what her friends had said too? Betty, Doris, Dolly, even Frank. That's what they'd said. They were all so much more logical than she was. Wiser, more astute. They must be right. There was a time when Betty hadn't received a letter from her William for weeks on end, but it had turned out okay. The letters had just gone missing. It was a simple explanation. Logical. No need to assume the worst.

So, this grave man, propping her up, stopping her from falling, shattering into a thousand tiny pieces on the floor – he was wrong. Maybe he wasn't even real? Maybe this was all a bad dream, and she was going to wake up any second now.

Twenty minutes earlier, she'd been in The Welly with her friends from Vickers, reminiscing about how she and Bert had first met and fallen in love. Their chance meeting on the tram when he was working as a conductor, and she didn't have enough change in her purse for the fare. How he'd paid for it himself, asked her out on a date . . .

'Please, Mrs Edwards.' There he was again. The man trying to burst her bubble of happiness, pierce all her hopes and dreams.

But then her mind drifted to the weeks of sleepless nights, counting the hours until dawn, tormenting herself with a thousand different, and harrowing, scenarios. Bert held by German troops or being tortured for information – she'd heard those things were common practice in war. Or maybe he was injured, so badly hurt he couldn't write. What if he'd been abandoned by his platoon, left alone to fend for himself, in a split-second decision during an assault by Jerry.

The idea of him coming to any harm had haunted her through the wee hours of the night, infiltrated her every thought, prevented her eyes from closing. At least when it was daylight, she had jobs to do, things to keep her mind busy. Billy and Linda needed their breakfast, before she dropped them off with her neighbour, Doris. Then she would go to work and embark on a gruelling, labour-intensive day at Vickers, but it kept her busy. It helped to take her mind off things. But as she sat thirty feet in the air, in the heavens of the factory, Bert always crept back into her thoughts, the worry about where he was in France and if he was safe. The news in the papers and on the wireless reporting on the small ships making the dangerous trip across the English Channel to Dunkirk, to rescue the Allied troops who were pinned against the Flanders shoreline, forced to retreat after Hitler had taken France. Yachts, fishing craft and paddle steamers, could they really get all those men to safety? How on earth could they make that journey with the Luftwaffe overhead? It was nonsensical, a death trap!

'No!' Nancy cried again, only this time the heart-wrenching guttural protest that echoed down Prince Street brought the terrifying reality sharply back into focus. All hope faded. This wasn't a dream. It wasn't even a nightmare.

No one was about to tell her everything was okay. She knew that now.

Nancy's knees buckled. Her whole body began to crumple. The officer caught her just in the nick of time and gently ushered her, in her dazed state, into the small kitchen and to a chair, next to the wooden family dining table.

'Can I get you a drink, a cup of tea maybe?'

Nancy shook her head. Nothing would help in this moment.

Summoning up all the courage she could muster, Nancy took a deep breath, as she firmly placed one hand in the other, to stop them shaking. 'Just tell me. Is my husband alive?'

The man, his kind eyes full of concern, sat down next to Nancy, the envelope placed conspicuously on his knee.

'I need to know,' Nancy asserted, temporarily recovering her voice. Despite how much she really didn't want to know, having lived on the principle 'no news is good news' for the month, she knew deep down, in her heart of hearts, she had to understand what had happened with Bert. Although living in limbo had meant she had avoided any seismic life-changing blows, Nancy knew she couldn't carry on like that forever.

'Firstly, please let me introduce myself,' the well-spoken man started. 'My name is Captain Samuel Clark. I am one of the senior officers in your husband's battalion.'

Nancy stared at him. She didn't need his name, but she did wonder how many times this man had been charged with delivering bad news. Was he used to it now? But then, how could he be? Only two months ago, everyone was still talking about the 'Phoney War', nothing was happening. Yes, there had been the odd false alarm, causing people to take cover under the stairs and in air-raid shelters, and warnings to carry gas masks at all times, but nothing sinister had happened. But then after the invasions of Czechoslovakia, then Norway, Denmark, Luxembourg and now France, all that had changed. Maybe Captain Clark had become used to delivering brown envelopes, had his announcement finessed, could cut off his emotions. How, in that moment, Nancy envied his stoic, perfectly composed demeanour.

'Please,' she reiterated, her whole body cold, despite the warm June evening. 'I don't think I can bear it. I need to know.'

'I'm sorry. Of course.' Captain Clark nodded. 'In this envelope, it states your husband is missing in action.'

Nancy clenched her eyes shut, her fingernails sharply digging into the palms of her hands. This was it, the news she had been dreading. This godforsaken war had finally caught up with her.

'Where?' was all Nancy could manage. *Norway? France?* She assumed the latter, but in all honestly, she didn't really know.

'France,' the officer confirmed. 'As I'm sure you are well aware, the Allied troops have been forced to retreat to Dunkirk in the last week. We had men all over the country.

Not all of them made it back to the Flanders coastline. I'm afraid Bert was one of them.'

'Do you think he's . . .' But Nancy couldn't actually say the word. To say it would make it real, and she wasn't ready for that. Not now. Not ever.

'We don't know is the honest answer. Our best hope is that your husband has either taken shelter somewhere, or he has been captured and is being held as a prisoner of war.'

'A prisoner?' Nancy gasped. 'What does that mean? What will happen to him?'

'As I said, we can't know anything for sure at this stage. If he's hiding out somewhere, he may be able to make contact. That's the best-case scenario.'

'But the worst case. What happens then?'

'Unfortunately, I have no concrete answers for you but please, Mrs Edwards, have hope. There is no evidence to show your husband has been killed.'

'Yet,' Nancy whispered. 'No evidence yet.'

Captain Clark didn't answer.

It was all the confirmation Nancy needed. No one knew where Bert was, and even more horrifying, they had no idea if he was dead or alive.

'Nancy, whatever is it?' Doris asked, alarmed as she took one look at her friend who had just appeared in her kitchen, her blotchy face sodden with tears.

'Where's Billy and Linda?' Nancy wiped her cheeks with the palms of her hands. She couldn't let them see her like this. Until she knew what had happened to Bert, she had to keep things as normal as possible for her children.

'They're in bed. I thought you'd taken my advice and stayed out with the girls, so they are topping and tailing with Joe and Alice. You don't mind, do you?'

Nancy looked at her watch. It was nearly ten o'clock. She hadn't realized it had got so late.

'No, no. It's probably for the best. I don't want them seeing me like this. Thank you.'

'Are you going to come and sit down?' Doris asked, concern etched across her face. 'And tell me what on earth has happened?'

'Oh, Doris,' Nancy sobbed. 'I don't think I can bear to say it.' After Captain Clark had left, the tears she had been holding back finally erupted. Nancy thought they would never stop. She had just about managed to pull herself together, assuming she would have to collect the children, but Doris's well-intentioned question had set her off again.

'Come on now, luv,' Doris soothed, putting her arm around Nancy's slender back and encouraging her to sit down. 'Whatever it is. You can tell me, but first let me get you a drink.'

Instead of picking up the kettle, Doris opened the cupboard next to the range and pulled out a bottle of Rémy Martin and two crystal glasses. Nancy tried not to dwell on the fact that they were the very ones Doris and George had received as wedding presents.

After pouring two generous measures, Doris came back

to the table. 'Have a sip of this, luv, and then you can tell me what has left you so upset.' Bewildered, she watched Nancy wrap her hands around the glass and slowly bring it to her lips. A few hours earlier, she'd waved Nancy off for a night out with her friends. Doris knew she'd felt guilty for leaving Billy and Linda after working all week and had taken some persuading before coming around to the idea that the outing would do her the world of good. She didn't know Nancy's work friends that well, but she'd only ever heard nice things about them, and couldn't imagine they would ever do or say anything to upset her.

'Is it Bert?' Doris asked tentatively. She knew Nancy had been fretting for weeks. The lack of letters and any news had really taken its toll.

'Yes.' Nancy managed to nod between sobs.

'Oh, luv. What's happened? Have you had a letter?'

'Yes, but it's worse than that.'

'What do you mean, luv?' Doris prompted, now more worried about what had got Nancy in this state.

'A telegram. One of Bert's senior officers was waiting for me as I got home.'

'What did it say?'

'It's just too awful,' Nancy said, carefully placing the glass down on the table, bringing her hands to her face.

'Oh, Nancy,' Doris gasped, once again on her feet and by her friend's side. Her late husband, George, may not have been a soldier, but she knew there were only a couple of reasons telegrams were hand-delivered. 'He's not . . .' But, like Nancy, Doris couldn't bring herself to say the words.

'No. Well, they don't think so. Not at the moment at any rate.'

Doris listened as Nancy repeated what Captain Clark had told her.

'He could be anywhere,' Nancy cried. 'And no one can tell me if he's alive or not.'

Instinctively, Doris wrapped her arms around Nancy, letting her friend's head flop onto her chest.

'It's going to be all right. I promise, whatever happens, we will find a way through this together,' Doris soothed, stroking Nancy's mass of blonde curls.

'But what if it isn't? What if they can't find him and he doesn't come home? How can I ever tell Billy and Linda? They would be heartbroken. They love Bert so much. I don't think I'm strong enough to give them the support they will need. And what sort of mother am I? I'm working all the hours God sends at the factory. I always thought I'd stop when Bert came home, but now I could be slaving away at Vickers forever, hardly ever seeing Billy and Linda.'

And with that, another avalanche of tears erupted from the corners of Nancy's already red and swollen eyes.

'Now stop that,' Doris said firmly. 'You're thinking too far ahead and jumping to all sorts of conclusions. We need to take one day at a time. There's no point thinking about the ifs and maybes yet. We have to deal with what we know.'

'It's just I know what it feels like to be scared you will never see a parent again.'

'What do yer mean, luv?'

'My dad. He went off to fight in the Great War when I was twelve and months would pass with no letters and we had no idea if he was dead or alive. My mum tried to hide it, but she was a right mess and I would lay awake night after night willing him to come home. My big sister Lucy tried to be brave, but I would catch her crying too. More often than not, we would sleep in the same bed, just so we could comfort one another.'

'But your dad came back, didn't he?'

'Yes.' Nancy nodded. 'About a month after the war finally ended, he walked through the back door one day. We had no idea he was coming.'

'Well then, luv, that just shows yer, you have to have hope.'

'Do you really think Bert will be okay?'

'I don't know the answer to that, luv,' Doris said honestly, as Nancy sat back up and looked at her. 'But what I do know is your Bert isn't the sort to give up easily. He's a fighter and he loves you and those kiddies with all his heart, so will be doing everything he can to get back home to you all.'

If the truth be known, Doris didn't know what to think. The idea of Bert being *missing in action* sounded ominous, but Nancy didn't need to hear that right now. What she needed was a reason to get up every morning, to keep going and to never give up. More than ever, her friend needed hope, and she was going to do everything she could to keep Nancy's spirits lifted.

'I hope you're right,' Nancy whispered, as she tried to stop the stream of tears that had formed rivulets down her cheeks, streaking her make-up.

'Until you receive any news to the contrary, you can't give up on your Bert. Besides which, imagine how cross he would be.'

This thought brought a hint of a smile to Nancy's face. She knew Doris was right. Bert was always the positive one. His glass half full, never half empty. She needed to try to at least think like he would. Bert would never give up on her or Billy and Linda. Doris was right, if he was alive, he would be doing everything he could to get home.

'What will I tell the kids? Linda is already asking every two minutes why Bert hasn't written to us for weeks on end.'

Doris took a moment before answering, taking a sip of brandy. She'd always gone by the philosophy that honesty is the best policy, but the reality was Nancy didn't know what the truth was. Yes, Bert could have been killed. From what she'd heard on the BBC news on the wireless, the Battle of France had been brutal and despite the Allied troops putting up a good fight, there was no denying the fact, Hitler was succeeding in taking the country.

'I think,' she said hesitantly, 'you have to think carefully about how you answer their questions. They aren't daft and pick up on more than we think. Maybe, when they next ask, explain the war is preventing letters getting through, and Bert is very busy. That's all you need to say to keep them from asking more questions for the time being.'

'Oh, Doris. You always know exactly what to do. I wish I was more like you, or Betty. You are both so strong and logical.'

'Now don't be putting yerself down,' Doris gently chastised. 'You are doing a grand job. You've got this far, and we will all do everything we can to make sure we get you through whatever happens next, but you have to have hope. Without it, you are no use to anyone.'

Nancy nodded, too exhausted and wrung out to speak. As she took the last sip of brandy from her glass, she just hoped Doris was right, but was struggling to fight off the worry that she would never see her beloved Bert again.

Chapter 2

Monday, 3 June 1940

'I just don't know whether I'll ever set eyes on him again,' Nancy said, fighting with all her might to hold back her tears that had, once again, been threatening to erupt all morning.

Nancy had looked pale since she'd arrived at Vickers, as if she had the weight of the world on her shoulders, but hadn't had a chance to tell her friends before the morning hooter had rung out what had happened after she'd left them on Saturday night. Now as they sat and ate their dinner together, Nancy had repeated what Bert's senior officer had told her.

Everyone listened in shocked silence and the gang of workers all looked utterly aghast at the news they'd just heard. Each one of them had truly believed that no harm would come to Bert and, like the rest of their menfolk, that he would eventually come home and life would return to normal.

It was the first bad news any of them had been dealt since the start of the war. But as they took in how visibly shaken and distraught Nancy was, the reality of Hitler's bombastic actions began to hit home, and an increasingly unfamiliar feeling of uncertainty hung over them all like a sinister and dark cloud.

Patty, who was still holding her untouched sandwich, glanced at Archie. She didn't really understand what was happening with the war, but she suddenly felt very lucky the man she loved was by her side.

Betty, too, was feeling uncharacteristically shaken. From the moment her William had announced he wanted to join the RAF she had worried about the consequences and had spent countless nights fretting something awful would happen to him. Now as she and her group of friends digested what Nancy had revealed, the weight of this war hung much heavier on her shoulders. What Nancy was now enduring was exactly what Betty had feared.

'I'm so sorry, luv,' Dolly said, breaking the stunned silence around the table, pouring Nancy a second cuppa and adding a heaped teaspoon of sugar. She had been terrified a naval officer would knock on her door and deliver a telegram concerning one of her boys, who were out at sea. 'What a bloody horrible shock for you,' she added. 'I don't suppose you have managed to get much sleep this weekend. Or is that a daft question?'

'Not really. I can't have had more than a couple of hours at most. Believe me, it wasn't for a want of trying. I tried, I really did, but every time I closed my eyes, I started imagining Bert in some awful situation. I just keep envisaging him in a ditch somewhere, badly injured and miles away from anyone who can help. Then, the odd time I did drop off, I'd wake up shaking, convinced Bert was . . . Well, you know what I mean.'

'That's awful, luv,' Dolly said kindly. 'How are Billy and Linda?'

'I haven't told them anything yet. Doris had them overnight on Saturday, which I was grateful for, as I was in no fit state to look after them. But in a way, it was harder going home to an empty house. It just made me think about how our family is falling apart at the seams. Then, yesterday, I just about held it together while I cooked them a roast. I'm sorry I didn't get to The Skates, Dolly.'

'Gosh, don't you be fretting about that, duck. If I'd have known, I would have taken your two for you.'

'It's okay. The thought of them not being next to me would have made me worse and I'd have had too much time on my own to worry.'

Dolly could certainly relate to that. If it wasn't for her granddaughters, both the spitting image of their dads, she would have felt very lost in life. Their very presence was her something concrete to hold onto, and ensured she never gave up hope.

Frank, who was also sat at the end of the table in the busy factory canteen with Archie, discreetly folded his *Daily Mirror* and moved it out of sight. The paper was full of stories about Hitler combatting France. Despite the reported success of Operation Dynamo, the mission to rescue soldiers from the now-taken country was making the headlines. The last thing Nancy needed to see was the struggle the Allied troops were still facing, not only getting to Dunkirk, but also the logistical difficulties in transporting those battalions back across the Channel to England. The Luftwaffe had been relentless in their deathly airstrikes across the French shoreline, targeting the Navy's ships that were desperately trying to help carry troops to Dover. Hundreds of thousands of soldiers from the British Expeditionary Force were relying on small ships to take them home. Thankfully, by some miracle and the incredible determination of man's ability to rise to the occasion, so many of the soldiers were back on home soil, but there were still thousands waiting to be rescued. And from what Nancy had just explained, Bert hadn't even managed to get to Dunkirk.

No wonder she's out of her mind, Frank thought to himself. *The poor bloke could be anywhere.* Like Bert's commanding officer had said, they just had to hope he was in hiding or been captured by German troops, who would have to follow protocol on how prisoners of war should be treated. It was well known that some were more ruthless than others, and more often than not, Allied troops were at the hands of their unpredictable goodwill. *Please, God, keep Bert safe*, Frank thought, his heart going out to Nancy, who looked so fragile as though she might shatter into a million pieces at any moment.

'Nancy, you know we will always be here for you,' Betty said, turning to her friend and desperately trying to hide her own shock at the news. After her fiancé, William, had signed up, she remembered, all too clearly, how worried she'd been when not a single letter from him had arrived for over a month. And even now, while he was relatively safe, training to be a RAF pilot in Canada, there still wasn't a day that went by when she didn't fret or get jittery about what the future held, especially as the war was now picking up pace.

'Thank you.' Nancy nodded gratefully. 'I just want to know Bert is alive. I can't imagine . . .' But with that, tears began to roll down her cheeks.

'C'mon, luv,' Dolly said, doing an admirable job of disguising her own fears and determined to stay positive for Nancy's sake. She didn't know for sure, but there was something her sons had both said in their last letters that made her think they were in one of the Navy destroyers, which were part of the Dunkirk rescue operation. The idea of them being in the open sea, visible to Jerry, had made her blood run cold. She wasn't daft and knew they too would be a prime target for the Luftwaffe.

Passing Nancy a large white hankie from the pocket in her blue-and-white gingham apron, she added: 'I know nothing I can say can make you feel better, but we are here if you need anything.'

'Thank you. I'm sorry for being such a misery guts. I promise, I don't mean to be. I'll try to get myself together.'

'Now, enough of that,' Dolly admonished, her matter-of-fact persona, which helped her cope with her own worries, shining through. 'The fact that you managed to get out of bed this morning, sort those little kiddies out and get here is an achievement in itself. There aren't many that would be able to manage even a fraction of that.'

'I'll second that,' Frank added, hoping to bolster one of his best crane drivers. 'And if you need to take any time off, I can speak to the gaffers. I'm sure they would understand.'

'Thanks, Frank, but I couldn't leave you all in the lurch. We're already overrun with orders, and besides which, I think I'd go mad at home, staring at my own four walls all day.'

'I know what you mean, duck, but if it all gets too much, the offer's there. All you have to do is say.'

'For what it's worth,' Betty interjected, 'I think you are better off working too. I know it's not quite the same, but when I was worried about William, I'd have gone half-crazy if I didn't have this job to keep my mind busy. It still keeps me on an even keel now. Besides which, we'll all look after you when you are here.'

'You are all so kind,' Nancy said, dabbing her eyes with Dolly's lavender-scented hankie, aware of how blotchy her face must look. 'I really don't know what I'd do without you all.' Nancy was once again reminded that ever since Bert had left, nine months earlier, to go off to war, her newfound friends at Vickers had continually kept her buoyed, surrounding her with love and support when she needed it the most.

'That's what friends are for,' Betty reiterated, gently

patting her friend's arm. 'You have and would do the same for any of us.'

'I just don't feel as strong as you all are,' Nancy confessed. 'I'm frightened I'm going to fall apart at any moment, but worse than that, I'm scared I won't be strong enough to protect Billy and Linda. And they need me more than ever now. It will do them no good if I end up in a heap on the floor.'

'Oh, Nancy,' said Josie, who had come to clear up the mugs. 'I promise you, that's not going to happen. I know it's hard to believe right now, while you are in the thick of it, but you can and will get through this.'

'I'm really not so sure.'

'Of course you can. You're a mum, and that alone gives you an unbreakable strength, one you don't even know you are capable of.'

'She's right, duck,' Dolly added. 'There's summat built into us when we give birth to our little 'uns that makes us determined to always be there and protect our kids, no matter how hard life gets.'

Gathering up a couple of empties, Josie turned to Nancy. 'Dolly's right. Most of the time it comes naturally, but sometimes life becomes so hard, you can't always see it and need a bit of a helping hand. Don't you remember how you told me last Christmas how I had to keep going for my girls? That I had to keep fighting, despite how low and poorly I felt.'

Nancy nodded, as she recalled how their chat, just the

two of them, one mum to another, had encouraged Josie to go and see the doctor after she thought she was dying and it would be her final Christmas with her husband, Alf, and their daughters, Daisy, Polly and Annie.

'Well,' Josie added, 'I was convinced there was no point in carrying on. I'd mentally prepared myself I wasn't for this world any longer and I was a gonner, but it was you who convinced me not to give up and go to hospital. And look at me now.

'I suppose what I'm trying to say is, somewhere inside us, if we look hard enough, we can always find a way through. And Nancy,' she said, touching her friend's shoulder, 'I know you can.'

Once again, Nancy anxiously pinched her fingers tightly into her palms, her now bitten-down nails no longer leaving an imprint. Subconsciously she firmly rubbed her index fingers against her rough, hard-worn thumbs, something she had found herself doing a lot on Saturday night. She wanted to believe her friends. She was desperate to believe them, but no matter how hard she tried to convince herself, she really didn't know how she could muster up the strength to hold it together.

Sensing Nancy's trepidation, Betty was already thinking about how she could help her friend, knowing, now more than ever, they were all going to have to support her through the coming weeks and months.

'We're going to get you through this,' Betty assured her friend. 'I promise.'

Chapter 3

'Are you sure we can't persuade you to come for a drink, Nancy?' Betty asked.

'I promise we won't be late, and Hattie is coming too. I'm sure she would love to see you,' Patty added, desperate to do something to lift her friend's spirits.

'I really wouldn't be much company,' Nancy sighed, as the group of women gathered outside gate three. 'Besides which, with all the extra overtime I've done this week, I need to spend some time with Billy and Linda. I hate putting on Doris if I don't have to.'

'You don't need to explain.' Daisy smiled empathetically. She recalled only too well how she would dash home from work to look after her two younger sisters during her mum's illness and help out her aunt, who had stepped in to hold the fort.

'Maybe next time,' Nancy replied, trying to be polite. If the truth be known, though, despite how much she knew friends were only trying to help, the last thing she wanted to do was paint on a brave face and try to be jolly. It would be hard enough pretending everything was okay in front of Billy and Linda. She'd barely slept a wink since the officer had turned up on her doorstep last Saturday and just wanted to curl up on the couch with the kids and listen to them chatter about their week for a dose of normality.

'Well, get some sleep if you can,' Dolly said. 'And please eat.' It hadn't gone unnoticed how Nancy had only picked at her sandwiches all week, and even today, after Dolly had served her up an extra big portion of her Friday special, mince and onion pie, she'd only managed a few mouthfuls.

'I'll do my best.' Nancy knew she looked pale and gaunt, but every time she tried to swallow even the smallest morsel of food, her throat closed and went as dry as parchment. Doris hadn't commented on how sickly Nancy looked but had sent her home with a pan of pureed vegetable soup a few days earlier. 'Maybe just try a small mugful or take some in a flask for yer snap at work,' she'd suggested kindly. 'Pretend it's a cup of tea.'

Nancy knew her friends were just trying to help, but all she wanted was to hide away from everyone, so she didn't have to be brave or pretend she was coping. Bert hadn't left her thoughts for a single second. He was on her mind constantly and the pain was like nothing she'd ever felt before. It was as though there was a big gaping hole in her heart and until she knew her husband was safe, it was impossible to seal it back together.

'Anyway, I better be off,' Nancy said.

'Okay, luv,' Betty said. 'We'll see you tomorrow. Only one morning at work left, then a full day off.'

'I can't chuffin' wait,' Patty harked up. 'I swear these weeks got longer, with each one that passes.' But as the words left her mouth, she immediately regretted it. Every day must feel like a lifetime to Nancy right now, as she waited for news about Bert.

But if Nancy did pick up on the innocent but ill-thought comment, she didn't say anything. 'See you all tomorrow.' She feebly waved as she set off down Brightside Lane, the dazzling afternoon sunshine a sharp contrast to Nancy's heavy demeanour as she trundled down the cobbled street, her shoulders slumped.

Fifteen minutes later, Dolly, Betty, Daisy, Patty and Hattie were sat around a table in their normal corner of The Wellington, each nursing a drink.

'Cheers,' Patty said, raising her glass of lemonade.

'Not long now until you join us in having a port and lemon or a shandy,' Hattie replied, raising her drink as they all clinked their glasses together.

'What's this?' Betty asked immediately. 'Is it your eighteenth birthday soon?'

'It is! On the thirteenth of July.'

'Well, that is definitely cause for a celebration,' Betty said.

'I'm hoping Archie is going to organize something! I've dropped enough hints.'

'I'm sure he will.' Hattie laughed. 'It's such a big occasion. He's bound to make a big deal about it and go to loads of effort.'

'Do you think?'

'Definitely,' Hattie enthused. 'Archie adores the bones of you. He will want to spoil you.'

'We should definitely do something special,' Dolly said. 'Heaven knows we all need something to smile about.'

'Do you think it's appropriate?' Patty asked, the excitement in her voice replaced by concern.

'What do you mean, luv?' Dolly asked.

'Well, just with Nancy. It might feel a bit selfish to celebrate when she's in such a state, worrying about Bert.'

Taking a sip of her drink, Dolly frowned. 'I know what you mean,' she said, thinking over Patty's concerns. 'But, I think she would feel worse knowing you had cancelled your birthday arrangements on her behalf, especially a big one like your eighteenth.'

'Do yer think?'

'I do,' Dolly confirmed. 'Nancy might not be up for celebrating, but she certainly wouldn't want you to change your plans, I'm sure of it.'

Patty looked to Betty for reassurance. The last thing she would want to do is cause Nancy any more upset, even if it was a milestone celebration.

'I agree,' Betty replied. 'I can't imagine, for a single second, she'd want you to miss out.'

'Sorry. Has something happened?' Hattie interrupted, oblivious to the events of the weekend before.

'Nancy's not so good,' Betty answered, taking a sip of her small glass of port and lemon, before explaining the news about Bert.

'I can't even begin to imagine what she's going through,' Hattie proclaimed. 'What an awful worry.'

'It is.' Dolly nodded and, once again, thought about her own two sons, whom she hadn't heard from for a couple of weeks. Determined to stay positive, she reminded herself of the age-old mantra, no news is good news. If something was wrong, then surely, she too would have had a visit from one of their senior officers. No good would come of fretting about something that might or might not have happened. 'And John?' she asked Hattie, conscious he was part of the Allied forces in France too. 'Have you heard anything?'

'I have, actually! I got a letter this morning. He's back in England and is hoping to get some leave soon and come home for a couple of days.'

'Oh, Hattie, that's wonderful. Why didn't you say sooner?' Patty trilled.

'I was just keen to hear how Nancy was. I knew she would be out of her mind with worry. All the terrifying news about Dunkirk. I know it's a bit naive, I suppose I was just hoping all those troops would just get home in one piece. I really am sorry to hear about Bert.'

'I know, luv,' Dolly said, lifting her half pint of pale ale to her lips, for Dutch courage. 'But it's great news about John. Did he say much else in his letter?'

'Not really,' Hattie said. 'Just that he'd been rescued by

a fishing craft. I got the impression he'd written it in a rush to get it in the post. I suppose he knew I'd be desperately waiting for news. Poor Nancy, her worries seem a million times worse.'

'It's all relative,' Betty agreed. 'But you're right. She's going to need all the support we can offer her.'

'She is that, luv,' Dolly added, hoping if she could concentrate on Nancy, it would keep her own mind busy.

'M' mom would be happy to have Billy and Linda over to play with my brother and sisters,' Patty suggested.

'Same here,' Daisy said. 'It's the least we can do after all the kindness Nancy showed our family last Christmas, and if it helps lighten the load a little, we'd be more than happy to help.'

'I'm sure Nancy will be very touched,' Betty commented. 'My only worry is, she won't want to spend a minute longer that she has to away from those kiddies. I know she feels so guilty relying on Doris to have Billy and Linda, before and after school, and on a Saturday, and even more so now, what with all the additional overtime.'

'You're right, luv,' Dolly said. 'We need to think of a way to help Nancy that involves the kids too.'

'I did have something in mind actually,' Betty replied, popping her glass down on the table.

'Of course you have!' Patty exclaimed good-heartedly.

'We wouldn't expect anything less,' Dolly added, chuckling.

'Do tell,' Daisy said, once again in awe of her friend who was always thinking of ways to help others.

'It's really nothing too dramatic,' Betty answered modestly.

'Well, come on then. Spit it out,' Patty ordered.

'All right.' Betty laughed, holding her hands up in defence. 'I know there's nothing we can do to get Bert home, and no matter what we do, Nancy will still always worry, but I wondered if we could set up a rota to help her out, and include Billy and Linda, of a weekend.'

'How were you thinking it would work, luv?' Dolly asked.

'My thoughts were, we could set up a little system, to invite Nancy and the kids over for tea of a weekend. It means we could ensure she is eating properly and hopefully she can relax a little. Between us we could keep Billy and Linda entertained, and that way Nancy won't feel like she's permanently got to put on a brave face. I've already spoken to Ivy about it, and she was all for it. I think it brought back memories of how she struggled during the Great War. I don't like to pry but I've always got the impression she had a pretty torrid time of it. Anyway, she was adamant she wanted to help Nancy.'

Dolly also recalled the horrors of the last war all too clearly. How any power-hungry dictator thought any good could come of sending hundreds of thousands of soldiers into battle against one another was beyond her. No good ever came of it and never would.

'I think that's a great idea,' she said. 'This war is testing us all but take it from me, having yer pals nearby to lean on is a huge comfort.' From her own experience, Dolly knew that what Nancy needed right now, even if she didn't realize it herself, was a circle of friends to keep her upright. They might not be able to change the outcome but having a shoulder to cry on or a distraction from your own fears went a long way to helping you get through each day.

'I'm glad you think it's a good idea,' Betty replied. 'I was racking my mind, trying to think of something useful, and this was the best I could come up with. I don't want Nancy to feel like she is a charity case, as we all know that will only make her feel worse. So, if we just sort it out among ourselves to take it in turns, and for it to seem quite normal then we can just casually invite her, without making a big deal of it.'

'You really are one of the most thoughtful and caring people I know,' Daisy interjected. 'You never stop thinking of other people.'

'Any one of you would do the same,' Betty answered, modestly shrugging away the compliment.

'But we didn't!' Daisy reiterated, determined her friend should take the recognition she deserved.

'Well, let's not worry about that. I just wanted to make sure you all thought it was a good idea.'

'We do,' Dolly said encouragingly. 'You really have thought it all through, luv. And I agree about not letting Nancy know that we've had this chat. I think you're right; it might upset her more if she starts thinking we are worried she can't cope. Yorkshire pride and all that.'

'I'll second that,' Daisy reinforced. 'You know what

my mum was like when she discovered you were all just trying to be kind, so I would hate your good intentions to backfire.'

'You're right,' Betty agreed. 'And if we take it in turns to suggest things it won't seem overwhelming or too deliberate.'

'That sounds like a grand plan, luv.' Dolly nodded. 'Just tell me when you need me to invite Nancy and the kids over. My granddaughters come over most Sundays, and they will be over the moon to have a couple of extra friends to play with. We could even go to the park with a picnic, now the weather is as lovely as it is.'

'My sisters will love having a couple of extra friends to play with too,' Daisy affirmed.

'And m' mom is never happier than when the house is crammed full of people,' Patty enthused. 'If Archie doesn't come for at least one meal a week, she wants to know why.'

'A woman after my own heart.' Dolly chuckled.

'I do love it when a plan comes together,' Betty announced, taking the last mouthful of her port and lemon, delighted her latest mission to help a friend was falling into place. 'Ivy is keen for me to invite Nancy, Billy and Linda next Sunday, so I'll suggest it to Nancy either tomorrow or Monday.'

'Count me in for the week after,' Dolly said. 'I'll see what rations I can save. Maybe I can set the kids off baking some biscuits before nipping to the park.'

'Well, if you need any eggs,' Betty offered, 'we have plenty. The hens have been a resounding success so far.'

'I might just take you up on that. Those chuffin' dried ones really don't come close.'

'And I'll speak to my mum,' Daisy said.

'Me too,' Patty echoed.

'I'm so sorry,' Hattie interjected. 'I feel a bit useless. My house is no fun right now, so probably not the best option for Nancy and the kids, but I would love to help in any way I can. I don't feel like I'm doing much at all towards this awful war.'

Patty didn't say anything, but discreetly tapped her friend's knee under the table, knowing Hattie's dad didn't always make life easy.

'Give me two ticks, luv,' Dolly said, rising to her feet. 'I'll just nip to the bar and get us all another drink and then we can chat more about this.'

'You don't need to do that,' Betty protested.

'Nonsense! I'm happy to. Everyone want the same again?'

A few minutes later, Dolly was handing over freshly filled glasses, and had placed a couple of bags of pork scratchings on the table for everyone to share.

'Now then, Hattie,' she continued, 'have you given any more thought to joining us all at Vickers? I think you said last week you were going to have a chat with your mum.'

'Sorry, this week's been a bit of a roller-coaster, with waiting to hear from John after Dunkirk, but I have, and my mum is all for it. She's obviously a bit nervous and worried I'll end up with some dreadful injury. She's heard a few horror stories about workers suffering nasty burns or losing a limb on one of those great lathes.'

'Aye, well, it does happen. There's no denying it,' Dolly sighed. 'But mainly when folk are being daft and haven't taken heed of what their foreman has told them.'

'Or, in my case when you go racing far too fast up a crane ladder!' Patty said, rolling her eyes as she recalled how she knocked herself out and was left nursing a badly sprained ankle not long after starting at the factory, and all because she thought Archie was being off with her and had been in a huff.

'I think I'd still like to give it a go,' Hattie insisted. 'As I said before, selling lipsticks at Woolies doesn't feel like I'm doing anything worthwhile. I would really like to do my bit and do something useful to help with the war effort. I feel like I'm the only one who isn't and if I'm perfectly honest, the extra money from the overtime definitely wouldn't go amiss right now.'

'I dunno,' Patty interrupted, her mind wandering to make-up and clothes. 'A girl has got to look good for her fella. I wouldn't be seen dead without my lippy outside of this place.'

'Patty!' Betty implored. 'It's not quite the same, and let's not forget, you also left Woolies to come and work here.'

Looking slightly abashed, Patty's cheeks flushed. 'Yer right,' she conceded, 'but my intentions weren't quite as honourable as Hattie's. Remember, I only came to bagsy m'sen a bloke.'

'This is true!' Betty couldn't help but laugh as she recalled Patty's unscrupulous actions, something she had been blatantly upfront about from the first day she stepped foot inside Vickers.

'Well, at least you succeeded.' Dolly chuckled. 'Anyway Hattie, I have no doubt the gaffers will snap yer hands off if you want to come and work here.'

'I'll second that,' Betty added. 'We are run off our feet.'

'My foreman was only saying today how desperate they are for more workers,' Daisy added.

'And do you really think I'd be capable of the work? I've never used a machine in my life.'

'Neither had any of us,' Betty explained.

'And if I can get the hang of it, anyone can!' Patty chirped.

'This is true!' Hattie giggled, remembering how their officious manager, Mr Watson, was forever telling Patty off for knocking the rows of lipsticks flying.

'Oi!' Patty said, in a gasp of mock horror, but delighted that her best friend was now seriously considering coming to work with them all. She missed not seeing Hattie every day and knew it would do her the power of good to be surrounded by such a lovely group of women.

'Why don't we have a word with Frank tomorrow?' Betty suggested. 'Patty can let you know what he says.'

'If you don't mind, that would be wonderful. I think our boys having to cope with so much in France has made me really think about what I can do to help.'

'Not at all,' Betty enthused. 'Consider it done. Besides

which, it would be marvellous to have you at Vickers with us.'

'I'll drink to that,' Dolly cheered, raising her glass.

'Hear, hear,' Patty extolled, as the friends all clinked their glasses together for the second time that evening.

'Thank you.' Hattie smiled, feeling heartened by these remarkable women, who despite what life threw at them, always seemed to find a way to make life more bearable.

Chapter 4

'Hello, gorgeous.' Archie grinned, kissing Patty on the cheek as he joined her and Bill on the corner of King Street.

'What's this?' Patty laughed. 'Are you sweetening me up for something?'

'Does there have to be a reason?' Archie protested. 'Is a bloke not allowed to give his girl a kiss just because he wants to? What do you reckon, Bill?'

'No point asking me, son. I'm not sure I will ever fully work out how a woman's mind works, especially this one. She's a mystery to most of us.' He laughed, looking towards his bemused daughter.

'I don't know what you mean,' Patty replied incredulously. 'Anyway,' she added, turning back to Archie, 'are you going to tell me why you are so chipper at this godforsaken time of the day, when most of us would still rather be in bed?'

'Well, the sun is shining and it's only seven thirty in the morning and, you will be pleased to hear, I'm not on air-raid duty on Friday night, so I thought I'd treat you to a night at the pictures.'

'Now you're talking.' Patty grinned. 'I heard *Gone with the Wind* is showing at the Pavilion. Can we go and see that? Please?'

What Patty really wanted to add was, *Clark Gable is such a dream,* but she didn't want to hurt Archie's feelings, knowing how little confidence he had.

'Your wish is my command!' Archie replied. 'I might even treat you to a bag of strawberry bonbons.'

'Now you really are spoiling me,' Patty teased, linking her arm through Archie's. 'But don't be overdoing it just yet, after all it is m' eighteenth birthday next month.'

'Is it?' Archie replied nonchalantly, hoping his casual remark would give the impression he had no idea. The truth was he'd thought about nothing else for the last few weeks, determined to give Patty a birthday to remember.

'Don't tell me, you didn't know?' Patty exclaimed, flabbergasted Archie would forget something as important as *her* milestone birthday.

'It probably just slipped my mind,' Archie said, grateful for once his cheeks hadn't flushed with colour at his white lie. 'You know how forgetful I can be at times.'

'But . . .' Patty looked aghast. She knew he could be absent-minded, but not even Archie could be that clueless, surely? Patty had been secretly hoping he would be planning something very special for her. Maybe she should vocalize her thoughts on what a heartthrob Clark Gable is and give Archie a proverbial kick up the bum!

'Nancy's meeting us this morning, isn't she?' Bill asked,

interrupting the conversation in a bid to defuse the impending tension, which, knowing his daughter, could explode into an enormous and drawn-out strop if he wasn't careful.

'Er, as far as I know,' Patty replied, feeling somewhat discombobulated by Archie's thoughtlessness, but deciding this wasn't the time or the place to discuss it. Instead, she planned to drop a few more very big hints on Friday night, when she had Archie all to herself, before adding: 'I know she hasn't been sleeping too well, so she's probably just running a bit late.'

'The poor woman,' Bill sighed. 'This war is putting her through the wringer. How's she doing?'

'Not great, if I'm honest, Dad,' said Patty, forgetting about her own gripes for the time being and accepting there were far bigger issues going on in the world right now. 'She looks as though she hasn't slept for weeks and the weight is dropping off her. Her overalls are hanging from her and if she manages even half a sarnie at dinnertime, I'm exaggerating.'

'Flaming Hitler,' Bill admonished. 'That man has got an awful lot to answer for. How he's been allowed to get this far is beyond me. And now, according to the wireless this morning, he's got chuffin' Mussolini on his side. As if France and our troops haven't already taken a big enough battering, without Italy getting involved and starting on the south. God knows what they are planning, but now it looks like we are at war with two countries.'

'What does that mean, Dad?' Patty refused to listen to

the news, or spoil a good night at the pictures by watching the Pathé newsreels, which dominated the big screen before most feature films started.

'I'm not sure yet, sunshine, but the last thing our Allied troops needed was two armies firing at them.'

'Aw, here's Nancy,' Archie said, tactfully bringing the conversation to an end. The last thing he wanted to do was add to Nancy's worries, especially as there was still no news of Bert's whereabouts.

'I'm sorry, I haven't kept you, have I?' Nancy asked, as she quickly trundled towards them down King Street, looking as exhausted as ever. 'You should have gone without me. I wouldn't want you to be late on account of me. It's not like any of us can afford to have our wages docked right now.'

'Don't be daft, duck. I think we were just early today. It's these light mornings. I'm up with the larks,' Bill replied, hoping his harmless fib wasn't too obvious. But Patty was right, Nancy looked dreadful. He'd never seen her looking so washed out. Hoping he'd managed to hide his shock at her appearance, he added, 'Between that, and our Tom Tom deciding he wanted his breakfast the second he wakes up, there's no chance of a lie-in.'

'You wanna try sharing a room with him?' Patty exclaimed. 'I swear he was asking for porridge at five o'clock this morning. I thought the blackout blind across the window might help – it doesn't let in a fleck of light – but I think that boy has got an internal alarm that wakes him up at the crack of dawn.'

'Our Billy was the same as a toddler,' Nancy sympathized, the smallest glimmer of a smile emerging, but as soon as the words passed her lips, her eyes began to smart. The treasured memories of Bert lifting Billy into their bed before dawn had broken, day after day, when he sneaked into their room for an early morning cuddle, taunted her. Bert never once sent him back to bed, instead he placed his 'little soldier' between them, always insisting they were precious moments to cherish. Nancy didn't think it was possible to love her husband any more than she already did, but in those tender junctures of fatherly affection, she thought her heart would burst. But now, as the images flashed before her eyes, they acted as a cruel reminder of the desolate situation she had found herself in. Would her family ever share those moments again? Would Bert ever see their children again? The thought crushed Nancy, anchoring her to the spot, freezing her in the moment, as she desperately tried to rationalize and battle against her own cruel thoughts.

'C'mon, duck,' Bill whispered kindly, breaking Nancy's trance. As a young lad he'd been conscripted into the Great War and had witnessed enough horror to instinctively know when someone was fighting against the demons in their own mind. 'I know it doesn't feel like it right now, luv, but I promise all this will be over one day. Things will get better.'

Nancy stared at him blankly, her blue eyes glistening with tears and her whole body shaking. Numb with anger, she didn't say a word, her mind in turmoil. *How would he know? How on earth can anyone know this is going to get better? My husband is missing, possibly dead, so how in God's name can anyone say this feeling of utter emptiness will one day pass? My poor children might never see their daddy again. How does that get better?*

'Nancy,' Patty said softly, gently touching her friend's arm.

Nancy turned to face her but remained silent. It was as though her body was shutting down, preventing her from speaking or moving. It's safer this way. If time stood still, the worst couldn't happen. She could prevent the future destroying her life, her kids' lives.

Then suddenly a monstrously loud bang yards from where she was standing caused her to scream, sharply piercing the morning air. It was as though all the fear, upset, anger and frustration that had been mounting inside Nancy for the last eleven days had erupted. The tension and pain poured out of her. Startling herself, as well as Patty, Archie and Bill, the stomach-churning sepulchral cry jerked her back to reality.

'It's all right,' Patty whispered, protectively wrapping her arms around Nancy, who looked as though her body was about to give way underneath her. 'It was just a car backfiring. Nowt more than that, I promise. It's okay now.'

Nancy glanced at the road as a blue Morris Minor chugged away, plumes of thick smoke pouring from the car's exhaust, the driver oblivious to the panic he'd caused.

'I'm sorry,' she said, coming to her senses. 'I don't know what came over me.'

'There's nothing to be sorry for,' Bill replied kindly. 'I should be the one apologizing. I'm truly sorry, luv, if I said something to upset you. I didn't mean to.'

Guilt surged through Nancy. They were her friends. How could she be so mean-hearted and think so unkindly of them? They were only trying to help. 'You didn't,' was all she could manage. 'I'm just so tired and oversensitive. My mind's all over the place.'

'That's understandable. Any one of us would feel the same. Are you sure you're up to going in to work today?' Bill asked, his voice full of concern. 'I'm sure the gaffers would understand if you took a bit of time off. You don't need to work yersen into the ground, luv. It will do you no good.'

'M' dad's right,' Patty echoed, troubled by how distressed her friend was. 'Frank would put in a word. He wouldn't want you struggling on for the sake of it.'

'No! No, I can't.' Nancy furiously shook her head, her eyes, once again, full of fear. 'I'd go mad at home. I need to keep busy. I'm my own worst enemy when I have too much time to think.' If the truth be known, Nancy was terrified of being on her own. Lying in bed of a night in the pitch-black, her mind played the cruellest of tricks on her. Haunting visions of Bert hurt or being tortured prevented any hope of sleep. Nancy heard him calling out her name, begging for help. She almost willed Billy or Linda to wake up, so they would climb into her bed next to her, so she could hold one of them tight, clear her mind, and they could fill the huge gap Bert had left behind.

'Okay, luv, but here, have this as we walk.' Bill handed Nancy a cup of steaming tea he'd poured from his flask. 'Our Angie insists on sending me with one every day. She's even used the cream off the top of the milk this morning. Says she is spoiling me, but I think it's her way of making it taste better now she won't let me use the sugar rations in me brew. Not that I can blame her. There's barely enough to go round.'

'Thank you,' Nancy said gratefully, taking the flask lid, which doubled as a cup, and bringing it to her lips. A good cuppa wouldn't solve her problems, but right now the soothing hot liquid was exactly the restorative balm she needed to bring her round from the explosion of panic that had engulfed her.

'Have you heard from Hattie?' Dolly asked, looking at Patty. She gave the giant stainless-steel urn a shake to check how much tea was left inside.

'I have actually. She popped in again last night after she finished at Woolies.' Turning to Frank, she added: 'I told her what you said about speaking to the main gaffers. Anyway, she went to see them yesterday, and she's been offered a job. She needs to serve a week's notice but looks like she can start the back end of next week or the week after. I think, from what she said, they would have her start today given half the chance.'

'I bet they would, duck.' Frank nodded as he unwrapped his Spam sandwich. 'We are being overloaded with orders at the moment.'

Nancy clenched her eyes shut. Every time she heard Frank announce how busy they were, all she could think about was what that really meant. They were already working all the extras hours they could and still couldn't keep up with demand. Britain was obviously being forced to step up their effort; building more planes and producing even more munitions could only mean they were anticipating Hitler's bombardment on Europe intensifying. How many more countries did he want to overtake in his quest for domination? And what did this mean for Bert? Would he ever get home alive?

'Oh, that's marvellous,' Dolly enthused, interrupting Nancy's thoughts. 'Did they tell her what she would be doing?'

'They did,' Patty exclaimed, now twisting in her chair to face Daisy. 'She's going to be with your lot in the turner's yard.'

'Oh really? That's good news. It will be lovely to work with Hattie and see more of her.'

'Yeah, she's chuffed she will know someone. It's reyt 'ard being the new girl, isn't it?'

'You can say that again!' Daisy recalled how difficult it had been to make friends, especially after getting off on the wrong foot with Patty, all because a lad Patty had the hots for had taken Daisy to a dance at City Hall.

'God, I was ghastly, wasn't I?' Patty squirmed, reading Daisy's mind, and not for the first time feeling rather embarrassed by her impulsive and less than friendly behaviour.

'It's all in the past now.' Daisy smiled, keen to reassure Patty. 'I'm just glad Hattie will be joining us. I'll make sure I look after her.'

'Okay, I'll let you know. Thank you, Archie,' Betty said, interrupting the conversation as she and Archie joined the group at their regular spot in the bustling canteen.

'Where have you two been?' Patty quizzed. At the first hint of a confrontation, Archie's cheeks typically turned crimson.

'Sorry, it's my fault,' Betty quickly replied, thinking on her feet. 'I was just picking Archie's brain about signing up as an air-raid warden.' She surprised herself how quickly the blatant lie had sprung from her normally virtuous lips.

'What?' Patty gasped. 'You can't be serious?'

Equally as flabbergasted, Daisy and Frank looked up from their snap.

'Oh no. It's not for me,' Betty clarified. Then adding to her lie, said, 'My brother is thinking about it, so I said I would find out a bit of information for him.'

'Really? Doesn't he have enough on working down the pit?'

'I think, like most of us, he just wants to do what he can.' Quietly chastising herself for her little indiscretion, Betty crossed her fingers behind her back, hoping Patty hadn't noticed. Edward had no intentions of joining the air-raid patrol unit. He worked all the hours God sent as it was, but Betty had been forced to come up with something. She and Archie had been discussing Patty's birthday, hoping to surprise her with a party, but Betty was well aware Archie would get himself into a fluster if he tried to make up a spur-of-the-moment excuse, and the last thing Betty wanted to do was give their well-intentioned secret away.

'Anyway,' she said, quickly changing the subject, 'what were you saying about Hattie?'

'She's coming to work with me in the turner's yard,' Daisy explained. 'Isn't that lovely?'

'It is!' Betty enthused. 'It will be nice for her to join our little group.'

'And it sounds like being surrounded by friends will do her the world of good,' Dolly added.

'Yeah, I think you're right,' Patty replied, standing up to pour herself a brew. 'She's been a bit down in the dumps lately, so I'm hoping this will help.' Lifting her mug, she added: 'Does anyone else want one?'

'I wouldn't mind.' Betty smiled.

'Me neither,' Archie added.

'Make that three, will yer, love?' Frank grinned. 'I'm parched today. All that dust. It sticks in yer throat.'

'And this heat doesn't help,' Patty said. 'Not that I'm complaining. It's good to see some sunshine, but this place is hotter than ever because of it now summer is here.'

But as she turned round and placed her mug under the tea urn, she spotted Archie and Betty swapping a guilty glance.

'That was close,' Archie whispered.

'It definitely was,' Betty replied, gritting her teeth.

'What was that?' Patty called out.

'I was just saying it feels really close in here today,' he stuttered clumsily. 'The temperature and all that. It's stifling.'

Patty eyed him suspiciously. She couldn't quite put her finger on it, but she was sure there was something odd about his behaviour. Or maybe it was the heat getting to everyone. It really did feel like the furnaces were running at full pelt.

'You ain't wrong there, lad,' Frank interjected, before Patty could give it any more thought. 'But I have to say, between the showers we've been having and now all this sun, Ivy's veggie patch is coming along a treat. I popped some strawberry and rhubarb plants in a while ago, and they are about ripe for picking.'

'We'll all be coming round for tea then!' Archie winked, grateful for the change in conversation before he dropped another clanger.

'You would be more than welcome, son, but you might have to form a queue. I believe we've got Nancy and her two little 'uns coming this Sunday.'

'What's that?' Nancy asked on hearing her name but oblivious to the animated chatter going on around her.

'I was just saying you, Billy and Linda are popping over for dinner at the weekend?'

For a split second Nancy looked utterly bewildered.

'Remember?' Betty said gently, as she sat down to start

her dinner. 'I mentioned it on Monday. Ivy has invited you all for a roast, so Billy and Linda can see the hens. You never know, they might even find an egg each.'

'Sorry. Yes, you did. I'm such a clutter brain at the moment. If Ivy is sure it's not too much bother, we'll be there. I have to warn you though, I'm not great company at the moment.'

'Don't you worry about that,' Betty said in her most cheerful, upbeat voice. 'It will just be nice to see you outside of Vickers and spend a bit of time with Billy and Linda. And here, Ivy sent you this, it's one of the scones she made yesterday and a couple of jam tarts for Billy and Linda.'

'Oh. Thank you.' Nancy smiled. 'She really didn't have to.'

'It's nothing much,' Betty said, hoping that if she and their friends could all just contribute in small, but thoughtful ways, it would keep Nancy going. She really did look dreadful and Betty knew it was going to take more than the odd sweet treat, or the spoonful of sugar Dolly kept slipping into Nancy's tea, to keep her going.

'Anyway, you know how much Ivy likes to spoil little ones. She's so looking forward to seeing Billy and Linda at the weekend. We all are.'

'Betty's right, duck,' Frank added. 'And I might just have a few jobs lined up for those kiddies of yours, to keep them busy for an hour or so.'

'They will love that, especially our Billy. He's forever got his hands in a pile of dirt.'

'Well, he'll be right at home with me then.' Frank chuckled.

Nancy nodded gratefully. She knew her friends were trying to help, and an afternoon out would be great for the kids, but she wasn't sure she was in the right frame of mind to make polite conversation. Nancy was just about holding it together at work and for the couple of hours she spent with Billy and Linda of an evening. She really wasn't sure she had the strength to put on a brave face and make the effort to engage in idle chatter at Ivy's dinner table too. Maybe she should cancel, but what was the alternative? Trying to stay jolly and pretend everything was normal in front of the kids? No, that was definitely too momentous a task to pull off. She would go over to Ivy's and just hope to God she didn't fall to pieces if Ivy asked how she was doing.

Chapter 5

'Archie!' Angie, adorned in her usual flowery pinny, cheered as Archie let himself in through the back door and made his way into the Andrews's family kitchen. 'It's lovely to see you. Park yerself there,' she added, indicating to the table. 'I've just put the kettle on. I'll make you a cuppa.'

'As long as it's not too much trouble? I don't want to put you out.'

'Nonsense! Besides which, our Tom Tom will be down any minute. He is desperate to see you.'

'I was just about you ask where everyone is. It's quiet in here tonight.'

'For a change, you mean.' Angie chuckled. 'The girls and John are out playing with their friends. Bill is listening to the wireless in the front room. I can't bear to hear any more bad news, so he's taken it in there and Tom Tom is with Patty upstairs, while she gets herself dolled up for yer night out.'

'So, you're enjoying a rare bit of peace and quiet then?'

'Exactly, which is why I popped the kettle on,' Angie replied, carrying a pot of freshly brewed tea to the table.

'Let me get that,' Archie instinctively offered.

'No need. You just sit down. You've been hard at it all week. I'll just grab the jug of milk from the parlour.'

As always, there was a plate of homemade biscuits on the table. Despite the rations and several hungry mouths to feed, Angie always managed to muster up a few treats – this time an offering of tempting miniature tarts, with the lightest layer of strawberry jam.

'Help yerself,' Angie insisted as she plonked herself down next to Archie.

'Well, I wouldn't say no. They do look very tempting.'

'I probably shouldn't have,' Angie whispered surreptitiously. 'I'm trying to save some butter and sugar for next month to make our Patty a special eighteenth birthday cake, but I had a jar of strawberry jam left over from last summer, and the kids were all asking for something sweet.'

'I'm glad you mentioned that,' Archie started, as he helped himself to one of the little treats. 'Betty and I have had a few ideas too, although we are trying to keep them from Patty, which, as you can imagine, is easier said than done!'

'Oh, I'm sure,' Angie harrumphed.

'What ideas are they?' Patty asked, suddenly appearing in the kitchen.

'I didn't see you there. You were quiet as a mouse coming down those stairs. Where's Tom Tom?' Angie said, quickly changing the subject.

'Tom Tom has fallen asleep on m' bed, so I didn't want to wake him up.'

'I'm not surprised. That little tinker had me up again at five o'clock this morning, claiming he was too hungry to sleep!'

'Sorry, I did try to get him back to sleep but he was adamant he wanted to come and see you.'

'Don't worry, luv. I know how tired you are. I don't mind getting up with him. I just knew he would be shattered tonight. He hasn't stopped racing around all day.'

'Anyway,' Patty said, determined to find out what her mom and Archie were talking about before she interrupted them. 'What ideas?'

'Er . . .' Archie hesitated, taking a big gulp of his tea, his mind working ten to the dozen as he desperately tried to think of something to tell Patty, and hoped, yet again, he wasn't blushing. Betty was so much better at this than he was.

'Well, are you going to tell me?'

'We were just talking about ways to try to help Nancy,' Angie answered, without a flicker of hesitation. 'I was saying we could maybe arrange an afternoon at The Skates and then a chippy supper. What do yer think, luv? You know Nancy far better than me, do yer think she would go for it?'

'Yeah, maybe,' Patty replied, unsure whether that's really what her mom and Archie had been talking about. 'I don't know if Billy would want to go roller skating, but I can ask. And what were *your* ideas, Archie?' she added suspiciously.

The extra thirty seconds had given him just enough time

to come up with something. 'I was saying to yer mom, maybe I could take Billy off to do something else. I've got a box of toy soldiers and planes at home, from when I was a kid. Maybe I could fetch them over and he could sift through them to see if he wanted any.'

Guilt coursed through Patty as she silently chided herself for being so paranoid. Her mom and Archie were just trying to help and here she was doubting their good intentions.

'I'm sure Billy would love that,' Patty replied. 'It's a really thoughtful idea.'

'Right then,' Archie said, just pleased he hadn't been caught out for the second time in as many days. 'Shall we get going? I can't have you missing Clark Gable. I'll never hear the flamin' end of it.'

'Oi!' Patty laughed, giving Archie a playful dig in the ribs. 'You were the one who offered, remember?'

'I'm only teasing. Your wish is my command.'

'Well, have a good night, you two,' Angie called after them, just delighted to see the pair of them back on track. It was obvious they loved the bones of one another, even if they didn't always see eye to eye. And Angie had no doubt, Archie would do everything he could to make her daughter's eighteenth birthday a day to remember – he just had to find a way of keeping it a secret from Patty, which was proving increasingly difficult!

As the couple made their way down Thompson Street, Patty desperately tried to put her niggling concerns that

Archie was being a bit off to the back of her mind. It was a beautifully warm evening, the pavements were full of kids playing, and for a short while at least, it was easy to imagine there wasn't even a war going on, especially if she ignored the windows taped up to prevent the glass from shattering in the event of, heaven forbid, a bomb being dropped. But Patty couldn't help feeling, despite his plausible explanation, Archie was hiding something from her. Things between them had been going well for months now, but all those little chats Archie had been having with Betty and not a single mention of her birthday. *Was he planning to call their relationship off and maybe he'd been asking for Betty's advice?*

'Penny for them,' Archie said, putting his arm over Patty's shoulder, and bringing her back to the moment.

'What?' Had Archie asked her something?

'I was just wondering what you were thinking about. You seem deep in thought.'

'Do I?'

'Yes!' Archie replied, spinning Patty round to face him. 'I know you too well, Patty Andrews. Now, are you going to tell me what's wrong? I don't want you fretting when we should be enjoying our evening!'

'Well . . .' Patty hesitated.

Archie's eyes revealed he was genuinely concerned. 'Come on. Spit it out.'

'Well,' Patty started again, 'it's just, you would tell me if something wasn't right, wouldn't yer?'

'Hey. What on earth is all this about?' Archie said, pulling Patty to his chest. 'I promise you. You have nothing to worry about.' But as he said the words, Archie guessed Patty was starting to read more into his little chats with Betty about their plans, and vowed to try to be more discreet.

'I'm probably just being daft,' Patty mumbled, feeling slightly reassured by Archie's tender embrace and genuine-sounding words. But despite how comforted she felt, there was still something, although she had no idea what, that was causing her to doubt Archie.

A few streets away, Hattie had just finished drying up the dinner pots, following a light meal of corn beef hash, when the doorbell rang. 'Are you expecting anyone, luv?' Hattie's mum, Diane, asked, as she put their two plates back into the cupboard.

'No.' Not that anyone, apart from the occasional visit from Patty, ever called on her. 'Are you?'

Diane shook her head. Neighbours always used the back door, but they avoided popping in of an evening in case Vinny was home, knowing he'd probably had a drink and would find any excuse to pick an argument. As it happened, as soon as he got home from the pit this afternoon, had a wash in the kitchen sink and got changed, he'd disappeared to the pub. If past experience was anything to go by, he wouldn't be falling through the door until after kicking-out time.

A temporary flurry of panic soared through Hattie. 'It

won't be the debt man, will it, Mum?' She knew her dad had been draining the weekly finances, frittering most of it away at the pub. Her mum hadn't said anything specific, but Hattie wasn't daft. Despite giving up the majority of her wages every week to support the family income, her mum was scrupulous about not wasting a single penny. Even before rations had come into effect, she made sure every morsel went to good use, and she hadn't treated herself to a new pair of shoes in over a year, let alone enjoyed a dinner or a cake at Lyons.

'No. No.' But Diane couldn't hide her own sense of fear. Had she missed something? She was sure she hadn't, but for months she had been robbing Peter to pay Paul. It had become a juggling act and one that left her on tenterhooks constantly. No matter where she hid her separate jars of money, from her own wages as a cleaner, alongside the money Vinny and Hattie gave her, for the weekly house-keeping, they were always lighter than expected when she retrieved them. Diane knew Vinny was responsible, but she'd quickly learnt confronting him ended in her being on the receiving end of his volatile temper. She hated the fact Hattie was now witness to his outbursts. No child should ever see that, no matter how old they are. She felt she wasn't doing her job as a mother protecting her daughter.

'I'll get it,' Hattie said boldly, putting the tea towel on the worktop and making her way down the hallway, aware her mum was worried about who would turn up at the house past six o'clock on a Friday evening.

'Please don't let it be Dad having got himself into trouble,' she whispered to herself. It wouldn't be the first time he'd got into a barny with someone in the pub or started a row with a neighbour. Her poor mum was constantly on pins worrying about what he'd do next.

Taking a deep breath, Hattie opened the front door, but as she looked at the tall figure staring back at her, she gasped, a mixture of relief and shock. Frozen to the spot, Hattie had to look twice, assuming at first that her eyes must be playing tricks on her. The handsome man looking back at her, with a huge smile across his face, was the last person she'd been expecting.

'John!' she finally managed to utter. 'What are you doing here?'

'That's not quite the welcome I was expecting!'

Without another word, Hattie fell into John's chest, allowing his protective strong arms to sweep her up, until their faces were touching, and he tenderly kissed her on the lips.

'I've missed you so much,' Hattie whispered as their mouths parted, tears of joy falling down her cheeks.

'Not as much as I've missed you,' came the reply. 'I've thought about this moment every day since I left. It was the thought of seeing you again that got me through.'

'Has it been truly awful?'

'Why don't you invite me in, and I'll tell you all about it.'

'Of course. Sorry. Come on in. Dad's out but Mum's here. She will be so pleased to see you too.'

Ten minutes later, after more embraces and with a fresh pot of tea nicely brewing, Hattie and John, firmly holding each other's hands, and Diane were all sat round the kitchen table.

'How long are you home for? Have they given you much time off?' Diane asked, pouring tea into mismatched mugs and making sure she took the one with the small chip, something else she needed to replace when money allowed.

'Only the weekend, I'm afraid. I need to report back on duty Monday morning.'

Hattie bit her lip and tried to hide her disappointment, but John was already squeezing her fingers a little tighter.

'But it's only Friday night, which means we get to spend all weekend together,' he said.

'It does,' Hattie replied optimistically. 'Is there anything you would like to do?'

'I don't care, as long as it's with you, although I think my parents would like me to spend some time with them too.'

'I'm sure they would,' Hattie replied. 'We have all missed you so much.'

Diane took that as her cue to make her excuses and leave her daughter and John in peace. 'I'm just going to catch up on some sewing,' she said, standing up and taking her mug of still steaming tea. 'Make sure you shout goodbye before you leave, John.'

'I will, Mrs Johnson, and thank you.'

'Diane! You've known me for far too long for such formalities. Now, you two enjoy the rest of your evening.'

As soon as Diane had gently closed the door behind her, Hattie once again fell into John's arms. With her head leaning against his firm, solid chest, she asked tentatively: 'Was it horrible? Dunkirk, I mean. I've seen so many awful stories in the papers.'

John stroked Hattie's silky brown hair. They had known each other all their lives, growing up on the same street and going to the same schools, and he had never lied to Hattie, but could he really recount all the horror and bloodshed he'd seen? He wasn't sure he even wanted to think about it, let alone repeat the words out loud. Fellow soldiers shot and killed yards from where he stood, others left without limbs or with gaping bloody wounds, the unforgettable screams for help. No one should ever have to suffer like that, but John was certain he would never be able to forget the scenes of utter devastation which he'd witnessed.

'It was the worst thing I've even seen,' was all John managed to say. When he thought about those long and terrifying days on the open expanse of beach, where swarms of confused and often leaderless soldiers had gathered, running like startled rabbits in headlights to take cover as the Luftwaffe carried out their relentless aerial attacks and hundreds of German fighter planes indiscriminately showered the sand with bullets and bombs. They had swooped down, machine-gunning troops, thousands killed spending their final seconds sprawled out among the debris. The Germans had also succeeding in destroying one of the massive concrete moles, a structure which had, until then, protected the pier at Dunkirk.

The Allied troops, or at least those who were still capable of using a weapon, had fired back haphazardly from the sandy shoreline, but it was no surprise so many lost their lives, when they were competing against the monstrous killing machines in the sky. What chance did they stand? They were a prime target for the Third Reich which was swallowing up countries at a rate of knots. It wasn't just the foot soldiers on the beaches who were being aimed it. When John was safely back on English soil, after a fishing boat had delivered him to HMS *Anthony*, a naval destroyer, he'd heard several Navy ships, including the *Grafton*, *Grenade* and *Wakeful*, had been sunk. Others, including the *Jaguar*, packed with troops, had been hit too, but fortunately the soldiers had been rescued.

Like all his comrades, while he was still taking shelter on the beaches at Dunkirk, John had prayed the RAF would appear and save them. It seemed to take forever before the familiar sight of the Spitfires appeared, with their telltale red, white and blue circles painted onto the underside of their wings, and went into battle against the sinister-looking German Messerschmitt Bf 109s. Even then, as the overhead assault commenced, there were moments when John feared he and all the troops pinned against the Flanders shoreline wouldn't get off French soil alive or would be left at the mercy of Hitler. And not all of them did make it back to Blighty. Lads he'd marched through France with, fought with shoulder to shoulder, taken shelter in barns with until German soldiers had passed, were by his side one moment, but then dead on the ground the next, peppered with bullets or hit by shrapnel, and what was left of their shredded combats stained crimson. John knew he was one of the lucky ones. It was only for the grace of God he had arrived home in one piece, and his parents weren't being handed a telegram in a brown envelope.

'I'm sorry,' Hattie whispered, looking up at John. 'I can't even begin to imagine how awful it was.'

'No,' he sighed, as he attempted to blink away the haunting images that were resting heavily on his mind. 'But I wouldn't want you to. War really is a terrible thing.'

Relentless fighting had left soldiers exhausted, frightened and desperate. When the small ships had arrived, there had been an initial panic, in a desperate bid to get off French soil. The rush to escape the beach and board the fishing craft, ferries, excursion boats, cabin cruisers, Thames sailing barges and yachts caused the unshaven, ravenous and terrified soldiers, with bloodshot eyes and dirty, battered bodies, to abandon the long snaking line to embark, and dive into the ghastly grey water. Some created makeshift rafts from battered doors and planks of wood, others found old inflatable dinghies, and dozens clung to the sides of boats in a frenzied attempt to be rescued, all of them with their eyes firmly set on home. Some were fortunate, their plan worked, and their taxi home secured, but others fell backwards into the unforgiving and dangerous water, with no protection against a strong and wilful tide, which had already caused several boats to capsize.

Order was only resumed when an officer, with a clear mind for logistics, realized the system wasn't working and had also discovered, after one of the key moles had been destroyed, the walkway to access the boats was unstable. When he ordered troops to build a makeshift jetty from abandoned lorries and trucks that littered the beaches, John and scores of others had followed the command despite their overwhelming fatigue. They were aware they could all drown or be left stranded without a proper means to board the ships and boats that would ferry them to the Navy destroyers and minesweepers, which would finally take them back to England.

Covered in oil and grease and soaked to the skin, waist deep in grimy, filthy water, John had spent the last of his wavering energy to help move the now-defunct vehicles into position, load them with heavy sandbags and shoot tyres to hold them in place. He and his fellow soldiers had ripped decking from abandoned ships to create a plank walkway and they'd even found enough rope to create a railing, to prevent anyone falling off the side.

It had worked and allowed tens of thousands of worn-out troops to secure their passage home, after what had been weeks of hell, fighting for their own survival. Of course, there was still the risk the Luftwaffe would fire on them from above, but for once, the weather had been on their side. A heavy mist and thick clouds had kept the German bombers away.

'Do you know where they will send you next?'

John shook his head. 'They haven't told me yet, but I will do my best to get word to you.'

It was common knowledge soldiers couldn't give much away in their letters, which were heavily censored, in case they fell into the wrong hands and gave enemy troops an advantage.

'Okay,' she answered, trying to keep her voice neutral, aware this was as hard, if not harder, for John as it was for her. He needed her to stay strong. She couldn't fall apart, at least not in front of him, as Hattie knew John's army career was far from over and he needed to focus on staying alive. 'We just have to make the most of this weekend. At least you are home now, unlike poor Bert. Nancy is out of her mind.'

John clenched his eyes shut. 'He was part of the British Expeditionary Force too, wasn't he?'

'Yes, I believe so.' Hattie sat up and passed John his mug of tea.

'Does Nancy know if he got back to Dunkirk?'

'They don't know for sure, but it doesn't look like it.'

John grimaced, unable to hide the concern etched across his face.

'Is it bad?' Hattie asked.

'It's hard to say.' The escape routes back to Dunkirk had been fraught with problems. Both the French First Army and the BEF, the name given to the contingent of the British Army who had been sent to France after war broke out, had come under fierce attack from the German troops as they traipsed through burnt-out towns, made worse after the Belgians had surrendered on the 28 May, leaving miles of France exposed. Exhausted and worn down from weeks of battle, John and his heavily deflated troop had been left with no choice but to fight for their lives in daylight and trek cross-country overnight, with only the stars to guide them, hoping the darkness, at least, would give them the protection they needed.

'France is in a bad way and the Germans have sent in thousands of troops to conquer the country. That's not to say there isn't a way out, though.'

What John didn't say was at one point he and his platoon had taken shelter in a barn, but Hitler's soldiers had set fire to the surrounding farmland, so they'd been forced to make a run for it, as the menacing clack-clack of machine guns blistered the air around them. When one of his friends had fallen to the gun, bright red blood seeping from the back of his head, John instinctively bent down to help him, only to be pulled up and dragged away by another soldier. 'You will be next if you stop,' he warned. It really was every man for himself, but it didn't make leaving his mate, dead on the ground, abandoned hundreds of miles from home, any easier.

'I hope so,' Hattie sighed. 'The alternative doesn't bear thinking about.'

John forced a smile. 'Bert's a resilient bloke, from what I gather.'

But he knew only too well how easy it had been to get lost. John and his battalion had taken countless wrong turns. At one point they took directions to go down a rural road from what they thought was a priest, only to be bombarded by more gunshots. Word soon spread that German paratroopers were dressing in religious attire, or as innocent-looking students, to trap the Allied forces. They had even dropped leaflets from the sky urging Tommies to surrender, but the troops had soon seen through that tactic and had used the hordes of propaganda-filled paper as toilet roll.

How could John tell Hattie this, knowing she would be terrified when they were forced to say their goodbyes once again?

'Nothing's impossible,' was all John could muster, trying to offer some hope to Hattie's last question. 'From what I can gather, there are still rescue operations going on. Please tell Nancy not to give up hope.'

But John had also witnessed the worst of humanity, and knew in his heart of hearts, Bert would need nothing short of a miracle to survive the barbaric actions of the German troops.

He and his battalion trampled through canals in the pitch-black, knee deep in water, with blistered feet, their bodies often acting as a crutch for a comrade who was too exhausted or injured to carry on walking. Occasionally they would find a cellar or farm to take cover for a few hours, but more often than not, they slept in ditches in full combat gear, sometimes standing up, so they would be ready to move at the smallest hint of danger.

Fatigued and starving, when they finally arrived within spitting distance of Dunkirk, they had known their battle was far from over. Nearby towns had been razed to the ground, roads to the port were obliterated, full of ginormous craters where bombs had dropped, cranes left leaning at obscure angles, dozens of abandoned dogs wandering the streets and now-homeless cats howling through the night.

'Anyway,' he added, forcing a smile. 'Enough about me. Tell me what you've been up to. How is Woolies and what about your dad? Any better?'

'Where do I start?'

'Sounds ominous,' John said. 'Is everything all right?'

'Yes and no.'

'Go on.'

'Well, my dad hasn't changed. If anything, his drinking is getting worse.' Hattie had lowered her voice to little more than a whisper, frightened her mum might catch a snippet of their conversation and she knew it would upset her.

'I'm sorry,' John said sincerely. 'I was worried the war might make it worse.'

'It has. There's barely a night he doesn't see the bottom of God knows how many pints. Mum is having to hide money in her socks and under the floorboards to stop him spending all the housekeeping. When you knocked on the door before, she was terrified it was the debt collector or someone saying he'd got himself into trouble again.'

'Hattie, I feel awful I can't be here to help you cope and protect you from all of this.'

'Don't be daft. There's not much you could do. It's not like my dad will talk to anyone about whatever is causing him to drink himself senseless and leave Mum scraping to pay the bills.'

'But at least you could talk to me. Have you told Patty?'

'No. You know what she's like. Her head is in the clouds. It's not that I don't think she would care, she just wouldn't know what to say so I don't want to be a burden.'

'I suppose,' John nodded, 'but I hate to think of you carrying this all on your own.'

'I'm fine, honestly,' Hattie insisted, determined not to put a downer on the evening. 'Anyway, it's not all bad news. I have got something exciting to tell you.'

'Really? What's that?'

'I'm starting at Vickers on Monday. I've left Woolies!'

'What? When did this happen? I thought you loved your job.'

'I do, but I wanted to do something worthwhile to help with the war. I feel like everyone is doing something except me! Even Patty is working as a crane driver. She might have joined the works to bagsy herself a fella, but she's still doing her bit, and I wanted to do my bit as well. And it will pay more with the overtime, so I can help Mum out with money being so tight. She'd never say, but I know the extra wages coming in will help relieve how anxious she is.'

'Hattie, you really are amazing!' John announced. 'I am

so proud of you, always putting others before yourself. I knew there was a reason I fell in love with you.'

'Stop it,' Hattie protested but secretly fizzing with delight that her John was not only by her side for the first time in months but was still very much in love with her.

Chapter 6

Sunday, 16 June 1940

'Come in. Come in.' Ivy, wearing a neatly pressed navy-and-white pinstriped apron, warmly ushered Nancy, Billy and Linda in through the front door. 'It's so lovely to see you all. Thank you so much for coming.'

'I think it's us who should be thanking you,' Nancy replied gratefully. As much as it had felt like an enormous task, after next to no sleep, to traipse across town with the children, she knew Ivy had been as thoughtful as ever, and would have no doubt gone to a huge effort. It was easy to see why she and Betty got on so well. They were like two peas in a pod. 'This is so good of you.'

'Not at all.' Ivy waved off the compliment with a little shake of her hand. 'Now, I suspect you are all feeling a little parched in this heat. Why don't you come through to the kitchen and I shall get you all a nice, refreshing drink?'

Billy and Linda looked at their mum for guidance. 'It's okay,' Nancy indicated, stifling a yawn.

But she would have to do a better job than that to disguise her exhausted demeanour from Ivy. Betty had warned her landlady how wretched her friend looked. Nancy was the gauntest Ivy had ever seen her, with heavy dark circles under her eyes, hollow cheeks and slumped shoulders. Ivy had given Frank firm instructions to keep the children entertained, so Nancy could have a rest and a natter – if she needed it.

'I have a big jug of iced barley water waiting.' Ivy smiled at the two children. 'And if Frank hasn't pinched them all, there should be a little plate of biscuits waiting on the table too.'

'Oh goody. I'm starvin',' Billy piped up, his eyes lighting up at the thought of a sweet treat.

'Billy!' Linda and Nancy both exclaimed in unison.

'Aha.' Frank chuckled as he popped his head round the kitchen door and made his way down the hallway. 'You come with me, son,' he said, grinning at Billy. 'I know where Ivy keeps all her extra goodies.'

Billy didn't have to be asked twice. He dashed off towards the kitchen, the thought of food too tempting to resist.

'Sorry!' Nancy said. 'I can never fill him up. I swear he has hollow legs.'

'Well, it's a good job I've made a big dinner then. I was going to do a roast, but I thought due to how warm it is we'd all appreciate something a little less heavy, so I've made a quiche. I hope that's okay?'

'Of course.' Nancy nodded. 'You really didn't need to go to as much trouble. We would have been happy with a quick sandwich.'

'Nonsense! It's no bother at all, so please don't worry, and I have to say it's rather nice to have guests to make the effort for.'

'Nancy, you're here!' Betty interjected, as she trotted down the stairs into the hallway, looking the epitome of summer in a pale blue cotton skirt and cream blouse with a Peter Pan collar. 'I'm so glad you made it.'

'Shall we go and have a cup of tea?' Ivy suggested, leading Nancy and Linda towards the kitchen, where Billy was tucking into a rectangular shortbread biscuit in one hand and holding a glass of the refreshing cordial in the other.

'I hope you said thank you,' Nancy said, grinning at her son, who was never happier than when he was eating.

'He did,' Frank replied, helping Billy out, who was nodding furiously, a dusting of crumbs around his lips and his cheeks bulging, which was preventing him from speaking.

'Would you like one?' Frank asked Linda, lifting the plate of homemade biscuits.

The complete opposite of her brother, she instinctively looked towards her mum for permission.

'It's okay, poppet,' Nancy replied. 'You can have one.'

'Thank you,' Linda said, as she politely took one of the treats.

'Right, you two,' Frank started. 'Who would like to come and see if we can find any eggs and check what veggies are ready for picking?'

'Yes, please!' Billy boomed. 'Are we allowed to eat what we pick?'

'Billy!' Nancy scolded. 'Where are your manners today?'

'Don't you be worrying about this little tyke.' Frank chuckled, affectionately patting Billy on the head. 'He's a lad after me own heart. Now what about you, Linda? Do you fancy helping me keep your big brother under control?'

Once again, the shy little girl looked towards her mum. 'It's fine,' Nancy encouraged. 'You will have fun.' Turning towards Billy, she added: 'Remember to do as you're told. Don't be getting up to any mischief.'

'Promise.' Billy grinned, now wiping his lips with the back of his hand.

'Right then, let's find you two a basket and a pair of gloves each and see what fun we can have,' Frank said, ushering Billy and Linda out the back door.

'Well, that should keep them entertained for a while.' Ivy smiled. 'Now why don't you take a seat and I'll pop a fresh kettle of water on the hob.'

A few minutes later, Ivy, Nancy and Betty sat round the kitchen table, each with a dainty china cup and saucer in front of them.

'Shall I play mum?' Betty offered, already lifting up the matching rose-decorated teapot.

'I feel very spoilt,' Nancy exclaimed, in the cheeriest tone she could muster. 'Between Doris helping me most nights and all of this, I'm barely doing a thing.'

'Enjoy it,' Ivy enthused. 'You all work so hard in the factory. You deserve a little break every now and again.'

But Nancy wasn't daft. She knew her friends were pulling

out all the stops to help her since it had been declared Bert was missing in action. Doris wouldn't hear of Nancy taking it in turns to cook tea and had even insisted they all eat dinner together on Saturday too.

'Everyone is being so kind,' Nancy said.

'Is that a good thing?' Ivy asked tentatively, remembering her own conflicting feelings when her Lewin was missing, and how everyone had fussed around her.

Nancy chose her words carefully. The last thing she wanted to do was offend anyone's good nature. 'I'm so tired, so obviously it really does help, and I am very grateful.'

'I sense a "but" coming on.'

'It's just,' Nancy sighed, lifting up the teacup, 'it almost magnifies how horrible everything is right now. It's like a constant reminder of what's happening and how awful things are. I know people are just helping because I've got myself into such a state, but that's the problem, I then feel worse, that I'm putting people out. Not only that, I know everyone's lovely gestures are because Bert isn't here. Does that make sense? I don't mean to sound ungrateful. I promise I am thankful for everything everyone is doing, as it really is a great help, and I probably wouldn't be able to manage without it. I just . . . I mean, I'm just so worried . . .'

No matter how hard Nancy tried to extricate the words, she couldn't, in fear they would set off another avalanche of uncontrollable tears. She had hoped and wished with all her might for some good news about Bert, praying a letter with information about his whereabouts would be waiting for her on the doorstep when she got home after work, but there had been nothing.

By some miracle Nancy was still managing to remain composed and keep it together for Billy and Linda in their presence, even coming up with a multitude of white lies about why no letters from their Daddy had arrived. 'The postal service is in disarray,' she'd told Linda. 'I heard there's a backlog at the sorting office.' Anything to avoid telling them the awful truth, that the man they loved with all their hearts was missing and no one had the faintest idea where he was, or if he was even alive.

But Nancy didn't have to say another word. Ivy knew exactly how the poor woman was feeling. After Lewin had been declared missing during the Great War, she'd felt like every minute had lasted an hour, every hour a day and each day a lifetime. Unlike Nancy, she had turned in on herself, refusing to talk to anyone, hiding away, barely coming out of her bedroom. The not knowing had consumed every fibre of her soul, leaving her thoroughly drained, as she prayed and begged her fiancé would be found and come home.

'I know you are already doing this, and a grand job you are doing of it too, but staying busy does help,' Ivy empathized. 'Having too much time to think can be dangerous.'

'That's exactly why I want to keep on working. I'd go mad with worry if I was at home all day. It's hard enough of a night when I'm in bed alone. Last night, our Linda got up for the loo, and instead of putting her back to bed, I let her come in with me. I probably shouldn't have. She's only a little girl and I shouldn't be using her to bolster me, but I hate being by myself of a night. It feels like the loneliest place in the world. It was hard enough when I knew where Bert was, but now it's just unbearable. I can't remember the last time I dozed for more than half an hour at a time, before some horrible image of Bert hurt or in danger woke me up with a start, and then I can't get them out of my head or fall back to sleep. I must see every hour.'

'Oh, Nancy,' Ivy sympathized, placing her own warm hand upon her friend's, vividly recalling how for months she felt so alone, barely sleeping a wink, haunted by endless harrowing possibilities of what had happened to her beloved Lewin. 'I don't think having Linda in with you on the odd occasion will hurt. All children climb into bed with their parents and it's probably reassuring for Linda too, knowing she can come and get a cuddle. I really do understand what you are going through.'

'Do you?' The words came out a little bit sharper than she'd intended. Nancy didn't want to sound self-centred, but once again she questioned how *anyone* could know what it was like to be her right now.

'Unfortunately, I do. You see, when Lewin, the man I was engaged to, went missing during the last war, I spent months torturing myself about where he was and if he was okay. I barely ate or slept, and I spent most of it sobbing into my pillow.'

Betty and Nancy exchanged a quick glance. Betty had always had a strong inkling her landlady's heart had been broken. The black-and-white photo of a young, dark-haired uniformed soldier still adorned the mantelpiece in the living room and the previous September, Betty had comforted Ivy after she'd got uncharacteristically upset when Neville Chamberlain's sombre declaration of war had brought back painful memories.

'I'm sorry,' Nancy whispered. 'I didn't realize, and I didn't mean to sound so disparaging. I'm not thinking straight.'

'No need for apologies. You couldn't have known. It's not something I talk about very often, if at all. I just wanted to let you know I really do understand how hard this is for you.'

'Thank you. It must have been so hard for you too,' Nancy managed, but didn't dare vocalize what else she was thinking. What had happened to Lewin? This was the first time she'd heard Ivy mention his name and there were no obvious signs of him ever living at the house. Did that mean Ivy's fiancé hadn't survived the war? That he too had been missing but hadn't come home? Nancy fought back all the questions, knowing the answers would send her into an even darker place.

But Ivy was far too astute not to realize what Nancy was thinking. 'You must have hope,' she said intuitively, squeezing Nancy's hand a little tighter. 'Not all stories end the same way.'

He had died then. Nancy bit down hard on her bottom lip. She wasn't naive. She knew tens of thousands of stories had ended in exactly the same way. If only she had a crystal ball, and could see the future, but then again, what if it was bad news? She wouldn't be able to cope with that.

'Am I being selfish by saying I hope so?'

'Of course you aren't, dear. I wouldn't want anyone to suffer the pain I was forced to endure.'

Nancy took a sharp intake of breath, as the thought of a future without Bert momentarily froze her.

'I know it's easier said than done, but you mustn't think the worst,' Ivy said instinctively. 'Without hope, you haven't got anything.'

'Ivy's right,' Betty added, topping up Nancy's cup. 'There is no evidence to show Bert is anything but missing. If there was, you would know.'

But what if they'd found his mutilated body and he was so badly injured, he was no longer recognizable, Nancy thought. These were some of the harrowing images that kept her awake of a night, but she couldn't say these ominous words out loud, because that would be tempting fate.

'I hope you're right,' was all Nancy could muster.

'You have to believe we are,' Ivy reiterated. 'I know it's hard, but if you dwell on the ifs and maybes, you won't get through each day.'

Nancy knew in her heart of hearts her friends were right but no matter how hard she tried to stay positive, she had a sinking feeling in the pit of her stomach that more bad news was just around the corner.

'Reyt then,' came Frank's booming voice half an hour later, as he bounded through the kitchen door, Billy and

Linda not far behind, 'I reckon we have pulled out a wheelbarrow full of weeds and collected nearly a dozen eggs.'

'In that case,' Ivy laughed cheerfully, 'I think you all deserve your dinner. Go and wash those mucky hands and I'll serve up.'

After the three of them had scrubbed their hands clean, they joined Ivy, Nancy and Betty around the kitchen table, which was now adorned with a vegetable quiche, a bowl of salad made with radishes and tomatoes from the garden, and a generous plate of homemade sliced bread accompanied by a few butter curls on the side.

As Billy and Linda competed to chat about how they had found the most eggs hidden in the coop and who had pulled the biggest weeds, Nancy momentarily put her worries to the back of her mind. Her friends had been right, the distraction was good for her and the kids. They were full of smiles and after an hour of weeding couldn't eat their dinners quick enough, especially Billy, who didn't hesitate to ask for seconds, much to Ivy's delight.

After a dessert of apple crumble, evening was drawing in and it was time to leave but not before Ivy had parcelled up an extra portion of quiche and a handful of biscuits. Nancy had to admit they were going home a lot happier than when they'd arrived thanks to a hearty meal and good company.

'Thank you,' she said, as she ushered Billy and Linda out of the door. 'It really has been the tonic I needed.'

'That's what friends are for,' Ivy replied, hoping the

few hours of respite had helped Nancy take her mind off things, even if it was only a temporary fix.

Across town Hattie was delighted to see John on her doorstep again.

'I'm so glad you could make it,' she said, grinning. 'Are you sure your mum and dad didn't mind?'

'I've promised I will have tea with them later. Besides which, I couldn't go back on that train tomorrow without seeing you at least once more.'

'Well, you better come in,' Hattie said, her tummy all aflutter at the thought of spending the next few hours with her lovely John.

'Is your dad at home?' John asked, almost whispering.

Hattie nodded, averting her eyes towards the kitchen. 'Mum's making him a coffee. He's a bit worse for wear. He didn't get home until after closing time last night.'

'Oh dear,' John sympathized. 'Don't let it ruin today. I tell you what, why don't you grab your bag and shoes? I just want a quick word with him.'

Alarmed, Hattie looked at him quizzically. 'Is everything all right?'

'Yes, absolutely. It will only take a minute. Now quick, grab your stuff. My mum's made us a picnic to have in the park and I want to enjoy this sunshine while I can.'

'Okay,' Hattie hesitatingly agreed. 'You're not going to say anything, are you? Dad would make Mum's life hell.' She'd confided in John about her dad's volatile drunken outbursts and how her mum had borne the brunt of his temper more times than she could remember, but never assumed he would say anything. The idea of John confronting her dad filled Hattie with dread. Knowing this could be the last time she saw John for months on end, she'd been hoping today, of all days, would pass without any trouble.

'Nothing like that. I promise you.'

Before Hattie could press John any further, he threw her a reassuring wink, before making his way down the hallway.

In a confused fluster, Hattie dashed upstairs, quickly applied some lippy and dabbed rouge onto her pale cheeks, before slipping on a pair of sandals and throwing a red-and-white polka dot scarf into her bag, in case she needed to keep the sun off her head.

Within a few minutes she was back downstairs, desperately trying to concentrate on the time she had with John, as opposed to what on earth he needed to talk to her less than hospitable father about.

'All set?' John asked, walking back down the hallway towards her.

'Yes!'

'Let's go then,' he said, a huge smile spread across his face as he opened the front door.

'Okay.' Hattie was still somewhat mystified, but didn't question John's happy mood, a pleasant contrast to his sombre state from a couple of nights earlier. The weekend home must have done him the world of good to lift his spirits.

'Have a good day, luv,' Diane called with a wistful smile, popping her head round the kitchen door.

'Thanks, Mum.' But Hattie couldn't help but notice the change in her mum's earlier downtrodden demeanour, when she'd been quietly tiptoeing around the house as though she were stepping on egg shells, desperately trying to avoid another fallout with her dad after one of his sessions at the pub.

'I thought we could nip to High Hazels Park. I've got a blanket, a couple of bottles of shandy and some of Mum's Spam sandwiches.'

'What more could a girl ask for?' Hattie replied, linking her arm through John's, as they made their way down West Street.

Twenty minutes later, the homemade patchwork rug was spread out on the grass, and a plate of sandwiches, accompanied by a bowl of strawberries, and two bottles of shandy were in front of them.

'Well, this really is rather lovely,' Hattie exclaimed, forgetting for a moment the horror in the world around them. Even the sight of the huge silver barrage balloons in the distance couldn't dampen her mood. 'Thank you for doing this,' she added, giving John an affectionate kiss on the cheek.

'I just wanted to make today special for you. After all, tomorrow is a new start for you.'

'Yes!' Hattie beamed. She hadn't expected to start at Vickers quite so soon, but after she'd told Mr Watson her plans, he'd applauded her for being so patriotic and conscientious, agreeing to let her go a few days early.

'Are you excited?' John asked, offering Hattie a sandwich.

'Yes, I suppose I am but, if I'm honest, a little nervous too. I've only ever worked at Woolies, so it will feel very different, but I will have Patty and all her friends to support me.'

'Have they said what you will be doing yet?'

'Just that I will be in the turner's yard – whatever that means. I guess I'll find out soon enough. Whatever it is, it will keep me out of mischief, I'm sure. I promise I will tell you all about it when I write.' What Hattie didn't say was the work would also act as a welcome distraction. With John heading off to God knows where and her dad's drinking increasing with each week that passed, having something to keep her busy could only help, and the fact the wages were slightly better meant she would be able to tip up a bit extra to her mum.

'I don't want you constantly worrying about me,' John said. 'You must promise me that you will try to enjoy yourself too while I'm away. Get out with the girls, go to the pictures and enjoy some of those extra wages you will be earning.'

'Oh, John,' Hattie said, edging closer towards him, their legs now touching. 'Of course I will miss you. How could I not? I will be counting down the days until you are next home. You promise me, you will be careful.' Hattie had picked up enough from listening to chatter at Woolies and reading the papers to know, life as an infantry soldier was as dangerous as it was unpredictable. They were on the ground and would come face to face with Hitler's troops, and their job was to bring them down or capture the enemy forces. It was a case of who was the fastest. One wrong move could cost a soldier his life.

Is that what had happened to Bert? But as quickly as the terrifying thought had entered Hattie's head, she shook it away. Like Nancy, she had to stay positive.

'I will be doing everything I can to get home to you,' John promised, as he reassuringly wrapped his tanned, muscular arm around Hattie's slender back. 'And once this blasted war is finally over, we can spend the rest of our lives together.'

'I'd like that,' Hattie mused, her head falling sideways onto John's shoulder.

'Would you?'

'Of course.' Hattie giggled, amused by how melancholy John had suddenly become. He really was acting very strangely today.

'Well, that's good news,' he started, his right hand reaching into the pocket of his navy cotton slacks.

Unsure of what John was trying to say exactly, Hattie looked at him curiously. He was never normally so cryptic.

'Hattie,' he said, quite formally, taking a small navy velvet box from his pocket, as he shifted himself round to face her.

Oh my goodness. He's not! Hattie's mind was a whirl-wind of emotions.

But as he took her left hand in his, Hattie knew, *He was!* John looked straight into her glistening eyes and flipped the lid of the box to reveal the most delicate gold and emerald ring. 'Will you marry me?'

For a split second, she was speechless, a mixture of shock and happiness like she'd never felt before flooding her.

Then just as quickly an explosion of excited sentiments poured from Hattie. 'Yes. Yes. Of course, I will. I couldn't think of anything that would make me happier. I love you with all my heart, John Harrison. You have made me the happiest woman alive.'

And with that, the pair fell into each other's arms, Hattie's tears of joy soaking John's warm, flushed cheeks, before they swapped long, elated kisses, sealing their devotion and commitment to one another.

When they finally parted, John took the beautiful ring from the cushioned box. 'I'm praying it fits. I must admit, I did have to guess.' But as he placed the band onto Hattie's finger, it glided into position with ease.

'You know me so well!'

'I should hope so. I've known you all your life.'

'But you still managed to keep this a secret from me.' Hattie beamed, her eyes flitting from John to the beautiful ring. 'When did you manage to get this?'

'I went into town with Mum yesterday. I wanted to surprise you before I went back.'

Hattie tried not to dwell on the last few words, knowing they only had a few precious hours left together. 'Well, you certainly did that.' She grinned, determined not to spoil their afternoon.

'A toast,' John announced, picking up the bottles of shandy and handing one to Hattie, also adamant their final day together should be one of celebration.

'To us!' Hattie cheered.

'And to the rest of our lives,' John exclaimed, as the pair clinked their bottles together.

'I really can't think of anything better. Wait until I tell Patty, she will have kittens at the thought of a wedding.'

'Let's not leave it too long,' John insisted. 'I don't know when I'll next get some leave, but as soon as I know, why don't we just do it?'

Hattie didn't want or need a big wedding. What she desired most in the world was knowing she and John would one day be able to spend every spare moment of their lives together. She also knew John, more than ever, needed to envisage a future free from war. Whatever he'd witnessed in France and on the beaches at Dunkirk had taken their toll. He hadn't said much, but Hattie knew it had cast a shadow, made him aware of how fragile life is. Alive one second, gone the next. He, like everyone else, needed something to look forward to. A reason to keep going.

Chapter 7

Monday, 17 June 1940

'Hattie!' Patty trilled excitedly, as her best friend made her way across the busy canteen, with Daisy by her side. 'How did you get on? Come and sit down and tell me everything. Did you enjoy it? Was it as hard as you expected?'

'Take a breath!' Archie laughed. 'And let the poor girl get herself settled.'

'I will. I will.' But the reality was, Patty couldn't stop herself, even if she tried. 'Sorry, Hattie. Come and sit down. I've saved you a chair. Let me get you a cuppa too. Dolly always puts on a big urn for us, knowing we will all be parched.'

'I'm certainly that,' Hattie agreed. 'I hadn't realized how dusty the factory was. I know you warned me, but I didn't imagine it would be this mucky.'

'Probably best that way, or you would never have come,' said Betty, who was sat on the opposite side of the table. 'It's quite the shock, isn't it?'

'It's definitely very different to Woolies, that's for sure.' Hattie nodded, sitting in the chair Patty had kept for her.

'And what are you doing? Are you where you thought you would be?'

'Yes. I'm with Daisy in the turner's yard, shaping steel into rods. At least that's what we were doing today.'

'Oh, I'm so pleased you are together. It won't feel as daunting.'

'It was certainly a nice surprise,' Hattie agreed, turning to Daisy and smiling. 'I didn't feel nearly half as nervous with a friendly face there as I would have done if I had been surrounded by a group of strangers.'

'You are part of the gang now!' Patty cheered, plonking a mug of scalding tea in front of her.

'I must admit, it does feel rather nice to be here with you all, and it will keep my mind busy.'

'It's certainly good for that,' Betty agreed. 'I'd go up the wall if I didn't have this place to keep me busy. I don't suppose you have heard from your John, have you?'

'Erm.' Hattie lifted her mug to her mouth. In normal circumstances, she would have told Patty straight away about her news, but with Nancy sat just a few feet away, looking as though her world was collapsing around her, Hattie had been reluctant to share the events of the last few days.

'Hatts,' Patty probed, sensing her best friend was holding something back. 'Has something happened?'

Instantly all eyes were on Hattie. *Oh goodness*, she thought, kicking herself for avoiding Betty's question.

'Is everything okay? I'm so sorry, I shouldn't have pried,'

Betty said solemnly, also feeling guilty for putting Hattie on the spot.

'Everything is fine, don't worry.'

'Have you heard something?' Patty pushed, never one to pick up on a hint.

Flustered, Hattie's cheeks reddened. She'd never been very good at thinking up excuses in a rush, especially under pressure. 'Well, yes, I have actually,' she finally confessed, simultaneously admonishing herself.

For a few seconds the whole table fell into silence. What with Nancy's recent and worrying news about Bert, the group of friends were naturally on high alert.

'Is John all right?' Betty gently asked, hoping with all her might that Hattie's sweetheart wasn't also missing in action.

Putting her mug of tea down, Hattie nervously gripped her hands together under the table. 'He's absolutely fine.'

'How do you know?' Patty insisted, still completely oblivious to how awkward her friend was feeling. 'Did you get a letter?'

Oh blast, Hattie silently cursed. She really didn't want to make this announcement in front of everyone. She had been hoping to tell Patty quietly at the end of the day if she could catch her friend by herself. 'No,' she started hesitantly. 'It wasn't a letter. John came home on Friday.'

'What?' Patty quizzed. 'You mean, you have seen him? Why on earth didn't you say? Is he okay?' As always, her unrelenting questions came thick and fast.

'Sorry! I promise, I was going to tell you later.'

'Well, you better tell me everything now,' Patty enthused.

Nancy, who was picking at her beef sandwich that Doris had given her after she'd dropped Billy and Linda off this morning, was suddenly alert. John had come home! She tried to bite back the pang of jealousy that was threatening to make her feel resentful of poor Hattie, who had done absolutely nothing wrong. Nancy knew it was wonderful John had made it home, but she couldn't help begrudge the fact that Bert, *a husband and a father*, hadn't been granted the same fortuitous and indiscriminate luck.

'We need to hear every detail,' Patty insisted.

But Nancy wasn't sure she could bear it. Spotting a few women gathering at the Swap Club box a few metres away in the corner of the canteen, she stood up rather abruptly. 'I'll erm . . . I'll just go and check if they need any help,' she announced.

'I'll come over too,' said Dolly, who had heard the tail end of the conversation as she came to check if the tea urn needed topping up. After Betty had set up the Swap Club eight months earlier, she'd been happy to help keep the initiative running, knowing how much it helped folk.

'No. No. You take a minute and have a rest, I haven't got much of an appetite.'

'It's fine,' Dolly said, seeing that Nancy was battling to keep herself together. 'I wanted to have a word with a couple of the women anyway.'

Betty and Dolly exchanged a knowing glance, instinct

telling them now wasn't the time to try to convince Nancy to sit down to eat something and put some fat on her increasingly gaunt frame.

After Nancy took her leave, Patty, now looking utterly crestfallen, turned to her best friend. 'I'm sorry,' she whispered apologetically. 'That was very tactless of me. As usual I didn't think. I just thought you were being shy.'

'I didn't want to say anything in front of Nancy as I was worried it would upset her, and by the look on her face as she stood up, I think I probably have,' Hattie replied glumly. 'I was trying to avoid harping on about my news about John, when Nancy is out of her mind with worry about her Bert.'

'Don't be thinking like that,' Betty said authoritatively. 'Nancy may be going through a difficult time right now, and we all feel for her, but that doesn't mean you can't be happy. I'm sure she doesn't begrudge you some good news. Heaven knows, this damnable war is testing us all. You have been through your fair share of worry too. We all need something to make us smile.'

'Betty's right,' Patty reiterated, hoping she was also off the hook for being so thoughtless, but in the same breath added, 'Now, are you going to tell us everything that happened this weekend with John?'

Conflicted, Hattie hesitated, taking a sip of her now cooling mug of tea. Still feeling apprehensive, she quickly glanced over her shoulder to check Nancy was out of earshot, before explaining how John had appeared completely out of the blue on Friday night. 'He was the last person I was expecting to see on the doorstep.'

'I bet! Did he say how bad it was? In Dunkirk, I mean,' Patty asked, never one to hold back.

'Not in any great detail, but I could tell from how guarded he was that he'd seen some awful things.'

Betty momentarily closed her eyes. She'd seen the reports in Frank's *Daily Mirror* about the RAF going into battle with the Luftwaffe over the English Channel and the French shoreline. Once again, she was grateful her brave William was still training in Canada, but in his latest letter, he'd excitedly explained how quick he was progressing, and Betty knew in it was only a matter of time before he too would be sent into active service to help defend Europe from Hitler.

'I know it's a long shot, but I don't suppose he saw Bert, did he?' Betty asked. She was sure they were both serving with the King's Own Yorkshire Light Infantry.

'I'm afraid not,' Hattie replied, gently shaking her head. 'I only know as I explained there was still no word from Bert.'

'We mustn't give up hope,' Frank interjected. 'There's plenty of reasons why Bert may not have made it back yet. We definitely shouldn't be assuming the worst yet.' Although the news reports didn't look good; thousands of soldiers had been killed, but the last thing Frank needed was his team of sturdy female workers giving up hope. He needed to do everything he could to keep up morale.

'Absolutely,' Betty reinforced, galvanizing Frank's point, refusing to even consider the alternative.

'So, when will you see John again?' Patty asked, keen to avoid dwelling on the doom and gloom of the war.

'I'm not sure. He couldn't say. I don't suppose he has any way of knowing.' But as Hattie lifted up her left hand to unwrap her snap, Patty spotted the shiny gold band on her friend's ring finger.

'Is that what I think it is?'

Hattie instantly blushed, partially out of modesty after Patty had once again thrown her into the spotlight, something she always avoided, but also because she couldn't help flushing with happiness as she recalled John's romantic and unexpected proposal.

'It is.' Hattie grinned as she looked down at her engagement ring, which still felt strange on her finger.

'Why on earth didn't you tell me the minute you saw me?' Patty gasped, virtually jumping out of her chair to take a closer look at the beautiful piece of emerald and gold jewellery that sat proudly on Hattie's finger. 'It's gorgeous! Was it ever so romantic? Did he go down on one knee? When's the big day? Are you going to go dress shopping? Please make sure it's on a day I can come too. I don't want to miss a single thing, besides which I want to make sure you choose something utterly gorgeous.'

'Patty!' Archie exclaimed, laughing at his overenthusiastic girlfriend. 'One question at a time. It's not an interrogation.'

'Sssh,' Patty said, dismissing Archie's suggestion, refusing to contain her excitement. 'This really is the best news. An engagement and a wedding!'

'Hold your horses.' Hattie grinned. 'We haven't set a date yet. It's impossible to say when John will next get some leave.'

'All the same, this is wonderful news,' Betty interjected, before poor Hattie was bombarded with another deluge of questions. She glanced around to check Nancy couldn't hear the conversation, especially Patty's very excitable shrills.

'It really is lovely,' Daisy added, tapping her new workmate on the arm.

'I'm delighted for you and no doubt, this one,' Archie winked, giving Patty a gentle nudge in the ribs, 'will keep us all posted on any developments.'

'Oi! It's my job, as Hattie's best friend, to be excited. Anyway, you could always pick up a few tips!'

The remark wasn't lost on Archie. 'I'm only teasing,' he replied, chuckling. 'Besides which, I don't think I do too bad.'

'Mmmm,' Patty mused. 'Time will tell,' she added, hoping she was dropping a big enough hint about her eighteenth birthday, which was now less than a month away. She had clearly forgotten already how Archie had treated her like a princess on Friday night when they'd gone to see Clark Gable in *Gone with the Wind*, spoiling her with sweets and complimenting her on how pretty she looked.

'Congratulations, duck,' Frank piped up, keen to stop Patty falling down another never-ending rabbit hole and keep the focus on Hattie's happy announcement, raising his mug of tepid tea by way of a toast. 'I'm sure that young man of yours will be doing everything he can to get home as soon as possible so he can walk you down the aisle.'

'Well, that would be nice,' Hattie agreed.

'We must arrange a few drinks at The Welly to celebrate,' Betty enthused, also eager to stop Patty having a pop at Archie, especially in the midst of Hattie's exciting news.

The group of workers sat around the table weren't the only ones to hear about Hattie's engagement. Nancy, who was now stood with Dolly at the Swap Club corner, had also caught the gist of the latest revelations. She knew she should be delighted for Hattie, recalling how she had been on cloud nine after Bert proposed, but she just couldn't bring herself to join in the round of celebrations; the demons in her head telling her it would be disloyal to her husband. How could she join in when he was either in some godforsaken hellhole or, heaven forbid, cruelly taken from this world, preventing him from ever having the chance to feel joyful about anything ever again?

While her friends were all deep in conversation with Hattie, Nancy made her excuses to Dolly and slipped away through the canteen, telling herself she was better off thirty feet up a crane, where she didn't have to pretend to be happy for anyone.

Knowing she couldn't do anything to help Nancy right now, Dolly made her way back to the gang of steelworkers. 'Did I hear The Welly being mentioned?'

'Yes,' Betty replied. 'I'm not sure how much you heard but Hattie got a surprise visit from John at the weekend, and he proposed!'

'Oh, that is marvellous news. Many congratulations, luv. I'm thrilled for you.'

'Thank you.'

'And, I agree with Betty, this is cause for a celebration. Let's arrange another get-together soon.'

'Any news from your lads, Dolly?' Frank asked.

'Actually, yes,' Dolly replied, her smile widening, as she picked up a couple of empty mugs. 'I didn't get a visit, but a letter was waiting for me on Friday when I got home.'

'All good, I hope?' Frank asked.

'Yes! Both Michael and Johnny were on one of the naval destroyers that helped ferry some of those poor exhausted soldiers home. I got the impression it was quite the mission. They did four trips across the Channel, but it sounds like they managed to get over three thousand of our lads home.'

'Well, that is grand news,' Frank agreed. 'You must be so proud, let alone relieved.'

'I am, duck. They've all had such a terrible time of it, but what an amazing feat. I heard on the wireless hundreds of thousands of Allied troops were brought back from Dunkirk.'

'Hitler certainly didn't see that coming, that's for sure. Anyway, I hope you get to see your lads soon.'

'I'm not sure when they will get some leave, but I'm just happy they are both okay.'

'Do you know what ship they were on?' Hattie asked, folding up the greaseproof paper her ham sandwiches had been wrapped in, so she could use it again tomorrow.

'Let me think. They did say. It began with an A.'

'It wasn't HMS *Anthony*, was it?'

'Yes. Yes, it was, duck. Why do you ask?'

'Really? That's the same craft John was brought home on.'

'Well, I never. What a coincidence. It really is a small world. I wonder if they came across one another. I'll ask my two in my next letter.'

'I'll do the same.'

'Right, ladies,' Frank said, scraping his chair backwards to stand up. 'I hate to break up the chatter, especially on such a good note, but we better get back to work, or we'll all still be here at midnight.'

'Chuffin' 'eck,' Patty sighed, looking at the huge clock on the canteen wall, indicating it was already twelve thirty. 'I'm sure that half an hour goes faster every day.'

'Time flies when you're having fun.' Frank chuckled.

'Whatever you say!' Patty rolled her eyes, as she took a final slurp of her tea. 'You would tell me owt.'

Picking up her bag, Patty waited for Hattie, before they zigzagged their way through the jigsaw of tables to the canteen doors. 'I hope your afternoon goes well. I might not see you at four o'clock. Frank has asked us to stay on and do some overtime, but I'll see you tomorrow. And I am really chuffed about you and John. It's the best news.'

'Thank you, and I promise you will be the first to know when we make any more plans.'

'I better be!' Patty said sternly, in mock authority. 'You cannot go dress shopping without me!'

Chapter 8

Friday, 21 June 1940

'I know we always ask, but are you sure we can't tempt you to come for a quick drink?' Betty asked Nancy, as the group of women gathered outside the great black iron gate after finally clocking off.

'I'd love to, but I don't want to put on Doris any more than I have to,' Nancy half lied. The reality was the last thing she wanted to do was go and celebrate Hattie's engagement when she'd still had no word of Bert's whereabouts. It was hard enough trying to keep it together at work; Nancy knew her friends were concerned but she was too weary to pretend to be happy, besides which it was already gone six o'clock and she really needed to get home to see Billy and Linda.

'Well, I hope you get some sleep tonight,' Betty said empathetically, patting her friend's arm, expecting her to politely excuse herself.

'Thanks.' And before she was pulled into another conversation, as Betty predicted, Nancy quickly waved a polite goodbye and joined the sea of workers heading home, keen for a hot meal before a warm soak in the bath, a typical

Friday night routine where the dirt, dust and grime of the week could be washed away.

'I really hope I haven't upset Nancy,' Hattie said, turning to her friends. 'She's barely said a word to me all week. I feel awful. Maybe I shouldn't have mentioned John getting weekend leave and proposing.'

'Now, don't you be thinking like that, luv,' Dolly said sternly. 'We are going out to toast your good news and that's exactly the way it should be. Nancy will be happy for you in her heart of hearts, she just can't see the wood for the trees right now. She'll come round in time.'

'I hope so.'

'She will, duck. Take my word for it. Now, no more fretting, let's go and have a little drink to celebrate.'

Ten minutes later, Hattie, Betty, Daisy, Patty and Dolly were all comfortably positioned in their regular corner of The Welly.

'To Hattie and John,' Patty applauded, raising her half-pint glass of iced lemonade.

'To Hattie and John,' the rest of the group echoed in unison, their glasses clinking.

'And to your first week at Vickers,' Patty added. 'You are definitely part of our factory gang now.'

'Hear, hear,' came the cheery response.

'Thank you so much. You really have all made me feel so welcome,' Hattie replied.

'Are you finding your feet?' Betty asked. 'It can take a bit of getting used to.'

'I have to admit, it's a world apart from Woolies. I don't think I've seen so much dust in my entire life, or been surrounded by so much noise, but, in a funny sort of way I'm really enjoying it. The work is obviously a lot harder, and I've got a lot to learn. I'm still terrified I'll not position the steel properly or overturn it, but I finally feel like I'm doing something useful. Does that make sense?'

'You don't have to convince me,' Betty replied. 'I know exactly what you mean. I think everyone thought I was crackers for giving up a comfy job in a solicitor's office to work at Vickers, but I wouldn't change it for the world. Between that and the work Daisy and I do at the WVS, it makes me feel as though I'm doing something useful.'

'How's that going?' Dolly asked.

It had been over three months since Betty had joined the Women's Voluntary Service at the depot in Fulwood, after Ivy and her friend Winnie had started contributing some of their free time to make hospital supplies.

'Well, we are always busy. I don't like to overthink why so many extra bandages are needed, but it's good to know we are helping in some small way.'

'If the snippets John hinted at, about what he'd witnessed in Dunkirk and getting through France, are anything to go by, then I should imagine all your efforts are greatly appreciated,' Hattie replied.

'My dad was saying he reckons we lost a lot of men even if all the official talk is about what a success it was,' Patty sighed.

'I should imagine he's right, duck,' Dolly added sombrely, but determined to keep the mood buoyant, she added, 'At least it looks like more were saved than lost.'

'Yes.' Hattie nodded, relieved her John was one of them.

'Do yer think Nancy's Bert will be all right?' Patty asked, rubbing a smudge of black dirt streaked across the top of her hand. 'I've never seen her look so worried. I'm not very good and don't know what to say to her to make her feel better.'

'All we can do is be there for her, duck,' Dolly replied. 'None of us can really appreciate what she is going through. It must be hell on earth, especially when she has those little 'uns to think of too, all we can do is keep reminding Nancy we are there for her.'

'She's bringing the kids round to our house tomorrow afternoon after work. I said I'd take Linda and my sister to The Skates, and Archie is going to do summat with Billy, while my mom has a natter with Nancy.'

'That'll be nice.' Dolly smiled. 'If we can all just help keep her busy, it might help a little.'

'If anyone else wants to come, yer more than welcome,' Patty added. 'The more, the merrier.'

'I might bring out Polly and Annie if you don't mind?' Daisy asked.

'Of course. It will be nice for Linda to be surrounded by lots of girls roundabout her age.'

'Dolly, how about your granddaughters? Would they fancy it?'

'Our Milly is only three. Is she a bit young?'

'Not at all,' Daisy replied. 'They start them tiny and she can just stay on Mug's Alley, with all the other beginners. To be honest, I doubt our Polly will be good enough to go upstairs. It's a bit fast.'

'Yer know what, I might just bring them. It will give their mums a break and will be a treat for Milly and Lucy.'

'Brilliant,' Patty said. 'How about you, Betty? Fancy another afternoon at The Skates? And you, Hattie, can you make it?'

'Aw, I'd have loved to,' Hattie answered, 'but I promised my mum we'd go get a cake and a cuppa as a treat, at Browns tearoom, to celebrate my first week at Vickers.' What Hattie didn't say was she was determined to spoil her mum with the extra money she'd earned working at the factory, before her dad got his hands on it all and spent it down the boozer.

'Sorry, I'm going to have to give it a miss too,' Betty added. 'I promised I'd put in a few hours at the depot and then I must write to William. With all the extra overtime we've been doing this week, I haven't had chance to put pen to paper. You don't mind, do you?'

'Gosh, not at all. I think there will be plenty of us to keep Linda entertained. She will be spoilt for choice on who to play with.'

'It's nice Archie can help out with Billy too,' Betty said, taking a sip of her port and lemon. 'He's not too busy with his air-raid work, then?'

'He's done all his training now, so he's free tomorrow afternoon but on duty tonight and tomorrow night. Hopefully he's coming for dinner on Sunday, though. We might be able to get out for a walk or summat afterwards if the weather stays nice. I hope so. He seems a bit distracted at the moment,' Patty mused. 'I hope he's not planning on taking on more war work and hasn't told me. I'll flamin' throttle him if he is. I'm not sure I can go through all that worry again. He hasn't said anything to you, has he, Betty? I saw you chatting the other dinnertime at work. There's nothing I should know about, is there?'

Betty took another rather large mouthful of her drink, buying herself a few seconds to quickly think on her feet. She had no idea how people managed to keep secrets. Betty had found the whole thing quite testing and had even woken up in the middle of night fretting about making a mess of all the planning. Even though she knew she was doing everything with the best intention, being dishonest really wasn't her forte. Organizing events was one thing, but telling lies, especially to a friend, was leaving her in a right old state, but she knew Archie would never forgive her if she whispered a single word of what they had been getting up to in secret.

'Er, no. Not as far as I know,' she finally said, hoping her initial hesitation didn't further rouse Patty's suspicions.

'What were yer both chatting about?' Patty quizzed, never one to hold back if something was troubling her.

'Oh, Archie was just asking if my brother had thought any more about becoming an air-raid warden.'

'Is he thinking of volunteering?' Dolly interjected, oblivious to the blatant lie Betty had just told.

'Maybe,' Betty said, internally admonishing herself for getting herself into such a pickle. 'I was telling Archie he's just keen to do something extra to help with the war effort.'

'That's very admirable,' Dolly praised, inadvertently making Betty feel even worse about her fabrication, which she and Archie had clumsily concocted as a way of covering their tracks.

'Talking of which,' Betty said, keen to move the subject on. 'Are you all still happy to do some knitting? We've got some money in the Swap Club kitty, so I can go and buy some yarn and Mrs Rafferty from the WVS has said they have had donations of old jumpers and the like, which can be repurposed.'

'Definitely,' Hattie enthused. 'I know at the moment it's blisteringly warm, but by the time we get a parcel together and it gets sent off, I'm sure the woollies will be much needed again. John was telling me how much he and all his comrades appreciated the hats, scarves and socks. And he said, a few of them found a few missives concealed in the packages with addresses of girls to write to!'

'So, it really does happen?' Betty chuckled, recalling how one of the women in the canteen, Carol, had told her about the plan by some of her mates to bag a soldier.

'From what John said, it reyt cheered a few of his pals up. Some of the girls had even included a photo, which they kept in their chest pockets.'

'Well, if it helps keep up morale, that can only be a good thing.' Dolly nodded, lifting her glass of pale ale to her lips.

Betty's thoughts instantly tracked back to when her lovely William had promised he would always keep the black-and-white photo of them walking arm in arm along Cleethorpes promenade last summer close to his heart. She had a copy of the same photo framed on her bedside table. 'Yes, I think a little bit of comfort and a reason to keep going can only help those poor boys who are hundreds, if not thousands, of miles away from home.'

'All right,' Patty exclaimed. 'I get what you mean but let's not get all maudlin like. Tonight is meant to be about Hattie and her engagement.'

'It's fine,' Hattie said, happy not to be the centre of attention. 'I'm just glad we can do our bit to help out as many troops as possible.'

'I agree, but Patty's absolutely right,' Betty confirmed resolutely. 'Tonight is all about toasting your good news. Let me go and get a round in and we can have another drink to celebrate.'

Before there could be any arguments about whose turn it was to go to the bar, Betty was already on her feet and grinning to herself as she heard Patty announce, more than ask, 'I assume I will be your maid of honour when you finally do get hitched.'

*

'Hello, I'm back,' Nancy called, as she opened Doris's back door, the comforting aroma of corned beef hash filling the kitchen and reminding Nancy she'd barely had a thing to eat all day. She had been unable to swallow more than a couple of mouthfuls of Dolly's normally irresistibly tasty mince and onion pie at dinnertime.

'We're just in here,' Doris called, but her guarded tone, a sharp contrast to her normal cheery inflection, set off alarm bells and Nancy instinctively knew something was wrong.

'Is everything all right?' she asked hopefully, more out of habit, as she dropped her gas mask and cloth bag. *Please, God, not more bad news. Don't let Bert's commanding officer be stood there, solemn-faced, waiting on attention.*

But as Nancy walked into the uncharacteristically quiet room, absent of Little George's incessant demands for food or roars mimicking speeding motor cars, a heartbreaking scene instantly assaulted her, causing every hair on her body to stand on end and sent a frightful shiver down her spine.

'Linda, what on earth has happened?' Nancy dashed in two long steps across the room to where her ruddy-cheeked daughter was sat on Doris's knee, tears flowing down her crumpled face, as she clutched her much-loved rag doll. Alarmed, Nancy looked to Doris to get to the bottom of what had happened.

'Linda's had a bit of a tricky day,' she offered by way of explanation.

'Come here, poppet,' Nancy soothed, opening her arms wide to offer a comforting hug.

'You go to your mummy,' Doris said, releasing the clearly devastated girl from her affectionate grasp. 'Have a nice cuddle while I pop the kettle on.'

She didn't need to be told twice. Within a second, Linda had taken the few steps into Nancy's grip, wrapping her little quivering arms tightly around her mum's bony back.

Nancy lifted Linda into her arms, then carefully manoeuvred them both into one of Doris's wooden kitchen chairs. 'Now, now. I'm here. I promise whatever it is, it won't be as bad as you think,' Nancy whispered, stroking Linda's mass of long white-blonde ringlets that were hanging across her puffy, tired face. 'Why don't you explain what's caused all these tears?'

'I can't, Mummy. It's just too horrible,' she sobbed, another avalanche of tears exploding from Linda's eyes.

Doris, who was scooping fresh tea leaves into the sturdy brown pot, explained, 'I'm afraid a few of the children at school gave Linda an unnecessary and unjustified scare today.'

'What do you mean?' Nancy quizzed, still none the wiser to what had caused such a spectacularly emotional outburst from her daughter. Linda had always loved school, and had made lots of friends since starting there nearly two years earlier.

'Would you like to tell me what happened?' Nancy, once again, gently coaxed.

Linda shook her head, determined not to breath a word about why she was so devastated.

'I can't help you, poppet, if you don't tell me.'

This time Linda's head flopped onto Nancy's chest, the onslaught of tears soaking into her mum's mucky overalls, no doubt leaving dirty steaks down Linda's face.

Nancy felt utterly helpless, her own eyes now glistening, as she struggled to hold herself together. Throughout all her own panic-stricken moments of fear and anxiety, since Bert had gone off to war, and even more recently as she felt completely broken not knowing where her husband was, she had always been able to comfort her children and make them believe everything was going to be all right. But now, seeing Linda so distraught felt like the final straw. At the same time guilt coursed through her. Had Linda sensed how fragile she was and was this why she was hiding something from Nancy?

Now frightened her own resolve would shatter into a thousand tiny pieces at seeing her daughter so uncharacteristically inconsolable, she turned to Doris, who was always the trustiest of stalwarts in times of need.

Shaking her head sadly, Doris explained, 'I'm afraid I have been barely able to get a word out of her since she came home, but her teacher did give me what I feel is the shortened version, when I went to collect them all this afternoon.'

As if she instinctively knew what Doris was about to say and do, without any warning Linda jumped off her mum's knee. 'I need the toilet,' she cried, dashing towards the back door and the outside lavatory.

Mashing the pot of tea with a spoon, Doris sat down opposite. 'Come on, luv. You can get through this. Try to stay strong, but I must tell you this,' she started, 'Mrs Duke was waiting for me when I arrived to pick them all up. She was holding Linda's hand, and I knew from how upset the little love looked, something must have happened.' Nancy, who despite feeling like her heart was about to break, nodded for her to carry on. 'Anyway,' Doris continued, 'she instructed Linda to stand with Billy and my lot, took me to one side and explained another little girl's daddy has been declared dead.' What Doris tactfully omitted was the poor man had not come back from Dunkirk. 'Anyway, when Linda had said Bert still wasn't home, some of the kids had suggested maybe . . .' Doris took a breath, feeling ghastly for having to repeat the remarks that were more than likely unintentionally cruel.

'It's okay,' Nancy said, her voice breaking, stopping Doris before she said the words that would confirm Nancy's worst fears. 'You don't need to say it. It's never far from my own thoughts.' But Nancy knew she had to momentarily put her own anxiety to one side. She might be thinking exactly the same as those unwittingly intuitive children, but right now Linda needed her to be strong and offer her reassurance.

Nancy steeled herself.

A minute later, Linda returned, a fistful of scratchy toilet roll in one hand, her rag doll in the other. 'Come and sit on my knee and have a drink of milk,' Nancy coaxed, trying her best to remain composed, despite how broken she was feeling. Obedient as ever, Linda did as she was asked, her eyes still glistening, but the flow of tears had stemmed, for the time being at least.

'Mrs Duke told Doris what the other children said to you today in school.' Nancy felt Linda stiffen. 'I want you to know . . .'

But Linda was one step ahead of her. 'Has Daddy gone to heaven, Mummy? Have the angels taken him? Is that why you cry in bed of a night?'

Nancy froze. She had been expecting the first two questions but not the latter. Sitting stock-still, she quietly chastised herself. She thought she had been so careful, so diligent about when she'd allowed her emotions to take over and run free. Had she woken Linda, as her sobs fell unbidden, or had her daughter heard her on waking to go to the toilet? It was her job, as a mum, to protect her children from the cruelties of the world, not cause them undue worry.

Nancy took her daughter's small hand into her own, letting the screwed-up tissue fall onto her lap. 'I'm so sorry,' Nancy said, unable to hold back her own emotions any longer.

'Mummy,' Linda gasped, at the sight of her mum so upset.

'I'm sorry, poppet.' Nancy desperately tried to stem her own flow of heavy tears. 'I didn't mean to cry.'

'It's okay,' Linda whispered, taken aback by how visibly shaken her mum was. 'I can give you a cuddle.'

Nancy took a deep intake of breath. How had it happened that her little girl was now comforting her? 'Thank you,' she answered. 'I think I'd like that.'

As Linda wrapped her tiny arms around her mum, Nancy was overwhelmed by guilt. She had vowed to remain strong while Bert was away, to keep her little family together, but now Linda was looking after *her*.

Nancy nestled her face into her daughter's mass of curls, taking in the smell of her lavender-infused shampoo. She needed a minute to pull herself together, to regain her strength. Feeling Linda's hands against her back was exactly the gentle reminder she needed that, despite how hard life was right now, she was still a mum and had to find a way through.

'Okay,' she finally said, sitting upright again, her eyes puffy and swollen but her resolve slowly returning. 'I need you to promise to listen to what I'm about to tell you,' Nancy said, finding her voice.

'Are you feeling better now?' Linda asked softly.

'Yes,' she reassured her daughter. A look of resounding trust filling Linda's eyes, confirming Nancy's intuition, that what her daughter needed was an authoritative voice, someone who could diminish all her fears.

'Like you, I miss your daddy, and that's why I sometimes have a little cry when I go to bed or, like now, when things feel a little hard. I also want him to come home. I try to be brave, but sometimes, even mummies aren't always as strong as we would like to be.'

Linda, who had also sat up, squeezed Nancy's hand in her unshakeable, affectionate manner of showing her mummy she was there for her too.

Grateful, but now determined not to fall apart again, Nancy continued, 'Your daddy is doing a very important job right now. With lots of other daddies he is working very hard to keep us all safe. And that's why he doesn't always have a lot of time to write letters at the moment. It's not because he doesn't care or has forgotten about us. He loves us all very much and is doing everything he can to get home as soon as possible, but there's just a few more things he has to do.' Nancy knew she was treading on fragile ground, and that one day, she might have to sit both Linda and Billy down and deliver some very different news, but now wasn't the time to dwell on such matters.

'Do you promise?' Linda asked, her little eyes almost pleading for her mummy to be right.

Detaching herself from the words she was somehow managing to say, Nancy answered with all the conviction she could possibly muster, 'Yes,' then once again enveloped her little girl in her arms, hoping she had said enough to instil hope in Linda that her daddy was still alive. She hated lying to her daughter, but Nancy was acutely aware, if she as a grown woman was struggling to come to terms with the lack of knowledge about Bert's whereabouts, she could hardly expect a confused little girl to cope with it.

As Nancy peered down at Linda, she realized not only had the shuddering stopped, but like her own, her daughter's tears had dried up too. *Thank goodness!* By some miracle, Nancy had managed to placate her daughter. If only she could somehow manage to soothe herself.

'Are you feeling a little better now, Linda?' Doris asked, penetrating Nancy's thoughts.

'I think so.'

'Would you like to go and play with Alice for a little while? Do you feel up to that?'

Doris's gentle prompt was answered with the faintest of smiles, and an accompanying nod.

'Good girl,' Nancy added, bending her head down to once again kiss Linda's crown of curls. 'And tomorrow, we will get your writing set out and you can write Daddy a letter. Would you like that?'

'Yes, please. And I will tell him what a good job he is doing too.'

'That's very thoughtful.' Nancy smiled, hoping beyond hope she wasn't setting her sensitive and trusting daughter up for an even greater fall.

As soon as Nancy heard the patter of Linda's feet on the stairs, she turned to Doris, energy draining from her, and said, 'I'm so annoyed with myself for getting upset. Do you think I convinced her?'

Without a hint of hesitation, Doris's affirmative reply came. 'Yes, I do. As I keep saying, you are doing a grand job and, for what it's worth, I don't think it will do Linda any harm to see you are finding life tricky too. She needs to know even adults find things difficult at times too.'

'Why do I feel so terrible, then?'

'Because, you are a mum, and the one thing we all want to do, which is virtually impossible, is make sure our children never suffer a single ounce of pain.'

'It's the fact I've lied to her too,' Nancy sighed, taking a sip of her tea.

'You had no choice, luv. To do anything but, would be cruel. She's too young to come to terms with the ifs and maybes. Now, let me get your tea out of the oven. You must be starving.'

But instead of feeling reassured, Nancy felt as though the world was tumbling in around her, and there was nothing she could do to stop the barrage of feelings that were threatening to suffocate her under a heavy and airless cloud of dread and horror.

Chapter 9

'Shall we go grab a cake and a cuppa?' Patty turned to Archie as the gaggle of workers made their way out of the roasting hot factory into the equally sweltering midday heat.

'Oh, sorry, Pats,' Archie replied, employing the affectionate nickname he used especially when he needed to keep her sweet. 'I can't.'

'Why not?' Patty looked abashed by this unexpected rebuff. 'You aren't on air-raid duty until later.'

Archie shot Betty a cautious glance, but despite how discreet he'd tried to be, it wasn't lost on Patty, who seemed increasingly perturbed.

Rather more quick-witted than normal, Archie replied, 'I'm nipping back with Betty, so Frank can give me some tips on planting a few veggies. My nannan is keen to be a bit more self-sufficient.'

'But you've only got a backyard, not a great whacking patch of fertile land!'

Giving himself a proverbial kick in the shins, Archie silently admonished himself for not thinking his alibi through.

Seeing her partner in crime was struggling and it wouldn't take much to rouse Patty's suspicions, Betty jumped in. 'Didn't you say your family are thinking of taking an allotment?' Betty astonished herself at how easily the lie slipped from her tongue.

But Archie, who was quietly thanking her unfaltering resourcefulness, nodded appreciatively in affirmation. 'Yes. Yes, she's badgering me and my dad that we should be following Frank and Ivy's Dig for Victory lead.'

'I see,' Patty replied sagely, trying not to sound too much like a petulant toddler. She knew it would be churlish of her to complain when all Archie was trying to do was help his family cope with the depressing onslaught of rationing, but why couldn't she help feeling rather put out. Patty could have sworn on her Tom Tom's life, Archie hadn't mentioned an allotment before now. *Please, God, don't let him be hiding anything from me. But surely Betty, of all people, wouldn't be complicit in any of his daft plans? After all, she was her friend, not Archie's!*

'I guess I might see you tomorrow, then?' she added hopefully.

'Er, yes. Maybe.' But seeing the confused look on Patty's face, a mixture of hurt and bewilderment, he quickly backtracked. 'I'll explain to my nannan we will have to go and look at allotments early, and then I'll come straight to yours.'

'Don't put yerself out!' Patty quipped defensively, half stung, instinctively raising her barriers.

'I promise we'll do something nice. Maybe we could go to The Skates after all the fun you had last weekend with the girls, while I was building dens with Billy and yer brothers.'

It was true the previous weekend's afternoon excursion had helped bring poor Nancy's daughter out of the doldrums for a couple of hours, but from what Patty's mom had said after everyone had gone home, Angie hadn't had the same luck with Nancy, who looked more fragile by the day. Despite the raging heat inside Vickers, and the glorious weather Sheffield had been privy to, Nancy was more pallid than ever, her complexion deathly grey, and the dark, imposing circles under her eyes were evidence of how little sleep she was getting.

'All right then,' Patty said, appeased.

'We will have a nice day,' Archie promised, quickly giving Patty a peck on the cheek. 'I may even treat you to a bag of sherbet lemons.' He winked, all too aware that after the enormous clanger he'd dropped, he was going to have to work extra hard to stop Patty's suspicions being aroused any further.

'You don't half know how to treat a girl!'

Sensing Patty was at sixes and sevens with herself, Hattie linked her arm through that of her friend's. 'If you're free then, would you like to nip for a cuppa with me and then help me choose my mum a new pair of shoes? I thought I'd treat her as a surprise with my latest wages.'

'I may as well, considering I've been binned for a pile of mucky tatties and carrots!'

'Pats, don't be like that,' Archie pleaded, keen to avoid one of her prolonged sulks.

'She'll be fine, once she sets eyes on that make-up counter in Banners,' Hattie reasoned. 'Now. Come on. Shall we all get going before we waste the rest of this gloriously sunny afternoon?'

'Sounds like a plan,' Betty agreed, hoping to avoid having to think up any more white lies to throw Patty off the scent.

'Where's Nancy?' Betty checked, scanning the crowd who were now traipsing out of gate three.

'She must have shot off,' Patty answered, their workmate nowhere to be seen.

'Oh dear,' Betty sighed. 'I do hope she can relax a little this weekend and get a bit of sleep. She really doesn't look well.'

'She's at Dolly's tomorrow?' Hattie commented, as she and Patty made to set off. 'There was talk of them all going for a picnic. Hopefully, that will be a bit of respite for her.'

'Let's hope so,' Betty mused optimistically, but she knew the only cure to Nancy's heartache was knowing her husband was safe and well, but with each day that passed, it was hard to fend off the increasing sense of trepidation.

News had spread quickly that the French government had signed an armistice a week earlier, dividing the country in two. The north was now under direct control of the Germans, and the south of a puppet regime, led by the former general Marshal Pétain. It had taken Hitler just eighteen days after Dunkirk to capture France. Rumours had circulated quicky that tens of thousands of Allied troops were still missing.

'Sorry! I haven't kept you too long, have I?' Frank said, as he zigzagged through the maze of exiting grimy-faced workers, interrupting Betty's thoughts. 'One of the top gaffers needed a word about how far along we are with orders. Apparently, there's going to be no let up any time soon.'

'Not at all,' Archie replied. 'We were all just going to walk darn' cliffe. Patty and Hattie are about to go off for something to eat and some shopping, and I'm going to come back with you and Ivy, so you can give me hints about growing veggies.'

'Are you?' The befuddled look on Frank's face revealed his surprise at this unexpected news.

'If it's not convenient, I can come another time,' Archie stammered, acutely aware Patty's eyes had travelled back towards the group and were now flitting like a ping-pong ball, between him and Frank.

'This is my fault,' Betty hastily interjected, once again coming to Archie's rescue. 'I mentioned it to Ivy earlier in the week. She must have forgotten to tell you. Archie's nannan is keen to start a veggie patch. I said, I was sure you would be happy to advise on how to get started.' Betty cursed herself for the hole she was digging and her shame at having to tell so many lies.

'Ah yes. That's no bother at all, son,' Frank answered. 'I'm still learning m'sen, but I have to say, I've become rather green-fingered over the last few months. Ivy tells me my rhubarb is the pinkest she's ever seen, and don't get me started on the size of m' cucumbers.'

'Ooh er, vicar!' Patty harrumphed.

'Patty!' Betty exclaimed, her eyes wide at the innuendo.

'What?' Patty exclaimed. 'I wasn't the one going on about the size of m' cucumbers.'

With that the group were overcome with laughter, and to Archie's relief, for the time being at least, the attention had been deflected from his bumbling excuses.

Twenty minutes later, after waving Betty, Frank and Archie off at the tram stop, Hattie and Patty were secured at a table in a shady corner of Browns tearoom.

'I don't know about you, but I think I'd rather have a glass of lemonade than a brew,' Patty said, brushing away her mass of strawberry blonde curls and using a paper napkin to wipe her perspiring forehead.

'Yes, I think I would too. These overalls weren't made for the summer, were they?'

'They chuffin' weren't! You can tell a man flamin' designed them. Not an ounce of thought put into them.'

After the waitress had taken their order for two glasses of ice-cold lemonade and a bowl of vanilla ice cream to share, Hattie continued, 'Do I get the impression men aren't high on your Christmas list, right now?'

'That obvious?'

'Just a bit. Is something bothering you?'

'Promise you won't think I'm being daft?'

'I'll try.'

'It's Archie. I just get the impression he's hiding something from me.'

'What on earth makes you think that?'

Rolling up the rough, suffocating sleeves of her thick khaki overalls, Patty took a deep breath and shared her worries with her oldest friend. 'He's constantly in cahoots with Betty. First summat about her brother wanting to be an air-raid warden. God only knows why, and then today about this allotment thing. I swear he's never mentioned this to me before, and it's not like I don't see his parents and nannan a fair bit, and I've never heard them breathe a word of it either. I just can't help thinking he's up to summat no good.'

'Patty, don't you think you are jumping to conclusions? Have you considered you might be putting two and two together and getting five?'

'I dunno. I hope so, but the other thing is, he hasn't mentioned my eighteenth birthday once. Not a single flamin' word. Don't you think that's odd? If it was his birthday, I'd be making a reyt big deal of it. I'd be planning all sorts. You wouldn't be able to stop me.'

Hattie found herself in a flummox. She could see this latest conundrum had left Patty in quite a fix.

'I don't know all the answers, but it's obvious to me, and anyone else who has seen the way Archie looks at you, he loves the bones of you.'

'I thought so too, but I'm telling yer, summat ain't right.'

Before Hattie had time to answer, the waitress reappeared,

expertly holding a tray with their much-needed drinks and ice cream, an elixir to combat how stiflingly warm both Patty and Hattie felt in their completely inadequate factory clobber.

'Thanks.' Patty smiled, almost salivating, desperate to quench her thirst that had been made worse by how much dust she had breathed in during her unbelievably hot four-hour shift. As soon as the drinks were placed on the table, Patty picked hers up and drank it down in one go.

'Gosh, I needed that. I was absolutely parched,' she said, her throat no longer as dry as sandpaper.

'Would you like another?' The waitress grinned, placing the silver stainless-steel bowl of ice cream in the middle of the two women.

'That would be grand.' Patty nodded. 'How about you, Hattie?'

'I'm okay.' She chuckled in amusement, looking down at her untouched glass.

Now eyeing up the bowl of equally tempting ice cream, Patty continued her one-sided rant about Archie. 'So, yer don't think he's up to no good, then?'

'I really shouldn't imagine so. I know he didn't tell you about his heart condition until he ended up in hospital, but I doubt he'd be that daft again.'

'Mmmm. He also lied to me about the air-raid warden's job, remember?' As much as Patty now understood Archie's motives for taking on the dangerous war work, especially after he had come to the rescue of Daisy's sister, who'd broken her wrist from a fall during an air raid, the memories of how he'd failed to mention his new role for several weeks made her question if Archie was, once again, hiding something from her.

'Yes, but the two were interlinked, and you have talked all this through now. I just don't think Archie would be as naive again to keep anything from you.'

'Maybe, but that still doesn't explain why he hasn't mentioned my birthday! And it is only two weeks away.' Patty was now feeling particularly obstinate.

'You know what men are like. It probably won't even occur to him until a couple of days before, then he'll go into a blind panic, and rush around at the last minute like a headless chicken to find you the perfect present.'

But Patty wasn't convinced and still had an uneasy feeling in the pit of her stomach. Archie wasn't the type to leave everything until the last minute. She was sure something wasn't right, but if she was honest, there was also a part of her that wasn't sure if she wanted to know the real reason behind Archie's baffling behaviour.

'Oh, I don't know,' she sighed. 'But talking of men, have you heard from your John? Any news when he might next be home so you can plan this wedding?'

'I have had a letter, but he can't say when he will be next home. I don't suppose I can moan, after all, I have only just seen him.'

'But you've got to admit, it would be nice to book a date and then we can go shopping for dresses. It will be my job, remember, as maid of honour to ensure you look your absolute best!'

'Of course, and I promise you will be the first to know.'

As Patty tucked into what was left of the ice cream, Hattie allowed her mind to wander as she imagined what life would be like after she got married. Until the war was over there was a good chance she would remain living at home with her parents, but when John returned to Sheffield for good, they would get their own house. The idea of the two of them planning their future and spending every spare moment they had together made Hattie smile to herself, but just as quickly, a feeling of angst came over her. As much as she would love to escape her dad and his turbulent moods, the thought of leaving her mum alone with him sent a cold shiver down her spine.

Chapter 10

Wednesday, 10 July 1940

Exhausted from another broken night's sleep, Nancy climbed the long metal ladder up to Mildred, the nickname given to the monstrous crane she had been assigned since starting at Vickers ten months earlier. Just putting one foot in front of the other, as she ascended into the heavens of the factory, left her feeling light-headed.

'Are you sure you should be going to work today?' Doris had asked her when she'd delivered Billy and Linda to her concerned neighbour at seven thirty that morning.

'I'll be all right once I get going. I just need my coffee to kick in.'

Doris had known she wouldn't be able to persuade Nancy to take a day off work, but she was worried. Not only could she count on one hand how many cups of coffee she'd seen Nancy sup in the whole time they had been friends, and most of them were in the last week, it was obvious she was struggling and on the brink of collapse. Despite how much Doris and all Nancy's friends at Vickers had rallied around to try to keep her upright, it wasn't enough. 'Please eat this on yer break, luv,' Doris had encouraged her, handing over a sliced chicken sandwich, the leftovers from a salad she'd made for tea the night before; but again, Nancy had barely touched it. 'You can't be manhandling one of those great machines with nothin' inside yer. You need to keep yer strength up.'

Nancy had nodded, absent-minded, putting the snap in her cloth bag on autopilot. Doris could almost guarantee it would still be there when Nancy picked her little 'uns up later. 'Maybe don't do any overtime tonight,' she had advised. 'Get yersen home. You did a couple of hours last night. From what you have told me about Frank, he'll not mind.'

Ever since the afternoon Linda had come home from school worried her daddy had died, Nancy had plummeted further into her own dark despair. She was walking around like a zombie, functioning out of necessity; it was all just too hard. Despite telling her daughter Bert was doing a very important and brave job, the playground banter had felt like a sinister warning. Those innocent children might have meant no malice, but it seemed the ominous outcome Nancy was desperately praying Bert would avoid. She really had no idea what to do, but she was certain of one thing, trying to reassure them with any level of conviction was now beyond her. She didn't have a shred of energy left to keep up appearances. Without Bert, there was no point at all.

So, if the truth be known, for the first time, much to her own horror, the extra couple of hours in Mildred every night was a more appealing alternative than trying to paint on a brave face for Billy and Linda.

Guilt coursed through every fibre of her soul for not wanting to spend time with her children but she really did believe Billy and Linda were better off being looked after by Doris, who, unlike herself, wasn't on the verge of tears every two minutes and could manage a jolly and upbeat conversation without her voice faltering.

They needed someone who could rally them, bolster them after a difficult day, assure them everything was going to be all right, not a wilting, gibbering wreck who could barely string a coherent sentence together. What was it Dolly had said to her on Sunday, when she had taken Billy and Linda to spend the afternoon with her and her granddaughters? 'Whether you think of the worst-case scenario or the best case, the end result will most likely be somewhere in the middle.' Well, the best case was that Bert had never gone off to fight this damnable war in the first place. The worst, well, every fool knew how that ended, even Linda's six-year-old school friends. The bit in the middle? What in God's name was that then? She knew Dolly meant well, heaven knows she's been through her fair share of worry, two sons in the Navy, at the mercy of German U-boats, and an absent husband whom she never spoke about, something had clearly gone very wrong there, but like Nancy she didn't have a crystal ball to hand either. So, whatever this thing 'in the middle' was, common sense at least told her, no one really knew.

Now, back in the moment, she carried on walking up the rigid ladder, the enormity of her thoughts consumed her, turned everything as black as coal, and temporarily paralyzed her. The solid stone shop floor, only a couple of feet below her, started to move, as though she was on a ship looking at the ocean, whirling, no longer stable. Wouldn't it be easy just to plunge into that dark mass, allow it to swallow her whole and put an end to all her misery, disrobe her of the never-ending pain that haunted every single second of her waking hours, and then sharply and brutally penetrated the few rare moments when sleep finally took her, jerking her back to the cruel reality of her life? Yes, that would be the best solution, but then a voice, somewhere in her consciousness, disturbed her, bringing her back to her senses.

'Nancy, are you all right, duck?' Frank called out.

'What? Sorry?'

'Are you okay, Nancy?' Frank repeated.

'Sorry. Yes. Yes, I am,' Nancy managed, realizing she was wavering, and quickly tightened her grip on the ladder.

'Are you sure? Have a minute if you need it,' he urged with a concerned tone that had become so familiar to her, from everyone she knew, since Bert had been declared missing.

'No. It's okay. I was just trying to remember if I'd given the kids their PE kit this morning.' She knew her lie was as unconvincing as it sounded, but she didn't have the energy or inclination to care any more.

'Just take it steady, duck, and take a break whenever you need it.'

'Will do. Thanks, Frank.' The interruption had brought Nancy back to the present, and a momentary prism of focus gave her the spurt she needed to finish climbing the ladder and hoist herself into the snug cabin, where she could be left alone for the next four hours until the hooter alerted the factory to the first sitting for dinner.

Positioning herself, Nancy had, she assumed, enough free space in her mind to listen for instructions from below. She could just about see the blond mass of hair on the top of Archie's head, and not far away, Frank keeping a watchful eye. The orders would start soon.

And, as she knew they would, the quick directions began. Before moving the hook into position, Nancy quickly fanned herself. It felt hotter than normal. The factory's windowless cavern allowed for not a single wisp of fresh air. The blistering heat was overwhelming. She looked down into the base of her cabin. She'd forgotten her water.

'Just focus,' Nancy murmured to herself, but even her own voice sounded distant, detached.

On autopilot, Nancy moved her gear stick that controlled the ginormous crane, positioning the machine into place to pick up and drop the giant slabs of steel, ready for them to be moulded and moved on to other parts of the factory for refining.

The minutes passed. Nancy concentrated as hard as she could, listening out for Archie's and Frank's commands as they hollered above the deafening cacophony that reverberated across the walls of the workshop, but their far-off words were no longer crystal clear, more like an indistinct mumble.

'Listen, you need to listen,' Nancy chastised herself, as harrowing images of her once strong, fearless Bert lying lifeless in a filthy mud-drenched ditch appeared before her eyes. She blinked. *Not now.* Blinked again. This time Bert was holding out his limp arms, calling her name. *Help me. Don't leave me here.* The same chilling images and desperate pleas that had invaded her dreams for weeks, abruptly jerking her awake, leaving her shaken and drenched in sweat, as she reached out across the bed to Bert's usual spot, until the equally harrowing realization kicked in that her husband wasn't there and hadn't been for ten months. This time Nancy clenched her eyes shut, internally screaming for the cruel, haunting flashes of Bert to stop. Wasn't she suffering enough? Weren't her children being subjected to the most agonizing of times too?

In a moment of absent-mindedness, Nancy took her right hand off the lever and squeezed her rough, bitten-down fingernails into her clammy palms. 'Please let it all end,' she pleaded, overwrought with fear. Her head dropped to her chest, where her heart was pounding, racing ten to the dozen, causing her to desperately gasp for breath. As Nancy opened her eyes, flashing white specks danced in front of them, and no matter how hard she tried, she couldn't stabilize her erratic breathing. Nancy blinked harder, quicker, but when she looked straight ahead, the perimeter of her crane cab blurred, the outlines of her hands, which Nancy lifted towards her face, were distorted and the usual high-pitched screeching of steel on steel that accompanied her every working hour had stopped. She could see little and hear nothing, and despite how excruciatingly hot she was, her whole body was shaking uncontrollably. Nancy's bony, angular knees were now banging together, her feet were vibrating up and down in an inconceivable manner and her heart was pulsating so fast she was convinced it would burst through her chest wall.

Opening her mouth, she tried to shout, scream for help, call for Frank, Archie, anybody, but no matter how hard she channelled her concentration, not a single sound escaped her, not even the quietest of mouselike murmurs.

A heart attack. I must be having a heart attack.

Billy. Linda. Their beautiful, innocent faces flashed before her. Their hands reaching out for hers. '*Mummy. Mummy, don't go. We need you.*'

Terrified, Nancy once again tried to cry out, but her throat was tightening, constrained. It was so dry, she couldn't even manage a whimper. This was it. She was going to die. Her children, they would be left with no mummy and a daddy missing in action. How could she leave them now? Why in God's name was this happening? It was too cruel. Surely, if there was a God, he wouldn't allow this, but still, she couldn't cry out for help.

It was as though she were looking down on herself,

watching helplessly as her body battled against an invisible force that was rapidly sucking the life out of her.

'Nancy. Nancy!' The sound of someone urgently calling her name penetrated her consciousness. Was it in her mind?

'Nancy. It's me.' There it was again.

Slowly, she turned her head to the side of the cab. She could see a figure. A man calling her name.

'Nancy,' he said again. 'Are you okay?'

The image started to solidify. The lines became less blurry.

'You're going to be all right,' the gentle voice promised.

Her eyes focused. It was Archie. Nancy stared at him blankly but was still unable to find any words.

'Do you think you can climb out and come down the ladder?' Archie asked kindly.

Get out? Somewhere deep inside her mind, Nancy knew she still had hours of her shift left before dinner. Incredulous; why would she leave her crane now?

'I think you just need a little break. Why don't I help you down?'

Nancy looked from Archie to her still trembling hands. Reality pierced her trance. Why wasn't she holding the control lever? Wasn't that one of the first things she'd been taught? Never let go when operating the crane. In the wrong hands, it was a lethal weapon, and could leave an unsuspecting worker out cold, or, heaven forbid, even worse. A cold shiver coursed through her, almost waking her. The hook, designed to lift tonnes of steel, weighed enough to kill a man. *What have I done?* The shock brought Nancy to her senses. Her vision gradually returning to normal, she glanced over the side of the cab, into the bowels of the workshop. The heavy crane hook, which she normally kept firmly under control and handled with precision, according to Frank, was swinging perilously close to the side of one of the wagons the steel slabs were loaded into. In fact, it wasn't just close, it was swaying like a pendulum, side to side, in and out of the truck, through a huge gaping hole in the side canopy.

Alarmed, a wide-eyed Nancy turned to Archie. 'What happened?'

'Nothing to fret about. Don't you worry, but I think we should get you down and you can have a breather.'

Nancy didn't argue. Her breathing was calming down, and her heartbeat wasn't thundering at the same terrifying rate, but she still felt fragile and woozy. She followed Archie's instructions and slowly descended to the factory floor, which instead of being a bustle of activity, was stilted. As Nancy looked round, she realized dozens of pairs of curious eyes were watching her, searching for an answer to whatever it was she had somehow done.

'All right, you lot. Less slacking and back to work now,' Frank ordered firmly, as he crossed the shop floor towards Nancy, his eyes full of concern.

'Are you okay, duck?' he asked affectionately, gently touching her arm.

'I'm sorry, Frank,' Nancy whispered in horror, suddenly

alert. 'I really don't know what happened. Please tell me I didn't hurt anyone. I really am so sorry.' And with that, the tears Nancy normally kept for behind closed doors betrayed her as they slipped down her dusty cheeks, making streaky rivulets.

'Now, come on. There's no need to cry. No harm done at all, duck. Let's go and have a minute in the office and I'll get one of the lads to fetch you a cuppa.'

Then turning to Archie, he said, 'Can you send one of them up to Dolly in the canteen and ask if she could possibly make a quick brew? Ask her to pop a couple of sugars in, if she can spare it? Then could you take charge while Nancy and I go and have a natter?'

'No problem, boss.' And looking at Nancy, Archie added, 'You take it steady now. You've had a nasty old shock.'

Five minutes later, Nancy's slightly trembling hands were wrapped round a steaming, restorative mug of Dolly's sweet Brooke tea.

'Are you sure nobody was hurt?' Nancy asked again, her voice on the verge of breaking, aghast by her lapse in concentration.

'Positive!' Frank confirmed. Then, trying to make light of the situation, said, 'That's the advantage of working in this place. We are always on high alert. If I had a penny for every near miss, I'd be living the life of Riley, with m' feet up, a glass of port in one hand and a plate of caviar in the other.'

'I really am sorry for all the damage I caused. You can

deduct the cost from my wages.' But even as Nancy said the words, she had no idea how long it would take to replace the canopy. Even with a couple of nights' overtime, she only earned four pounds a week at the most.

'Nonsense,' Frank protested. 'Accidents happen, duck. And, like Betty here, you are normally one of m' best crane drivers.' Betty, who had seen all the commotion that had brought the shop floor to a standstill, had come down from her crane, guessing Nancy might need a bit of friendly support.

'I don't feel much like it today,' Nancy replied.

'Do you want to talk about it?'

Nancy looked from Frank to Betty, taking in their caring, kind expressions, as she desperately tried to recollect exactly what had happened. One minute she had been operating Mildred, the next Archie was helping her down the ladder. *Bert!* Once again, he had invaded her thoughts, harrowing images assaulting her, temporarily paralyzing her, blurring her vision and causing her heart to race.

'It's hard to explain,' Nancy started, then repeated what she could remember, before adding, 'I've never had a funny turn like that before.'

'That doesn't sound very nice, duck,' Frank empathized. 'How are you feeling now?'

'Honestly?'

'We're just worried about you and want to make sure you're all right,' Betty reassured her, reaching across to Nancy and taking hold of her friend's arm.

'I feel like such a fool,' Nancy confessed wearily. 'I really don't know what came over me.'

'May I suggest something?' Betty began tentatively.

Nancy nodded, her eyes bloodshot and cheeks puffy and blotchy from crying, although she dreaded what her friend was about to say.

'I think you are trying to cope with a lot and everything got too much. From what you have described, it sounds like you had a panic attack up there,' Betty started. 'I have no doubt your friend, Doris, will have said the same, but do you think you maybe need to slow down a little?'

'I can't stop. Not now.' Her reaction was impulsive. A guttural, desperate plea. The idea of having time on her hands filled Nancy with dread. Being busy was the only thing keeping her sane, well until this morning.

'No one is suggesting you do, but maybe you could just take it a little easier? You are coping with so much right now. You are working here, looking after those two little children of yours and trying to put on a brave face about Bert. Nobody is that strong. Please remember you are only human, not a robot.'

'What choice do I have?' The deflated lilt in Nancy's voice was a mixture of annoyance and utter desolation. She didn't like being told what to do, but the other part of her knew, she couldn't carry on like this indefinitely.

'Maybe I can offer a solution,' Frank suggested.

Nancy's eyes swung to her foreman. 'Please don't lay me off. I can't be at home all day. I will go out of m' mind.'

'Hang on,' Frank exclaimed, raising his hands in the air. 'Who said anything about laying you off? Besides which, I'd be flamin' crackers to get rid of one of m' best workers.'

'Maybe not after today,' Nancy sighed, resigned to the fact she really wasn't capable of doing a good job of anything at the moment.

'Now, enough of all that. There's not a chance I'm letting you go, but . . .'

Nancy took a deep breath.

'Let me finish, duck.'

'Sorry.'

'There's nowt to be sorry for, but I agree with Betty, that something a little less strenuous might be a good idea right now. And before you start thinking this is some sort of punishment for what's happened today, it's not. I don't give a monkey's chuff about the lorry, but what I do care about is you. If you haven't got yer health, duck, you haven't got anything.'

Biting down on her bottom lip, Nancy felt tears swimming in her eyes. She really was an emotional wreck.

'I just don't want to see you get hurt, duck. The shop floor can be dangerous enough when you have got yer wits about yer, and I'm just a little concerned you could come to some harm.'

Nancy hated the idea of Frank thinking she was now more of a hazard than a help, but despite how much she had tried to pretend she was okay, Nancy was also fully aware she was at breaking point. Not only that, but it was nothing short of a miracle that her little episode hadn't left someone else dead, and Nancy knew she wouldn't be able to live with herself if her own clumsiness had caused the unthinkable to happen.

'What are you suggesting?' Nancy asked tentatively.

Both she and Betty looked towards their kindly foreman, curious about what he was going to say next.

'Don't look so alarmed. I promise it's nothing too drastic.'

'Go on,' Nancy quietly prompted.

'Well, there's two options that you might like the sound of, but before I tell you them, I want you to know, they are both only temporary, so don't be thinking I'm trying to get rid of yer.'

Nancy managed half a smile, aware Frank was doing his utmost to reassure her.

'The first is,' he carried on, 'Dolly was telling me she was a bit pushed in the canteen and could do with an extra pair of hands.'

'Oh,' Nancy mouthed, the suggestion taking her completely by surprise. She'd really thought Frank was going to insist she took some time off. 'What's the second?'

'I heard the gaffer saying they needed some typists in the office, and I wondered if you fancied lending a hand over there for a few weeks.'

It wasn't ideal to be missing one of his crane drivers right now, Frank thought, but it was better to let Nancy work elsewhere in the factory than lose her altogether.

As much as Nancy hated to admit defeat, she could have hugged Frank for being so thoughtful. Whatever had happened up in Mildred, a panic attack is what Betty had called it, but whatever it was, Nancy knew it was a warning. She wasn't daft enough to think it wouldn't happen again, but there had to be safer places to have a *funny turn*.

'I still feel like such a fool,' Nancy admitted, taking the final mouthful of her much-needed mug of tea.

'You mustn't,' Betty and Frank said in unison.

'Thank you,' Nancy replied humbly. 'All the same, I feel so stupid. And as much as I don't want to admit it, I know you're both right.'

'Maybe something not quite as intense might be helpful,' Frank suggested. 'Just for a few weeks until things feel a little easier.'

Nancy nodded. 'It's okay. I know you both mean well and I really do appreciate it.'

'Things will get easier,' Betty said reassuringly, once again gently placing her hand on her friend's.

'I hope so.' What Nancy didn't say, as she felt as though she had been a big enough burden already, was that she couldn't see further than the next hour, let alone what the weeks ahead had in store for her.

'Will you consider my offer?' Frank gently prompted.

'I don't need to.'

Betty and Frank both froze. Surely Nancy had seen Frank was only trying to help.

'Sorry. What I mean is, if you don't mind, I think maybe

a break from operating a crane all day might be a good idea.'

The look of relief on Frank's face was visceral. 'Again, I don't want you to think it's some sort of reprimand, because it isn't.'

'I know,' Nancy interrupted. 'I thought being up in Mildred was probably good for me, but after today, I can see it's allowing my thoughts to take over, and right now they are my own worst enemy.'

'We've all been there, duck.'

Nancy looked at Frank. She knew he'd suffered his own fill of heartache, and his words weren't just empty platitudes to make her feel better.

'Thank you.' She nodded.

'And you just give it some thought about where you'd like to work for the next few weeks.'

Nancy didn't need any time to think about it. She had no doubt the women in the office were a lovely bunch, but the idea of trying to make new friends, or explain why she was so gloomy, filled her with dread. She might not be thinking clearly right now, but the one thing she was certain of was that she needed, more than ever, her friends who didn't ask questions or judge her when she was uncommunicative.

'If Dolly will have me, the canteen would be perfect. I'll try not to break any plates or drop any dinners.'

'Don't give it another thought, duck. You'll be grand and I have no doubt Dolly will be grateful for another pair of hands. We are taking more workers on by the day, so that means more mouths to feed. I reckon folk are taking advantage of how subsidised the meals are and if they can have summat hot and decent here, they don't have to use up as much of their rations.'

'I've heard women say the same in the canteen queue,' Betty agreed.

'When should I start?' Nancy asked.

'No time like the present, duck. Why don't me and you have a wander up to see Dolly now? I bet she will snap you up. And Josie is up there too, so that's two friendly faces. Unless you'd rather take the rest of the day off. No one will mind, luv.'

'No!' Nancy replied, adamantly. 'I'll feel like a fool if I go home now. I'd rather be busy.'

'That's that, then.' Frank smiled, standing up. 'But I want you to promise me one thing.'

'What's that?'

'As soon as you are feeling up to it, you come back down here. I don't want to lose one of my three musketeers permanently.'

'Of course.' Nancy managed a weak smile, once again grateful to be surrounded by such thoughtful and kind friends.

Chapter 11

'What's with the long face, luv?' Angie asked, as her sullen daughter trundled into the kitchen. 'You look as though you've lost a shilling and found a h'penny.'

'I may as well have done,' Patty sulked obstinately.

'That bad?'

'Yes!' Patty exclaimed, dropping into one of the kitchen chairs.

Angie poured Patty a mug of strong tea. 'Want to tell me about it?' she asked innocently, despite knowing full well why her eldest daughter looked so miserable.

'You must know!'

For the umpteenth time, Angie was filled with guilt. 'You don't know what tomorrow will bring yet, luv. Why don't you just wait and see?'

'It's my flamin' eighteenth tomorrow and all Archie has said is that he will take me to the pictures. It's hardly anything special. I just thought he might have put a bit more effort in, that's all.'

'You know what men are like, luv. They leave everything

until the last minute. I'm sure he will have something else up his sleeve too.'

'Excuse me! What's this?' Bill said, walking into the kitchen, holding Tom Tom's hand. 'I shall let you know, I always plan ahead.'

'Well, you haven't said owt about m' birthday either,' Patty reproached.

'Aw, so that's why yer so touchy this morning.'

'Wouldn't you be?' Patty scowled, as she picked up her mug of scalding tea.

Angie threw Bill a warning glance. This wasn't the time to tease their daughter. She was already wound up like a tightly coiled spring. It wouldn't take much for her to burst into a fit of hysterics.

'Yer know yer dad and I will always make a fuss of you on yer birthday,' Angie said, placing a bowl of freshly made porridge in front of Patty.

'And me,' Tom Tom added, as he climbed onto his sister's knee.

'You're just after m' breakfast, aren't yer?' Patty sighed, but the tone in her voice softened as she smiled at her little brother, who still had sleep in the corner of his eyes; that and his ruffled blond hair indicating he had just woken up and hadn't done anything to bear the wrath of Patty's foul mood.

'Here's yours, greedy guts.' Angie laughed, placing a second bowl of porridge on the table.

'I just thought Archie would have made more of a fuss,

that's all,' Patty lamented, feeling rather sorry for herself. 'The girls at work haven't said much either. It's as though no one is that bothered.'

'I thought you said you were going to do summat with Hattie and Daisy?' Angie asked.

'I am. It's just I thought we would have done something a little more exciting and that all the girls, especially Betty, would come along,' came Patty's nonchalant reply.

'There is a war going on, sunshine,' Bill said, as he took the bowl of hot breakfast Angie had handed to him. But as soon as the words had passed his lips, Angie shot her husband a fierce look. She'd meant for him to go easy on Patty, show a little empathy, but instead he'd gone in like a bull in a china shop, with his giant size tens.

'I know,' Patty replied, considering her dad's words. Despite how fed up she was feeling, she also knew he had a point. Archie was busy with his air-raid patrol work; Betty was juggling her time with the factory, the WVS and helping Ivy with her veg patch; Hattie was getting used to a new job and trying to help her mum, who from what she could gather was struggling with her dad; and poor Nancy was only just about managing to get through each day. *Maybe I am being a little self-centred*, Patty thought to herself. *After all, it is only a birthday, even if it is a bit of a milestone.*

'I'm sure you will have a lovely day. We will make sure of it, won't we, Bill?' Angie said reassuringly, as she dug her knuckles into a ball of dough, the third one that morning.

'Of course we will, sunshine,' Bill agreed. 'When have we ever forgot yer birthday?'

'Thanks,' Patty accepted before blowing on her spoonful of hot porridge. *I just hope Archie at least remembers, even if he hasn't arranged anything special.* War or no war, she didn't think she would be able to ever forgive him if he just let the day pass without any sort of acknowledgement.

'How are you getting on?' Betty asked Nancy as she approached the canteen counter, where her friend had swapped her mucky khaki overalls for a blue-and-white gingham apron.

'At work or just in general?'

'I suppose I meant in your new role.'

'Not too bad. I've only dropped two plates so far,' Nancy replied, more upbeat than normal.

'That's only one a day.' Betty smiled, trying to make light of the situation, pleased to see Nancy looking a little less anxious. She still had bags under her eyes, which were as heavy and dark as ever, but Betty agreed with Frank, Nancy was probably better off cooking and serving up dinners, than trying to operate a monstrous and potentially lethal crane. By the looks of things, a couple of smashed plates was a far better alternative than losing control of a great metal hook.

'Take no heed,' Dolly interrupted. 'Nancy is doing a grand job. I've been known to drop two plates in the same number of minutes. Two plates in two days is actually quite commendable!'

Nancy smiled gratefully at Dolly, and then added, 'I have had some good news.'

'What?' Betty quizzed. 'Nancy, has something happened?'

'Go and take a quick break now,' Dolly encouraged knowingly. 'I can man the fort here.'

'Are you sure? It's getting busy.'

'You've been hard at it all morning. Besides which, this news can't wait. Go on and I'll manage the rabble with Josie.'

A couple of minutes later, Nancy was sat at their usual table, nursing a cup of tea.

'So, are you going to tell us?' Betty asked, not wanting to tempt fate but hoping her gut instinct was right.

'What's this?' Patty asked.

'Nancy has some news,' Betty announced, now secretly praying it was what they had all been hoping for.

'It's Bert,' Nancy announced.

Silence fell across the table, the anticipation was palpable as they waited for Nancy to finish.

'We've had word. He's back in England.'

'That's wonderful!' Betty cheered.

'I think I'm still in shock,' Nancy started, taking a sip of her brew.

'Don't leave us in suspense,' Patty urged, delighted to see her friend looking so happy for the first time in weeks.

'There was a letter waiting for me when I got home after work yesterday,' Nancy began, reaching into her apron and pulling out a white envelope.

Betty immediately clocked the colour, smiling at the fact it wasn't the conspicuous brown that was now associated with the ominous news that came in the form of official telegrams.

'It's from a nurse in a hospital in Portsmouth. Bert was admitted about a week ago. I don't know how he got there or how seriously ill he is, but he's alive. My Bert is really alive.' And with that, an avalanche of tears cascaded down Nancy's flushed cheeks. 'Sorry, I'm just so relieved and happy. I thought this day would never come.'

'Nancy! This is the best news,' Betty enthused, wrapping her arms around her friend.

'It really is,' Daisy added, her own eyes glistening.

'I'm so happy for you,' Patty said, echoing the sentiments once Betty had pulled away from Nancy.

'Thank you. Sorry, I was going to try to catch you all later. You have all been so kind. I just wanted everyone to know.'

'Not at all. We'd have been so cross if you hadn't come and told us.'

'Hear, hear!' Patty enthused.

'Anyway, I better get back to work. I don't want Dolly thinking I'm taking liberties, especially as it's only my second day,' Nancy said, standing up.

'I'm sure Dolly won't mind,' Frank interjected. 'I really am so pleased for you. You deserve some good news, duck.'

'That's very kind of you to say. I do still feel wretched for messing you about.'

'Don't!' Frank admonished. 'Archie is operating Mildred.' Then turning to Archie, he added, 'You're rather enjoying it, aren't you?'

'I am!' Archie grinned. 'It makes a pleasant change from using the ground cranes and trying to get the lads to listen to me. I've never been reyt good at giving orders.'

'You'll not want me back,' Nancy sighed.

'Nonsense,' came Frank's booming retort. 'As soon as yer ready, duck, I'll have you back in a heartbeat. You just have to say the word.'

'Thanks, Frank.' Nancy nodded, making to turn back to the serving counter. 'You really have all been so supportive.'

'That's what friends are for,' Patty affirmed. Then taking the bull by the horns in a desperate bid to see if she could encourage Archie and the rest of her friends to help her celebrate her birthday, she added, so everyone else could hear, 'I think this calls for a double celebration. I was thinking of having my first legal drink with Hattie and Daisy in The Welly after work tomorrow, at dinnertime, if you would like to come along.'

'Oh luv, of course. It's your eighteenth, isn't it?' Nancy said. She had heard about Betty and Archie's secret plan but had been told not to say a word.

'Yes!' Patty exclaimed, making a point of throwing Archie a pointed smile.

'Would you mind if I let you know tomorrow, luv?'

Nancy asked. 'I need to check with Doris and just see how Billy and Linda are.'

'Yes, of course.' Patty nodded. At least Nancy, she noted, who still looked exhausted, despite the bit of colour that had returned to her cheeks, had a good reason for being hesitant. The poor woman didn't look as though she'd had a peaceful night's sleep in months. She couldn't, however, say the same for Archie!

Despite how much she tried to remember what her dad had said about the war, she couldn't stop focusing on the fact Archie still hadn't mentioned her birthday, not once. Was it really so much to ask? Surely, with all the gloomy news coming out of Europe, they all needed something to smile about. She couldn't help but feel disappointed at his lack of effort.

On the other side of the table, Archie's brain was working overtime, but whenever he was in a muddle, he couldn't think straight. He was desperately trying to come up with a convincing reason as to why he couldn't go for a celebratory drink with Patty on her birthday. He knew she wasn't daft and had sensed something was amiss.

Before the rising tension could take over Nancy's happy news, Betty inhaled deeply and said, 'Hattie, Daisy and I were talking about this earlier in the week, Patty. We thought you would enjoy having your first alcoholic drink in The Welly.' She had to ensure Patty didn't go straight home from work, and was fully distracted at the pub while she and Archie put all their plans into place.

Now, far more okay with telling lies than she ever thought possible, Betty added, 'I'm really sorry, though, I can't get there at dinnertime, I promised Mrs Rafferty at the WVS I would go over and help. Can I pop over and see you afterwards?'

'Yes, sure.' Patty tried, but failed, to hide her disappointment. Of all people, she had been sure Betty would have been there. In fact, she was convinced Betty would have been the one leading the event, encouraging everyone else to come along. Isn't that what she always did? Was her birthday really that insignificant?

'How about you, Archie?' Patty asked. Surely, despite the fact he hadn't been very forthcoming with any plans, he wouldn't let her down.

But as Archie's cheeks turned a telltale red, Patty's heart began to race. 'Can we chat about this later?' he asked quietly, aware everyone around the table was looking at him.

'So, that's a no then!'

'I can explain,' Archie whispered, hoping to avoid a scene.

'Yer joking, aren't yer? In fact, don't tell me. You have some flamin' air raid thing to do.'

'It won't take long. Just a couple of hours and then I'll come over to yours and we'll go to the pictures tomorrow night.'

'Oh, forget it! Don't put yourself out. I'm clearly not that important,' Patty rebuffed, the mixture of hurt, anger and upset, which had been churning inside her for weeks, now exploding out of her like a volcano. *How could Archie be so selfish? Surely on my birthday, of all days, he would put me first?* she silently screamed.

'Pats, don't be like that. I'll see you first thing in the morning . . .'

'What! As we walk to chuffin' work! Hardly very special, is it? Is that all I'm worth on m' birthday of all days. And my eighteenth birthday at that!'

'I promise, after I've done what I need to do, I will spend the rest of the day with you,' Archie said, trying to placate Patty.

'Why flamin' bother!' Patty wasn't sure if she wanted to wring Archie's chuffin' neck, burst into tears or tell him in no uncertain terms how flamin' useless he was being, or a mixture of all three. Incandescent, she pushed her meal away, noisily scraped back her chair and stood up.

'Oh Pats, don't be like that?' Archie pleaded again. 'Don't ruin your special day before it's even got here.'

'What would you care?' Patty retorted sulkily, turning her back on Archie.

The next twenty minutes passed under an air of tension. Desperately trying to lighten the mood and feeling tremendously guilty her and Archie's plans were now leaving Patty feeling as though they didn't care about her, Betty tried to change the subject. 'It really is just wonderful that Bert is back in England, isn't it? I'm so happy for Nancy.'

'It certainly is,' Daisy agreed.

Finally, the end of their thirty-minute dinner break arrived.

'Right, gang, I'm afraid it's time we got back to it,' Frank said, standing up.

'I'll be glad to get back to work anyhow,' Patty sighed, her blood boiling, feeling more worn down than ever after the lukewarm response to her suggestion for a birthday drink.

'I'll be there in a minute,' Betty said, lifting her tray up. 'I just need a quick word with Dolly about something.'

As Patty headed out of the canteen, flanked by Hattie and Daisy, she realized Archie wasn't with them. Turning round she spotted Betty and Archie deep in conversation and could have sworn she caught the glimpse of a conspiratorial smile between the two of them. Bewildered, Patty was momentarily frozen to the spot. There was something about the familiar way they looked at one another, as though they were sharing a secret, that made Patty's stomach lurch. It wasn't the first time she'd caught them in cahoots, and now, something about their *convenient* explanations made her feel sick. In her heart of hearts, Patty knew she was being paranoid, and neither Betty nor Archie would ever be that deceitful, but something was clearly amiss. Unable to stand it a second longer, she shook her head in a bid to dispel the awful thought from her mind.

'Some friend and boyfriend they have all turned out to be!' Patty audibly muttered, in a state of confusion, tears burgeoning in the rims of her eyes.

'Come on, Patty!' Hattie soothed, hoping to calm her friend down. Unlike Patty, she knew Betty and Archie's conversation was well intended and she just had to hold her end of the bargain to keep Patty distracted in the meantime.

'Sorry. I'm just fed up. It's my eighteenth birthday tomorrow, for God's sake, and Archie hasn't said a word about any plans, apart from a chuffin' trip to the pictures. It's hardly very special, is it?'

Hattie, Daisy and Frank, who had heard Patty's furious comments, all looked at one another. Quickly, trying to placate her friend and defuse the situation, Hattie said, 'Don't be so hard on him. Remember what I said. It doesn't mean he's forgotten.'

'What else can it mean?' Patty sighed in frustration, no longer convinced by Hattie's excuses about men leaving everything until the last minute. *How much later could he chuffin' well leave it?* Patty thought to herself. *It's not like there was much time left.*

'Why don't you just see what tomorrow brings?' Hattie said, trying to appease her.

'I'm not holding out much hope, but I don't think I have much choice, do I? Anyway, please tell me you are coming to The Welly after work tomorrow?'

'Yes, of course I am. I wouldn't miss it for the world.'

'And you, Daisy? Can you still make it?' Patty asked.

'Yes, I'll be there for a quick one.'

A quick one! Patty tried to bite her tongue. She had been talking about her first alcoholic drink for months and now it was finally about to happen, the people she thought would most want to share her special moment with her suddenly didn't seem that bothered and she couldn't help but feel let down by her friends.

Chapter 12

Saturday, 13 July 1940

'Pat, Pat. Wake up. It's your birthday!'

As Patty opened her eyes, she saw her little brother pulling at her pink floral eiderdown. 'Wake up,' Tom Tom insisted.

'All right,' Patty yawned, 'I'm awake.' She lifted her chubby pyjama-clad brother onto the bed and he repaid her by landing a sloppy kiss smack-bang onto her lips.

'Happy birthday,' he repeated, looking as pleased as punch with himself.

'Thank you!' she replied, before thinking to herself, *At least someone's remembered.*

'Get up,' Tom Tom demanded, tugging at her arm. 'I'm hungry.'

'Well, there's a surprise!' Patty looked at her little foldaway clock on her bedside table. 'Six thirty,' she groaned. 'Aw well, I've got to leave for work in an hour, so I don't suppose I'd have got a lie-in anyway.'

Ten minutes later, dressed in her overalls and her strawberry blonde curls tied into a top knot, Patty trundled into the kitchen, with Tom Tom by her side.

'Happy birthday, luv!' Angie beamed, rushing to her daughter's side, and giving her a huge hug. 'Who'd have thought my little girl is now eighteen. A fully fledged adult.'

'Thanks, Mom,' Patty replied.

'Now, sit yerself down and let me make you some breakfast. The others are all still fast gone, but yer dad will be down in a minute. I've got bacon and eggs, and the bread has just come out of the oven.'

'Really? That makes a change from porridge!'

'It is yer birthday. Now, have this mug of tea and I'll get everything in the pan.'

'And me!' Tom Tom piped up.

'Of course.' Angie chuckled, ruffling her youngest son's nest of curly blond locks. 'It's more than m' life's worth to forget about you!'

Just as Patty got Tom Tom comfortable on her knee, Bill marched into the kitchen. 'If it isn't the birthday girl,' he cheered, then pecked his daughter on the cheek. 'Eighteen. I don't feel old enough to have a daughter who is now an adult.'

'I'm not sure I feel like an adult either,' Patty exclaimed. 'Does this mean I have to be really grown-up now?'

'I'm not sure there's much hope of that!'

'Oy!' Patty exclaimed. 'I'll let you know I can be very grown-up when I want to be.'

'He's only winding you up, luv. Just ignore him,' Angie interrupted, handing Bill a steaming mug of tea. 'Now, tell me, what are yer plans for after work? Are you still going to nip to The Welly with Hattie and Daisy?'

Angie silently prayed the answer was yes. Patty had come home from Vickers in a vile mood the night before, ranting about Archie paying no interest in her birthday and Betty bailing out of going for a birthday drink, convinced the pair of them were hiding something sinister from her. Angie had tried to reason with her, explaining how busy everyone was, but her words had fallen on deaf ears, and Patty had gone to bed spitting feathers. Fortunately, as far as Angie could tell, Patty had woken up in much better spirits, and maybe her birthday wouldn't be a disaster after all.

'Yeah, I think so,' Patty replied. 'At least they are willing to celebrate with me.'

'Now, come on, luv. Don't wind yerself up. Not today. You need to enjoy yer birthday,' Angie replied, flipping the bacon in the pan, which was now sizzling away.

'Mmmm,' Patty sighed. 'I just thought . . .'

'Yer mom's right, sunshine,' Bill interjected. 'It's a special day. You should enjoy it.'

'What time can we expect you home?' Angie asked, keen to move the conversation on, before Patty got herself in another tizz, as she cracked the first egg into the large frying pan.

'Erm. Probably about half one, maybe two o'clock at a push. Is that all right?'

'Yes. Yes, it should be.'

Patty looked at her mom quizzically. 'What do yer mean?'

Caught off guard, Angie hesitated. 'Er. Sorry, luv. I just wondered if you would like your cards and present now, or later?'

The idea of a gift instantly lifted Patty's spirits, allowing her to momentarily forget about how cross she felt with Archie's lack of effort. 'Actually, can I wait until later?'

'Yes. Absolutely.' Angie and Bill swapped a bemused grin.

'What?' Patty asked. 'There's nowt wrong with that, is there?'

'Not at all, sunshine.' Bill laughed. 'It's just, normally you're chomping at the bit to rip open yer presents.'

'I know,' Patty agreed. 'It's just, well, it will be nice to have summat to look forward to later when I get home. I was hoping Archie might have planned to take me out somewhere special, but I reckon I'll be lucky to even get to the pictures at this rate. I'm not sure he'll even come round later after what I said to him yesterday. I was pretty horrible to him.'

'I'm sure he will have forgotten all about it,' Angie sympathized, dividing the now cooked bacon and eggs among three plates.

'I wouldn't be too sure. I didn't 'alf give him what for, and I didn't wait for him to come down from his crane cab to walk home with him either.'

Bill raised his eyebrows and rested his chin in his left hand, wondering if his headstrong daughter would ever learn that jumping off at the deep end was very rarely the best way to resolve a situation.

'I'm sure he will be waiting for you to walk to work,'

Angie said, determined to keep Patty buoyant. She hated seeing her daughter in such a fix, and especially on her birthday.

'Do yer reckon?'

'Yes!' Angie and Bill said in unison.

'How do yer both know?'

Bill glanced at his wife, before saying, 'Take it from me, sunshine, that lad loves the bones of you, and the last thing he would want to do is cause you any upset, especially on your birthday.'

'Then why hasn't he made more of a fuss?' Patty scowled petulantly, convinced Archie really hadn't put in more than a minute's thought regarding her birthday.

'Now tuck into this. It will make you feel better,' Angie said tactfully, placing Patty's cooked breakfast in front of her.

'Thanks.' Patty smiled. The last thing she wanted was to feel utterly miserable on her big day, but she still couldn't help feeling miffed about how little attention Archie, and Betty for that matter, had granted her. She just hoped whatever Archie had to do at dinnertime was of utmost importance, if it meant he couldn't come and celebrate with her.

Just before seven thirty, Patty and her dad picked up their gas masks, shouted their goodbyes and made their way out the door. As Bill predicted, Archie was waiting for them on the corner of Thompson Street. 'Happy birthday!' he cheered, giving Patty a big kiss on the cheek and handing her a pink envelope. He'd clearly chosen to forget Patty's outburst the previous dinnertime and the fact she hadn't hung around so they could walk home together.

'Thank you,' she said, smiling weakly. At least he hadn't completely forgotten. 'Can I open it later? I was going to save everything until after work.'

'Of course.' Whether he felt a little put out or not, Archie didn't show it, keeping his tone light and cheerful. 'I promise I'll nip round as soon as I'm done.'

Nip round! Is that all he can manage? Patty silently grimaced, her fury mounting once again. *It's my eighteenth birthday and by the sounds of it, he can only spare a few minutes. Well, that's chuffin' charmin'!* Patty's determination to enjoy her birthday was rapidly diminishing.

'Okay,' she snapped at Archie, more sharply than she'd intended.

Archie anxiously looked towards Bill, who was shaking his head in dismay. 'Right, let's get going or Nancy will think we've abandoned her.'

Somewhat deflated, Patty carried on walking in between her dad and Archie, until they reached Nancy, at the top of King Street, a few minutes later.

'Morning, luv,' she said. 'And a big happy birthday,' she added, handing Patty a bag. 'There's just a little something in there from me and the kids. I don't mean to be a misery guts, but I don't think I'll get to The Welly. I feel so guilty putting on Doris and I've hardly seen the kids all week.'

'Oh Nancy. Thank you so much. You really didn't have

to,' Patty said, and she genuinely meant it. Nancy was the one person she couldn't be cross with for not being able to join in the celebrations. Despite Nancy looking a little bit happier, the gaunt expression replaced by a smile, the poor woman really had been through the mill of late.

'I hope you slept a little better last night,' Patty added.

'I have to admit,' Nancy confessed. 'I was still tossing and turning but more with excitement than worry.'

Guilt coursed through Patty. Here she was moaning but even though Archie might be driving her mad right now, at least he was close by, and up to now, thankfully, his role as air-raid warden hadn't brought him to any harm. 'We can organize another trip to The Skates if yer like to give you a rest. Linda loved it last time.'

'Thank you,' Nancy replied gratefully. 'I'm sure she would love that. You really have all been so kind.'

'It's okay,' Patty said, knowing exactly what her friend was about to say. 'Isn't that what friends are for?'

Linking Nancy's arm, almost pleased to have a reason not to chat to Archie, she picked up the pace as the group made their way to Vickers. Patty knew she needed to stop being sulky with Archie, but she couldn't help feeling hurt, which then led to anger. No matter how much she tried to supress her frustration with Archie's apparent indifference about her birthday, it kept bubbling up inside her and she was worried her increasing resentment was about to reveal itself, yet again.

Fifteen minutes later, after Bill had left his daughter,

Archie and Nancy at gate three, the group were all stood in line, ready to clock in.

'There you are,' Hattie called, as she, Daisy and Betty joined the queue. 'Happy birthday,' the three of them said, in almost perfect synchrony.

'Thank you.' Patty grinned, her irritation temporarily subsiding at their warm greeting.

'Have you had a good morning so far?' Hattie asked. 'Have you been very spoilt? I was going to give you my gift in the pub if that's okay, when we have more time.'

'Me too,' Daisy interjected.

'Yes. Yes, that's all fine. Thank you,' Patty replied. 'I didn't open my present off my mom and dad, as I wanted to save it until later. M' sisters and John were still in bed when I left, so it didn't seem right to open it until they were about.'

'That's very restrained for you!' Hattie remarked, amused.

'I must be growing up.' Patty laughed. 'I *am* eighteen after all.'

'You are a case,' Hattie replied. 'Well, you can open my gift in The Welly, if you are sure you can hold out that long?'

'I think I can manage that!'

'And I'll call round later,' Betty added. 'If that's okay?'

Patty made a concerted effort to dam her chagrin. She was still feeling rather dismayed at Betty. Between the cosy chats she and Archie had been having and the fact she wasn't going to come for a drink at dinnertime, Patty was beginning to question her so-called friend's excuses. But what was it her mom used to say, when she chastised her as a little girl for being argumentative in public? 'It's not the time or the place.'

Instead of making a snide quip, as she seemed quite capable of when it came to Archie, no matter where they were, she just nodded and said, 'That's fine. I'm just going home after The Welly.' The latter part of her pointed remark was less forgiving, and aimed at Archie, to reiterate the point that on her eighteenth birthday, he hadn't arranged anything out of the ordinary; not even a meal out – just a possible trip to the Pavilion to watch a picture. *What sort of flamin' boyfriend was he?*

Chapter 13

'Cheers! And a huge happy birthday to you,' Hattie said, as she clinked her glass with Patty's and Daisy's.

'Thank you!' Patty grinned, determined to enjoy her little celebration with her two friends.

Taking a sip of her port and lemon seemed very grown-up, after years of nothing more than a lemonade or a dandelion and burdock whenever she went to the pub. 'Oh, it's rather nice, isn't it? I think I could get used to this.' Patty's eyes sparkled.

Hattie laughed, delighted to see Patty smiling after how cross she had been with Archie. The icy atmosphere in the clocking-on queue this morning had been obvious, and Hattie hated seeing her friend so miserable, especially on her birthday. 'Now, would you like your gift?'

'Well, I'm hardly going to say no, am I?' Then thinking about how much Hattie was trying to help her mum, Patty added, 'I hope you haven't spent too much.'

Hattie placed the perfectly wrapped box on the table. 'Don't you worry about that. Just open it.'

Patty carefully untied the baby pink ribbon and

unwrapped the floral paper to reveal a small carboard box. 'It's the only way I could get them wrapped up as one,' Hattie explained.

As Patty looked inside, a huge smile appeared on her face. She picked up the new pearly pink lipstick, a mascara compact and some coral-coloured rouge. 'You know me so well,' she said. 'This is perfect. Thank you so much.' Patty leant across the small round table in the corner of The Welly and hugged her best friend. 'As soon as I get home and out of these mucky overalls and wash m' face, I will try them all out.'

'You are very welcome.' Hattie grinned, delighted her choices had gone down a treat.

'And this is off me,' Daisy said, passing Patty an equally meticulously wrapped gift, only this one had a lilac ribbon around some crisp brown paper.

As Patty unwrapped the present, a delicate pink-and-white dotted satin neck scarf fell into her hands.

'It's beautiful,' Patty gushed. 'I love it.'

'I just saw it and thought of you.' Daisy smiled. 'You can wear it on a night out with Archie.'

'You really are both so kind,' Patty said, a little tearfully, feeling slightly overwhelmed, or maybe it was the port making her feel tipsy.

'Not at all. It's your birthday,' Daisy exclaimed.

'I really do appreciate it. You have both been so thoughtful and kind, which is more than I can say about Archie and Betty right now.'

'Let's not think about that now,' Hattie insisted. 'I'm sure Betty didn't mean to double-book herself and I would be stunned if Archie didn't have something up his sleeve.'

'Mmmm,' Patty said, less enthusiastically. 'But yer right. I'm not going to spoil the moment.'

For the next hour or so the three girls chatted and laughed as they enjoyed a second port and lemon each, Daisy and Hattie insisting there was no need for Patty to rush off.

'I do feel a bit woozy.' Patty giggled after taking the final sip of her drink. 'Maybe I should get home and have a cuppa or I'll end up slurring m' words like one of those old lushes you see falling out of the pub at kicking-out time.'

Hattie quickly glanced at her watch. It was just after one thirty. 'Why don't Daisy and I walk home with you?'

'I'm not that tiddly!' Patty gasped.

'Well, I wouldn't mind seeing yer parents. It's been a while.'

'And I haven't got any other plans now,' Daisy added. 'M' mum told me to take all the time I needed.'

'Well, if you insist,' Patty said, shrugging. 'It will be nice to have you around to help me celebrate for a bit longer yet. I've got nowt else on.'

'Perfect!' Hattie said, pushing her chair back and standing. 'Shall we make a move then? I'm sure yer mom will be desperate to see you.'

'At least someone is!' Patty couldn't resist.

Throwing each other a knowing glance, Daisy and Hattie hurried Patty along, determined to keep her in good spirits.

Fifteen minutes later, the three women were walking up Thompson Road towards Patty's house. Suddenly, Patty began to feel anxious. What if Archie didn't show up or only did pop in for ten minutes? What would that say about their relationship? She really wasn't sure she would be able to forgive him.

'Come on,' Hattie encouraged, reading her friend's mind. 'Let's go and have a cuppa with your mom.'

As they made their way up the gennel, a whisper of hushed voices, which Patty assumed were that of her siblings, emanated from the backyard. 'At least they have stayed in to see me,' she mused.

But as the three women turned the corner, Patty stopped in her tracks. 'My goodness,' she whispered, astonished by the sight before her.

A huge, colourful homemade banner, with the words 'Happy 18th Birthday, Patty', was pinned to the wall, and balloons, gently swaying in the sunny afternoon breeze, were anchored with string to chairs around a table covered in an array of buffet food.

Her parents, brothers and sisters, Ivy, all her friends from Vickers, including Betty, were there. Then Patty's eyes darted to the one man she really wanted to see. Archie was right at the front, smiling from ear to ear like a Cheshire cat, gazing back at her, his hand raised, poised for a toast.

'Oh!' was all Patty managed, completely stunned by the surprise welcome that stood before her.

'Happy birthday,' the chorus of excited voices cheered, as everyone lifted their glasses in Patty's direction.

'I don't know what to say,' Patty exclaimed, momentarily stumped. 'How on earth did you manage to arrange all this without me knowing?'

'Well, you don't make it easy, luv, that's for sure.' Angie laughed, coming over to her daughter and giving her a big hug.

'Oh!' Suddenly everything fell into place for Patty. All of Archie and Betty's clandestine chats, their excuses not to meet up, her mum asking what time she would be home, the exchanged knowing glances between her friends. 'You were all in on it!'

'Will you ever forgive us?' Betty asked sheepishly.

'Forgive you!' Patty's fury had dissipated quicker than she could say her name, as guilt over her dreadful thoughts surged through her. 'This is the best surprise ever.'

Then Patty looked over to Archie, whose recent frowns had been well and truly turned upside down.

'I'm sorry,' she cried, running towards him. 'I don't know whether to burst into tears or kiss you.'

'I'll take the latter.' He grinned, and before Patty could argue, he pulled her towards him until their lips touched. 'I love you, Patty Andrews, and I hope you have the best eighteenth birthday ever.'

'Did you plan all of this?' she asked.

'I had a fair bit of help,' he replied, glancing towards Betty.

'But it was all Archie's idea,' Betty interrupted. 'He was determined to make your birthday a day to remember.'

'I'm so sorry,' Patty said again, feeling somewhat abashed. 'I've been so mardy and jumping to all the wrong and most ridiculous conclusions.' To think she had even allowed herself to think Archie and Betty could have been up to no good. What a silly fool she had been.

'Maybe it was a little mean of us to let you think we hadn't made any effort for your birthday,' Betty replied, conciliatory as ever.

'I must admit, I did think you weren't bothered.'

'I promise, it was never meant to upset you.'

'I hope we have made up for it now?' Archie asked.

Looking at both Archie and Betty, she replied, 'You really have. I don't know what to say.'

'Well, that'll be a first, duck.' Frank chuckled, appearing at her side, looking all dapper in a navy blue, short-sleeved shirt, with Ivy next to him, as elegant as ever in a long peach tea dress, her hair curled up at the front, making her even more chic than normal.

'You both knew too?' Patty asked.

'Guilty as charged,' Frank replied.

'How on earth did you manage to keep it a secret?'

'It was testing at times,' he said. 'But it was worth it to see the look on yer face when you walked into the yard.'

'Happy birthday, Patty,' Ivy added, handing over a carefully wrapped gift. 'This is from Frank and myself; I hope you like it.'

Patty unwrapped the present to reveal a cream-coloured clutch bag.

'It's beautiful and perfect for a summer's night out. Thank you.'

'Exactly my thoughts, dear,' Ivy agreed. 'A young lady can never have too many bags.'

'I couldn't agree more.' Patty giggled.

The yard was now abuzz with family and friends engrossed in conversation and children dashing in between legs, playing tig, while simultaneously calling for cake and biscuits.

'Before we bring out the cake,' Angie interrupted, 'why don't you nip upstairs and get changed?'

'I'd completely forgotten,' Patty gasped as she looked down at her grubby overalls, dusty hands and heavy steel-toe-capped boots.

'I'll come with you,' Hattie said.

'Me too,' Daisy added, as the pair of them picked up their bags.

'Have you got clothes in them?' Patty asked in surprise.

'Of course!' Daisy laughed. 'You didn't think we would come to a party dressed in this mucky clobber, did you?'

'Is there nothing you lot didn't think of?' Patty laughed.

'I hope not,' Hattie answered. 'It's been weeks, if not months, in the making.'

Upstairs in Patty's bedroom, a delicate pink-and-white polka dot dress, with capped sleeves and a nipped-in waist, lay on her bed.

'What's this?' Patty cast her eyes over the pretty silky dress.

'Open the card,' Hattie nudged.

To Patty,
I know you will look a million dollars in this.
Happy birthday!
All my love,
Archie xxxx

'It matches the scarf you bought me perfectly,' Patty exclaimed, turning to Daisy. 'How on earth did he choose this?'

'I think you've got Betty to thank for that shopping trip.'

Another surge of guilt coursed through Patty. She really had been most mean-spirited.

'Don't worry,' Hattie said reassuringly. 'We all knew we were taking a risk not telling you, but just wanted you to have a lovely surprise.'

'Thank you. It really is.'

Patty, Daisy and Hattie spent the next fifteen minutes using the bowl of hot soapy water Angie had left in the room, having a quick wash. They carefully applied their make-up, Patty keen to try out what Hattie had bought her, and did their hair, before slipping into their party outfits.

'Twit twoo,' Archie whistled as they made their way back into the yard. 'You all look stunning.'

'Thank you for my dress.' Patty grinned, performing a functionary twirl, before planting a kiss on Archie's cheek. 'It's perfect!'

'I'm so glad you like it. I must confess, Betty did help me choose it.'

'Daisy just told me. I've been just a nitwit, haven't I? I got myself in such a state imagining what you two were up to.'

'Don't worry about that now. Anyway, I've got another little something for you,' Archie said, holding out a small navy plush-velvet box.

'Shall I open it now or later, with everything else?'

'It would be nice if you opened it now,' Archie urged.

Sensing how important this was, Patty gently opened the lid to reveal a silver heart-shaped locket. 'It's beautiful,' she exclaimed, feeling slightly overwhelmed by Archie's kindness and generosity. 'It must have cost you a fortune, what with this and the dress.'

'You're worth it.' He smiled, delighted his choices had gone down a treat. 'Would you like to wear it now?'

'Yes, please, but hang on a minute.' Patty gently unclipped the delicate clasp to open the locket, but when she realized the little heart frames were empty, she looked at Archie quizzically.

'I was scared you would still be cross with me.'

'You daft apeth.' Patty laughed. 'Of course I'm not mad with you. Now pop this necklace on me and tomorrow I will find the perfect photos to go inside.'

Patty spent the next hour talking to all her guests, still

stunned by how much trouble everyone had gone to for her. Dolly had given Patty a pair of diamante hair slides and Nancy had arrived with a beautiful bouquet of pink roses in a delicate glass vase.

Beside the table holding the rest of the gifts, there was another adorned with decanters of sherry and port, bottles of Babycham, a jug of pale ale, and several of barley water for the children. It turned out, Angie had recruited Josie, Ivy and Betty to help with all the catering. Between them they had produced a buffet fit for King George VI; there were enormous platters of egg and cucumber sandwiches, crustless quiches, sausage rolls, a selection of mini jam tarts, an array of almond and Garibaldi biscuits, and, goodness how, but the biggest plate of fruit scones.

'My hens have been rather productive,' Ivy explained, chuckling.

'And I've been kneading bread dough for nearly twenty-four hours non-stop!' Angie laughed. 'My arms are aching. I even sieved out the grain from that god-awful National Flour.'

'My hens are grateful!' Ivy replied, taking a small sip of her glass of sherry. 'As I'm sure are most of the children.' The wholemeal government flour had been far from a hit with the younger generation, who all missed their simple and much-loved white bread, but Ivy's hens loved the grain Angie had saved for them.

'Where on earth did you get all the butter from?' Patty asked.

'We all chipped in,' Dolly explained, then tapped her nose in a conspiratorial manner, adding, 'I may also have a few extra supplies.'

'Dolly!' Patty gasped in mock horror, but knew better than to ask any more, assuming some could have come from the Vickers canteen or one of Dolly's contacts on the black market.

'Can I get your attention, please?' Bill said, interrupting the conversations as he tapped a spoon on the table from the other side of the yard, while Angie quickly topped up everyone's glasses.

'Thank you,' he started. 'Now, I'm not reyt good at speeches, so I won't keep yer long, but I couldn't let today pass without saying a few words about our Patty.'

Patty instantly blushed, taken aback by her dad's unexpected announcement.

'As you all know, she can be a bit of a drama queen . . .'

'Dad!'

Bill threw his daughter an affectionate smile, and added, 'And the run-up to today has been no exception. I think we all came close to giving the game away at points.'

Archie put his arm around Patty's shoulders, who was now looking a little sheepish. 'Sorry!' she mouthed.

'Anyway,' Bill continued, 'despite all the drama and shenanigans, our Patty has brought me and Angie more happiness that we could have ever imagined. I named her my ray of sunshine the day she came into the world, and to this day she still makes us both smile, and we are proud to be her parents. So, if I could ask you all to raise your glasses . . .'

The request was met with utmost enthusiasm, even from the dozen or so children, who lifted their beakers of barley water in the air.

'To our Patty. Happy eighteenth birthday, sunshine.'

'Happy birthday,' came the jubilant response, as glasses were clinked and cheers of 'Hear! Hear!' reverberated around the now crammed backyard.

Once the adulation of birthday wishes settled, Bill once again tapped his spoon. 'I promise I'm nearly finished, but I couldn't let this moment pass without also saying how pleased we are Nancy's husband, Bert, is back on English soil. So, if we could once again raise our glasses, and I'm sure we will all be counting down the days until we can welcome Bert home.'

'To Bert,' came the poignant, heartfelt cries.

'Thank you all,' Nancy whispered, dabbing her eyes with a handkerchief. 'Your thoughts and kindness mean so much.'

'Now without further ado—' Bill started but was abruptly interrupted by his youngest son.

'Cake!' Tom Tom called.

'Give us a second, lad.' Bill laughed. 'If you would have just waited, I was about to say, will you all join me in a chorus of "Happy Birthday"?'

And with that, Angie, who hadn't stopped dashing about, now emerged from the kitchen proudly, but tentatively balancing in her hands a triple-layer Victoria sponge, adorned with eighteen mini candles, their flames all shimering in the afternoon sun.

The mood buoyant, a joyful rendition of the celebratory song could be heard up and down Thompson Road, as Patty blew out her candles. 'Don't forget to make a wish,' Angie whispered as she held the plate in position.

Patty didn't need to think twice. *I wish to always be as happy as I am right now*, she silently mused. *And for this chuffin' war to be over quick sticks.*

The afternoon turned into early evening. The pleasant temperature and happy atmosphere meant no one was in a rush to leave. A gramophone had been sourced and as the sweet lyrics of 'I've Got You Under My Skin' by Cole Porter played, Archie took Patty's hand and, his confidence boosted by the two or three pints of beer he'd consumed, said, 'Let's dance.'

'Your wish is my command.'

And, in the middle of the yard, the couple, feeling blissfully content, swayed in each other's arms.

'Thank you,' Patty whispered, her head resting on Archie's shoulder. 'I really have had the best day. I feel like the happiest girl alive. I don't think I'll ever be able to thank you enough.'

'Just promise to trust me in future and I promise I'll do my best never to make you worry again.'

'Sounds like a plan to me.' Patty smiled, sealing their pact, and the end of a very special and memorable day, with a gentle, lingering kiss.

Chapter 14

Nancy's heart raced as she spotted a white envelope lying on the doormat, instantly recognizing Bert's distinctive handwriting. She picked it up and rushed back into the kitchen, where Billy and Linda were sat with a glass of milk and a biscuit each.

'Look what's arrived!'

'What is it, Mummy?' Linda asked, while Billy wolfed down his sweet treat.

'It's a letter from Daddy.'

'Really?' Billy's interest suddenly piqued. 'What does it say? Is he coming home? Will we see him soon? I hope so. I've got so much to tell him and I want to know what he thinks about my latest paper aeroplane. I'm sure he's going to love it, though.'

'Slow down.' Nancy laughed. 'I haven't opened it yet. Let me pour myself a cuppa and I'll read it to you.'

It had been ten days since Nancy had received the news that Bert was alive and back in England, albeit in a hospital, with goodness knows what injuries. The relief had been immeasurable, and Nancy's once overwrought tears had been replaced with those of joy. She'd been unable to stop smiling and still had to pinch herself, knowing Bert was only a couple of hundred miles away. For the first time in months, Nancy had managed to sleep for more than a few hours at a time, the heavy bags under her eyes gradually reducing, and the grey pallor in her cheeks brightening with colour. Although she was still painfully thin from the stress of the last few weeks, it hadn't gone unnoticed by Dolly that she was putting a bit of meat back on her bones now her appetite had returned.

After the letter from the thoughtful nurse who had been looking after Bert, Nancy, Billy and Linda had all written straight back, overwhelmed with excitement that they had finally heard news of the man they loved most in the world. Linda had told her daddy about Patty's birthday party and the enormous cake they had all shared, while Billy had told him how he had become a master in making paper aeroplanes and had just started reading the Biggles books, and now wanted to be a pilot and adventurer just like the main character. Whereas Nancy had filled her missive with declarations of love and affection, expressing her joy that Bert was finally back on English soil.

Now, as she held Bert's letter in her hand, she was a mixture of excitement and apprehension. There was obviously a reason he was in hospital, and she suddenly felt a sense of trepidation for what she might be about to discover. *Maybe I should have read it first, before announcing to Billy and*

Linda a letter had arrived, she chastised herself. But after she poured herself a steaming brew, she composed herself as she slowly opened the envelope.

'Come on, Mum,' Billy insisted. 'You're taking ages. What does Dad say?'

Nancy bit her lip, and hoped beyond hope his letter was full of good news. 'Hold yer horses,' she replied, playing down her concern. 'Right. Let me sit down and read it first, then I can tell you what Dad has said.'

Linda and Billy nudged closer, and although they were both good readers, she felt confident they wouldn't be able to decipher Bert's scrawl. Then to Nancy's relief, she realized there wasn't one letter, but three. On each neatly folder sheaf of paper was each of their names.

'Daddy has written to us all,' Linda exclaimed, her sparkly blue eyes lighting up.

'Can I read my own?' Billy pleaded, fit to burst. 'I can read lots of long words now. Daddy must have known that, otherwise he wouldn't have sent me my *own* letter.'

'Of course. Here you go.' Nancy grinned, handing over the letter, glad to see her children looking so happy after months of waiting for news from Bert.

'Will you help me with mine?' Linda asked, her voice ever so slightly faltering. Nancy knew how much her daughter had desperately missed her daddy. Out of her two children, it was always her sensitive little girl who wore her heart on her sleeve and would wake up in the night upset that she was missing Bert. It wasn't that Billy hadn't hoped to see his dad, it was just he revelled in the adventures he imagined Bert was having. In his eyes, his dad was a hero, so he was happy envisaging Bert driving a huge tank, or in his words 'fighting the baddies' with untold gumption.

'Of course I will, poppet.' Nancy kissed the top of her daughter's head, her mass of wild blonde curls falling haphazardly down her rosy pink cheeks.

'Can I read mine first?' Billy pleaded. Nancy knew there was no point in arguing; she wouldn't get a second's peace until her impatient son had read the letter at least twice.

'Go on then. Read it out to us all.' As always, Linda, compliant as ever, didn't protest.

Billy puffed his chest out, sat up tall and began.

Dear Billy,

I'm sorry you haven't heard from me for a little while. I've been a bit busy being a . . .

'What does that say, Mum?'

'Soldier.'

. . . soldier. I didn't manage to drive any tanks but I did see lots of planes.

Nancy took a sharp intake of breath, dreading to think what atrocities he'd witnessed by the German Luftwaffe.

Undeterred, Billy continued.

I hope you have been a very good boy for your mum
and you are working hard at school.

 Are you still making paper aeroplanes, and having
Swallows and Amazons . . .

'Adventures,' Nancy interjected, as Billy struggled to read
the word.

 . . . adventures with Joe next door?

Nancy assumed Bert mustn't have received their letters they
had all written before penning these.

 I can't wait to see you. I am hoping to be home very
soon. I just have a bit of a sore leg, but as soon as
that's better, I will be coming back to see you all.

'So that was it.' Nancy shuddered, knowing Bert would
have underplayed how serious his injury was. But Bert was
back in England – that's all that mattered and hopefully he
was on the mend.

 Until then, my little soldier, carry on looking after
your sister and Mum for me.
 Lots of love,
 Daddy xxxx

Finishing the letter, Billy gripped the piece of white paper, a smile the size of the moon emerging across his freckled face. 'Daddy is coming home!' he finally exclaimed. 'Do you think he will be back before the school holidays start this week?'

Nancy wrapped her arms around her delighted son. 'I'm not sure about that but hopefully we won't be waiting too much longer.'

'He can look after us while you are at work.'

'Maybe,' Nancy smiled, 'but Doris has offered to take care of you in the meantime.'

'At least I can play with Joe all summer.'

'You can,' Nancy said, giving Billy's mop of brown hair an affectionate ruffle.

Climbing onto Nancy's knee, Linda looked up at her mum. 'Please will you read my letter now?'

'Of course I will, poppet.'

Unfolding the paper, Nancy took in Bert's writing, feeling closer to her husband than she had in for what seemed like forever.

Dear Linda,

How are you, my little poppet? I hope you and Billy are both being good for Mummy. I'm sure you are.

I am very sorry it has taken me a long time to write to you. I hope you aren't too cross with me. I promise it wasn't because I didn't want to. Sometimes being a soldier means you are very busy, but the good news

*is I will be home soon, and I can't wait to see you all.
I have missed you, Billy and Mummy very much and
I'm looking forward to lots of big cuddles.*

*You can tell me what you have been up to at school
and what new books you have been reading.*

*I have a bit of a sore leg so it might be a few weeks
before I am allowed to leave the hospital, but as soon
as I can, I will be on my way back to you all.*

*If you do get the chance, will you write me another
one of your lovely letters, telling me what you have
been up to, on that pretty writing set you got for your
birthday? And maybe you could draw me a picture
too. I can stick it next to my bed and then I will have
something nice to look at. I would like that.*

I promise I will see you soon.

Lots of love,

Daddy xxxx

Nancy placed the letter down on the table and took a sip
from her cup of tea. As she'd read Bert's words out aloud,
she could almost hear his voice and for the first time in
months felt like there was some light at the end of the
tunnel.

But as Nancy looked down at Linda, she saw tears gently
sliding down her little girl's face. 'What is it, poppet? Don't
cry. Isn't it lovely to have a letter from Daddy?'

'I'm not really upset, Mummy. They are happy sad tears.'

'Oh sweetheart.' Nancy pulled Linda a little tighter

towards her chest. 'As long as they are more happy than sad. Daddy wouldn't want you to be miserable. And isn't it wonderful that he might be home soon?'

'Yes. Can I draw him a picture now before I go to bed?'

'Of course you can.'

'And can I make Daddy a paper aeroplane?' Billy piped up. 'I want him to see how good I've got.'

'I'm sure he would love that.' Nancy chuckled and was also secretly relieved their attention was diverted. She could read her letter from Bert later, once both children were in bed, and she didn't have to be quite so brave if emotions overtook her.

It was a couple of hours later when Nancy was sat back down, her cup refilled with freshly brewed tea, and the letter from Bert before her. Billy and Linda had fallen asleep smiling, after a chapter of *Swallows and Amazons*, but Nancy knew the real reason was they each had a letter under their pillows from Bert. Seeing them both, but Linda especially, so content after months of apprehension had made Nancy's heart swell with happiness.

Now as she picked up her note from Bert she was determined to savour the next few minutes as she read the words her husband had sent to her knowing he was one step closer to coming home.

Dear Nancy,
I'm so very sorry you haven't heard from me for
so long. I promise it wasn't because I didn't want

to write to you. I simply couldn't. It's too long of a story for a letter, but one day, I will tell you why.

I have missed you, our Billy and Linda so much. It was thinking about you all every day that got me through. The thought of seeing all your faces again was the only motivation I needed.

Anyway, I didn't write to you to be all maudlin. The good news is, as you now know, I'm finally back in England. Unfortunately, I went and got myself injured, and my leg is a bit of a mess. I'm hoping it will start to heal now I'm in hospital, but the doctors aren't making me any promises, but you know me, I'm not one just to give up. I guess what I'm trying to say is it might be a little while before I get home. I don't think the staff here are keen to let me go anytime soon, but please don't worry. I might not be able to run any races, but I'm keeping everything crossed that it's just a matter of time.

I hope you are managing to keep your chin up. I know you will have worried yourself witless when you didn't hear from me, and just knowing that made me feel dreadful, but it also made me do everything I could to get back to England.

I hope our Billy and Linda have been good. I'm sure they have. They've always been good kids.

Please write to me as soon as you can. I haven't had any letters from you in a while. I know it's not because you haven't written to me; they just couldn't

get to me. Maybe they will find their way to me soon,
but in the meantime, I would love to hear about
what you have all been up to. Tell me everything
when you can.

And lastly, but definitely not least, I really hope
you have been looking after yourself. I know how
hard the last few months must have been, and you
will have been worrying yourself sick, and for that
I am so sorry. This war has a lot to answer for.

Give our Billy and Linda a big kiss and cuddle
from me. I can't wait to get home and hold you all
in my arms again.

All my love,
Bert xxxx

Nancy carefully put the letter on the table, placed her face in her hands and wept, tears flowing unbidden into her clammy palms. It wasn't that the letter was overly sad or full of bad news, quite the opposite, it was just so overwhelming. The enormity of hearing from her husband, not just the nurse, but her actual Bert, after all these months, was palpable. Even the four little kisses, where he'd ended the letter with his trademark sign-off, representing the four of them, had left her overwrought with emotion.

She had waited so long for this moment, hoping beyond hope it would happen but equally terrified it would never come. For what seemed like an eternity, her every waking hour had been overtaken with worry, an overriding feeling of fear that something awful had happened. And now, here, before Nancy's very eyes was his letter, and it had completely engulfed her. She was happy, beyond happy in fact, that finally she, Billy and Linda could at least write to him, and know they would receive a letter back. No longer did Nancy have to think up excuses for why a letter hadn't arrived and then pray she wasn't inadvertently causing her children any further suffering by the white lies she was telling. Just knowing Bert was alive and in England was the greatest gift she could ever hope for.

Nancy picked up the letter again and slowly reread it. Her husband's natural positivity was there, his determination to get home, the desire to be a normal family again, the four of them, it was just like the Bert she had always known and loved. Nancy knew he'd felt conflicted when he went off to war, his moral conscience battling against how upset she, Billy and Linda would be, but like so many men, he'd felt compelled to go and fight against that godforsaken German dictator. She could still remember the heart-wrenching moment they had said their final goodbyes at the Midland train station in Sheffield, as if it was yesterday; all of them struggling not to break down in the middle of the crowded platform. That was ten months ago now; a different life, so much had changed.

But Nancy was determined to remain optimistic, just like Bert always was. He never allowed himself to get sucked into the rights and wrongs but always looked to the future.

Holding the letter to her chest, Nancy closed her eyes.

Her relief of knowing Bert was all right was all that mattered. That night as Nancy climbed into bed, instead of tossing and turning, she quickly fell into a contented and happy sleep, knowing her husband would be back home soon and they would all be a family, once again.

Chapter 15

'I hope you don't mind me saying, luv, but you look dead beat today,' Dolly commented, as Hattie approached the canteen counter.

Hattie smiled weakly at Dolly, knowing her comment wasn't meant unkindly, but was said more out of concern. 'I didn't get much sleep.'

'Has summat happened, duck? Nothing's happened with your John, has it?'

'No. No. Nothing like that,' Hattie replied, taking the steaming plate of Dolly's special Friday mince and onion pie and mash. 'My dad just came home late, and he was a bit worse for wear.'

What Hattie left out was that her dad hadn't just come home late, he had been rip-roaring drunk and had hammered on the front door, managing to wake half the street, before Hattie and her mum rushed downstairs in a daze to let him in. As usual, there was no apology, just the ramblings of a man who had seen the bottom of far too many pint glasses. As Hattie's mum, Diane, tried to persuade him to go upstairs so she could get him to bed, Vinny had not only rebuffed her gentle encouragement but had lashed out. Hattie winced at the harrowing memory of her dad, swinging his arm in brutal resistance, sending her mum flying across the hallway. Vinny hadn't even looked sideways at his wife, crumpled on the floor. Blind drunk, his eyes glazed over, it was doubtful he had even realized what he'd done, so any chance of an apology was non-existent. Hattie had instinctively rushed to her mum's side, appalled her dad could be so callous. She'd suspected he'd been violent in the past, but this was the first time Hattie had witnessed her dad carrying out such a cold-hearted attack. Diane, her maternal instinct kicking in, had tried to brush it off. 'He didn't mean it, don't worry. I'm fine. It was just an accident,' she'd whispered, holding back the spasm of tears, which were threatening to erupt. 'It's nothing, honestly. Your dad didn't mean anything by it. He wouldn't deliberately hurt me.' But despite all Diane's well-intended claims, Hattie knew she was simply pretending for her benefit.

Whether her dad had meant it or not, he'd done it, and what had made Hattie feel so desperately frightened was how he'd stormed at her mum in his drunken stupor.

Hattie had helped her mum into the kitchen and made her a cup of tea, as they listened to him banging about upstairs, trying to take off his clothes, until the house fell silent, her dad no doubt collapsed onto the bed.

'Has he done this before?' Hattie had asked. Her mum

didn't answer but the worn-out expression on her face betrayed the truth she refused to admit.

After their second cup of tea, Hattie had tried to persuade her mum to sleep in her bed with her, but Diane had refused, insisting her daughter needed a good rest before the morning. Chance would have been a fine thing. Hattie had tossed and turned when she finally turned in, unable to get the image of her dad so drunkenly assaulting her mum out of her mind. Hattie's worst fears of what her dad was capable of when he'd been on the drink had become a reality. He really was a nasty brute. When she'd got up this morning, Diane was still at the kitchen table, where Hattie had reluctantly left her, her head resting heavy on her arms.

'Oh Mum,' Hattie had sighed. 'You shouldn't have to put up with this.'

'It will pass, luv.' Diane attempted to insist but exhausted, she said the words with little conviction, the weariness in her voice revealing she didn't believe for a second that would be the case.

'Are you sure you are all right?' Dolly said kindly, bringing Hattie back to the present.

'Yes. Just a bad night's sleep. That's all. I'll be okay.'

'Well, you take it steady today, duck,' Dolly replied, not convinced by Hattie's explanation.

'I'll do my best.'

Dolly recognized all too well the fatigue in Hattie's face, mixed with a fragile and resigned acceptance, but also knew now wasn't the time to probe too deeply. She couldn't quite put her finger on it, but she sensed that something was up.

'Well, get this down yer, and hopefully it will see you through the rest of the day,' Dolly said, nodding at the plate of food, 'and make sure you try to get an early night if you can.'

'Thanks, Dolly. I'll certainly try.'

As Dolly watched Hattie join the rest of her friends at their regular table, she made a mental note to keep a closer eye on her. She'd overheard the young lass mentioning her dad spending a fair bit of time in the pub, and had hoped it wasn't anything too serious, but now she wasn't so sure.

'Is everything all right?' asked Nancy, who had stood alongside Dolly dishing up meals to the hordes of hungry workers.

'Not sure, but I hope so.'

'That sounds cryptic.'

'Sorry, it wasn't meant to. I just don't want to say summat and get it all wrong.'

'Fair enough.' Nancy smiled tactfully, scooping a helping of pie onto another plate, and handing it over the counter. 'Anyway. How about you? Are you and the kids feeling a little better?'

'We are,' Nancy replied cheerfully, her cheeks now showing a little colour and the bags under her eyes receding. 'Billy and Linda can't wait to see Bert again, and I must admit, neither can I. It's been far too long.'

'Any idea when he might get home?'

'Afraid not. I guess he will let me know. I did wonder if I could go to Portsmouth and see him but it's too tricky. It would take me away for at least a couple of days and I can't ask Doris to do any more than she already does.'

'I'm sure Doris wouldn't mind under the circumstances,' Dolly suggested.

'Maybe not, but if I'm honest, I'd struggle to leave our Billy and Linda. I've never left them before for any length of time and it would cost a fortune to get to Portsmouth. It's such a long way. I think I'll just have to wait until he gets home. I'm just praying it won't be much longer.'

'I'm sure it won't be,' Dolly said with optimism. 'And at least now you have something really special to look forward to.'

'I do!' Nancy enthused, the uplift in her voice indicating a mixture of relief and excitement.

Apart from Betty, who was busy chatting to a trio of women in mop caps at the Swap Club corner, the gang of workers were tucking into their regular Friday dinnertime treat at their usual table.

'I don't know how Dolly does it, with rations 'n' all, but I swear this pie gets tastier by the week,' Frank praised, as he tucked into his steaming scran.

'Or maybe we get hungrier!' Patty exclaimed.

'Patty!' Archie mock-admonished.

'I was only joking, but I am chuffin' starving.'

'You always are.'

'It's hungry work up those cranes,' Patty puffed in defence.

'I'll give you that.' Archie nodded, throwing his sweetheart an affectionate wink.

Hattie, who didn't usually have a jealous bone in her body, couldn't help but feel the slightest twinge of longing for John, especially today. More than ever, Hattie felt as though she needed his support. Working at Vickers had been the distraction she needed, and Patty's friends had given her a warm welcome that had helped galvanize her a little, but she hadn't had the strength or energy to confide in them how hard things really were at home. She'd never had to spell it out to John; although he'd never bore witness to the worst of her dad's actions, he'd seen and heard enough to know when Hattie needed a restorative arm around her. Not even Patty, her best friend, knew the extent of her dad's increasingly volatile moods. It wasn't just that Patty lived in her own little world, keeping the explosive drunken incidents to the confines of her own exhausted mind had allowed Hattie, until today, to compartmentalize what was happening at home – leaving those nights behind her back door, and allowing her to enter through the gates of Vickers six mornings a week. It had felt safer that way. But today was so much harder. Hattie knew that news about the rescue operation at Dunkirk had amplified her dad's alcohol-fuelled moods, churning up memories of his own experiences serving in the Great War, but she just couldn't understand why he had to take it out on those who would try to help him the most, given half the chance.

Even so, Hattie was determined not to sour her new life with the one she wished she and her mum could somehow escape. Instead, painting on a smile and listening to everyone else's woes meant she didn't have to think about her own for up to ten hours a day. It didn't stop her worrying about her mum, but she knew daytime was always the calmest at home; it was when her dad was either working down the pit or sat at the kitchen table on his occasional days off, reading the paper, barely uttering a word, despite how much the news across Europe fuelled his need to drink, night after night. Besides which, how could she even compare her own troubles with those of the others, after what Nancy had been forced to endure over the last few weeks? Where would she even begin?

And she had to remember that not everything in her life was horrendous. At least her John had got home from Dunkirk in one piece and wasn't hauled up in a hospital at the other end of the country. She knew she should be grateful even if John had now been, according to his latest letter, stationed in the middle of nowhere on the Salisbury Plain on a mortar course, whatever that was, and was far away when she needed him most.

'Are you all right?' Betty asked gently, pulling Hattie back to the noise and chatter of the factory canteen. 'Penny for them. You look a million miles away.'

'Oh, sorry. Just a bit sleepy today. End of the week and

all that.' Hattie quickly smiled, hoping her little white lie was enough to convince Betty that she was just feeling the strain of working tooth and nail.

'Anyway,' she added, changing the conversation, 'did the women you were just chatting to find what they needed in the Swap Club?'

'They did and donated some bits too.'

'Is it still going well?' Daisy interjected, remembering how it was that very box that had acted as the catalyst to her becoming friends with Betty, Nancy and Patty.

'It is. I didn't know if the novelty would wear off but barely a day passes without someone having a rummage through or somebody donating a skirt, or a blouse they no longer wear.'

'It's true what they say, one person's junk is another's treasure,' Daisy mused, remembering how she'd been over the moon to find winter woollies for her two younger sisters, not long after starting at Vickers.

'You've certainly helped a lot of folk out,' Frank enthused, in between mouthfuls of pie and mash.

'I do hope so. That's all I ever wanted,' Betty replied.

'Talking of good deeds, Ivy was telling me you are still as busy as ever at the WVS.'

'We are. In fact, Daisy and I are heading over there after work tomorrow for a couple of hours. There seems to be a constant demand for hospital supplies.'

'I'm sure they're gratefully received, duck.'

Frank had quietly been picking up what bits of news he

could on the wireless, mainly when Ivy was busy tending to their vegetable patch or checking on the hens, determined to avoid her worrying.

Although the evacuation of troops at Dunkirk had been declared an enormous success, France hadn't been able to overcome the German troops and the country had fallen to the power-hungry dictator. Even more worryingly, snippets of news were filtering through that the Luftwaffe had attacked shipping convoys in the English Channel and night raids had started along the south coast. He hoped poor Nancy hadn't heard anything, knowing it would cause her another overwhelming wave of worry about Bert, who was hospitalized not far from where the Germans were targeting. Even for Frank's liking, who always tried to remain calm and positive, telling himself the RAF were a force to be reckoned with, it felt a bit too close to home.

Hattie, who had been quietly picking at her dinner, exhaustion and worry diminishing her appetite, had hoped when she started at Vickers that she would also be able to join Betty and Daisy at the Fulwood depot. But she didn't like to leave her mum any longer than she really had to, and after last night she was even more hesitant to spend more time away from her. She had thought about asking her mum to come along to the WVS with her but knew her dad would kick up a stink about her not being at home 'where she belonged', and Hattie couldn't bear the thought of giving him reason to start yet another needless argument.

'What about you two?' Frank asked, looking towards Archie and Patty, determined to keep the mood buoyant.

'I think we're off to The Skates tomorrow afternoon with our Sally and Emily, then Archie is on shift with the ARP. I was going to ask Nancy if she wanted me to take Linda and Billy too, so she could have a break,' Patty replied, after shovelling the last forkful of her dinner into her mouth.

'I'm sure she'd appreciate that.' Frank nodded. 'It's been a rough old time for her. She's coming over to us on Sunday. Ivy is determined to make sure she takes a break and is cooking up some dinner.'

The 'us' wasn't lost on Betty, who couldn't have felt happier to see her landlady and Frank's relationship evolve. This war was testing each and every one of them in different ways, but alongside the relentless worry and fear, there were still plenty of reasons to smile. She'd learnt long ago, dwelling on the negatives did no good at all, but celebrating the little things that made her happy made life far more bearable.

Chapter 16

Saturday, 27 July 1940

'That was more exhausting than I thought.' Daisy yawned as she and Betty made their way out of the Fulwood depot of the WVS. The pair had spent the last two hours making hospital bandages after Mrs Rafferty had explained the need for supplies was as great as ever. 'Maybe I'm being naive, but I thought things might have eased off a bit, especially after Dunkirk.'

'It doesn't sound like there's going to be any let up any time soon,' Betty sighed, trying not to overthink the implications.

'I know what you mean. I overheard my dad talking to one of the neighbours about the Germans coming for England next. Do you reckon he's right?'

The thought had crossed Betty's mind more than once in the last twenty-four hours, and despite her normally optimistic outlook, she'd asked herself the same question.

It still felt inconceivable that France was now occupied, despite the admirable fight the Allied troops had put up. Until Operation Dynamo and the mammoth support of the small ships, France had seemed a million miles away, a foreign land that had no bearing on England, but suddenly it felt much closer. If fishing boats and trawlers could get there and back in a day, then the Luftwaffe wouldn't have any problems soaring across the skies to Blighty.

But will they really invade Britain? she silently pondered. *Is that Hitler's next plan?* There had been rumblings that England could be his next target. Betty had to give her head a little shake to stop the thoughts, which were threatening to consume her.

'Do you fancy coming to the funfair with me and my sisters?' Daisy asked, pulling Betty's attention back to the here and now. 'I promised I'd take them.'

'That would be wonderful,' Betty agreed, keen to ignore what was going on in her mind, which had been niggling away at her since she'd got home from work the night before. A happy distraction was just what she needed. *There's no point in fretting over something that hasn't happened*, she quietly reminded herself of the advice she had handed out to Nancy countless times since her Bert had gone off to war.

'I think there's a merry-go-round and a helter-skelter as well as a few stalls selling sweets.'

'Do you know, that sounds just the tonic,' Betty replied as she fell into line with Daisy and they made their way to the tram stop.

An hour later, Betty and Daisy were sat behind Polly and Annie, who were squealing with delight as the four of them bopped up and down on the Victorian carousel.

'This is so much fun!' Betty laughed. 'I can't remember the last time I came to the fair. It must be years.'

'Me too.' Daisy giggled.

It didn't take much cajoling from Polly and Annie to queue for a second turn and when they begged Daisy and Betty to have a go on the helter-skelter, they were met with little resistance.

Their sides hurting from laughing, the two women finally collapsed on the grass, after Betty had insisted on buying them each a refreshing glass of lemonade while Polly and Annie went to try their chances on Hook a Duck.

'I think it's fair to say we have earned this,' Daisy declared, taking a long gulp of her drink as the afternoon sun beat down on them.

'You won't get any argument from me on that one. But I must admit I don't think I've had so much fun since before the war.'

'I'm not sure any of us have.' Daisy lay back, propped up on her elbows, her long legs outstretched before her. 'And to be fair, what with all the overtime and helping out at the depot, you barely get a minute to yourself, and I bet you've been helping Frank and Ivy with the vegetable patch at home too.'

'I have, but that's quite relaxing, and I get a real sense of achievement when we pull up some potatoes and pick the peas, knowing we grew them all ourselves. We've even had some deliciously tasty beetroot. Ivy is in her element coming up with new recipes and serving up fresh vegetables every night. I feel guilty saying it, but with what Ivy creates, I sometimes forget that we are on rations.'

'Don't feel guilty! Ivy is so generous. I know we are grateful for the extra eggs and veggies she keeps sending our way. They have been a godsend and have saved us from those flaming awful dried eggs that are meant to be a substitute for the real thing.'

'It makes Ivy happy to know she's helping. It was the whole reason she started the veggie patch and bought the hens. It makes her feel like she's doing something useful, which she obviously is.'

'Please thank her from me again,' Daisy reiterated, placing one hand above her eyes to shade them from the late afternoon sun. 'Now tell me, have you heard from William lately? How's he getting on in Canada?'

'I have actually,' Betty replied, swallowing back the knotty ball of angst that she'd been trying to repress, determined not to spoil the fun she'd had. 'There was a letter waiting for me last night when I got home,' she added, recalling the missive from her fiancé.

My lovely, sweet Bet,

William's letters always started in the same manner.

You won't believe it but as I write this, I can see the Canadian Rockies, and even now in July, there is snow on them. And a few days ago, we were given a day off to go and watch some chuckwagon racing, which was really good fun as teams of men drove horses round a circuit very fast, pulling a wagon. The locals relished in it, even when a few drivers were injured. I have to admit, though, I was on the edge of my seat.

Anyway, it made a change from being in the sky, but you'll be pleased to know my instructors say I'm doing well. I'm about to start taking part in some cross-country flights with the other cadets and will be taking it in turns to fly and then navigate. Apparently if we get lost, all we need to look out for is the Canadian Pacific Railway, and that will help guide us. I hope they're right as I've also been told sometimes this isn't always possible due to all the forest fires in the summer making visibility poor. Anyway, don't you be worrying though, Bet. I'm in good hands and the instructors aren't going to let us do anything daft.

Now enough about me. What you are all up to? How's your veggie patch coming on and has that funny hen, Houdini, done any more disappearing acts?

Did Patty have a good birthday after all your secret preparations with Archie? I bet it was a right surprise, wasn't it? I'd have loved to have seen the look on her face when she realized what you had all

*been planning. I hope she had a great day and you
all celebrated in style.*

*And how's Nancy and her little ones doing? I've
been thinking about them a lot. Any news on Bert
yet? All that worrying really is rotten for them. I'm
keeping everything crossed he's on his way home to
England very soon and is safe and well.*

Clearly her last letter, which she'd penned a couple of days
after Patty's eighteenth birthday, filling him in on all the
details, hadn't got to William yet. Betty had got used to
the time lag between their correspondence, knowing by the
time their latest news reached one another, it was already
a few weeks old.

*Please promise me you are relaxing a little too. It
sounds like Daisy has been good for you, making
you stop for a minute and have a bit of fun. You
deserve it. I know how hard you work between the
factory and now putting in as many extras hours
as you can with the WVS. Have you been back to
The Skates? I'm holding you to that promise to
teach me how to glide around the floor on wheels
as soon as I'm back.*

*I better sign off now. It's getting late and we've
got another early start tomorrow, so I should get
some sleep. I need to be focused when I'm up in
the sky.*

*Please take care, Bet. I don't know when I'll be
back in England, but you are always in my thoughts
and I kiss your picture, next to my bed, every night
before I fall asleep.*

All my love,

William xx

'And?' Daisy's question pulled Betty's attention back to her.

'Sorry! I didn't mean to start daydreaming. William has finished his Chief Flying Instructor's Test and has moved on to the next stage, which means he's been moved to Calgary to train in a different plane called an Airspeed Oxford. It sounds quite cumbersome, but he seems to be getting the knack of it, from what he's said in his last couple of letters.'

'That's good, isn't it? Will that mean he's one step closer to coming back to England?'

'I assume so, but he's not mentioned when that might be yet.'

'Hopefully it won't be too much longer,' Daisy enthused, lifting her glass up to take another sip.

'Possibly not.'

'You don't sound overly excited. Is there something wrong?'

'That obvious?'

'Afraid so. What is it? Do you want to talk about it?'

The little ball of tension that had been bothering Betty finally rose to the surface. 'I'm probably overthinking it, and I know I always tell everyone else that's the worst thing you can do, but Frank had the wireless on last night in the living room, while Ivy was in the kitchen. I think he thought I was with her, but I was just about to go and have a sit-down when I heard mention of air raids across the south coast.'

'Really?' Daisy had heard her dad surmising but she hadn't thought too much of it, putting it down to hearsay. Her parents were always cautious not to have the latest news broadcast on while her younger sisters were about, not wanting to frighten them. 'I hadn't realized.'

'I'm trying not to overthink it. I know it's the worst thing I can do. Heaven knows, isn't that what I've been telling Nancy for months, let alone Patty when she got in a tizz over Archie joining the ARP, but if Jerry is targeting England, it will probably be William's job, once he's fully trained, to defend the skies.'

Daisy took a moment to think about her reply. It wasn't like Betty to worry; she was always the voice of reason and eternally positive.

'I know it's easy for me to say,' she started tentatively, 'but none of us knows what tomorrow will bring, let alone the next few months. Maybe the RAF will scare the Germans off before William even leaves Canada. Surely Hitler won't want to start attacking England as well as France?'

Betty wasn't so sure. The beast of a man had already marched through Czechoslovakia, Poland, Denmark, Norway, Belgium, Netherlands, Luxembourg and now northern France, while Italy had entered the south. She feared that there was no stopping him.

'I guess none of us really know,' Betty conceded, if only to try to steel herself.

'We don't,' Daisy affirmed. 'But I do know, if the shoe was on the other foot, you would be telling me there was no point in fretting until something actually happened.'

Betty couldn't help but smile at her friend, knowing she had hit the nail on the head. Wasn't that exactly what she'd thought to herself the previous afternoon, as she recalled how wonderful it was to see that Frank and Ivy's relationship had blossomed and grown? Daisy was right, no one knew what was around the corner.

'I'm sorry. I didn't mean to be such a misery guts, especially when we're supposed to be relaxing and forgetting about work and this godforsaken war for an hour or so.'

'Don't be daft.' Daisy reached over and placed a hand on Betty's. 'You've listened to me countless times. I'm glad I can return the favour. Isn't that what friends are for?'

'Thank you. You really are a good friend. And thank you for inviting me this afternoon. William is always telling me to relax and have fun in his letters and I really have enjoyed today.'

'I'm so glad. Your William is right. You should let your hair down more often. You work so hard and deserve it. Now, promise me you will chat to me in future when things feel a little overwhelming. It's no good keeping everything trapped inside. It will only feel a million times worse.'

'I promise,' Betty said, reaching across the grass and gently squeezing Daisy's hand, simultaneously counting her blessings that she was fortunate enough to have someone she could turn to when her own thoughts started playing havoc with her normally stoic and pragmatic composure.

'Right,' Daisy added, jumping up. 'Let's go and join my sisters.'

With that the two women ran over to the carousel where Polly and Annie were calling for them to have another go. As Betty jumped back on the ride, her worries floated away, for the time being at least.

Chapter 17

Sunday, 28 July 1940

'Come in. Come in,' Ivy said, greeting Nancy and her two children as she opened the front door. As usual, Billy was hopping from one foot to the other, a cheeky grin across his face, while Linda was tightly holding onto her mum's arm with one hand, and carefully gripping a bunch of pretty pale-pink chrysanthemums in the other.

'Is Frank here?' Billy asked, jumping over the threshold onto the black-and-white-tiled floor, not waiting to be asked twice. 'I want him to help me test out my design for my latest paper aeroplane.'

'He certainly is.' Ivy chuckled, holding the door open as Nancy and Linda made their way in. 'He's in the garden. Would you and Linda like to nip out and see him? You might even find a few eggs in the hen coop if you're very lucky.'

Billy didn't need any further encouragement as he shot down the hall, not once looking back.

'Would you like to go out too?' Nancy gently asked her daughter.

'Okay,' she quietly answered, then looked at the flowers, unsure what to do with them.

'You can give those to Ivy,' Nancy prompted. Obediently, Linda held her arm out.

'Thank you, sweetheart.' Ivy smiled graciously. 'They are lovely, but you really didn't need to.'

'It's the very least I can do. You have been so kind to us,' Nancy replied.

'Nonsense.' Ivy brushed off the compliment and led Nancy and Linda towards the kitchen. 'But I shall get them in a vase straightaway. I don't want them to wilt in this heat.' Entering the room at the back of the house, they came upon a tantalizing aroma of freshly baked biscuits, which were cooling on a wire rack on the worktop.

'Linda, why don't you take a saucer of these almond thins out into the garden for you, Billy and Frank?'

Once again, the shy little girl looked towards her mum for approval. 'It's okay,' Nancy gently reassured her.

With a nod from her mum, Linda obligingly took the treats into the garden, where, through the kitchen window, Nancy and Ivy could see, Frank was admiring Billy's latest creation.

'That should keep them entertained,' Ivy said. 'Now what can I get you to drink? A cup of tea or something cooler?'

'Water would be lovely. It's so warm out there.'

'I think I can do better than that.' Ivy trotted off to the pantry, returning a few seconds later with a jug of barley water. 'Now sit yourself down and I'll pour you a glass.'

'You really are very thoughtful,' Nancy said gratefully.

'Now enough of that. I have time on my hands and after many years being on my own, it's a real joy to have friends over. How have you all been?'

But before Nancy had chance to reply, Betty, wearing a navy cotton dress, popped her head round the kitchen door. 'Sorry, Nancy. I was upstairs writing a letter to William and didn't hear the door. Have you been here long?'

'No. Only a few minutes. Are you coming to join us?'

'Yes, of course,' Betty replied, plopping herself down at the table. 'Ooh, is that barley water? I'm parched.'

Instantly Ivy produced another glass. 'Nancy and I were just commenting on how hot it is. We mustn't complain. It beats rain, although my garden wouldn't turn down the odd shower or two.'

'Thank you for all the veggies and eggs you keep sending in with Frank and Betty. That last lot of peas were delicious. Billy and Linda loved shelling them. I think they ate more than went in the pan.'

'We've got plenty more where they came from. In fact, I'll get Frank to pick some with your two after dinner and you can take them home.'

'You really don't have to. I wasn't hinting.'

'I know you weren't, and we have loads, so you would be doing me a favour. There's no way Frank, Betty and I can get through everything we have grown. There's enough to feed an army.'

'Ivy's right,' Betty reiterated. 'We can never get through it all.'

'Now tell me,' Ivy asked again. 'How have you been? You must be so relieved about Bert being back in England.'

'I am, and the children were so pleased when they both received a letter from Bert, especially our Linda.'

'And I assume you got a letter too?'

'I did. They all came in the same envelope.' Nancy picked up her glass of barley water and took a large gulp to quench her thirst.

'Any news on when Bert may get back to Sheffield?'

'Not yet, but I'm hoping it won't be long. I'm trying not to get too excited, but I must admit it's hard not to. I have all sorts of plans running through my mind about what we can do.'

'I'm sure,' Ivy replied. 'It's wonderful that you have something happy to think about.'

'I was thinking we could maybe nip to the seaside for the day on the train. It's not much and while this war is still going on, it's probably the best we can do in place of a holiday. And it will still be a lovely treat for Billy and Linda.'

'That sounds lovely,' Ivy said. 'I can't imagine many people will be going far with fuel being rationed.'

Betty didn't like to burst Nancy's bubble but the last time she and William had been to Cleethorpes, just before war broke out, mines were being planted in the sand as a way to stop enemy forces. Instead, she said, 'A few days out, no matter where you go, will be perfect. I bet Bert won't care where he is as long as he is with you, Billy and Linda.'

'Yes. You're right. He could even come and watch them at The Skates or have a picnic at High Hazels Park and help Billy fly his paper aeroplanes.'

'The simple things are often the best,' Ivy added. 'And don't forget, Bert will have seen a lot and maybe he just needs time to readjust. I'm sure what he wants more than anything is to get home so he can see you all. He will have missed you so much.'

The thought made Nancy beam. How much she had longed for the moment when they could all be a family again and Bert had made it abundantly clear he couldn't wait to come home. It really would be magical.

Conscious she had been talking about herself non-stop since she arrived, Nancy turned to Betty. 'How about you? Any word from your William? How's the training going?'

'Yes, I had a letter a couple of days ago, actually.'

'Ah, lovely. And how is he?'

'He seems really well. He's now somewhere near the Rocky Mountains and has even had the odd day out. He went to see some sort of rodeo recently, which sounded a little bit wild, but I think he had fun.'

'And how about his training?'

Betty quickly clenched her hands together under the table, determined to remain composed. Nancy was the happiest she had been in months and Betty really didn't want to spoil the moment and cause her friend to start worrying about what was still to come.

'Really well, from what I can gather. By the sounds of it, he seems to be progressing fast.'

'That's excellent news,' Nancy enthused, as Ivy topped up all their glasses, and placed a saucer of the now cooled almond thins in the centre of the table. 'Does that mean he might be back in England soon?'

Despite her best efforts, Betty's voice slightly faltered. 'I actually don't know for sure. He didn't exactly say in his letter.'

Nancy and Ivy quickly made eye contact. 'Is everything all right, dear?' Ivy asked, kindly.

'Yes. Yes. Sorry. I was just thinking about William in one of those ginormous planes,' she replied, hoping her white lie wasn't too obvious. As much as she missed her fiancé, unlike Nancy, instead of willing William to come home, she had quietly concluded he was better off where he was, despite the risky flying manoeuvres.

'I'm sure the instructors will know what they are doing,' Nancy said, hoping to reassure her friend, glad to be the one offering support for a change after everyone had rallied around her the past few weeks.

'I agree,' Betty said enthusiastically. Then before she could stop the words escaping her lips, added, 'He's probably in the safest place.'

'What do you mean?' Nancy quizzed. Having Bert back in England had felt like the best news she'd received in months; surely, Betty would want the same for William. Although Betty always put on a brave face and remained stoic in the most testing of times, Nancy also knew she desperately missed William.

Betty silently admonished herself for letting the words slip out in front of Nancy. She'd only told Daisy about how she was feeling, as she worried Nancy would start worrying about how safe Bert was; after all there was a strong possibility Bert would be sent back to the front line. It had helped, talking about her concerns, but she'd still struggled to fall asleep the last couple of nights as anxiety-inducing images of what the future held flashed before her.

'It's not like you, dear, to sound so fretful,' Ivy commented. Betty hadn't even mentioned William's last letter. She'd of course known it had arrived, recognizing the airmail envelope and William's handwriting, but had assumed there was nothing to cause Betty any concern, as she hadn't confided in her. Then again, when she thought about it, Frank had been around most evenings and was always here of a weekend. 'Is there something worrying you?'

Betty suddenly felt lost for words. Although she didn't know exactly what had happened to Ivy's first love, Lewin, she felt pretty sure her landlady would have given anything for him to return to England in one piece. This alongside everything Nancy had endured, praying with all her might her husband would return home, made Betty feel rather selfish. After all, she was in a much luckier position than most. Her William was safe, for the time being at least, and hadn't endured a fraction of what Bert had. And despite not knowing all the details, she knew Ivy had suffered immeasurable heartache during the Great War, recalling how upset she'd got when Neville Chamberlain had announced Britain was at war, for the second time in her lifetime. It was obvious how distraught she'd been, it had brought back painful memories. By comparison, Betty really had nothing to complain about and now felt even more guilty for mentioning it at all, despite the angst that refused to dissipate.

'Betty?' Nancy probed, snapping her friend from her thoughts. 'Is something playing on your mind?'

Betty sighed, more out of frustration with herself. How on earth could she vocalize her thoughts without sounding utterly self-absorbed? Taking a deep breath, she tried to prepare her answer, aware Nancy and Ivy were both now looking at her intently, and clearly slightly bewildered by her off-the-cuff comment.

'I'm sure we'll understand whatever it is,' Ivy added instinctively, sensing Betty had got herself in a bit of a muddle.

'Dear me,' Betty finally said heavily. 'I'm sorry, but I think I'm being rather selfish.'

Now Nancy and Ivy did look somewhat confused. 'Selfish' was the last word they would use to describe their generous, good-natured and caring friend.

'I find that somewhat hard to believe,' Ivy protested.

'Why don't you tell us what's bothering you, and let us be the judge?'

Resigning herself to the fact she really had no choice but to reveal what was on her mind, Betty tightly enveloped one hand in the other on her knee. 'Please don't think I'm being insensitive, I promise I'm not, it's just I really don't want William to come back to England, well not for the moment, at least.'

'Why ever not?' Ivy enquired further.

'I know. I'm sorry. That really does sound awful, doesn't it? I assure you, I don't mean it to.'

'Why don't you slow down and tell us exactly what it is that's got you so flummoxed?' Ivy said kindly.

Betty glanced from Ivy to Nancy, hoping what she would say next wouldn't cause either of them to think any less of her. 'It's just I'm frightened what will become of William if, sorry, when he becomes an active pilot with the RAF.' And with that, the tears Betty had up until now refused to let surface, pierced the back of her eyes.

'Oh, my poor dear,' Ivy said, instantly on her feet, and her arm wrapped around Betty's quivering shoulders. 'There, there. Of course you are worried. You wouldn't be human if you weren't. It's completely understandable.'

'But you have both endured so much, while William is relatively safe,' Betty whimpered.

Reaching out, and gently placing her hand on Betty's, Nancy added, 'It's not a competition. We all want the people we love to be safe.'

'I just feel so guilty. Ever since I read William's last letter, I've been willing for his training to last longer, so he doesn't have to risk his life against Hitler's Luftwaffe.'

'There's nothing wrong with that,' Nancy reiterated.

'You've had to cope with Bert being missing.' Then turning to Ivy, Betty added, 'And I know you've had to cope with bad news too.'

'Now come on. You mustn't think like that,' Ivy said firmly, as she sat back down. 'Just because we've had to deal with difficult times, doesn't mean we would wish it upon you.'

'Exactly,' Nancy exclaimed. 'I wouldn't wish the pain and endless tears I've shed on my worst enemy. I'd hate you to have to worry in the same way I've had. I really would.'

Ivy momentarily closed her eyes as she bit the inside of her lip. Betty was like the daughter she'd never had and seeing her in such a state of unease pained her. Like Nancy, Ivy desperately didn't want to see Betty go through all the harrowing emotions that came with having your loved one away at war, and would do anything she could to bolster her, but she also knew the reality, that, unless a miracle happened to put a stop to Hitler, William would be called upon to actively defend the country.

It went against Ivy's conscience to lie to Betty, so instead she decided the best thing she could do was endeavour to keep her spirits up. 'None of us know what's around the corner and as you have reassured Nancy here, many times, it's best to try not to think about the ifs and maybes.

Believe me, it doesn't do anyone any good, especially the person fretting.'

'Ivy's right,' Nancy reiterated. 'Look at how ill I made myself, thinking about what could have happened to Bert. Every scenario possible had flashed before me. In my darkest moments, I imagined he would never be found, and I would never see him again. I barely slept, hardly ate and went round in circles thinking about how me and the kids would come to terms with losing Bert, but then I got the news he was in hospital, something I'd virtually given up hope of. I guess what I'm trying to say is, none of us can predict what will and won't happen. But look at me, I started to think the worst, got m'self in a right old state, and all for nothing.'

'I'm sorry, you've to cope with so much,' Betty said.

'But that's my point. I could only think about the worst-case scenario, and I made myself quite sick in the process. I don't want you getting yourself in the same awful state.'

'I feel terrible. I really didn't mean to offload all my worries on you both, especially you, Nancy. You don't need to hear me harping on about something that hasn't even happened yet.'

'Now enough of that, dear,' Ivy instantly affirmed. She didn't want Betty worrying, but she certainly didn't want her then admonishing herself for just expressing how she felt. 'I'm sure Nancy will agree with me, but I for one am glad you have told us how you feel. You must never keep something like this trapped inside as you will only end up catastrophizing and getting yourself in more of a pickle.'

'You mean like I already have?'

'Well, yes. You should have told us sooner, and we could have maybe assuaged your fears.'

Betty didn't like to say she had already told Daisy, who like Ivy and Nancy, had tried to reassure her, but still she felt uncharacteristically uneasy. It wasn't like her to be so worrisome, but when it came to William her normally galvanized approach to problems seemed to crumble. She'd been exactly the same when William had signed up for the RAF, and then when he'd been transferred to Canada, and now she didn't want him to come back. What a muddle!

'I was worried it would come across a little insensitively and you would all think I was—'

'I agree with Ivy. You must never think like that,' Nancy insisted. 'You have been the greatest of friends and I would be so upset if you thought you couldn't share what was on your mind with me, especially after how much you have helped me.'

'Thank you. I feel very lucky to have you as a friend too.'

'Now,' Ivy said. 'Before Frank and the children come back in, and I serve out dinner, my final piece of advice is when you get yourself in a fix, imagine what the best outcome would be, then the worst, and nine times out of ten, the reality will be somewhere in the middle.' What she hadn't said was that in her case, her worst fears had become a reality, but it also didn't take a genius to know that was last thing Betty needed to hear.

Feeling emotionally exhausted, but simultaneously

grateful to Ivy and Nancy for being so kind, Betty's eyes glistened. 'Thank you.'

'You have nothing to thank us for,' Nancy replied, giving Betty's hand a final squeeze. 'As you have said to me countless times, that's what friends are for.'

'And you know I will always be here for you,' Ivy said, reinforcing the sentiment.

'I really am very grateful.'

'No need to be,' Ivy said. 'Just promise me you will talk to us sooner in future. It might save you a couple of sleepless nights, if nothing else.'

'I will.' Betty nodded, dabbing her watery eyes with a hankie. 'You have both made me feel a little better.'

But as Ivy stood up from the table and made her way over to the oven, where a vegetable quiche was cooking, she couldn't help but think, despite her morale-boosting words, that for both Betty and Nancy, their worries were only just beginning. This damnable war was testing them both, and she would need to muster all her fortitude to give Betty and Nancy the support they needed over the coming months.

Chapter 18

Thursday, 1 August 1940

'Goodnight,' Nancy called as she finally made her way down the stairs after story time with Billy and Linda, reading a new chapter of *Swallows and Amazons*. It was Nancy's favourite time of the day and she cherished those special moments when they all cuddled up on one of their beds, both her children snuggled up next to her, their eyes slowly closing, before she tucked them in under their own blankets, told them how much she loved them and wished them sweet dreams.

In the kitchen, light still streaming in through the window, Nancy made herself a fresh pot of tea, then fell into a chair, tiredness getting the better of her.

Nancy knew she needed the warmth and comfort the steaming liquid would offer as she picked up her favourite china cup and saucer. She'd been eagerly waiting for this moment since she'd seen the letter, with Bert's familiar handwriting adorning the envelope, on the doorstep a couple of hours earlier. Nancy had quickly retrieved it and slipped it into her gingham apron pocket, determined to wait until the children were asleep and out of the way before she could cherish the words without any distractions.

Just like last time, there were three separate letters for each of them. Nancy placed the ones for Billy and Linda to one side, knowing it would be a lovely surprise for them in the morning.

Then she unfolded the piece of paper with her name on it and took a quick sip of her tea. 'Oh Bert,' she whispered, as though he was in the room, before instructing her eyes to focus on the handwritten words.

Dear Nancy,
Thank you so much for the letters from you, Billy
and Linda. They cheered me up no end. I see our
Billy is his same cheery self. I'm glad to see this
blasted war isn't affecting him, unless you count
his determination to make the best paper aeroplane
possible! I have Linda's drawing pinned up on the
wall next to me, and it makes me smile every time
I look at it. I can't wait to give them both a big
cuddle, even if, due to no fault of my own, I won't
be chasing them round the yard any time soon.

'They will be so excited,' Nancy sighed, images of days in the park flooding her thoughts, not really taking in the last part of Bert's sentence.

Anyway, it won't be long until you find out. I've been told I can come home next week. I don't know what day for sure yet, but I'll try to get word to you as soon as it's confirmed.

I know I sound a bit of a misery, but I promise I really am looking forward to seeing you all so much. The only thing that has got me through the last ten months or so is imagining holding you in my arms. It was the incentive to keep going, to stay alive, to find my way home.

'Oh, my love, we can't wait to see you too.'

I should warn you, though, I'm not the man I used to be. I will do my best to be the husband and father you all deserve; I hope you aren't disappointed by the broken man who comes back to you.

The last sentence took Nancy by surprise, but as she thought about how the war had started to wear everyone down, she guessed Bert was just explaining he was pretty wrung out too. After all, he'd been in France for months and now, what with him being in hospital, he was bound to be feeling a little out of sorts. He was probably being oversentimental and fretting that Nancy would see a few changes in him, but that was perfectly understandable. She could never be 'disappointed' in him. She had loved him since their very first date and couldn't imagine ever feeling otherwise. 'I will always love you,' Nancy whispered, emerging from her daydream. 'We just want you home so we can take care of you and be a family again.'

Believe me when I say, I will do my best to get better, but the days feel very dark at the moment, and the nights pitch-black. This blasted war has a lot to answer for and I hate what it's done to my mind. I am sorry for putting all this down on paper, but felt it only fair I should warn you about the state I'm in, as I didn't want it to come as an awful shock to you when you see me. I know I'm asking a lot of you, but please forgive me for the person I've become, and I give you my word, I will try to find, within me, the husband you married.

All my love,

Bert xxxx

As Nancy finished reading, she realized the letter was now damp from her own salty tears. Her emotions had overtaken her as it occurred to her Bert was only a week, maybe days, from coming home. Of course he would need a little time to recover, but nothing a good dose of tender love and care couldn't rectify.

Bert was just letting her know he was tired of this war, but wasn't everyone? He'd always been so considerate, so incredibly thoughtful and determined that his own feelings came second to anyone else's, and here he was again, explaining why he might not be quite his normal self. 'Well, there's no need!' Nancy said out loud. 'I will take care of you.'

Bert had always been the strong one, the one who picked her up when she was upset or worrying, who could make Billy and Linda laugh when they'd fallen over and scraped their knee or woken up grumpy and tired. Bert had been the one to convince her, when she'd silently pleaded against the idea, unable to vocalize her terrified thoughts, that going off to war was the right thing to do. His admirable and selfless determination to fight for King and country had always buoyed Nancy, made her think about the bigger picture, the greater good, causing her to admire and love her husband even more.

'We will get through this,' Nancy told herself, full of optimism.

Nancy imagined what Bert would do if the roles were reversed, and she was poorly. Without a shadow of a doubt, he would take control, look after her, and ensure Billy and Linda were also taken care of.

Nancy had felt galvanized since the news had arrived that Bert was back in England and now, even though it was obvious Bert wasn't quite himself, her hopes for the future were shining the brightest they had since war had been declared.

Until this moment, Nancy could never have ever envisaged having to be the strong one. It wasn't a role that came naturally to her. Even after Bert had gone off to war, she had relied on Doris, and then her new friends at Vickers to bolster her. Without them, Nancy was quite convinced she would have fallen to bits. They'd kept her going with pep talks, kindness and love.

And when Bert had gone missing, Nancy had been out of her mind, barely functioning, haunted day and night by harrowing images, not knowing what had happened to her husband. Her family had been through so much already but, strengthened by the fact Bert would be home soon, her spirit had been lifted and her energy for life restored.

A resilience like never before had been building in Nancy over the last couple of weeks. She wasn't naive enough to think that the weeks and months ahead were going to simply resort back to how they were a year ago, after all she had her job at Vickers, but their evenings and weekends as a happy and contented family would be just like old times. This war might not be over yet, but Nancy was looking forward to a greater sense of normality.

Taking a final sip of her tea, Nancy started making plans. Firstly, she would tell Doris that she would be taking her turn to make a few evening meals over the next week or so, determined to repay all the favours her neighbour had done for her. Then Nancy began thinking about the summer holidays and the fact the kids would be off school. Bert coming home was perfect timing. He could take care of Billy and Linda while she was working and even help Doris out with her brood. Nancy had decided she would also ask Frank if she could have a few days off so they could enjoy some family days out. The four of them could have lazy days in the sun with picnics and ice creams in High Hazels Park or make a trip to one of the nice cafés in town for a cake, or if the mood took them, they could nip to Flathers for a chippy tea. They might not be able to enjoy a proper holiday, but Nancy didn't mind; Bert was coming home, and she couldn't wait to enjoy the summer with her family, which would feel complete for the first time in nearly a year.

Chapter 19

'Right, girls, who fancies a quick one at The Welly?' Dolly had joined her gang of friends gathered outside gate three. 'Nancy's had word from Bert, and I reckon she could do with a glass of something.'

'That sounds like good news,' Betty replied.

'Yes. It's very good news!' Dolly affirmed.

'Well, whatever it is, let's go and toast it. I don't need to get straight off.'

'Me neither,' Patty echoed, quickly followed by Daisy, Josie and Hattie.

'Well, that was easy.' Dolly grinned. 'No time like the present. We may as well walk down there now, before it gets swamped with workers.'

Hattie quickly glanced at her watch. Just after four o'clock. Her dad would already be in the local boozer. He always started early on a Friday. What time he would stagger home was anyone's guess, but she surmised her mum would be okay on her own for a couple of hours yet. *I'll just stay for an hour*, Hattie thought to herself, erring on the side of caution, although she couldn't deny being away from the family home, which was increasingly fraught with tension, was appealing. Since her dad had struck her mum, he hadn't had a pleasant word to say. Hattie didn't want her mum left to face her drunken dad on her own later on, but she was confident he wouldn't be home for a while yet.

'Are you okay?' Patty asked, seeing her friend was deep in thought, as they joined the throng of workers making their way down Brightside Lane.

'Sorry. Just daydreaming.' Despite Patty being her best friend, Hattie'd never told her about the gravity of her dad's volatile behaviour. It hadn't been a conscious decision, more that the opportunity hadn't arisen, and she also worried Patty wouldn't really understand. Hattie suspected her friend might also fall into a complete panic, and that was the last thing she needed. 'Where's Archie tonight?' Hattie asked, quickly changing the subject.

'He's on air-raid duty tonight and tomorrow night. I'm trying not to moan about it. He's promised to take me out for cake after work tomorrow, so I'm not complaining.'

'At least you get to see him most days,' Hattie replied in an effort to cheer her up.

'Gosh! Listen to me. Tactless as ever. I do. Sorry, have you heard from your John recently? You must be missing him like crazy.'

'I am a bit but he's okay from what I can gather from

his letters. He's busy training and the fact he's still in this country is an absolute blessing. I worried myself sick when he was in France. It feels as though he's safer here.'

'That's true.' As much as Patty didn't like Archie putting himself at risk week after week, up to now, apart from the south coast, the country hadn't been subject to any raids by the Germans. 'Maybe he will get some more leave soon.'

'I'm hoping so.' Hattie nodded. In fact, it was the one thing she'd wanted more than anything. John always knew exactly how to take away the angst she felt about her dad. Just having him around made her worry less; maybe because he visited her house most nights and her dad was generally less confrontational when John was about.

'Try to keep yer chin up,' Patty encouraged, linking her arm through Hattie's, sensing her friend was feeling a bit down in the dumps.

'I'll be fine,' Hattie said, adamant not to allow herself to get into a tizz. She had to, for her mum's sake if nothing else.

But before Patty could probe her any further, they'd reached the corner of Upwell Street and The Welly.

'Reyt then,' Dolly started as they made their way inside the busy pub. 'Why don't you lot find us somewhere to sit and I'll go to the bar. Is everyone having their usual?'

'Let me help you,' Betty insisted. 'Besides which, you can't be buying all those drinks. It will cost a fortune.'

'Betty's right. Why don't we all throw some money in?' Josie suggested.

'Whatever works,' Dolly said, heading towards the bar. 'I'll grab some pork scratchings to nibble on too. It is Friday after all. We might as well treat ourselves.'

'Eee. Yer don't 'alf know how to push the boat out!' Patty laughed.

Ten minutes later the group of friends were all collected around a couple of tables that they shunted closer together, drinks in one hand and helping themselves to the savoury snacks Dolly had bought.

'Well, here's to another week!' Patty said, lifting her half pint of pale ale.

'I'll drink to that, luv,' Josie hailed, as the women clinked glasses.

After taking a delicate sip of her port and lemon, Betty turned to Nancy. 'Are you going to tell us your good news?' Normally the two women would have made time for a quick chat at dinnertime, but the canteen had been busier than ever, and Nancy hadn't stopped for a second, so didn't managed to nip over to their usual table for a natter.

Nancy took another quick slurp and a deep breath, and excitedly announced, 'Bert is coming home!'

'Hey!' Patty exclaimed.

'That's brilliant, I'm so happy for you,' Daisy enthused.

Dolly, who was sat next to Nancy, gave her friend's arm a reassuring pat.

'It is,' Nancy replied, placing her glass on the table. 'I can't wait. It will be wonderful to have him back. The kids are really excited as you can imagine. I just want things to be back to normal. Well, as normal as they can be with this war going on.'

'It really is marvellous.' Betty grinned, delighted for her friend. 'You deserve a bit of happiness after everything you have had to cope with.'

'You do,' Patty trilled. 'And is Bert okay? Yer know, with him being in hospital 'n' all.' Tact had never been her strong point.

Nancy looked taken aback. She hadn't really thought too deeply about Bert's injuries, assuming he was in good hands and on the mend.

'Yes, I think so. He'd injured his leg somehow, but I presume it's getting better if he's allowed home.'

'Has a nurse from the hospital been in touch?' Betty asked.

'No. Nothing like that. I got a letter off Bert yesterday and he told me himself.'

'And does he seem fine in himself?' Betty asked tentatively.

Nancy was about to answer and affirm Bert seemed absolutely fine, but before the words left her lips, his letter flashed through her mind. *Please forgive me for the person I've become, and I give you my word, I will try to find, within me, the husband you married.* A lump formed in Nancy's throat, but she quickly swallowed it away, telling herself she was overthinking the throwaway comment. 'I think he's a bit tired but I'm sure once he's home and can rest in his own bed he will feel a lot better.'

Dolly, who was determined to keep her friend buoyant after the last few months, rested her hand on Nancy's. 'I'm sure you're right, luv. Everything is going to be all right. He's been through the wringer so it's understandable if he's tired and worn down but your Bert will be as reyt as rain once he's home.'

Betty, who now felt immensely guilty for dampening the moment, added, 'Dolly's right. Your Bert will be on cloud nine to be home. It will be the best tonic for all of you.'

'Thank you.' Nancy nodded. 'I know it sounds daft, but I hadn't really thought about him being in a bad way. I was just so pleased he was alive and back in England.'

'Oh luv, we know that,' Dolly said reassuringly. 'Please don't start fretting now, and if Bert is struggling, I have no doubt you will be able to help him.'

For the first time since she'd received the good news about Bert, she started to wonder if she had been a little naive. Bert had hinted in his letters the war had changed him and he felt changed. Nancy had been so thrilled to simply hear from him, she hadn't really thought about any further meaning in his letters.

Sensing her friend was beginning to get herself in a pickle, Betty reached across the table and patted her hand. 'Come on. Don't worry. It's brilliant news that your Bert is coming home. You have so much to look forward to and you know if something doesn't feel right you can talk to us. Things are bound to feel a little different. Your life has changed too, but that doesn't always mean it's a bad thing. Look at how much stronger you are now.'

'That's right,' Dolly interjected. She had quietly questioned if Nancy had thought that Bert might be in a bit of a bad way psychologically when he came back. She knew from experience what war could do to a man. 'There's always a friendly ear or two here who can help with anything. If things do get a little heavy at home, you will still have us lot to natter to.'

'What do you mean?' Nancy asked, quickly turning to Dolly, feeling slightly affronted. Even if Bert was a bit poorly, Nancy couldn't imagine ever needing a break from Bert. It would be her job to look after him and she was determined, if that was the case, to nurse him back to full health.

'Sorry, luv. That didn't come out very well. What I meant is sometimes we all need a bit of respite when we are looking after someone, and you know we will all be here to help you and just listen if you need a chat or would like some advice. What I'm trying to say is, we can't look after your Bert, but we can look after you.'

Nancy suddenly felt guilty for thinking her friends were insinuating she might not be able to cope with her beloved Bert. 'Thank you,' she whispered, her chagrin replaced by gratitude. 'You really are all so kind.'

'What do I keep telling you?' Betty said kindly. 'That's what friends are for.'

'I know and I am so grateful, I really am, but I just

have such a good feeling about the future. Even if Bert needs a bit of help or time to recover, I can't help thinking about how nice life is going to feel having him around again.'

'Of course it is, luv,' Dolly replied. 'I guess all we were saying is if you do need a little help, then we are on hand.'

'I do appreciate it, and you're right, I will probably need the odd bit of advice.' But if the truth be known, Nancy was just being polite, convinced no matter how weak or exhausted Bert was, she would be more than capable of looking after the man she loved so deeply.

'Well, all you have to do is say but I have every faith that you will be fine,' Dolly said reassuringly, hoping beyond hope she was right.

'Dolly's right,' Josie chirped up. 'Look at what my Alf had to suddenly do when I wasn't so clever. I'd always been the one keeping everyone together, while he was at work, and suddenly I was fit for nothing.'

'Mum!' Daisy exclaimed. The memories of how poorly her mum had been the previous Christmas still upset Daisy.

'It's true though, luv, isn't it? You and yer dad suddenly had to take charge, and luckily for me, yer both did a grand job.' Turning back to Nancy, she added, 'And if it wasn't for you, I might never have gone to the hospital and got the help I needed. I guess what I'm trying to say is you will know what your Bert needs and know exactly what to say – just like you knew what to say to me. You're a damn good person, with a big heart, and when you love someone, like you do Bert, helping them comes naturally. There's no instruction manual, but you'll know what the right thing to do is.'

'Thank you,' Nancy mused. 'I just want things to be like they used to be. I know I can't fix what's wrong with his leg, but I'm sure the doctors will be on with that. I suppose, more than anything, I am simply looking forward to us all being happy again.'

Hattie, who had listened in silence, nervously rubbed her fingers under the table. Is that what her mum had thought she could do? Had she hoped things would go back to normal after the Great War? Had she vowed to make sure the man she married would eventually return to his happy self? Hattie prayed for Nancy's sake that Bert would be a better patient than her own dad had turned out to be and that his experience didn't leave him with a temper that would turn his whole family against him.

'And you will be,' Josie said with hope, interrupting Hattie's sombre thoughts. 'Take it from me. I'm living proof of what love and determination can do.'

'You really are and thank you,' Nancy replied. 'I'll definitely ask for help if I need it. I don't want to get m'self in a pickle again.'

'We won't let you,' Betty implored. 'And you can guarantee Ivy will be keen to help out in some way too. She loves having Billy and Linda over, so I'm sure if you need a bit of time for just you and Bert, we can gladly keep them entertained for an afternoon.'

'You've done so much already,' Nancy said. 'I don't want to keep putting on you all.'

'We wouldn't offer if we didn't want to help. Besides which, it's lovely seeing Billy and Linda helping Frank with the veggies and the hens, and he's in his element with his two extra little helpers.'

'I have to say, they are loving it. They have a competition going on who has collected the most eggs.'

'There you go then,' Betty confirmed. 'We can't stop their fun now.'

The encouraging, and now upbeat, chatter among all but one of the women continued. Hattie still hadn't said a word, lost in her own thoughts, but her unusually subdued silence hadn't been lost on Dolly, who was sat on the other side of her. Although Hattie was normally happy to join in a conversation, it wasn't the first time Dolly had seen the young lass looking perturbed and ashen-faced.

'Are you all right, duck?' she asked discreetly, as the rest of the group continued to spur Nancy on.

Hattie looked up; her fingers still clenched. 'Sorry. I'm just a bit tired.'

Dolly didn't doubt it. Hattie had dark circles under her eyes, and she looked as though she could sleep for a week.

'You not getting much kip, duck?'

'Not as much as I'd like recently. In fact, do you think anyone would mind if I got off? I promised m' mum I wouldn't be late.'

Dolly didn't argue, but she knew it wasn't even five o'clock – not what most people would call late, especially for a young 'un like Hattie.

'I don't think anyone would mind at all. I can't imagine Nancy will stay much longer. She likes to get home to her kiddies. I tell yer what, I'll walk out with you. I've got my granddaughters coming round this evening, so I need to be getting back too.'

'Please don't leave on my behalf.'

'I'm not,' Dolly insisted, happy to tell a small white lie to help Hattie feel better that she wasn't the first to leave.

'Nancy, luv,' she said, before Hattie could argue. 'If you don't mind, Hattie and I are going to get off. I've got our Lucy and Milly nipping round soon and Hattie's mum is expecting her back for some tea.'

'Of course not,' Nancy answered. 'I'm grateful to you for making me come out. It's been nice to just have a minute to relax.'

'I don't think any of us will argue with that.' Then standing up and picking up her bag, Dolly added, 'It's lovely to see you looking like your normal self again.'

'Thank you. I do feel so much better.' Then noticing a pale-faced Hattie, Nancy added, 'Thank you for coming too. I do appreciate it.'

'Sorry I've been quiet. I'm just a bit tired this week.'

'Oh luv, don't apologise,' Nancy insisted. 'This job is exhausting. I'm not surprised.'

'But you've not even touched yer drink,' Patty trilled. 'You can't let it go to waste!'

'Sorry, I think what I really need is a cuppa. You can have it.'

'Ooh thanks, Hatts,' Patty exclaimed, picking up the glass, not needing any further encouragement, completely oblivious to the fact that something else could be bothering her friend. 'I'll not say no; after all, there's no point it sat there gathering dust.'

The rest of the group burst into laughter. For someone who hadn't touched a drop of alcohol until a couple of weeks ago, Patty was certainly making up for it.

'Right! On that note, we'll see you all tomorrow.' Dolly chuckled as she and Hattie grabbed their gas masks and headed towards the exit.

'See yer tomorrow,' came the chorus of chirpy replies.

'Come on, duck, I'll walk part of the way with yer,' Dolly said to Hattie. 'I'm in Darnall too.'

'You didn't leave early on my account, did you?' Hattie asked, feeling guilty.

'No, but if I'm honest, I got the impression you could do with some company on the way home.'

Desperately trying not to reveal her true feelings, Hattie steeled herself. 'I'm all right, honestly. As I say, just a bit tired.'

Dolly was no fool, but she was also tactful enough to

realize pushing Hattie would only make her close up even more. After all, isn't that what she'd done when her life felt as though it was spiralling out of control? 'Okay, duck,' she replied kindly, as they crossed over the road. 'But, let me just mention one thing, if you don't mind?'

'Of course.'

Taking her time to reply, Dolly gently touched Hattie's arm, before saying, 'Although I come across as happy as Larry these days, I promise you I haven't always been this chipper. There were moments when I couldn't see past the day ahead and I was worried sick about what each night would bring.'

Slightly bewildered, Hattie looked at Dolly. 'I didn't realize.'

'There's no way you could have, duck. It's not something I talk about much, and back then, I didn't tell a soul about the problems I was having, until it was too late.'

'I'm so sorry to hear that.'

'Don't be. Just promise me one thing.'

'What's that?'

'That you won't keep whatever is worrying you to yerself forever. Take it from me, it does no good in the long run.'

With tears threatening to betray Hattie's true feelings, she took a deep breath, and nodded. There was no point in denying there was nothing to worry about, but she still wasn't quite ready to reveal quite how bad things had got at home. 'I promise,' was all she could manage. 'And thank you, Dolly.'

'You don't have to thank me, luv. Just know you can come and talk to me if it all gets too much.'

'I will.' Hattie wasn't sure if she meant it or not, but simply knowing there was someone who she could turn to was a huge comfort.

Chapter 20

The sun beating down on her, Nancy made her way up Prince Street, happy to be getting home to her children. *Maybe I can take Billy and Linda for a walk around High Hazels Park,* she thought to herself, keen to enjoy the nice weather and lighter nights while it lasted. Since she'd started working in the canteen she was home not long after four o'clock every day, meaning she got to spend an extra couple of precious hours with Billy and Linda. *I could take Doris's little ones too. Heaven knows she needs the break.* The start of the school holidays had meant her good-hearted neighbour was surrounded by kiddies all day. Doris was adamant she didn't mind, insisting they spent most of the day playing on the street or in the backyard together, but it didn't stop Nancy feeling guilty, and trying to find a few hours here and there to give Doris some respite.

Her mind made up, she sped up as she approached the gennel between hers and Doris's terraced houses. She'd gather all the kids up and take them out for an hour and then insist on cooking tea. But as she entered Doris's yard, instead of being greeted by a rabble of children, all playing different games beneath the washing lines full of the laundry her neighbour had taken on to earn a living, there was an unusual and slightly ominous silence.

Maybe Doris has conceded to let them play Swallows and Amazons upstairs, Nancy reasoned. *Or, more likely, they are begging her for a biscuit before tea, claiming they were starving. She'll definitely be ready for a break!*

But as she opened the back door into Doris's house, a voice from the kitchen stopped Nancy in her tracks. 'I didn't but I did sit in a tank at one point.'

'Was it huge? Are the wheels really as big as me?' Nancy heard Billy ask.

And then, just in case she was in any doubt, which she wasn't, came the reply and all the confirmation she needed. 'They are, son.'

Speechless, Nancy strode into her neighbour's kitchen. And there he was, sat at the table with Billy and all of Doris's children, with Linda perched on his left knee, her arms tightly wrapped around his diminished frame.

It took a second for Nancy to find her voice. 'Bert,' was all Nancy could manage, barely more than a whisper, overwhelmed by the enormity of seeing her husband for the first time in eleven months. 'You're here.'

Nancy's presence brought the delighted chatter to an abrupt halt, as everyone turned to look at her, but the momentary silence was quickly pierced by Billy's cheer.

'Mum!' he gasped. 'Dad's home and he's been in a ginor-mous tank.'

'I can see,' Nancy stuttered, too shocked to formulate a full sentence. She couldn't take her eyes off Bert, who was still the man she had longed to see every day since the previous September. She couldn't believe how much he'd changed – his once thick mop of brown hair was now shaved close to his head, his brown eyes now surrounded by heavy grey circles and his once chiselled cheeks alarmingly gaunt, emphasizing his uncharacteristically sickly pallor.

'Aren't you going to give him a hug?' Billy exclaimed incredulously.

'Yes. Yes, of course.' Nancy smiled, her eyes brimming with tears, as she crossed the kitchen. 'It's so good to see you,' she whispered, approaching Bert. 'We have all missed you so much.'

'I've missed you all too,' he replied, reaching out his free hand while the other held onto Linda, who was snuggled into him as though she would never let go. 'I'd stand up but I'm a bit wobbly and I'm not sure this one will actually detach herself from me.'

'It's okay,' Nancy replied, taking her husband's visibly shaking and bony hand. 'I'm just glad you're here. When did you get back? I'd have tried to get the day off if I'd have realized. Hardly the best of welcomes back, coming home to an empty house.'

'It was all a bit last minute. I knew I couldn't get a letter to you in time. I didn't mean to shock you.'

'Well, you certainly did that, but it doesn't matter.' Nancy attempted a chuckle, but it got lost in her throat and was replaced by a stifled gasp.

'Kids,' Doris interjected. 'I've got some biscuits. Why don't you take them out into the yard and let Bert go and settle into his own house?'

Billy and Joe didn't have to be asked twice, jumping up quicker than the speed of light, followed by Doris's other three children, Katherine, Alice and Little George, but Linda didn't budge, squeezing her arms tighter around Bert's chest, revealing how much his once firmly built frame had visibly shrunk. Nancy wasn't sure if her daughter had noticed how much her dad had physically shrunk, but she was stunned by his frightfully slight frame.

'Would you not like to do some skipping with Alice?' Doris prompted Linda but the girl fiercely shook her head, burying herself deeper into Bert, her riot of blonde curls falling over her anxious face.

'Don't worry, poppet. You can stay with me,' Bert said, reassuringly, but there was a weary strain in his voice that Nancy didn't recognize.

He's probably exhausted from all the travelling, or maybe his leg is still giving him a bit of gyp, Nancy mused.

'It's been a long day for you both,' Doris empathized. 'Why don't you get yerselves home? I've got a couple of pies in the pantry. Take one home with you and it will save you cooking.'

'Oh Doris, I couldn't possibly. You've already had my two all day,' Nancy protested.

But her neighbour cut her off before Nancy could say another word. 'No arguments,' she said firmly. 'It's the very least I can do. Besides which, I can't imagine you will fancy cooking tonight. Just slice up some bread, and jobs a good 'un.'

'You really are very kind,' Nancy replied, as she looked at Doris, further conveying her thanks and gratitude.

Bert gently coaxed Linda from his knee. 'Come on, poppet, you can help yer old dad across the yard.'

The words weren't lost on Nancy. As she watched Bert pull himself up and lean with one hand on the wooden walking stick by his side, it suddenly dawned on her she hadn't appreciated, from her husband's letters, how weak he was.

Once settled around their own kitchen table, teatime passed with Billy asking countless questions about guns, tanks and planes, which Bert barely had time to answer, before their good-natured, but unrelenting son began on another inquisition. Nancy was grateful for the distraction, diverting the attention away from how exhausted Bert looked. Normally he'd have laughed at Billy's persistent demands for answers, but he'd only managed clipped mono-syllabic replies. Thankfully, Billy, in his overexcitement at seeing his beloved daddy, hadn't noticed. Linda, on the other hand, hadn't left her father's side all evening; tightly holding his hand, she had eyed him curiously. Nancy was also trying to adjust to her husband's stark appearance. His now brusque and weary voice, his almost bedraggled and sickly appearance, his quiet demeanour, all of it a sharp contrast to the man she had remembered and cemented in her mind – an image she'd held on to for so long.

A couple of hours later, after many hugs and kisses, Nancy had finally torn Billy and Linda away from Bert and got them tucked into bed.

'Will he be back to normal in the morning?' Linda had asked as Nancy tucked her into bed, loosely nipping the cotton sheet under the mattress.

Nancy was taken aback. She thought Linda had been delighted to have Bert home and hadn't realized she must have picked up too on how changed he was from the dad who'd left them. Sitting down on the edge of the single bed, Nancy used her index finger to gently stroke Linda's cheek. 'Your daddy has had a bit of a tricky time. He's very tired and just needs to rest.'

'But then will he be happy again, if he gets a lot of sleep?'

The poignant words struck Nancy. She'd hoped, probably naively, Billy and Linda wouldn't have picked up on how downcast Bert had looked, but she realized now that had been wishful thinking. Silently accepting she couldn't protect her children from everything, Nancy rested her free hand on Linda's arm.

'Of course he will,' Nancy finally said, in her most optimistic voice. A couple of months ago, this question would have broken her, left her crumbling, but Nancy knew now, more than ever, she needed to stay strong. She couldn't, and wouldn't, allow her children to see both their parents fall apart. 'But it might take a little bit of time, and we might need to be especially patient. Do you think you can do that for me?'

Linda's tired and confused eyes stared back at Nancy. 'We can make it our little job,' Nancy said reassuringly.

'To stop Daddy being sad?' Linda asked.

Nancy took another deep breath. How could she put such a ginormous task on a little girl? The thought of Linda bearing such a huge responsibility made Nancy shudder. If it didn't work, she knew Linda would forever blame herself.

'Maybe I didn't explain that very well,' Nancy started again. 'What I meant to say is, shall we try to let Daddy have lots of rest, so he can catch up on all the sleep he's missed?'

'I could make his breakfast and read my storybooks to him, like he used to do for me.'

'Oh, sweetheart,' Nancy said, drawing her daughter into her arms, and resting her own head on top of Linda's, if only to stop her daughter seeing the tears she was desperately trying to blink away. 'I'm sure Daddy would love that. You can show him how good you are at reading now.'

Nancy felt her daughter's head ever so slightly bop up and down, willingly accepting the task.

'I'll start tomorrow,' Linda announced, easing herself back from Nancy, a smile now adorning her little rosy-cheeked face.

'That's a lovely idea. Now why don't you get some sleep? It's a bit later than normal and you have got to get up early in the morning.'

'Do we still have to go next door, even though Daddy is home?'

'Just for a little while,' Nancy said soothingly. 'So we can let Daddy catch up on his sleep.' Doris had discreetly caught Nancy before they had all left, insisting she still look after Billy and Linda while she was at work, guessing it would be too much for Bert. Nancy had nodded in agreement, accepting for the time being at least, it was probably for the best.

'Okay, Mummy,' Linda obliged and although Nancy was grateful, she knew this was her daughter's way of helping her daddy get better.

'Right then, poppet. You get some sleep and I'll see you bright and early for breakfast.'

'Night-night, Mummy,' Linda said, her voice already drifting towards a sleepy slumber.

'Love you,' Nancy whispered, as she turned and made her way out of the door, thankful that at least her daughter was falling asleep, a little less anxious about what lay ahead.

By the time Nancy got downstairs, Bert had propped himself up on the armchair in the front room. 'They're all settled,' she said. 'I'll just make us a fresh cuppa and I'll come and sit down.'

'It's all done,' Bert announced, exhausted. 'I just couldn't carry it in. This blasted leg is a hindrance. I'm sorry.' The resentment in her husband's voice wasn't lost on Nancy, nor was the sight of Bert's walking stick, which was lying on the floor where she guessed he'd dropped it in frustration. 'Don't worry,' she said cheerfully. 'I can fetch it. Would you like anything else to eat?'

Bert shook his head. 'Doris's pie is the biggest meal I've had in months, I'm stuffed.'

Nancy had worried Bert would think she had been a bit mean with the portions, which had gradually got leaner as rations had taken hold, but looking at Bert's emaciated frame, she guessed he'd been surviving on meagre offerings for quite a while.

A few minutes later, Nancy was pouring Bert another strong, sweet cuppa, happy to use her sugar rations to try to fatten Bert up a bit.

There was so much she wanted to ask her husband that she hadn't brought up in their letters. *What happened in France? How did your leg end up so badly injured? How did you get home? Will you have to go back?* But somehow, the questions didn't feel appropriate, not tonight at least. Instead, not wanting to overwhelm her husband, as she handed him his mug of steaming tea, she asked: 'Are you tired? It's been a long day for you.'

'No more than usual. Every day seems to last forever.'

The trite remark momentarily stumped Nancy but she put it down to Bert being so tired after the long train journey from Portsmouth. Nancy placed her rose-painted china cup and saucer by her foot. 'I'm sure you must be very tired and I can't begin to imagine what you have been through over these last few months. But hopefully things will feel a little easier now you are home.'

'Maybe . . .' But Bert stopped himself before he said anything else.

Nancy watched as he stared down at his rigid right leg, his eyes a mixture of sadness and an uncharacteristic anger, which she had never seen before. 'Being home can't fix this,' he snapped, his mood now a sharp contrast to a couple of minutes earlier.

Nancy took a quick intake of breath, the unfamiliar cutting words slicing through her. In the whole nine years they had been married, Bert had never spoken to her in such a despondent and dismissive manner. But, in a show of strength that surprised even herself, Nancy didn't falter, determined to stick to her vow, to do whatever it took to help her husband recover. *It will take time*, she quietly reminded herself. *He's just needs a good night's sleep.*

'Let's see what tomorrow brings,' Nancy replied optimistically.

Bert, at least, had the decency to looked slightly abashed. 'I didn't mean to sound so ungracious,' he muttered, looking into his mug of tea, unable to make eye contact with his wife.

'It's okay,' Nancy said empathetically, despite the lack of remorse in her husband's voice, but also acutely aware Bert was dog-tired and convinced things wouldn't seem so difficult in the morning.

In a bid to lighten the atmosphere, Nancy began telling Bert about how the children were getting on at school. Linda's teacher had praised their hardworking and diligent daughter for her beautiful handwriting, love of reading and aptitude in her spelling tests, while Billy was always commended for his vivid imagination and his natural affinity with maths. 'I'm sure they will tell you all about school over the next couple of days and no doubt want you to help with their homework once they go back next month.'

'Mmm,' was all Bert managed in response.

His noncommittal response once again stumped Nancy. Bert had always been the most dedicated of fathers, never once shying away from helping Billy and Linda with whatever they needed, whether it be learning to ride a bike or reading their bedtime stories.

Another thought suddenly struck Nancy, sending a shiver down her spine. 'You will still be here next month, won't you?' Maybe she was being naive and had foolishly jumped the gun. Maybe he would be expected to return to his battalion after a couple of weeks rest.

'It looks that way,' Bert sighed indignantly. 'I can't imagine I'm much good to King and country in this state.'

Nancy bit down on the inside of her lip. On the one hand she was grateful Bert wasn't going to be called back to war anytime soon, but his obvious disappointment at having to be at home had stung. Didn't he want to be here, with her? With Billy and Linda? Wasn't this where he'd dreamt of being? Hadn't Bert said in his letters he couldn't wait to see them, that it was the only thing keeping him going? Nancy could still clearly recall the words from his letters. Surely, this was where he could be safe and get better.

Scared of what Bert might say next, Nancy didn't probe any further, not sure if she would like Bert's answers. Instead, finishing her tea, she looked at the little clock on the mantelpiece. It wasn't even nine o'clock, but she felt wrung out, and she only had to take one look at Bert to see how exhausted he was. She then told herself, again, this was probably why he was being so despondent. She knew only too well how a lack of sleep could zap the enthusiasm out of anyone.

'Shall we turn in for the night? A good night's sleep in your own bed might help.'

Once again, Bert avoided making eye contact. 'If it's all right with you, I'm just going to sleep down here on the couch.'

'But . . . but won't you be more comfortable in a proper bed? That couch is years old and full of lumps and bumps. I can't imagine you will get much sleep.'

'I'll be fine,' Bert snapped.

The words took Nancy back. She thought she'd mentally prepared herself for Bert coming home and the fact he would be exhausted, but what Nancy hadn't ever considered was the only man she'd ever loved would so blatantly reject her. She quickly stood up and turned to the door to hide her tears. 'I'll just go and get you some blankets and a pillow,' she whispered, unable to draw enough breath to speak any louder.

When she came back downstairs, Bert was already laid down on the sofa, his eyes closed.

'Would you like a hand getting out of your clothes?' Nancy tentatively offered.

'I can manage,' came the blunt reply she'd steeled herself for. 'I'll see you in the morning.'

Abashed, pain searing through her, Nancy carefully placed the bedding next to the couch. 'Just shout for me if you need anything.' But even as she said the words, she instinctively knew, Bert wouldn't call on her help.

It was only as Nancy climbed the stairs to her bedroom, which now seemed emptier than ever, and stared at the double bed, which she had longed to share with Bert since the day he'd left, did she allow the tears to stream unbidden down her cheeks, dripping heavily from her quivering chin, onto her aching chest. This was far from the happy homecoming she been dreaming of for months.

Chapter 21

'Go and have ten minutes with yer pals and make sure you have a strong cuppa while yer at it,' Dolly insisted, giving Nancy her orders, as the canteen started to fill up. 'Josie and I can manage here.'

'I couldn't do that. You'll be rushed off yer feet.'

'It's not up for discussion,' Dolly said, firmly. 'We're lucky to have you here at all today, so go and take a break, before some poor starvin' bugger demands you dish up his scran.'

'I'll not disappear for long.'

'Go!' Dolly commanded. 'We are quite capable of manning the fort here.'

Nancy hated to appear as though she was slacking, but also knew Dolly, who had the biggest of hearts, would be offended if she didn't take up her offer, so doing as she was told, Nancy made her way across to the table next to the swap box, where her friends were settling down with their pack-ups.

'Ay up, duck. How are you? Have you come to check the

257

tea urn?' Frank asked, greeting Nancy, completely oblivious to the events of the previous evening.

'Oh sorry. Of course, let me check it.' Momentarily flummoxed, she automatically made her way over to the stainless-steel vat, giving it a cursory shake, instead of sitting down. 'There's still plenty in it.'

'Nancy, is everything okay?' Betty asked, instinctively guessing from how pale Nancy looked that something was wrong.

Where do I begin? she thought. Nancy closed her eyes for no more than a second. She'd known all morning, at some point, she would have to repeat the story she'd already told Dolly and Josie.

'Why don't you come and sit down?' Betty suggested. 'I'm sure Dolly won't mind if you have a minute.'

'That's exactly what she told me to do too.' Nancy half smiled, trying to hide how drained she felt.

Frank looked over, a mixture of concern and guilt. 'Sorry, duck, and here's me asking about the brew.'

'Please, don't apologise. I'd have checked it anyway.'

'Nancy,' Betty repeated, now convinced something was troubling her friend. 'Is it Bert? Has something happened?'

'You could say that,' Nancy answered, sitting down in the empty chair next to Betty, as everyone around the table turned to listen, acutely conscious of how befuddled their friend appeared.

Sensing Nancy was a little discombobulated, Daisy discreetly got up and went and poured her a cuppa and placed it in front of her.

'Thanks, luv. I meant to grab myself one.'

'Is everything all right?' Betty gently enquired again, praying the worst hadn't happened.

'Sorry. I don't mean to look like a wet weekend. It's just, well, Bert came home last night.'

'What?' Patty gasped. 'Were you expecting him? You didn't say.'

'No. Not just yet anyway. He was sat in Doris's kitchen when I got home. It was all a bit of a shock. Quite the surprise in fact.'

'That's great news, isn't it? You must be over the moon.'

'Yes. Yes I am.'

But the weariness in Nancy's voice didn't go unnoticed.

'Did something else happen?' Betty asked, sensing it hadn't been the happy occasion she knew her friend had wanted. 'Are things not quite as easy as you'd hoped?'

Nancy nodded, then sighed, taking a deep breath. 'It really is the best feeling having Bert home. Billy and Linda were beside themselves. Our Billy couldn't stop talking and Linda clung to Bert as though she would never let go.'

'They'd both missed their dad,' Betty said, smiling.

'Yes. Yes, they have and I suppose it was just how I imagined it and it really is wonderful to have Bert back.'

'I sense a "but" coming,' Betty prompted, noting Nancy's voice wasn't as enthusiastic as she thought it would be after eleven months without Bert.

'Dear me. I'm sorry. I really am over the moon, it's just Bert was so distant. I know he's tired and needs time to adjust, I suppose I just thought he would be a little more upbeat than he was.'

'What do you mean?' Betty asked.

'It's hard to put it into words, but he just seemed so deflated and not in the least bit excited to be home. Even Linda asked me when I put her to bed why her daddy was so sad. I tried to explain he just needed time to feel better, but I don't know. I expected him to be a little bit happier about being back with us. He kept telling me in his letters that's all he wanted, but you really wouldn't have known it last night.'

'Oh Nancy,' Betty said, comforting her friend. 'I know you don't need me to tell you this, but maybe Bert needs some time to adjust and come to terms with whatever he went through in France. And it must have been a tiring journey, which can't have helped things.'

'You're right,' Nancy replied hopefully, the tone in her voice slightly uplifted. 'Doris said the same to me this morning. I suppose it just left me a bit shell-shocked.'

'I'm not surprised!' Betty exclaimed. 'Especially when you weren't even expecting him home.'

'In my head, I'd had this lovely image of me and the kids welcoming Bert home with bunting and cakes, and him being full of smiles and enthusiasm about seeing us all. And don't get me wrong, I think he was pleased to see me and the kids, but he was just so deflated. I think I must be a bit worn out too.'

'I'm sure you are,' Betty empathized, rubbing her friend's

arm. 'Last night would have left you emotionally drained and I bet you barely slept, did you?'

'That obvious?'

'I'm afraid so.'

'I think the surprise of seeing Bert and having him home sent my mind into overdrive. I didn't sleep that well, so I guess I do feel pretty wiped out. When I finally got into bed, and accepted Bert was just exhausted, I started making plans for the rest of the summer, thinking about family picnics in the park and Saturday afternoons at the pictures. My mind was whirling ten to the dozen.'

Betty smiled at her friend in admiration. Only a couple of weeks ago, Nancy was on the edge of falling to bits, struggling to put one foot in front of the other, but here she was taking the lead and planning how she could ensure her family got back to normal.

'I know you are tired today, but I'm quite sure you wouldn't have it any other way,' Betty said, emboldening her friend.

'I know you're right. It really was the best surprise seeing Bert sat there in Doris's kitchen, even if it did take me a few seconds to register what I was seeing. I just hope Bert starts to return to his normal happy self soon.'

Frank, who had finished eating his Spam sandwich, was carefully folding up the piece of brown greaseproof paper that Ivy had wrapped his dinner in. 'For what it's worth, duck, I think everything you have just told us sounds completely normal. He's obviously pleased to be home but probably needs a bit of time to readjust.'

'Do you really think so?' Nancy asked hopefully.

'I do, duck. Sometimes, we men aren't very good in these situations.'

'What do you mean?'

'Well, we don't like to admit we can't do something. Our pig-headed stubborn pride means we sometimes act in ways that don't make sense to anyone but ourselves.'

'I'll second that,' Patty interjected, as she wolfed down the heel of a loaf covered in jam.

'Pats!' Archie exclaimed, giving his sweetheart a playful nudge.

'Well, you blokes can be chuffin' daft at times.'

Aware this wasn't the time to argue the toss, Archie rolled his eyes in mock jest.

'To be fair, Patty has got a point,' Frank added.

Nursing her steaming brew, Nancy threw the foreman a quizzical glance.

'Yorkshire pride, duck. It can be a reyt curse at times. We don't like to admit when things are tough.'

Something in what Frank said began to register in Nancy's mind. She took a moment to consider his words. Bert had always been the strong arm of their family, the one to buffer Nancy and their children from hardship, working extra hours as a conductor, to make sure they didn't have to go without, even when he was shattered. In his own way, was Bert trying to protect her?

'Do you think he's just feeling a bit unsettled after being away for so long?' Nancy asked.

'I wouldn't like to put words in your Bert's mouth, duck, but I wouldn't be surprised if he is. He's been away at war for the best part of a year and then walked back into his old life but hasn't had time to really deal with everything he's been through himself.'

It was as though a light had been switched on and Bert's uncharacteristically guarded behaviour started to make sense. Of course, that's what it was. As much as Nancy hated to think of Bert not feeling he could share his inner fears with her, she also knew he was a firm traditionalist, the man of the house. It was obvious now; Bert's pride would have kicked in.

'You're right,' Nancy muttered. 'He won't like me seeing him drained.' *No wonder he was so keen to get to sleep and maybe that explained why he wanted to sleep on the couch too, so he had a bit of space to try to process what he'd been through without worrying me.*

In her heart of hearts, Nancy knew there was a part of Bert that would see his physical and emotional injuries as a sign of weakness. She recalled how he had warned her in his letter he was in a dark place; now it was her job to help him find a way out and ease back into his old life.

'Listen, duck,' Frank said, interrupting Nancy's thoughts. 'I know you all need time to settle into a new routine and time to get used to Bert being at home again, but when you think your Bert is up for it, why don't you all come over one Sunday? I'm sure Ivy would love to see you all.' Then turning to Betty, he added, 'Wouldn't you agree?'

'Absolutely,' came the confirmation. 'And,' Betty added, 'a change of scenery is always good for the soul.'

'Thank you.' Nancy smiled in appreciation, her worries fading away. Determined to simply enjoy having her husband home, she added, 'I'll just give Bert a bit of time to settle in, and then I'll take you up on the offer.'

'Whenever you're ready, duck,' Frank said, standing up from the table. 'Now, as much as I hate to leave you all, I need to go and see one of the gaffers about this latest order.'

'Dinner ain't over yet, is it?' Patty protested. 'I was just about to tackle m' knitting.'

'No.' Frank chuckled. 'Don't fret. You've got a bit of time. I just need to sort summat out.'

'Thank God for that,' Patty exclaimed, pulling her half-completed bottle-green hat out of her bag. 'I feel like I've only just sat down.'

'Do you need a hand with that?' Daisy asked, seeing the befuddled look on her friend's face as she tried to work out where her wool, which seemed to be in a coiled knot, started and ended.

'Would yer?' Patty stated more than asked. 'I knew I should have kept to scarves.'

Betty laughed and encouraged her friends to keep knitting; with autumn not far off, there would be an increased demand, once again, by troops for winter woollies.

As the rest of the table chatted, Hattie, who was sat the other side of Nancy, couldn't help feeling uneasy. Her mum had always said it was the Great War that had destroyed her dad, turning him from a gentle, caring man to an unrecognizable brute. He'd always refused to talk about what he'd seen and endured, instead turning to the bottom of a pint glass to deal with whatever troubled his mind.

'I hope your Bert starts to feel a bit better soon,' Hattie said, turning to Nancy. She wouldn't wish the suffering her mum had been forced to endure on anybody, and especially not someone as kind and good-natured as Nancy. Her dad had come home half-cut every night since he'd left her mum in a heap on the floor, and during the day and when he was at home, he was either sat at the table snarling or demanding Hattie's mum hand over more of her meagre wages she earned from cleaning. 'I know, it's easier said than done, but if and when Bert is up to it, if you can get him to open up, that might help.'

'I'm sure he will.' Nancy nodded. 'We've never had any secrets in the past, so I can't see why he wouldn't now.' The thought of Bert not talking to her about what was going on in his head seemed inconceivable.

Is that what happened to my dad? Hattie quietly asked herself. *Did he suddenly clam up, preventing mum from helping him?* She had no living memories of them being happy together, but surely they must have been once?

Hattie didn't want to upset Nancy or spoil her happy moment, so instead just said, 'I'm sure when he's had a bit of time adjusting to being back at home, he will start talking, but if you ever want to just have a chat, I'm always happy to listen.'

'Thank you. I do appreciate it. Did your dad fight in the last war?'

'Yes.' Then added as tactfully as possible, 'Wars have a lot to answer for.'

'They certainly do, luv,' Nancy agreed. 'And I'm still trying to work out for what good.'

'I wish I knew the answer to that myself,' Hattie sighed, unable to hide the disillusion in her voice.

Nancy had always sensed Hattie didn't have the easiest of home lives. She'd made the odd comment when they'd been in The Welly about needing to get home for her mum, and taking her out for a rare treat. Part of her wanted to ask more, but something stopped her. Not only did Nancy not like to pry, but there was also another part of Nancy that was worried Hattie might tell her things that she wasn't sure she could cope with right now. It wasn't that she didn't care, far from it, she hated to think of Hattie having a tough time of it, but she needed to stay strong and keep telling herself she could help Bert so eventually, with a bit of time and love, her old husband would return, and they could be a normal, happy family again.

Chapter 22

Nancy had just sliced up the freshly made loaf she'd made the night before, and popped it on the table with a small portion of butter and an equally paltry ramekin of strawberry jam. It was by no mean a feast, but she hoped the simple, traditional breakfast would remind Bert of their pre-war family traditions.

Linda and Billy were already sat at the table, both patiently waiting for their dad, who had once again spent the previous night sleeping on the couch.

'I'm drawing Daddy a new picture,' Linda announced, her face deep in concentration as she bent over the piece of paper she was colouring in. 'Do you think he will hang it up in the front room?' she asked innocently, no idea the impact the words had on Nancy.

'I'm sure he will,' Nancy said, keeping her tone cheerful, even though she'd spent the last four nights, since Bert got home, tossing and turning, her double bed feeling emptier than ever and a painful reminder that the man she loved most in the world felt a million miles away, despite being in the same house.

'I wish he'd hurry up. I'm starvin',' Billy complained, thinking only of his stomach.

At least some things never change, Nancy mused, grateful her son hadn't been affected by how distant Bert had been. Nancy knew Linda was producing another drawing in the hope it would make Bert smile, whereas all Billy could think about was when he would next be fed.

'I'm sure he'll be through in a minute,' Nancy said, popping a fresh pot of tea on the table and ruffling her son's messy mop of thick brown hair with the other.

'What's that?' came Bert's tired voice from the kitchen door.

'Dad!' Billy exclaimed. 'Hurry up. I'm starvin' and Mum wouldn't let me start until you got here.'

'Sorry, son. Easier said than done, I'm afraid,' Bert replied wearily, as he hobbled unsteadily into the kitchen, leaning heavily on his walking stick.

Linda immediately looked up in bewilderment at seeing her daddy so frail. 'We saved you the crust,' she said, eager to please.

'Did we?' Billy protested indignantly, his stomach rumbling.

'Yes!' Linda said, throwing her brother a stern look.

'There are two crusts, one at each end of the loaf, so you and your dad can have one each,' Nancy interjected, hoping to both satisfy Billy and prompt Bert about how he always used to tease the kids; he would have the heal of the loaf if he beat them downstairs for breakfast.

But instead, as he dropped himself onto one of the wooden chairs, he announced, 'You can have both, Billy. I'm not that hungry.'

The downcast comment caused Linda to turn sharply to Nancy, her eyes bestowing how anxious she felt.

Billy, on the other hand, didn't need any further encouragement. 'Oh good!' he exclaimed, reaching over to the plate of wholegrain bread, and picking up a thicker than normal crust. 'I was hoping you'd let me have it.'

'Will you have a cup of tea at least?' Nancy asked carefully, feeling as though she was treading on egg shells, frightened she would say the wrong thing.

Bert nodded. 'Thank you.'

Totally unaware of the tension as he covered his bread in butter and bright red jam, Billy asked, 'Do you want to come and fly some paper aeroplanes with me today, Dad? My latest one can glide all the way across the yard now. Or we could go to the park and see how far they go there?'

Bert looked at his eager-faced son. He'd love nothing more than to spend hours watching Billy chase across High Hazels Park, whooping with delight as his paper creations soared through the air, but he knew he'd let him down. He could barely make it a few steps without sharp shooting pains leaving him wincing in agony. He had no chance of traipsing to Darnall and then across the tree-lined expanse of grass in pursuit of a replica fighter plane, the latter threatening to cause harrowing flashbacks that he really didn't want to relive. 'Maybe another day, son,' he half-promised, not even sure himself if he would ever be able to fulfil the simple request.

Silence draped the room and for the first time, Billy looked crestfallen, his hopeful face crumpling at the uncharacteristic rejection. His dad, *his hero*, the person he'd envisaged driving tanks, fighting off enemy soldiers and defending England against Hitler, couldn't even watch him launch his latest, and carefully produced, paper aeroplane.

Momentarily taken aback, Nancy, who had lifted the teapot to pour herself and Bert a cup of tea, stood stock-still. Bert's response was a far cry from his usual, pre-war enthusiasm to join in their children's fun. He had always been such a hands-on dad, the first one to offer to kick a ball about in the yard, or read bedtime stories, determined to embrace every part of Billy and Linda's childhood. Had she been kidding herself that a few good nights' sleep and a handful of hearty homemade meals could revert Bert back to his old self?

The look of hurt in Billy's eyes pulled at Nancy's heart. Her good-natured son never got upset or complained, always finding something to smile and laugh about, but his excitement had been instantly dampened.

Nancy glanced from her dejected son to her husband, who looked equally as upset as he stared down at the table, tightly wringing his pale bony fingers in his lap, his eyes watering. The despondent atmosphere was palpable.

Don't let your family fall apart. Nancy remembered the vow she'd made to herself. She couldn't allow Billy to think Bert was cold-heartedly dismissing him, especially when she knew how much her son idolized his dad. By the disconcerted look on her husband's face, he was suffering too.

Then Nancy recalled what Frank has said about Bert being too proud to reveal how much he was struggling. She had seen how he hobbled slowly from the living room to the outside loo in the yard, limping through the house, propping himself up on his stick, and still hadn't attempted the stairs. *It's all too much for him*, Nancy thought to herself, *but he doesn't want to say*.

Pulling herself back to the moment, Nancy carefully poured the tea, and as she handed Bert his steaming mug, suggested to Billy, 'Why don't I take you over to the park for a couple of hours and when we get back, maybe we all sit out in the yard and you can show your dad your planes? It's a lovely day and I can take a picnic. We could eat in the sunshine while your dad has a little rest.'

Billy, on tenterhooks, was too anxious to show any enthusiasm, in fear of being disappointed for the second time in the space of a few minutes. Instead, he sat rigid and stared straight ahead at his weary dad.

'I can read you my new schoolbook later too,' Linda offered, 'and show you all my pictures.'

Please don't reject them, Nancy silently pleaded.

Bert looked around the table, the anxious eyes of his

family all upon him. The backyard wasn't a big ask, and heaven knows, he could do with some fresh air. 'I'm sure I can manage that,' he stammered, trying to keep his voice intact.

'Thank you, Daddy.' Linda beamed, her eyes glistening in pure joy. 'I promise to try really hard with my reading.'

'I don't doubt it,' Bert whispered, smiling at his elated daughter.

'Does that mean I can show you my latest paper aeroplane?' Billy asked tentatively. 'I'll try it out first with Mum.'

'Of course.' Bert nodded.

Instantly the tense atmosphere evaporated and was replaced by a welcome, steady stream of chatter as the family tucked into a simple but tasty breakfast. Nancy hoped and prayed giving Bert some time to himself would revive him enough to give Billy and Linda the attention they so desperately craved. And she, too, needed to think about how she could help Bert, who, she was beginning to realize, really was a shadow of the man she'd waved off at the Midland station the previous September.

Later that afternoon, after a couple of hours in High Hazel Park where Billy had proudly demonstrated his latest paper flying machines, he found his best friend Joe waiting in the gennel. 'Wait until you see this,' Billy boasted, launching a paper plane into the air.

Leaving the boys to play in the yard with Linda, who had fetched her reading book and French knitting doll, Nancy went into the kitchen to pour a jug of fresh lemonade. As she glanced out of the window, if she hadn't known any different, Nancy would have believed life had returned to normal. Isn't this how they had spent many a Sunday afternoon, before Neville Chamberlain had made his sombre announcement?

'Penny for them?' Doris asked, interrupting Nancy's daydream, as she let herself in her neighbour's back door and stepped into the kitchen.

'Oh!' Nancy said, startled. 'Sorry. I didn't see you there, luv.'

'You were in a world of your own. Is everything okay? I just popped in as I could hear the boys outside and Alice wanted to come and see Linda.'

'Of course. We've just got back. I was going to wake Bert. He's having a nap on the couch and then I'm hoping we can all go outside for a while.'

'How is he?'

'Not doing great, I'm afraid,' Nancy said, lowering her voice so Bert didn't overhear. 'If I'm brutally honest, he looks more tired now than the day he got home.'

'Oh, luv. That's hard.'

'In all the excitement of Bert coming home, I think I underestimated how hard things were going to be. I don't think he's sleeping. I heard him shout a couple of times in the night. And, although he won't admit it, I think his leg is giving him some gyp.'

'Has he said what happened yet?'

Nancy shook her head. 'No, and I don't want to push him.'

'That's understandable. Hopefully, as he gets settled, he'll open up. Has he got some painkillers for his leg?'

'Yes, I think so. I've seen him swallowing pills, but I don't know if they are as strong as what they gave him in hospital.'

'And how are you feeling?'

'Honestly?' Nancy took a few beakers from the cupboard. 'I feel exhausted and utterly wrung out. I'm barely sleeping for worrying and my mind is in constant overdrive. Nothing is quite how I expected.'

'I don't think anybody can predict something like this,' Doris sympathized.

'You're probably right but maybe I should've been more realistic about how this war has affected Bert.'

'Don't beat yerself up, luv. How could you have possibly known?'

'Oh, I don't know. Bert did tell me he was in a dark place in his letters but, I think, if I'm being honest with myself, I didn't want to think about what that really meant. And now, I don't feel like I can switch off. It's like I'm trying to second-guess how he is feeling, but I'm determined to stay strong. I've had a few wobbles and shed a few tears, once the kids have been in bed, but the good news is I've surprised myself at how determined I've been to keep it together.'

'That's because yer a mum and much stronger than you ever given yerself credit for,' Doris praised. 'Having children gives us some unexplainable strength to carry on when times get tough.'

'You're right,' Nancy replied, taking the few remaining biscuits from the picnic bag and popping them on a plate. 'Tell Alice and Joe there's enough snacks if they want to stay and play?'

'Haven't you got enough on?'

'To be honest, they are a welcome distraction for Billy and Linda. It stops them focusing too much on Bert.'

'Fair enough.' Doris nodded. 'But send them home if it gets too much. And please, make sure you put your feet up for an hour too.'

'Thanks, luv. I'm going to take this lot out and then go and get Bert. I'm hoping the rest and a bit of peace and quiet will have helped and he will come outside for a bit.'

'I'm sure he will,' Doris said. 'Reyt, I'll leave you to go and wake him, but you know where I am if you need me.'

'I do and thank you.'

'Don't mention it,' Doris said with a wave of the hand as she left through the back door. 'And don't forget, I'll have the kids tomorrow.'

'How on earth will I ever repay you?' But Doris had already vanished, aware at how precious the family afternoon was for Nancy.

Placing the plate of biscuits and the jug of lemonade on a tray, Nancy took a deep breath, painted on her smile and made her way out to the yard.

'Oh goody,' Billy exclaimed, his eyes lighting up as soon as he caught sight of his mum and an array of food. 'I'm starvin'!'

'It wasn't that long since your sandwiches.' Nancy laughed, her son's insatiable appetite never ceasing to amaze her.

'It's been hours,' Billy proclaimed. 'Can Joe stay for summat to eat too?'

'Of course, and Alice too. There's plenty.'

'Thanks, Mum.' Billy grinned, before helping himself to a biscuit.

'Hold yer horses!' Nancy mock-admonished as she set the treats down on an upturned wooden crate.

'Sorry!' But Billy knew his mum never had the heart to really get cross with him.

'What's this? Are you starting without me?' came a voice from the back door.

'Dad!' Billy beamed. 'Would you like to see my paper aeroplanes glide through the sky like Spitfires now?'

'Okay.' Bert nodded as he hobbled to a chair.

'Would you like a biscuit?' Nancy offered.

Bert shook his head. 'I'm not hungry.'

'Are you sure? You barely touched your breakfast.' The words had slipped out unbidden, before Nancy could stop herself.

'I'm not a child!' Bert snapped.

The curt words left Nancy momentarily paralyzed. Bert had never once snapped at her in the past. His gentle, caring nature meant he had always spoken to her with nothing but kindness. Sharp tears burnt the back of her eyes, but Nancy forced them back, keeping them hidden, refusing to break now. *He's not well*, she told herself. *He just needs time.*

'Sorry,' Nancy finally managed to say. 'It's the mum in me,' she added, her cheerful tone, once again, emerging.

Bert glanced at her, his normally bright eyes weary. 'I might have something later.'

'You'll have to beat Billy!' Linda announced.

'That's true.' Nancy smiled. 'There's no filling that brother of yours. If I didn't know better, I'd be convinced he had hollow legs.'

Nancy was determined to keep the last hour or so of the afternoon as upbeat as possible, silently praying the children didn't pick up on any unnecessary tension. This war had impacted them enough, without their having to watch their mum and dad snap at one another.

'He's grown,' Bert observed a few minutes later, his voice softer and a look of sadness appearing across his weathered face.

'He's still a little tinker, though. Same Billy, just a bit taller.'

Bert stared intently at Billy and Joe, who in between wiping crumbs from their mouths, worked on perfecting their paper aeroplanes, slightly bending the wings and ensuring the nose was as pointed and precision-sharp as possible.

'He's been desperate to show you his creations,' Nancy added.

Bert nodded but remained silent.

What's going in that mind of yours? Nancy quietly mused, observing her husband's unfamiliar behaviour. *What's holding you back?* She didn't pressure Bert to explain, remembering Frank's likely theory, that his pride was probably preventing him opening up. Nancy couldn't pretend to fully understand it, but she knew she had to be patient and hope beyond hope, that with time, Bert felt comfortable enough to let his barriers down and allow her back into his inner thoughts, just like he always had.

'Daddy,' Linda chirped up, interrupting Nancy's thoughts.

Bert turned towards his smiling, eager-to-please daughter, lifting his thinning eyebrows in response.

Whether Linda was oblivious to Bert's nonchalant response or just keen to tell her daddy something, Nancy couldn't be sure, but either way, her daughter carried on regardless.

'Do you think if I make my French knitting long enough, I could turn it into a hat for a soldier? Mummy and her friends did lots of knitting so I thought I could too.'

Nancy watched her husband closely. His dark eyes, which had previously sparkled naturally, now glistened as water collected in them, and once again, he started nervously pulling and twisting at his fingers, something he'd never done before the war but Nancy had seen Bert do frequently since he'd come home.

When he didn't reply, causing a look of bewildered angst to appear across Linda's face, Nancy quickly interjected. She couldn't let her children suffer any more than they already had. 'What a lovely idea. I'm sure any soldier would love a warm woolly hat.'

But the sensitive little girl was still looking at her dad, waiting for *his* approval.

'Bert,' Nancy gently prompted, quietly pleading her husband would give their expectant daughter the encouragement she desperately needed.

'Your mum is right,' he finally said, without any emotion.

But Linda didn't mind. She had her dad's seal of approval and a huge smile spread across her face. Closing her eyes, Nancy exhaled in relief. She knew the children would have picked up on the change in their dad, but Nancy hoped she could shield them from the worst of it.

Chapter 23

Sunday, 18 August 1940

'Bert. Bert,' Nancy said urgently, as she gently shook her husband, who was in a deep sleep on the couch. 'You need to wake up.'

'What? What is it?' His voice tremored, his eyes, full of panic, suddenly alert, were scanning the room, darting frantically from one corner to the other. 'Get down,' he ordered. 'Get down.' Bert's body was now shaking, and Nancy could see droplets of perspiration appearing on his clammy forehead.

'Bert,' Nancy said, taking hold of her husband's arm, realizing he must have thought he was back in France. 'You're here, at home.'

'Get down,' he commanded.

'It's okay,' Nancy said, desperately trying to reassure him. 'You're dreaming. It's me. Nancy. I'm here. You're at home.'

For a few seconds, Bert looked completely terrified, his glassy eyes glazing over. 'But the noise. The sirens. It's a warning.'

'It is,' Nancy agreed. 'It's an air-raid siren. We need to

get to a shelter. That's why I'm waking you up. We need to get Billy and Linda to safety.'

Bert stared at his wife, his wild eyes settling, as he slowly came to his senses. 'A shelter,' he repeated. And then, just to reiterate Nancy's point, the high-pitched screeching of the air-raid sirens echoed through the room.

'There's a communal shelter down the road. We need to get there. I'll go and wake the kids.'

But right on cue, Billy, still half asleep, came trundling down the stairs and into the front room, dressed in his creased blue-and-white-striped pyjamas. 'The siren. It woke me up,' he muttered.

'Don't worry,' Nancy said instinctively, jumping up and rushing to her son's side. 'It's all right. We just need to get down to the shelter. You know what to do, don't you? Will you get your shoes and coat on for me?'

Quickly coming round from his sleepy slumber, Billy nodded. And then, as if on instinct added, 'Shall I pack the biscuits?'

'If you hurry,' Nancy replied, the deafening, spine-chilling alert keeping her focused.

Making her way towards the door, Nancy looked back at Bert, but he was stock-still on the couch. 'Please hurry,' she said, hoping to bolster him. 'I'll be back down in a minute. I need to get Linda.'

But just as she was about to make her way up the stairs, she was greeted by her tearful little girl. 'The sirens,' she cried. 'They frightened me.'

'It's all right, poppet,' Linda soothed, lifting her quivering daughter into her arms, her riot of blonde curls falling onto Nancy's shoulder. 'Mummy's here and Daddy and Billy are getting ready. We are going to go down to the shelter.'

Linda turned back into the living room where Bert was still frozen to the spot. 'You go,' he whispered. 'I'll slow you down.'

'No!' Nancy protested instantly, keeping her voice quiet but firm, to avoid frightening Linda. 'We all go together.'

'I can't,' Bert whispered, looking down.

'Why not?' Nancy panicked. She just needed to get her family out of the house and sharpish.

'I'm ready, Mum,' Billy called from the kitchen.

'Good boy,' Nancy replied. 'Just give us a minute and we'll all be ready.'

'You go,' Bert insisted again, pulling himself up into a sitting position on the couch.

'Daddy,' Linda pleaded, her little voice no more than a whimper, as she lifted her sleepy head from Nancy's now tense shoulder.

Aghast, Nancy stared at her husband. *Please. Think of the children*, she willed him.

Bert looked from Nancy to Linda, and then down at his gammy leg. 'I won't make it.'

Before Nancy could protest any further, there was a loud knock at the back door, followed by Doris's voice as she marched through the house to the front room. 'Nancy.

Come on, luv. We need to get these kiddies down to the shelter.'

'It's Bert,' Nancy explained. 'He doesn't think he'll make it.'

'Nonsense,' Doris said, sternly. 'These children need to get to safety, and you are not staying here, if I have to carry you myself.'

Bert was too stunned to respond, but his neighbour's blunt instructions sparked something inside him. 'Give me a minute,' he said and nodded.

'Right, I'll stay here,' Doris said matter-of-factly, 'in case you need an arm to lean on. Nancy, go and get your and Linda's coat. My lot are in the yard. I've got a big flask of tea and some biscuits. We need to get going.'

Nancy knew Doris was deliberately sending her out of the room, to prevent her from pandering to Bert any further. In the kitchen, she pulled Linda's anorak on her, knowing that despite the pleasantly warm evening, they might still feel a chill the later it got. It was already after nine o'clock; God knows how long it would be until the 'all clear' rang out.

'I found some cake in the tin, Mum, so I put it in this,' Billy said, proudly holding up a brown paper bag.

Nancy couldn't help but smile. The world could be collapsing around him, and her son would still think of his stomach. 'You are a case.' She grinned, bending down to help Linda into her summer sandals.

'We're here,' Doris said, supporting one side of Bert, who was gripping his walking stick with his free hand. He was already wearing his boots and had a sweater on over his polo shirt.

'Are you okay?' Nancy asked, noting the strain in her husband's face.

His reply came in the form of a slight nod, but Nancy knew this wasn't the time to get into a discussion, not that Bert was saying much of late.

A couple of minutes later, the two families were walking down Prince Street, surrounded by dozens of others all hastily making their way to the brick-and-concrete communal shelter on Thompson Street. Despite the countless false alarms, there had been a change in the atmosphere since Dunkirk. The war suddenly seemed closer to home and people were keen to stay safe.

Nancy, who had hold of Linda's and Alice's hand, kept glancing across to her husband. Bert's expression bestowing his sheer concentration as he hobbled down the street, relying on both Doris and his stick to walk. Nancy's heart ached at seeing Bert struggle, knowing every step was causing him immeasurable pain.

'Hello, you lot,' came a familiar voice, interrupting Nancy's thoughts.

'Bill,' Nancy gasped, as she spotted Angie, Patty and her brothers and sisters.

'Flamin' typical, isn't it?' said Patty, who was carrying a sleepy Tom Tom. 'I was desperate for an early night after all this overtime. Chuff knows how long we will be trapped in this shelter for.'

'Patty!' her dad reproached. 'This shelter could very well save our lives one day!'

'Sorry. I don't mean to be mardy. I'm just shattered and would rather be in m' own bed.'

'Wouldn't we all, sunshine.'

'Anyway,' Bill said, changing the subject and turning to Bert. 'I don't think we've met before. I'm Bill. My daughter and your wife work together and I'm at Vickers too.'

Despairingly, Bert looked at the steep concrete stairs that he somehow needed to tackle. His pride was already in tatters after being left with no choice but to rely on Doris to get this far, and he knew he couldn't manage the potentially lethal descent on his own. He'd end up going head over heels, and in a heap on the floor.

Bill noticed Bert gripping his walking stick tightly. Not wanting to immediately interfere, he held off a few seconds to see if Bert could manage. Only when Bill saw Bert was struggling to navigate the descent, did he add, 'Can I give you a hand down these steps?'

'If you don't mind, it's probably wise,' Bert said. 'Thank you, and sorry, pleased to meet you too.'

'No problem, pal.'

As Doris let go of Bert, allowing Bill to take over, she glanced at Nancy, who was watching her husband intently, with a mixture of concern and sympathy.

'He'll be all right, luv,' Doris whispered reassuringly, as she patted her friend's arm.

'At least he's here,' Nancy replied as she watched Bert

hobble unsteadily down the stairs, with Bill at his side taking the lion's share of his weight, before checking Billy and Joe were still nearby. 'I couldn't have left him at the house. I'd have been out of my mind with worry.'

'Of course you would, but there's no point fretting about that now. He's here and that's all that matters.'

'What on earth did you say to him? I haven't been able to get him farther than the backyard since he got home.'

'To be honest, I didn't say much else. I just told him to get a move on and that I wasn't leaving the front room unless he left with me.'

'Well, I wouldn't get on the wrong side of you either,' Nancy joked. 'Maybe I need to try that approach and get a bit sterner.'

'Don't be too hard on yerself, luv. Maybe just hearing it from someone else meant Bert didn't feel like he could argue.'

'Possibly.' Nancy nodded, feeling a bit put out that her own husband wouldn't listen to her but did exactly what their neighbour ordered.

'Right, kids,' Doris said, as she took Little George from her eldest daughter, and simultaneously commanded the attention of their combined brood. 'Let's get into this shelter and stick together. Find a space on the bench and get comfy. We could be in for a long night.'

'I don't like it down there,' Linda whispered, squeezing her mum's hand.

Nancy looked down at her daughter, her little face

already crumpling. 'I know, poppet, but you know I'll be sat right next to you.'

'And I'll hold your hand,' Alice added. 'I've brought some books too.'

Linda managed the smallest of smiles. Nancy knew how much her daughter hated the air-raid shelters, the wailing siren leaving Linda clinging to her.

'I promise we'll be fine and remember, Daddy is here too.' This final comment seemed to do the trick, and as the two families entered the shelter, Nancy sensed her daughter's worries were gradually evaporating.

A few minutes later, the families of Nancy, Doris and Patty were all huddled together in the cavernous chamber. Bill had perched himself next to Bert, directly opposite Nancy, and all the kids had commandeered a corner and were hurriedly unpacking the medley of toys they had quickly managed to grab.

'I brought you this!' Billy exclaimed, pulling Linda's French knitting doll and wool from his haversack.

'Thank you.' Linda beamed, then looked to Alice and exclaimed, 'We can take it in turns.'

Despite the circumstances, Nancy felt a sense of clam. *Whatever happens, at least we are together*, she thought.

'How's your Bert getting on?' Angie, who was sat next to Nancy, asked discreetly, keeping her voice low enough to prevent anyone from overhearing. 'Patty was telling us he's been finding it tough since he got back.'

'It's definitely been harder than I thought but I'm hopeful

it will get easier with time.' Nancy was determined not to lose hope, reminding herself it was now her job to keep her family intact.

'Let me know if we can do anything to help,' Angie said. 'It's no bother.'

'Thank you, but I'm sure you have enough on.'

'Not at all.' Angie pulled her knitting from a cloth bag. 'We all have to stick together in times like this, and I've probably got more time on m' hands than you. I've even managed to make a couple of hats and scarves for yer friend Betty's collection.'

'She will be chuffed.' Nancy smiled. 'I know Betty will want to get another care parcel put together for the troops.'

Nancy felt her husband's eyes upon her and glanced across the crammed, dimly lit shelter. His face was hard to read, but the sadness in his eyes was unmistakable. She nodded and smiled at her husband, hoping it was enough to reassure him, that she was there for him.

But before Nancy could gauge his response, a deafening whirring noise could be heard above their heads, and then another. 'Mummy,' Linda screeched, jumping to Nancy's knee.

'What the chuffin' 'eck was that?' Patty said, her eyes darting from the ceiling to her dad, and then zigzagging around the semipermanent subterranean shelter.

'The bloody Luftwaffe,' came one response.

'Those blasted Germans,' another sniped.

'It was only a matter of time,' someone else commented. 'Bloody Hitler has been gunning for us for months.'

As the sinister overhead sounds increased in frequency, the tension inside the shelter mounted. The fear palpable.

This is it. It's really happening, Nancy thought, as she held her daughter closer to her chest. 'Billy. Come here,' she called to her son.

Then, desperately trying to get her husband's attention, without alarming Billy and Linda, she turned towards Bert. 'Can you hear me?'

Bert didn't move his head an inch; it lay heavily encased between his rough, calloused hands, slumped against his bony knees.

Even though they were only a metre or so apart, Nancy felt as far from Bert as she had when he was across the Channel in France. The same brave man, who would have once been the first to protect his family, was now an unreachable quivering wreck.

'Is Daddy all right?' Linda asked, her little body tensing with every unfamiliar, and intimidating, roar that came from outside.

Nancy had prayed her children wouldn't have to witness the devastating impact the war had had on Bert, but she realized now it was impossible to disguise how damaged their father was. Whatever he'd endured on the battlefields wasn't going to be cured with a few homemade meals or the simple comfort of his own home.

Even Billy, who normally let most things wash over

him, was now staring at the unfamiliar sight of his terror-stricken dad, in a subdued state of confusion and bewilderment.

'He's just very tired,' Nancy lied, trying to reassure them.

'Does he want a cuddle?' Linda asked, the sight of Bert, looking so timorous, adding to her upset.

'Maybe in a little while. Just give him a minute.'

If only it was that easy, Nancy thought. If only a pair of loving arms, tightly embracing her damaged husband, could dissolve the heavy and destructive load he was carrying around with him. She'd naively assumed as soon as Bert was home, surrounded by his family, and smothered in love, he would be okay, that the memories of what he'd witnessed would dissipate, and he would return to his old self.

But now, as she watched her husband's once muscular, but now skeletal shoulders shudder, she really wasn't sure what it would take to fix him.

'Give him time,' Doris, who was sat the other side of Nancy, Little George on her knee, whispered, as if reading her friend's mind. 'It's still early days. He's got a lot to process.'

Nancy nodded gratefully, thankful she could offload her worries onto her friends. She also knew Doris was right. She needed to be patient. What else could she do but give him time? That, mixed with a large helping of love, was all she really had.

But did she? Another loud whistle from above instantly silenced the dozens who had rushed to take shelter in the public bolthole. Her maternal grip tightening on Billy and Linda, she shuddered. Her eyes were the only thing that moved as she looked around the shelter, desperately trying to rationalize her thoughts. But no matter how hard Nancy tried, all she could think was that every single one of them was trapped in this suffocating brick-and-concrete chamber, with no idea if they would get out in one piece, and if they did, what they would face. Admittedly, despite the ominous sound of what could only be military aircraft overhead, there hadn't been any loud bangs to indicate an apocalyptic explosion, but even so, there was no doubt about it, this air raid was different to all the others. Although the sirens always acted as a catalyst for folk to get to a shelter, as the early months of the war had passed, many had seen the spells in the underground caverns as a test at best, or at worst an interruption to their daily routines. But now, the Phoney War had long passed and all the news about the Luftwaffe taking to the skies across Britain, first on the south coast, and then across the country, had left Nancy and everyone else wondering what the Germans would do next.

Nancy had overheard men in the dinner queue prophesizing about what the future held, whether Hitler would try to occupy England, as he had in parts of France. She hadn't really paid it much heed, the concept so alien, and her mind so overtaken with Bert, but now as she took in the suddenly sombre mood, the enormity of the situation consumed her.

One hand on each of her children, Nancy couldn't even begin to imagine what lay ahead. Although Frank generally had a *Daily Mirror* with him most dinnertimes, she hadn't really picked up on exactly how the people of France had suffered. If the truth be known, Nancy didn't understand what an 'occupation' meant.

But the one thing she did know was the Allied and French troops had suffered untold losses as they'd tried to defend France. The thought of one person dying, a brother, a father or a son, made her shudder but she knew the numbers were far more harrowing than a single death. Is this what now lay in store for Britain? Was this what the future held? Days, weeks or, heaven forbid, months of fear and not knowing what each day would bring? Nancy couldn't envisage how this could become the norm. The enormity of it was just too hard to comprehend.

The clack-clack of anti-aircraft guns pierced Nancy's thoughts and as she slowly took in the almost visceral terror on the faces of those surrounding her, Nancy realized that she wasn't alone in her apprehension.

The scene of older siblings, parents and grandparents holding their loved ones closely was replicated around the densely occupied shelter. The usual chatter, the clacking of knitting needles or the communal sing-along of Vera Lynn's 'We'll Meet Again' had been replaced by a deafening silence that was reverberating off every wall. Not even the babies and toddlers were murmuring, the paralyzing shock of hearing aircraft above quelling each and every one of them.

Patty, who normally always had something to say, was deathly quiet, as she wrapped one arm tightly around her bewildered little brother, and another around the shoulders of her youngest sister, Emily. *She will be worrying about Archie*, Nancy imagined. *Please, God, let him be safe.*

Nancy looked across at Bill, who had placed one of his hands firmly on Bert's shoulder. She wanted to rush to her husband's knees, reassure him everything was going to be all right, but like everyone else, she didn't dare move. Nancy closed her eyes, forcing back the tears that were threatening to spill, the shock of what was happening diminishing her newly found fortitude to remain strong for her family.

Just when she thought she was about to succumb to her emotions, Nancy felt a squeeze on her arm. Opening her eyes, Nancy turned to her left. Doris was looking at her. She too was silent, but there was something reassuring in her familiar gaze. Nancy knew she was telling her to hang on in there, things would get better. Even in moments when words couldn't be spoken, Doris always knew how to fortify Nancy.

The next ten minutes seemed to last an eternity with the muffled sound of airplanes flying overhead. A hundred prayers must have been silently uttered, no doubt each one liberally bargaining with God, impassioned promises in return for the safety of themselves and their loved ones.

Nancy's eyes moved from her two children, who were

both snuggled into her, their little bodies quivering, to Bert, who never once looked up, his head remaining firmly downwards as he wrestled with his demons. In an act of unbidden kindness, Bill never once took his protective hand from his shoulder – something Nancy was grateful for.

Finally, the sinister whirring faded away, and with it a gradual, yet cautious, feeling of relief began to come over the temporary inhabitants of the shelter.

'Is it over?' Linda whispered to Nancy, her head still firmly enveloped in her mum's arm.

'I think so, poppet.' Nancy hated the fact her little girl could be so aware of the danger they all faced. She was just six years old. No child should ever have to bear witness to such torrid and frightening circumstances.

'The Germans know we will beat them, that's why,' Billy added, suddenly full of innocent bravado.

'That's right, son,' the air-raid warden, Fred Williams, said. 'Hitler doesn't know what he's playing with by messing with our brilliant RAF.'

'Hear, hear!' came a resounding cheer of encouragement from one of the older men. 'Let's hope they shot the bloody Nazis down. No less than they deserve if yer ask me.'

Nancy shuddered, instinctively putting her hands over Linda's ears, knowing back-room talk like that was enough to give her highly sensitive daughter nightmares for weeks.

'I'm not arguing with yer sentiment,' Fred replied, 'but

remember we have lots of kiddies in here tonight. Maybe that's a conversation for another day.'

'Sorry, gaffer. M' tongue often works quicker than m' brain.'

'No bother, pal. Anyway,' Fred added, 'at least it's gone quiet. We might still be down here for a while though, so I'm afraid yer might have to remain comfy for a bit longer yet.'

'Yer might have to install some beds,' another voice piped up.

'If only we had the room.' Fred chuckled. 'But I did manage to commandeer a couple of packets of biscuits if anyone fancies one?'

'Ay, pass em round,' came the reply.

'Can I have the food I brought, mum?' Billy quickly asked, suddenly remembering his appetite.

'Of course you can. I didn't think it would take you long to remember your stomach.' Nancy grinned. 'But remember to share it out.'

'I managed to throw a few bits in my bag too,' Doris said, indicating to her eldest daughter, Katherine, to do the same.

'We must have all been thinking the same,' Angie added, taking a biscuit tin out of her haversack.

Within a couple of minutes, the group of kids were once again collected in a corner of the shelter tucking into their late-night feast, their fear replaced by an excited chatter at the welcome sight of biscuits and a few slices of cake.

The women all turned to the huddle of now smiling

children, their web of hands in the tubs and tins, the contents disappearing at a rate of knots.

'At least they're happy,' Nancy commented, which was more than she could say for Bert, who despite the assurance Jerry had passed by was still doubled over, as if he was bracing himself for the inevitable.

Chapter 24

Monday, 19 August 1940

'Betty. Hattie,' Patty said, stifling a yawn as she caught up with her friends as they trundled wearily through gate three. 'Are you both okay? What an 'orrible chuffin' night that was. It didn't 'alf put the heebie-jeebies up me and I don't think I've had more than three hours' sleep.'

'I'm not sure any of us have, duck,' Frank sighed, as he came alongside the group of exhausted-looking women, not to mention Archie, who looked washed out with fatigue.

'It was certainly a long one,' Betty conceded, her cheeks pale despite the promise of another hot day. 'But I'm just glad you are all here and no one got hurt.' Then turning to Archie, she added, 'You didn't hear of any bad news, did you?'

'No, thankfully not,' he replied, shaking his head. 'And hopefully it will stay that way.'

'I've just bumped into a couple of lads who said a bomb was dropped near Blackbrook Road in Fulwood, leaving a gaping hole in the ground,' Frank interjected. 'And apparently another was dropped near Redmires Road and there's a great thirty-foot crater in the grass.'

'Goodness,' Betty gasped. 'Was anyone hurt?'

'Not that I know of, duck, but apparently it's destroyed a fair few houses nearby.'

'Those poor people,' Betty replied. 'You can't imagine your home being obliterated like that, can you?'

'Let's hope they have got family nearby they can stay with,' Hattie said.

'Did you and yer mum get to a shelter?' Patty asked.

'My dad refused to leave the house and my mum didn't want to leave without him, so we left him in the kitchen and went down to the cellar until the all clear.'

Patty was mystified. She couldn't understand why Hattie's dad would be so stupid and put his family's life at risk, but seeing how exhausted her friend looked, she had the good sense not to push it now, making a mental note to maybe arrange a little catch-up at the weekend, over a cup of tea and a slice of cake.

'How about you, Nancy?' Betty enquired, as the group made their way to the line to clock in. 'Did you all go to the communal shelter?'

'We did.' Nancy nodded. 'Patty and her family were there, as well as Doris and all the kids.'

'Was Bert okay?'

'Not really, I'm afraid. I think I underestimated what a bad way he is in. Whatever he saw in France really has taken its toll and last night brought it all back up.'

'Oh, I'm sorry. That was probably a daft question. How is he this morning?'

'I don't know,' Nancy sighed. 'He was still fast gone when me and the kids left.'

Conscious this wasn't the time to have a full-blown conversation, Betty squeezed her friend's arm. 'Do you think you might get ten minutes at dinnertime for a quick cuppa?'

'I'll check with Dolly.'

'Okay, but try to stay strong,' Betty said supportively. 'You know we're all here for you. In fact, while Frank, Ivy and I were in the shelter last night, Ivy came up with an idea. I'll tell you all as we have something to eat.'

'Yer know what our Ivy is like,' Frank interjected, rolling his eyes in mock jest. 'She's always thinking of something.'

Yet again, the 'our' wasn't lost on Betty, her heart gladdening at one of the positives that was coming out of the damnable war. Frank now stayed at the house several nights a week, something both of them seemed more than content with.

'I hope it doesn't involve knitting for England again.' Patty grimaced. 'I still can't get m' knit and pearl right.'

'You are a case.' Betty chuckled. 'It isn't that, although I am going to start asking for more woollies soon. It will be getting chilly again before we know it.'

'Don't say that!' Patty protested at asking everyone to get their knitting needles clicking a bit faster soon. 'Let's at least enjoy the rest of the summer first.'

'Don't worry! I think Ivy's suggestion will be right up your street and I promise it doesn't involve any knitting.'

'Thank the Lord for that!' Patty replied, taking her timecard from the left-hand metal rack.

'I don't know how you keep up, boss.' Archie chuckled. 'Between Ivy and Betty, there's always something being plotted.'

'Tell me about it!'

'You would be bored without us.' Betty grinned. 'Anyway,' she added, placing her card under the time machine. 'I'll tell you more at dinnertime.'

'Hopefully, I'll join you for a quick cuppa,' Nancy said, preparing to go in the opposite direction of her friends, who were all heading to their usual workshop.

'I hope so,' Betty said, hoping her friend was as well as could be, after what sounded like a distressing night with Bert. As she made her way through the maze of corridors to the factory floor, she once again felt grateful William was still in Canada. The thought of him being one of the pilots defending the skies of Sheffield sent a cold shiver down her spine. Although there had been no reports of casualties from the previous evening, Betty wasn't naive enough to think it would always be that way. The thought had gone through her mind dozens of times over recent weeks. Now as Betty prepared for another morning thirty feet high in the heavens of the factory, she was once again torn between desperately wanting to see her beloved William, who had been in Canada for five months, and willing him to stay thousands of miles away, in relative safety.

'Chuffin' 'eck. I'm shattered,' Patty exclaimed, as she plopped herself down in one of the canteen chairs. 'I swear I'll be asleep by seven o'clock tonight. I think I'll go to bed when our Tom Tom does.'

'I know it's little consolation,' Frank said, sitting down opposite Patty, 'but I'm very grateful that you all turned in today after such a turbulent night.'

'It's all right,' Patty yawned. 'There's no way m' dad would have let me stay off work.'

'Aye, yer old man is certainly a trooper.'

'We couldn't have let you down,' Betty interjected. 'It's hardly your fault the Luftwaffe decided last night was the night they were going to drop bombs on the city. Besides which, the only way we will defeat the Germans is if we keep making munitions to fight them with.'

'Well, there is that, duck,' Frank agreed, unravelling his egg and lettuce sandwich that Ivy had lovingly made that morning; as always it was wrapped in brown greaseproof paper and tied with string. 'Nonetheless, your efforts and commitment haven't gone unnoticed. And you'll be pleased to hear, I've had a word with the gaffers and they agree, no one has to do any overtime tonight.'

'Thank the Lord for that,' Patty trilled, tucking into her own snap, which consisted of dripping on bread and a small tart filled with a paper-thin scraping of jam. 'There is a God after all.'

'Patty!' Archie said, giving his sweetheart a gentle nudge. 'You aren't that hard done by.'

'I know.' She shrugged. 'I'm just tired. Just ignore me.'

'I think we're all feeling it today,' Frank empathized.

'Feeling what?' Nancy enquired, as she approached her group of friends.

Betty smiled. 'Have you got time for a quick cuppa?'

'Dolly insisted, so I guess I have.'

'Good,' Betty replied, already on her feet and heading to the tea urn. 'You sit down, and I'll fetch you one.'

'It's me who should be getting you all a top-up,' Nancy protested.

'Nonsense,' Betty said, waving off the suggestion. 'You're as busy as the rest of us.'

'She's not wrong there, duck,' Frank said, finishing a mouthful of his sandwich.

'I still feel guilty that I'm not back operating a crane,' Nancy commented, as she sat down in the empty chair next to where Betty was sitting.

'Don't be fretting about that! Archie is in his element up in Mildred, aren't yer, lad?'

'I'd be lying if I said no.'

'Yer see, duck,' Frank reiterated. 'Nothing for you to be worrying about. Besides which, from what Dolly tells me, you are doing a grand job here.'

'That's kind of her, but I promise as soon as things have got a bit easier at home, I'll be back.'

'And we'll be glad to have you, but only when you're ready. You need to concentrate on those kiddies and Bert.'

'How was Bert when he got home?' Patty asked.

Nancy lifted her mug of hot tea to her lips and took a sip. 'It's hard to say. It was so late, and we were all shattered. By the time I got our Billy and Linda to bed, Bert was already laid out on the sofa in the front room. I tried to talk to him, but he wouldn't say much, only that the noise of the aircraft brought back terrible memories. But please thank your dad again for me. I really don't know what I'd have done without him.'

'I will.' Patty nodded, wiping the crumbs and the traces of dripping from her lips. 'But I know he was just happy to help.'

'That sounds hard,' Betty interjected. 'For both of you.'

'I must admit, I really hadn't thought about how affected Bert would be. I keep thinking back to his letters that he sent me from hospital, and he told me then he was in a dark place, but I was so pleased that he was alive and back in England I didn't really consider what he meant.'

'Don't be hard on yourself,' Betty sympathized. 'You couldn't have known. No one could.'

Hattie, who had been listening quietly, discreetly bit down on her bottom lip. *Is this what happened to my dad? Is this why he turned into such a monster?*

'It sounds horrible, but Bert feels like a stranger at the moment. I think that's what I find the hardest,' Nancy sighed, hoping her comments didn't sound disloyal.

Betty reached out and placed her hand on Nancy's. 'I don't have any answers, but please say if we can do anything.'

'Thank you. I will, but honestly, you all do so much already. Just being able to talk about it is a great help.'

'Good,' Betty said, opening her pack up. 'That's what we are here for.'

As everyone tucked into their dinner, Hattie turned to Nancy. 'Do you mind if I suggest something?'

'Of course, luv.' Nancy nodded. 'I'm happy to hear any pearls of wisdom that might help.'

'I don't want to interfere or tell you what to do, so please don't think I am.'

'I would never think that.'

'Well, it's just from what my mum said about my dad after the Great War, I think she always regrets not pushing him to open up more.'

'What do you mean?'

Nancy wasn't the only one listening, Patty's ears had perked up to. Hattie rarely went into detail about her dad, always preferring to change the subject.

'It's just that, well, my mum always says if she'd got my dad to talk more when he'd got home, he might have . . .' Hattie stopped herself for a second, not wanting to scare Nancy. 'It's just, he clammed up a lot and my mum doesn't think that helped him in the long run.'

Nancy looked at Hattie inquisitively. In the last few weeks she'd picked up on hints of what Hattie and her mum put up with and suspected her dad's drinking was the main issue. Bert had never been one to turn to the bottle to cope with his problems, but maybe, once upon a time, neither had Hattie's dad. Had the last war left him so damaged that he'd turned to the demon drink? Nancy didn't want to push Hattie any further, but, if the truth be known, neither did she have to. Nancy already knew the answer and it terrified her. She couldn't, wouldn't, let Bert become so consumed by what he'd seen in France that it not only ruined the rest of his life but caused her, Billy and Linda to resent him. Bert was a good man. He deserved to be happy again and she would do everything in her power to ensure her husband found a way to get out of this dark place.

'Nancy,' Frank interjected, pulling her back to the moment.

'Sorry. Yes?'

'Do you think it would help if Bert got out a bit?'

'I do, but I've tried. Just getting him in the backyard last weekend was a struggle and if it wasn't for Doris, I doubt I'd have got him to the shelter last night.'

'Do you reckon he might like to go for a pint? Maybe me and Bill could nip to The Welly with him?'

'I'd love to say yes. I think it would do him the world of good, but I'm just not sure he will go for it. Our Billy really wanted him to go to High Hazels Park last Sunday, but there was no persuading him.'

'Do you reckon he would come for dinner this Sunday? Maybe I could try to convince him to come for a pint then?'

'It would do you good to have a break too,' Betty added.

Nancy took another mouthful of her tea as she

contemplated the offer. 'I would really like to. I'm just not convinced Bert will agree. I think he's worried about what people think of him. He hasn't said it, but I get the impression he feels as though he's failed because his leg has been so badly injured.'

'But that's just daft!' Patty exclaimed.

'I know it comes across like that,' Nancy reasoned. 'But I'm starting to realize whatever happened in France has really messed up how he's thinking.'

'Like I've said before,' Frank jumped in. 'His pride will be dented and none of us are given a manual on how to cope with war and everything that comes with it.'

'I wish there was a manual telling me what to do,' Nancy sighed. 'It's as though he's been sent home from hospital and just left to sort himself out. I know everyone is strung out dealing with this godforsaken war, but Bert can't be the only one left in this position.'

'He won't be, duck,' Frank agreed. 'Look what happened after the last war.' But as soon as the words left the normally tactful foreman's lips, he regretted them, as Hattie took a deep intake of breath.

'I'm sorry,' Frank said immediately. Like the rest of the gang, he didn't know what had happened to Hattie's dad, but he was astute enough to realize he'd come back from serving in the trenches a broken and changed man.

'It's all right,' Hattie said, quickly shaking her head. 'Everything you are saying is true. My mum blames the last war too.' Then turning to Nancy, she added, 'That's why I think you need to get your Bert out and about. If he can see other people and not be trapped in his own four walls, it might help. My mum said my dad barely left the house for months when he came home. I don't want to add to your worries but staying locked inside obviously didn't do my dad any good at all.'

Nancy bit back the overwhelming feeling of panic that was threatening to course through her. Bert deserved a happier future, they all did. She knew getting Bert out to socialize would be a mammoth task, but the alternative was far worse.

'Don't ask me how just yet, but I'll find a way to persuade Bert to come on Sunday,' she said with resolve, determination overtaking the feeling of dread she had become so familiar with.

'Only if you're sure, duck?' Frank answered.

'I am! Besides which, the kids love coming over and finding the eggs your hens have laid. As Betty said, it will do us all the power of good.'

'I'll let Ivy know.' Frank nodded. 'But if you can't make it after all, there will be another time.'

'Have you forgotten, Frank?' Betty said, quickly swallowing the last of her sandwich.

'Chuff me. All this talk about Bert, I did, duck, yes. Why don't you tell everyone?'

'Tell everyone what?' Patty asked, slightly befuddled. 'What have you forgotten to tell us?'

A huge grin appeared across Betty's normally serene face.

'What is it?' Daisy asked.

'Sorry.' Betty laughed. 'I didn't mean to keep you in suspense.'

'Get on with it then,' Patty said.

'Pats!' Archie scolded. 'Give Betty a chance. She can't get a word in edgeways.'

'Sorry. You know what I'm like. I hate not knowing something.'

'Never!' Archie grinned.

'Anyway,' Betty said, breaking up the playful banter, 'Ivy has decided she would like to host a little end-of-summer get-together in the garden.'

'Oooh. Really?' Patty trilled.

'Yes. She's decided that as we have that much salad, veg and an endless supply of eggs, she would like to share it with everyone and do a nice buffet before the good weather disappears.'

'How lovely,' Nancy commented. 'She really is a generous soul.'

'She is that, duck,' Frank agreed, his eyes gleaming with pride.

'So,' Betty continued, 'she would like me to invite you all and all your families.'

'Does Ivy have a date in mind?' Nancy enquired.

'She does. How does September the first work for you all?'

'Well, as you can imagine, my social calendar is over-flowing with engagements,' Patty joked, with an elevated hint of irony in her voice, as she mockingly tapped her index finger to her cheek. 'I may have to double-check.'

'Pats!' Archie scolded for the second time.

'I'm only teasing! Of course we'll be there. I don't have to be asked twice when food is involved.'

'I give up,' Archie sighed, shaking his head incredulously.

'That really is very kind,' Daisy answered. 'Are you sure it won't be too much for Ivy?'

'Nothing is ever too much for Ivy!' Frank announced, sealing the date.

As the gang all made their way back to work, Hattie held back as Nancy collected the empty mugs from the table.

'If you ever fancy a chat,' Hattie quietly said, 'please do say. My mum and I have been through it with my dad, so if there is anything I can do to try to help you with Bert, I'd be happy too.'

Nancy looked at Hattie. 'Thank you. I never liked to ask about your dad, but I am sorry for whatever you've had to cope with. And the same goes. If you just want someone to talk to, I'd be more than happy to listen.'

The two women exchanged an appreciative smile. Neither of them had to say another word, instinctively understanding what the other was coping with.

'War really does have a lot to answer for,' Nancy finally confirmed. 'Let's make sure we have that cuppa.'

Chapter 25

Wednesday, 21 August 1940

Kissing Linda on the forehead, Nancy whispered, 'Night-night, poppet.'

'Mummy?' the sleepy-eyed little girl asked.

'Yes?'

'Do you think Daddy will ever be happy again?'

The innocent question caused Nancy's heart to race. It wasn't that she was surprised by it, more saddened. Her maternal instinct had always been to protect Billy and Linda, but even Nancy knew she couldn't hide from her children what was right in front of their noses.

Clasping Linda's hand, she took a deep breath. 'I'm sure he will be. Daddy has been through a bit of a difficult time and that's why he's sad, but I'm trying my best to help him get better.'

'I miss our old daddy.'

'Me too, poppet,' Nancy said, forcing herself not to falter. 'But sometimes we all go through tricky times, and it takes a little while to feel back to normal.'

'Is that what's happened to Daddy?'

'Yes, but he's home now, so that's a good start.'

Linda nestled her head back into her pillow. 'Okay,' she whispered. 'I'll try to think of some more ways to make him happy.'

'You are a very kind little girl,' Nancy praised. 'Now you close your eyes and have a nice sleep. And I promise, I will think up something too.'

'Night-night, Mummy. I love you and tell Daddy, I love him lots too.'

'I will,' Nancy promised.

After gently closing Linda's bedroom door, Nancy made her way down the stairs, knowing her next conversation wasn't going to be an easy one. Despite how tired she felt, she stifled a yawn, and entered the front room, where Bert was already lying on the sofa, his injured right leg elevated on the arm rest.

'Shall we have a cuppa?' Nancy stated, more than asked.

'I thought I might settle down for the night. I'm pretty wiped out.'

'I am too but we need to talk,' Nancy insisted, unable to put off the frank conversation she needed to have with Bert any longer.

Besides Linda's pleas for her daddy to get better, the previous night had, yet again, revealed how hard Bert was finding life. The evening had been interrupted by the piercing wail of the air-raid sirens, and, like two nights earlier, it had taken as much persuasion to get Bert to the communal shelter. Nancy had naively hoped after Saturday night, he might have coped a little better when the call to get to safety came, but she'd soon realized whatever was haunting her husband wasn't something that was just going to disappear. He'd spent another fraught few hours with his head in his hands, and by the time he got home he was as white as a sheet and unable to say a single word.

Nancy could have just about dealt with Bert's reaction if it wasn't for the fact that both Billy and Linda had got upset by it and, when she'd finally tucked them into bed, had tearfully asked if their daddy would ever be like how he used to be. Like a few minutes earlier, it had taken all Nancy's fortitude not to break down in tears. Instead, she had done what she'd vowed she would, galvanized herself and remained stoic, promising her children she was doing all she could to help their daddy.

So, now, as she boiled a kettle on the range and scooped a heaped dessertspoon of tea leaves into the pot, Nancy knew she couldn't let Bert's pleas for an early night put an end to their chat before it had even started. Even if he didn't open up to her, Nancy had to make him understand the negative impact his melancholy mood was having on Billy and Linda.

'I am really tired, luv,' Bert protested a few minutes later as Nancy carried the tray of tea into the front room, and gently placed it down on the coffee table. 'Last night really took it out of me.'

Nancy refused to succumb. 'It did all of us. Billy and Linda's eyes were going before their heads hit the pillow.'

The mention of his children's names caught Bert's attention. 'Are they okay?'

'Not really,' Nancy replied, as she carefully poured them both a drink and passed Bert his mug.

'I'm sorry,' he whispered, looking down at his hands, which were now trembling despite the heat emanating from the steaming mug of tea. 'I am trying, Nancy. I promise.'

This wasn't the time to berate her husband, but Nancy knew she also needed to stand firm.

'It's hard for me to see that right now,' she confessed.

Bert's brow furrowed even more. He opened his mouth to say something, then slowly shut it again, a weary sigh taking the place of any words he might have spoken.

'That's part of the problem,' Nancy pointed out.

'What do you mean?'

'You won't talk to me. I have no idea what's going on inside your head.'

Bert looked at Nancy, noted the hurt in her heavy eyes, the desperation in her voice. He knew he was causing her untold pain, and he hated himself even more for it.

'We used to talk about everything,' Nancy continued. 'We didn't have a single secret between us, but now I feel like you are hiding everything from me.'

'I don't mean to.'

'Then why can't you just try to talk to me? I feel like we are strangers right now.'

'I can't,' he insisted, the inflection in his tone unfamiliarly brusque.

'Why not? I'm your wife.'

'You wouldn't, *couldn't* understand.'

Nancy grimaced. The 'couldn't' felt deliberately pointed. 'Try me. I can't understand if you don't at least give me that chance.'

But Bert didn't respond. In the place of an answer, a deafening silence filled the room, reverberating off every wall, and the already tense atmosphere increased, shrouding everything in a heavy cloud, and if Nancy didn't know better, she would have sworn it was her husband's deliberate intention to dispel the last remaining light from their already less than enlightening conversation.

Nancy bit down on her lip. Frank's words about giving Bert time to come to terms with what he'd endured came rushing back, echoing through her mind like a steamroller, urging her not to push Bert, but her own frustration was fighting against the well-intended advice. She really didn't know how much more of this she could take. Nancy was utterly exhausted, the new wave of air raids and presence of German aircraft over the skies of Sheffield taking their toll. But the real threat to Nancy's normally patient temperament was the fact Billy and Linda, after everything they had already been through, were desperately confused and upset by the father who had returned. And along with the fact there was no indication of when Bert might start to show any signs of recovery, she was running out of ways to reassure them.

'We can't go on like this,' Nancy finally said, breaking the silence.

Bert looked up. He knew his wife was right, but still didn't say a single word.

Nancy momentarily closed her eyes, running her fingers through her mass of blonde curls in exasperation. 'You can't keep ignoring me.'

'I'm not.'

'You are. You are avoiding my questions. Clamming up. Refusing to talk. It's not healthy.'

Bert shook his head, but his vexing inability to speak returned.

'You see. You're doing it again. Instead of trying to explain what's going on inside your head, you say nothing. Do you know how hard that is for me?'

'For you!' Bert blurted out, incredulously. 'For you.'

For a split second, Nancy was dumbstruck. This was another side of her husband she had never seen before. Bert had never once snapped at her or tried, so dismissively, to diminish her feelings, as though they were irrelevant and of no consequence.

She wouldn't be beaten, though. Not now. She had to save her family and she'd already overcome a lot. She refused to let this blasted war ruin the one thing that meant more to her than anything else in the world.

But before Nancy could answer, Bert suddenly found his voice.

'You have no idea what I've been through. What I've seen. The things I've had to do. All that, while you have been holed up here, surrounded by friends, food and in safety. You could go to bed every night in our bed, see our children, and walk down the street without fear of being shot or killed. And you moan that this is hard for you.'

The venom in Bert's voice temporarily paralyzed Nancy. Despite her furious determination to swallow them back, sharp, salty tears stung the back of her, now reddening, eyes. Who had her husband become?

'You think this has been easy?' she managed to say.

'Yes. Yes, I do. Compared to what I've had to cope with, I think it's been a walk in the park, and I'm fed up of you trying to make me better.'

Beaten, Nancy slowly shook her head in dismay. She looked at the small carriage clock on the mantelpiece. It was gone nine o'clock. She had to be up at six and was already exhausted after several nights of little to no sleep, weeks of tiptoeing around Bert and nearly a year of non-stop worrying.

He was clearly adamant he wasn't going to talk, and she couldn't risk Bert's heated and resentful words waking up Billy and Linda. It had already taken all her powers of persuasion and endless reassuring cuddles to get them to sleep.

Standing up, Nancy collected the half-empty mugs of cold tea, placed them back on the tray and, without saying another word, slipped out of the room, not once turning back to look at Bert.

Chapter 26

'I do appreciate you inviting us around again,' Nancy said, as she sat down at Ivy's kitchen table. The kids and Bert had already been ushered into the garden by Frank, who was keen to show off his ever-increasing crop of vegetables.

'It's nothing. I love having people over, besides which, Frank and Betty said you could do with a break. Am I right in thinking things have been a bit tougher than you'd hoped since Bert got home?'

'You could say that. I'd certainly be lying if I said life was easy right now.'

'I'm sorry to hear that,' Ivy sympathized, handing Nancy a glass of barley water.

'Thank you,' Nancy said taking a sip. 'I know I shouldn't complain. Folk have it much worse than me. At least Bert is at home, although, as much as I hate to admit it, there are times when I think it was easier when he was still being cared for in hospital. Don't get me wrong, I know I am one of the lucky ones. There's loads of women chatting in the canteen about their blokes still being hundreds of

317

miles away from home and some of them haven't had a letter in months. And those poor people whose houses were damaged after Tuesday night's air raid. A couple of the lasses had their windows blown out when that bomb dropped at the back of Jessop Road. You can't imagine dealing with that, can you?'

'No, you can't. I think this week has knocked us all for six. I read in the *Sheffield Telegraph and Independent* that a poor old man was sat in his armchair when the bomb went off and it knocked him clean across his front room. Can you imagine? The poor thing. By the time he realized what was happening, plaster from the ceiling was falling on his head. It must have been a right old shock for him. And Frank was telling me, one of the men at work only just got his little ones in the shelter before the wind from the bomb wiped the door clean off his shelter.'

'My goodness. That's awful. They must have been terrified. What a horrible shock.'

'Awful, isn't it?' Ivy sighed.

'Those poor little 'uns.' Nancy nodded. 'It's your worst nightmare as a parent, your kids being scared. I'd have been out of my mind. I dunno, maybe I was just being naive, but I really didn't think I'd see the day when Jerry would be bombing Sheffield.'

Ivy pulled out a chair and sat down opposite Nancy. 'I don't think any of us could have imagined it really happening. I mean, how can you? I thought everyone had learnt from the last war, but I guess greed and power will always be an incentive.'

'I think you're right. Anyway, sorry, I haven't even asked. Were you okay on Wednesday, during the air raid?' Nancy asked, quietly reprimanding herself for not enquiring sooner.

'Don't you be worrying about me, dear. I was absolutely fine. Frank and Betty were here, so we all just took ourselves off to the garden and into the shelter. We have quite the routine going now. I take a flask of tea. Frank brings a pack of playing cards and a torch and we manage a few games of seven card rummy to pass the time. I never thought I'd hear myself say it, but it's actually quite cosy in there.'

'That's good. Maybe that's what I need to do.'

'What do you mean?'

'I wonder if I could make under the stairs or the cellar a bit more appealing. That way, Bert wouldn't have to drag himself to the communal shelter and maybe he wouldn't be quite as withdrawn. The kids were so upset after seeing him rocking with his head in his knees. It's not the Bert they are used to. They both keep asking me if he will ever be happy again.'

'Oh gosh, that is hard. Was it really that bad?'

'If I'm honest, I'm not even telling you the half of it. There was no getting through to him. He wouldn't look at me and completely ignored Billy and Linda. I never thought I'd see the day when he didn't put the kids first. I am trying to stay upbeat. I keep telling them Bert is just poorly, but

I can tell they don't really understand what's going on. They have waited all this time to see their daddy again and they can't understand why he's so different. It's a lot for their little minds to take in.'

'I know it's not much consolation right now but try to take some comfort in the fact children are usually far more resilient than we are.'

'I keep trying to tell myself that. I look at Doris's kids. They have been through much worse and have all coped so well after they lost their dad, but you know what I'm like. I just can't stop worrying.'

'It's only natural, dear. You wouldn't be human or the good mum you are if you didn't fret about it, but you are doing a grand job and I'm sure those kiddies are benefitting from how strong you are.'

'I hope so. They are too young to have to deal with all of this. At their age, they shouldn't have a care in the word, but this war is certainly putting short shrift to that.'

'It will pass. I promise you. Everything always does. That's the great thing about time. Everything keeps moving forward. Nothing ever stands still. There were times when I thought the days would never end after the last war. I'd never felt so desolate in my life, but day by day, things did get easier. Take it from me, they will, and I bet my last shilling your two will come out of this war okay.'

'I hope so. I really do.'

Seeing Nancy's now drained glass, Ivy courteously topped it up from the jug she'd placed in the centre of the table. 'I know he's probably putting on a brave face, but Bert seems okay today. Has he picked up since Wednesday?'

Nancy took a deep breath and let out a weary sigh as she pursed her lips into an O shape. 'I wish I could say yes, but I'm afraid not. Don't get me wrong, he's been civil when he's spoken to us, but he's not very forthcoming and obviously won't talk about what's really going on inside that head of his. I feel sure if he just spoke to me, I could help him, but God knows, I've tried, and I can't get a bean out of him.'

'Do you think his pride is getting in the way or he just doesn't know how to articulate how he's feeling?'

'I really hope that's what it is,' Nancy answered. 'Because anything else doesn't bear thinking about.'

They were the same questions Nancy had asked herself over and over again. When sleep wouldn't come and her mind went into overdrive, she'd even started to wonder whether Bert still loved her. In the dead of night, she'd tossed and turned continually. Her mind played tricks on her and Nancy wondered if Bert had been changed so much by the war that he no longer saw her as the person he could share his life with. When she did drop off, the cruel thoughts had slyly crept into Nancy's dreams, causing her to wake up shaking, gripping the sheets, fear coursing through her.

'I'm sure it will be,' Ivy said, bringing Nancy back to the moment, as she reassuringly touched her friend's slender arm. 'You know it's true what they say, we often take things out on those closest to us.'

'I suppose you're right.' Hadn't Nancy taken her

frustrations out on Bert when she'd discovered he'd been called up for war, even though, she knew in her heart of hearts, he was the only one who could make her feel better?

'Maybe chatting to someone else will help too,' Ivy encouraged. 'He's been out in the garden with Frank for quite a while. Hopefully, that can only be a good thing.'

But before Nancy could respond, the door from the garden swung open. 'Did I hear my name being mentioned?' Frank enquired, cheerful as ever.

'Elephant ears.' Ivy chuckled. 'But as a matter of fact, you did. I was just saying you have been out in the garden for a while. Have you been showing off our harvest of veggies?'

'How did you guess? We really have got enough to feed an entire army despite how many bags full Betty keeps taking into the factory to share out.'

'What's that?' Right on cue, Betty, who was dressed in a pale blue-and-white gingham summer dress, made her way from the hall into the kitchen.

'Hiya, luv,' Nancy said. 'You look nice. Have you been somewhere?'

'Daisy and I just met up for a walk with it being such a nice day.'

'It really is. We certainly can't complain, and Frank here was just saying the veggie patch has been a huge success.'

'It has.' Betty beamed. 'In fact, I've just finished writing a letter to William. I've told him that he's in for quite a surprise when he sees how horticultural I've become, when he gets back to England.'

'Any news about that?' Nancy enquired.

'I'm not sure. In his last letter, he explained he's moved to a different flying school to pilot a different plane and do some training exercises at night. It sounds terrifying but, as always, he's staying upbeat. He says he's been swotting a lot as he's got some important exams coming up. He didn't really say if that meant he would be coming home afterwards. I guess he didn't want to tempt fate.'

'You must miss him,' Nancy empathized.

'I do, but after this week, I'm glad he's still in Canada.'

'I can understand that.'

'Sorry, ladies,' Frank interrupted. 'I hate to break up your chatter, but I just wanted to let you know I'm going to take Bert to the pub for quick pint before dinner if that's all right?'

'What! Really?' Nancy asked, visibly taken aback. It had taken all her powers of persuasion to convince Bert just to come out for dinner. When she'd first mentioned it, Bert had refused to even consider the possibility. It was only when Billy and Linda pleaded with him, desperate to show Bert the hens, that he'd started to come round to the idea. Nancy was sure if it wasn't for the kids, he'd never have agreed.

'I thought it might do Bert good.'

'No, sorry. I was just a bit shocked. I agree. It will do Bert the power of good. Thank you.'

'It's no bother, duck. We'll only be an hour or so.' Then turning to Ivy, added, 'Is that okay? We'll be back for dinner.'

'Of course. Go and enjoy yourselves.'

As Frank turned to leave, Nancy put her hands on either side of the chair to stand up. 'I better go and check on Billy and Linda, if Bert and Frank are going to the pub.'

'No, you don't,' Betty said, placing her hand firmly on Nancy's shoulder. 'You stay where you are. I'll go and entertain Billy and Linda. I don't think we've collected the eggs yet, have we?'

'No,' Ivy said, shaking her head. 'It was on my list of jobs.'

'Perfect. We shall do it. I know how much Billy and Linda love finding them. We can pick some veggies too. That will keep us busy for a while.'

'Are you sure?' Nancy asked. 'I feel guilty you taking care of them.'

'Don't! You have nothing to feel guilty for. Enjoy the rest, while you can. You never get a break.'

'Thank you. I do appreciate it.'

But Betty was already making her way into the garden, waving off Nancy's thanks as she went.

'So,' Ivy asked, confident Nancy's children and Bert were out of earshot. 'Maybe chatting to Frank will help Bert.'

'I hope so,' Nancy said sadly. 'As I said, I tried to chat to him after that last air raid, but it couldn't have gone any worse.'

A look of concern appeared on Ivy's kind face. 'Maybe Frank can help. It can be hard telling the people you care for most details that might upset them.'

'Fingers crossed, you're right. I'm not sure what else I can do. It's as though he's a different man. I hardly recognize him at times. Before this horrible war, Bert never snapped at me, and we'd barely had a cross word, but he was so sharp and dismissive on Wednesday night. I thought talking it through might help, but all it did was create an even bigger divide between us. He really didn't want to talk to me.'

'It's well-worn advice but time can be the greatest of healers,' Ivy gently suggested.

Exhausted, Nancy took a mouthful of her drink. 'I don't know, Ivy. I really want to believe that, but if the truth be known, I feel like I'm losing him, and I can't bear it.'

Chapter 27

'What are yer having?' Frank asked, as he and Bert, who was leaning heavily on his walking stick, made their way to The Bridge.

'A pint of bitter, if you don't mind.'

'Not at all.' Frank nodded, as Bert hitched himself onto a bar stool, using his arms to pull himself up.

A few minutes later both men were happily supping their drinks. The change of scenery had lifted Bert's mood. 'I'd like to thank you,' he said, looking at Frank.

'What on earth for?'

'For keeping an eye on Nancy at work. She told me in her letters and in the snippets of conversations we've had since I got home how good you have been to her. I just wanted you to know I appreciate it. I know she's found the last year hard, but you have all been there for her, when I couldn't be.'

'Anyone would do the same, pal.'

'I'm not sure they would,' Bert insisted. 'From what I can gather, working at Vickers and all the new friends Nancy has made have kept her going while I've been away. She's told me how kind and supportive you have all been.'

'She's a good 'un, but I'm quite sure you don't need me to tell you that. Nancy, and all the other women have been a godsend at the factory. We couldn't function without them.'

'I won't lie, it did come as a bit of a shock when I read in her letter that she'd started at Vickers. I could never have imagined Nancy in one of the steelworks, let alone up a great crane. She's always been such a gentle and quiet soul. It was the last place I thought she'd end up.'

'I think it was a bit of a culture shock for all of them, but your Nancy has come a long way over the last year.'

'What do you mean?'

'Well, as you know, she was ever so shy and introverted when she joined Vickers, but this war has made her come out of herself. I'm gathering she's been a good friend to your neighbour, Doris, and it was Nancy who convinced Daisy's mum to get medical help when Josie thought she was dying.'

'She's always had a huge heart,' Bert admitted affectionately.

'She certainly has,' Frank agreed. 'And your Nancy came out of her shell a bit more after that. Her confidence started to shine through.'

'At least summat good is coming out of this blasted war,' Bert conceded, a surge of pride soaring through him, before adding, 'Thank you again, for looking after her.' His voice was on the verge of breaking.

'As I've said, you have nothing to thank me for. I'm

just very grateful for every woman who has sacrificed her normal life to come and work at Vickers.'

Bert looked down at his pint glass. For the first time since he'd got home, he had been forced to think about what Nancy had been through. He hadn't meant to be so self-absorbed; the flashbacks that had constantly tormented him had taken care of that. But, at the same time Bert knew he could have tried a bit harder when it came to his family and he felt ashamed he'd barely even asked Nancy about her time at Vickers. Nancy was a good woman. He didn't need a bloke he'd never met before to tell him that, so why on earth was he being so chuffin' difficult?

'Listen, pal,' Frank said kindly, seeing Bert getting maudlin. 'It's not my place to pry or interfere, but it's obvious you've had a pretty rough time. I can't even begin to imagine what sort of hell you have been through, but if you just need to get something off yer chest or need a sounding board, I'm always happy to come and have a pint. We blokes aren't very good at dealing with stuff, not like women who can chat until the cows come home. Anyway, what I'm trying to say is, you don't have to cope with everything by yerself.'

Momentarily stunned, Bert looked at Frank. His mind a whirl of overwhelming and confusing thoughts, he was unable to find the words to articulate what he was thinking.

'Listen, why don't I get us another pint?' Frank suggested. 'I reckon we've got time for another quick one before Ivy serves up dinner.'

Bert nodded in appreciation. The last thing he wanted to do was face Nancy while he felt this rotten. He'd already failed her and the kids and didn't have the first idea about how to make it better. He was still struggling to get through a single hour without flashbacks reminding him of the atrocities he'd been forced to witness and endure in France.

A couple of minutes later, Frank was sliding another pint across the bar towards Bert. 'We all need a helping hand occasionally,' he offered. 'Take it from me, there's no manual out there on how to cope when life hits you with something that knocks you sideways.'

'Yer not wrong there.' Bert nodded, taking a slurp of his pint.

'I know it's different, so please don't think I'm trying to compare, but when I lost my wife, Mary, I was a reyt old mess. I couldn't speak to anyone and if I'm honest, didn't think anyone could ever understand what I was going through.'

'I'm sorry to hear that,' Bert replied sincerely. 'That must have been a rough time for you. I can't ever imagine Nancy not being around.'

'I won't lie. It was pretty tough and for quite a while I didn't think life would ever get any easier. I was in a dark place for a good couple of years.'

'I'm not surprised. Were you and Mary married for a long time?'

'Ten years. After she died, I didn't think I could be happy ever again, but here I am. I guess what I'm trying to say is, time is a great healer. I know it's a cliché, but it was true for me.'

'I hope you're right,' Bert sighed. 'If I'm honest, I'm struggling to see past the end of each day right now.'

'I remember those moments well. It's a pretty grim ride, I'll give you that, but can I give you a piece of advice?'

'I'm all ears.'

'I know it's easier said than done, but maybe try to concentrate on all the things you have in life that make you happy.'

Bert put his pint on the bar and dropped his face into his half-open hands. 'I'm making a flamin' pig's ear of this, aren't I?'

'I have no idea what's going on in your own house. I just get the impression you might be struggling and wanted to let you know there is always a way through.'

'I wish I could see it right now.'

'What exactly is it that's worrying you?'

Bert took a deep breath. He hadn't spoken to anyone about the overwhelming emotions that kept him awake most nights and in a frustrated state of anger during the day. He'd told Nancy in his letters how difficult he was finding life but since getting home he hadn't been able to vocalize his thoughts.

Frank didn't rush Bert, recalling how hard he found it to open up after he became a widow and life seemed an uphill battle. Instead, for the next few minutes they sat in companiable silence.

'I feel like a failure,' Bert finally confessed, the words heavy with sadness. 'This damn leg has left me in a right mess. I haven't told Nancy yet, as I know it will upset her, but I got shot on my way to Dunkirk and then the wound got infected, so it's left me with a nasty limp. The army will never have me back.'

Frank looked at his newly found acquaintance. Bert's deep-set eyes were watering, his cheeks sallow and his posture was that of a man who had all but given up on life. This blasted war certainly did have a lot to answer for. Frank knew he had a job on his hands to lift Bert's trampled spirits.

'What would make you feel better?' Frank asked, taking a different tack.

The question took Bert by surprise. He had spent so long thinking about what he'd been robbed of, he'd barely considered what would make him feel better, apart from wishing life could go back to how it was a year earlier.

'I just don't know what I can do. I can't get the memories of what happened in France out of my head. I'm virtually crippled and I'm making Nancy and the kids miserable.'

'That is a lot to disentangle,' Frank agreed.

'Yer telling me.'

'I am, but maybe you need something to focus on and the rest might slowly sort itself.'

'What on earth like?' Bert said, a little more sharply than he'd intended.

Frank took the rebuff on the chin, knowing it wasn't meant personally. Bert had every right to feel blighted.

Like thousands of others, he'd gone off to war, strong and determined to do his bit, but had come home broken and disillusioned, but Frank sensed the last thing Bert wanted to do was give up.

'There's things you can do here to help with the war effort.'

'With this leg?' Bert groaned, looking down in disgust at his injured limb that was still giving him gyp. 'Who on earth would want me?'

'How bad is it? You can obviously walk on it with the support of a stick. Is it improving?'

It was true. Bert had noticed, despite wallowing in self-pity, with each day he was getting a little stronger, and the pain was becoming more manageable. The doctors at the hospital had warned Bert the injury had meant he would never walk without a limp, or a walking stick, but he'd been lucky not to have lost his leg after how badly infected it had become.

'It'll never be how it was,' Bert said, despondently. He'd convinced himself in his own mind that his gammy leg meant he would never be able to move forward with his life.

'That's not what I asked.'

Bert threw Frank a sharp look, his defence mechanisms kicking in again. 'I'm fit f' nothin'.'

'I wouldn't be too sure about that,' Frank replied, keeping his tone neutral. 'I know going back to the front line might not be a possibility, but, like I said, there's plenty of jobs going here that you'd be able to do.'

'I couldn't work at Vickers. I'd be a bloody liability.'

'I wasn't thinking about the works, but I'm sure there would be an office job if you were interested.'

'I can't be a secretary,' Bert replied. 'I'd look a reyt one!'

'That's not what I was thinking either,' Frank said gently.

Bert had the humility to at least look slightly abashed by his curt comment. 'I'm sorry. I didn't mean to be snappy. I just feel so chuffin' useless and have no idea how to make a life for myself. I just want to look after my family and provide for them.'

'I get that, and I really didn't mean to sound like I was teaching an old dog new tricks.'

'You're not. I'm just not in a good place and I keep going round in circles and then getting myself in a bigger rut. I really thought being at home would make me feel better, but it just seems to have exasperated how I'm feeling. I haven't even been able to talk to Nancy.'

'Ah well, that's our daft brains for yer. For some inexplicable reason, we don't always find it that easy to talk to the people we are closest to.'

'I hate the fact I'm not the one protecting her and the kids.'

'That'll be our stubborn Yorkshire pride for yer.'

'I've been making her life a bit of a misery.'

'If I know Nancy, I'm sure she will forgive you. She will just want the best for you. Believe me, pal, you are all she's thought about for the last eleven months.'

Resting his elbow on the bar, Bert slumped his head into his hand. 'She deserves better than this.'

Taking a sip of his pint, Frank smiled warmly. 'I reckon you are doing yerself a disservice. Your Nancy just wants you to be happy.'

'I wouldn't mind myself.'

'I can't confess to having all the answers, but could I offer a suggestion?'

'Why not? I'm hardly doing a great job myself.'

'Have you heard of the Home Guard?' Frank asked, hoping Bert wouldn't feel he was interfering.

The call for ex-soldiers had come from the government before war had broken out, to help defend the towns and cities of England. Frank had heard from some of the lads at the factory that hundreds of men from Sheffield had signed up.

'Anyway,' Frank continued, 'I reckon they will be calling out for a bloke with your front-line experience.'

'But my leg? I'm hardly ready for combat.'

'But that's what I'm saying. From what I've heard, they are after blokes who can help with training and there will be office-based roles, and I very much doubt you would be hired as a secretary! It might be worth a visit to the Sheffield office.'

Something close to hope began to percolate in Bert's mind. Maybe he could do something and wasn't bound for the knacker's yard after all.

'Do you know, I think I might just do that. Thanks, Frank.'

Chapter 28

'What's this?' Nancy asked, making her way into the kitchen, where Bert was sat at the table with Linda and Billy. 'I nipped to Doris's but she said you were all here.'

'Daddy came to get us,' Linda replied, beaming.

'That's lovely,' Nancy exclaimed, slightly taken aback as she took in the scene. Billy was making what looked like his fifth paper aeroplane and Linda was drawing, her vast array of colouring pencils lined up neatly in front of her.

'I thought it would give Doris a break,' Bert explained. 'And I haven't seen much of these two lately.'

'I'm sure Doris appreciated it. She never stops and already has a house full of kids. Anyway, would you like a cuppa?' Nancy tentatively asked Bert, as she dropped her gas mask and bag down by the back door.

'I can make it,' Bert said, already putting his hands on the side of his chair to lift himself up.

'It's all right. You stay there with Billy and Linda. I'm already stood up.' Nancy walked across the kitchen to the kettle, happy for the distraction as she took in the far from familiar scene around her. She'd just about given up on how to help Bert but after he'd come back from the pub with Frank on Sunday, he'd seemed less pent up. Nancy had been astonished and delighted in equal measure when Bert had made small talk through dinner, complimenting Ivy on her veggie plot and repeatedly thanking her for having them over.

When Ivy had thrown her a discreet wink, Nancy had secretly prayed her husband was turning a corner, but her hopes had been dashed when they'd got home a few hours later, and Bert's sombre mood had returned, and he took himself off to the front room to lie down. Despairing, Nancy had been too tired to question Bert's sudden U-turn in mood and had nipped to Doris's to check she was happy to look after Billy and Linda during the week while she was working. As always, she'd instantly agreed, professing it was no bother at all, despite the fact she had her own four children to take care of.

Emotionally and physically exhausted, Nancy had, once again, gone to bed that night utterly drained, resigned to the fact Ivy had been right when she'd concluded you take things out on the ones closest to you. She hadn't given up on Bert, far from it, but needed a bit of time to think about how best to try to help him, without begrudging his erratic behaviour.

Now, as Nancy took her china teacup and saucer out of the cupboard and a mug for Bert, while she waited for the kettle to boil, she didn't know what to think. Apart from the few hours Bert had spent in the yard a couple of weeks earlier, this was the first time since he'd got home that Nancy had seen him do anything with Billy and Linda.

Somewhat discombobulated, Nancy wandered into the pantry, a thousand thoughts spinning round her mind, to retrieve the milk jug from the cold stone. *At least the kids are happy*, she thought to herself, but the moment of elation was quickly superseded by the overwhelming worry Bert might suddenly withdraw into himself and leave them feeling utterly bewildered all over again. *Please don't hurt them*, Nancy silently willed, as she poured the scalding water into the teapot, before carrying everything over to the table.

'Who would like a biscuit?' Nancy asked, carefully placing the tray down.

'Me!' Billy exclaimed. 'I'm starvin'.'

'Of course you are.' Nancy laughed, grateful to her son for his innocent ability to make everything feel so normal. 'You'll be pleased to know I picked some sausages up at Oliver's on the way home, so it's your favourite for tea too.'

'With mashed potato?'

'Yes!'

Turning to Linda, Nancy asked, 'Would you like a biscuit?'

'Yes please, Mummy.'

'Bert?'

'Why not? I am a bit peckish.'

'Have you eaten today?' Nancy asked instinctively, before she had time to stop herself.

But instead of snapping at her, resenting Nancy's naturally caring personality, he shook his head guiltily. 'Not since this morning.'

'Aw well,' Nancy said as lightly as possible, as she fetched the biscuit tin to the table. 'It's a good job I have a hearty tea planned.'

'Why don't you sit down for a bit?' Bert suggested. 'You have been cooking and serving up other peoples' dinners all day.'

Nancy didn't argue, worried the first wrong word would send Bert back to his dark mood.

For the next twenty minutes Nancy sat with her family chatting about their day and it was as if the war had never even started. Billy was full of jubilant tales about how he and Joe had conquered a few other lads on the street in a marble contest, while Linda and Alice had contented themselves playing schools, roping in Little Georgie to be their pupil, alongside their collection of dolls.

'It sounds like you've all had a wonderful day.' Nancy smiled.

'Can we do the same tomorrow, Mummy?' Linda asked. 'Georgie still needs to learn his alphabet.'

'I'm sure you can. And talking of school, you only have this week left before you go back.'

'Urgh. That's rubbish,' Billy groaned. 'Do we have to go back?'

'Of course you do.' Nancy laughed. 'How else are you going to grow up to be the greatest aircraft designer?'

'I reckon I could teach myself.'

'Good try, but it's back to school come what may next Monday.'

With that Billy successfully glided his latest paper aeroplane across the kitchen, as if to prove his own point.

Nancy, never able to get cross at her lovable little boy, suppressed an amused smile as she reached across the table and ruffled his thick mop of brown hair.

Then looking at Linda, who had her head bent over a piece of paper, a brown coloured pencil in one hand as she drew something with the other, Nancy asked, 'What's that you are drawing, poppet?'

'It's our family picture.'

'Can I see?'

Linda looked slightly hesitant.

'What is it, luv? Are you not finished?'

'Sort of.'

'Is it a surprise?' Nancy prompted.

'Not really.'

'You don't have to show us if you don't want to.'

'It's not that,' Linda whispered, her cheeks turning pink.

'What is it then, poppet?'

'It's a special wish.'

Nancy and Bert instinctively glanced at one another; something in their daughter's tone was causing them to question if everything was all right.

'Is it a *secret* special wish?' Nancy asked kindly.

Linda looked from her mum to her dad, frown marks appearing on her forehead, as she ever so slightly nodded her head up and down, then as if unsure, shook it from side to side.

'You can tell us,' Nancy encouraged. 'But only if you want to.'

Linda didn't say a word. Instead, she slowly lifted up the drawing she had been so quietly and diligently working on.

At first glance, Nancy couldn't spot what was worrying Linda. Her drawing, of the four of them, all stood in line holding hands, was no different to all the ones she'd sent to Bert while he'd been away.

'It's lovely, sweetheart,' she praised. 'But what's the special wish? I don't think Mummy understands.'

Linda's bottom lip began to tremble, and her eyes filled with tears.

'Oh, poppet. What is it?' Nancy asked, rushing to her daughter's side. Dropping her meticulously created drawing onto the table, Linda wrapped her arms around Nancy's waist and flopped her head onto her mum's chest.

'Now, now. Whatever it is, it can't be that bad. Why don't you tell me what's got you in such a state?'

But instead of revealing what was bothering her, Linda sunk deeper into her mum's arms, her tiny little shoulders shuddering as she sobbed. Nancy knew from experience there was no point in trying to stop her daughter's tears. Whatever it was, she needed to get it out of her system and only then would she be happy to disclose what was upsetting her.

Bewildered, Billy looked at his sister. He'd never been able to understand what got Linda in such a state. 'Is it because I didn't make you a paper aeroplane? I'll do you one now if you promise to stop crying. I'll make it a good one.'

Linda furiously shook her head, her mop of curls swishing from side to side down her back.

'I don't think it's that, soldier,' Bert commented, concern etched across his gaunt face.

Nancy looked quizzically at her husband, silently observing him. But like his distraught daughter, Bert couldn't speak. The weight of the world on his shoulders, he momentarily closed his eyes, knowing, despite how difficult he was finding life, he had to try to make his sweet-natured little girl feel better.

'Poppet,' Bert whispered, using the pet name he had adopted for Linda the day she was born.

The comforting sound of her dad's voice caused Linda to lift her head slightly.

'Why don't you come and sit on my knee?'

'It's poorly,' she muttered, in between the tears.

'I've got another,' Bert joked.

Nancy was watching her husband carefully, not quite sure what to think. A glimmer of hope started to increase, that her old Bert was re-emerging. This was the first time he'd laughed about his injury. Could her dependable husband really be resurfacing?

Linda slowly extracted herself from her mum, her little face now red and blotchy from crying and her eyes swollen and puffy.

'Come and sit with your old dad,' Bert gently encouraged, holding his arms out wide.

Linda looked at her mum for reassurance. Nancy silently nodded, still on tenterhooks, praying Bert did what was needed to pacify their highly sensitive little girl.

Linda nudged over from the chair she had been sat on to Bert's good knee. The feeling unfamiliar after months of her daddy being away, Linda sat bolt upright, her back as straight as a rod and her hands neatly placed on her knee.

'Shall I tell you my little secret?' Bert asked his anxious daughter, who looked as though she had been ordered to go and sit with a stranger, as opposed to her own father.

'Okay,' Linda whispered, a mixture of nerves and curiosity. She wasn't the only one. Nancy was also intrigued by what Bert was about to say.

Placing an arm around his daughter's back, Bert took hold of one of Linda's hands with his own and began, 'I think you and I have made the same secret wish.'

Linda's eyes were suddenly wide open, her interest piqued.

'Why haven't I got a secret?' Billy interrupted. 'I don't want to be the odd one out,' he added.

'Billy!' Nancy softly berated her son, knowing he didn't really have a jealous bone in his body. 'Let your daddy finish.'

'It's all right, soldier,' Bert said kindly. 'I have a funny feeling; we might all have the same wish.'

Nancy flinched, the unexpected words catching her by surprise. Still too apprehensive to question Bert, she remained silent, nervously biting the inside of her bottom lip.

'Do we?' Billy asked, confused by all the cryptic statements.

'I think so.'

'What is it then?'

Bert rubbed his daughter's fingers as he held her hand, and continued, 'I think your little sister just wants us all to be happy and things to be like they used to be.'

'You knew,' Linda exclaimed, her face a picture of delighted astonishment.

'It's what I've always wanted,' Bert confessed. 'I've just not been very good at talking about how I feel.'

'Oh, Bert,' Nancy gasped, putting her hand to her mouth, the tears that had been pooling in the bottom of her eyes now finding an escape route through the corners and trickling down her cheeks.

'I'm sorry,' her husband solemnly replied. 'I realize I haven't been a barrel of laughs since I got home, but I promise I'll try harder. Can you forgive me?'

'Of course I will.' And with that, she sat down in what had been Linda's chair and threw her arms around Bert, their daughter sandwiched in the middle.

'Hey!' Billy protested. 'What about me?'

'Come here, soldier.' Bert beckoned with his free hand, ushering his son over, and as Billy joined them, the whole family encased themselves in each other's arms, the feeling of love enveloping them in an invisible bond, knitting them back together.

After tea, Billy and Linda nipped into the yard to play with Doris's kids while Nancy wiped up the pots.

'Come and sit down,' Bert insisted. 'There's something else I want to tell you.'

Sensing Nancy's panic, Bert added, 'It's good news. Well, at least I think it is.'

Nancy sat down next to Bert at the table. 'What is it?'

'I've been doing some thinking and I think I have found a way to pull myself out of this horribly dark mess I'm in.'

'Really?'

'Yes. When I was chatting to Frank last week, he mentioned the Home Guard were looking for volunteers.'

'The Home Guard?' Nancy asked. She'd heard talk of the local defence unit at the factory and the fact they had a base in Sheffield. Nancy didn't know an awful lot more about them, apart from the fact they had been established to defend key areas.

'They are looking for ex-soldiers,' Bert explained.

'Ex-soldiers?'

'I haven't had official notice yet, but I can't see how the army will have me back. This leg has taken a hammering and I'm pretty sure I will be deemed medically unfit.'

'Bert. I'm sorry,' Nancy said, reaching over to place her hand on her husband's.

'I thought you would be relieved,' he joked, half-chuckling.

'Sorry. Well, yes. I suppose I am. It's just I know how much it meant to you to go and do your bit.'

'It did. It still does, and I've been feeling low not knowing what I was going to do but hopefully my skills can be put to good use here.'

'I just want you to be happy and have the old Bert back that we all love so much,' Nancy said.

'I know,' Bert whispered, edging forward on his chair so he was closer to his wife. 'And I promise from this very moment, I'm going to work harder at getting better.'

Nancy pulled her chair so it was touching Bert's and nestled her head into her husband's chest, the thought of him staying close by filling her with a sense of relief. For the first time in a year, she felt her shoulders relax and all the tension she had been holding inside her dissipate. Her emotions taking over, causing a stream of tears to flow unbidden down her cheeks, soaking Bert's blue cotton shirt.

Bert didn't stop her, knowing his wife had been putting on a brave face since he got back, and he had made her life a misery.

A few minutes passed before Nancy sat up, pulling a hankie from the pocket in her apron. 'I'm sorry,' she gasped. 'I didn't mean to get myself in such a tizz. I'm just so happy.'

'Good.' Bert grinned, brushing aside Nancy's riot of blonde curls and popping a kiss on her forehead.

'Just promise one thing,' Nancy said.

'Anything.'

Nervously, Nancy bit her lip.

'What is it?' Bert insisted.

'That you will start sleeping in our bed again.' Even as the words left her mouth, Nancy's cheeks burnt pink and for a moment she felt like the shy teenager she had been all those years ago when she and Bert had first started courting.

Sensing his wife's fear of rejection, Bert took Nancy's face in his hands and lovingly pulled her lips to his, Nancy melting into the tender embrace.

Bert grinned when they finally parted. 'Try to keep me away.'

For weeks she'd craved to hear that her husband still desired her, after beginning to believe Bert didn't even want to be home. 'Oh, Bert. You have made me the happiest woman alive!'

Chapter 29

Friday, 30 August 1940

'My round and I'm not having any arguments,' Nancy insisted as the gang of workers took up their usual spot in The Welly.

'Are you sure?' Dolly asked, aware of how tight money was for everyone.

'It's only a few drinks, and it's the very least I can do after how much you have all helped me,' Nancy insisted. 'But you can help me carry them all over to the table if you like?'

'I think I can manage that!'

A few minutes later, the group of friends were all sat round a table, clinking glasses.

'I'm so glad you could make it,' Betty said, turning to Nancy. 'I feel like we haven't had a catch-up for a week or so.'

'I know. I'm sorry. It's been manic in the canteen. None of us have stopped for a minute.'

'You can say that again, luv,' Josie interjected, taking a sip of half a shandy.

'You've both worked like troopers,' Dolly applauded. 'I'd have been lost without the pair of you this week.'

'Team effort,' Josie said, clinking glasses with Dolly and Nancy. 'I have to say we are going to miss you going back onto the cranes next week.'

'I'm going to miss you both too.' Nancy nodded. 'But I guess I had to go back at some point.' Feeling the strongest and happiest she had in months, Nancy had told Frank a few days earlier she was ready to return to her old job. 'But I better get some sleep this weekend, otherwise I'll be fit for nothing.'

'After that flamin' air raid last night, I'm amazed any of us are managing to keep our eyes open,' Dolly interjected.

'Archie was telling me it was the worst one yet,' Patty added.

'Was anyone hurt?' Nancy asked. Bert had still buried his head in his hands when they got to the communal shelter, but on the way home he'd held Linda's hand, reassuring her they were all safe. And when they'd got the kids into bed, he had held Nancy in his arms when they finally turned in for the night.

'Worse than that,' Patty answered. 'He says he heard from other wardens a handful of people died and there was quite a few injured and hundreds have been left homeless. Apparently one family woke up to find their bed on fire.'

'That's awful,' Nancy gasped, silently thanking God she hadn't suggested they all go in the cellar.

'I know,' Patty agreed. 'Do yer reckon the Germans were

heading for the steelworks? The houses that were damaged weren't a million miles from here.'

'It would make sense,' Dolly confirmed. 'They're bound to know we are making weapons to try to destroy them.'

'It doesn't 'alf put you on edge, doesn't it?' Patty sighed.

'It does, luv. I have to say, this war feels a bit too close to home now for my liking.'

There was a momentary silence as a sense of realization filtered through. Sheffield being attacked had brought home the fact no one was safe from Hitler's tirade.

'I hate this chuffin' war,' Patty finally exclaimed.

'Don't we all, duck,' Dolly concurred. 'Did Archie hear anything else?'

'Only that they have had to set up a few emergency centres in schools for the hundreds whose houses have been destroyed.'

'That's terrible,' Betty said. 'It must have been a tough night for Archie. I bet you were out of your mind, weren't you?'

'Not 'alf. My heart was in m' mouth. I was reyt pleased to see him this morning. I can't get to sleep after a raid, worrying about him, hence why I look like a dog's dinner today. I've got bags under m' eyes down to m' chin. Hitler is making me look at least ten years older.'

'Oh Patty!' Hattie reprimanded. 'I really think that's the least of your worries.'

'Well, I don't want Archie looking elsewhere . . .'

'Stop it,' Hattie reproached, more firmly. 'That boy loves

the bones of you, and I can't imagine he's too worried about whether you have got bags under your eyes or not.'

'Okay. Okay. I'll stop moaning.' Patty reluctantly succumbed, even if she was still quietly miffed by how puffy her skin looked.

Shaking her head in mock frustration, Hattie turned to Nancy. 'How's your Bert getting on? Any better?'

'A little bit,' Nancy said, putting her glass of shandy on the table. 'I can't say he's back to normal, far from it, but he's definitely better than he was.'

'Tell them about Tuesday,' Dolly encouraged.

For the next few minutes, Nancy recalled how she'd got home from work a few nights earlier to find Bert sat with both the kids, and how they'd all hugged after Linda's picture revealed all she wanted was everyone to be happy again, like they used to be.

'Goodness,' Betty whispered, when Nancy had finished. 'I can feel myself filling up. You must have been overwrought.'

'I was rather. I'd started to wonder if Bert would ever show any signs of getting better.'

'Did you manage to talk afterwards, once the kids were in bed, about how he's feeling?' Hattie asked.

'Yes. He's thinking of joining the Home Guard. I think it might be just what he needs and will give him a purpose again.'

'That's brilliant,' Betty said. 'And your Billy and Linda must have been over the moon?'

'They are. It's early days but, dare I say it, it's starting to feel like they have got their old daddy back.'

'How's he been since?' Hattie asked tentatively.

'Up and down. He's been chattier and has started having the kids with him during the day, instead of them going to Doris's. His sense of humour is even returning, but he still hasn't told me what happened in France.'

'That's lovely things are returning to some form of normality,' Betty replied. 'And I'm sure in time, Bert will open up.'

'I hope so but, as you say, I am pleased things are getting easier. He's still been having terrible nightmares, though, and shouts out in his sleep. I've had to wake him up a few times and he's always really bewildered when he comes round. It takes him a few minutes to realize where he. He's obviously reliving whatever he went through while he was in France – he looks terrified. I might be wrong, but I think Bert sees it as a sign of weakness and is a bit embarrassed.'

'It's very hard but your Bert has got nothing to feel embarrassed about,' Dolly sympathized. 'Whatever our lads went through, they deserve a medal for it.'

'I agree, but I don't want to push him, even though I hate the fact he still can't talk to me about it.'

'That must feel hard,' Betty empathized.

'It is, but it's not all bad. I've got to keep reminding myself that at least things are moving in the right direction, and he insisted I came out for a drink tonight.'

'That is a good sign,' Hattie agreed. 'I don't think my

dad ever got that far and look where he is now. He'd never have let my mum go out for a drink with her friends.'

'I'm sorry,' Nancy said. 'I shouldn't be moaning on.'

'You're not at all!' Betty chastised.

'I didn't mean to make you feel like you were,' Hattie added. 'I suppose, I just want you and Bert to have a happier ending than my parents. My poor mum has led a dog's life with my dad, and I can't see anything ever changing now. At least your Bert is trying. That can only be a good thing.'

'I hope so, and now I'm sorry. Your mum has had it really tough.'

'She has,' Hattie agreed. 'And I really can't see an end to it. She'll never leave him. He's left her feeling worthless and tells her repeatedly no one else would ever want her.'

'I'm sorry, I didn't realize,' Patty said, feeling ashamed that she'd never once asked her best friend about how tough things were at home. Hadn't her mum said to her a million times to think a bit more about her friends? Had she really been that blind to her friend's circumstances?

'Don't be. It's probably my fault. I don't like talking about it as it either upsets me or makes me angry, and I know neither of those things will help Mum.'

'Oh, duck,' Dolly interjected, flashbacks to her own turbulent marriage flashing before her eyes. 'Believe me, I know how hard it is, but don't try to cope with this on your own. I promise you it's too hard and we will always be here for you.'

'Thanks, Dolly. I do appreciate it and I promise I'm all

right. Working at Vickers and coming out for the odd drink is a huge help in itself.'

'Good but just remember, if you need a chin wag, you can come and have a cuppa with me anytime. There's always a brew on the go.'

'I'll definitely take you up on that if I need to.'

'And Hattie,' Patty said, overridden with guilt. 'Let's do more together.'

'That would be lovely.' Hattie smiled. 'I'll never say no to tea and cake.'

'I'll make sure we do it more often,' Patty promised, smiling at her friend as she silently vowed to make a concerted effort to think more about other people.

'Talking of tea and cake,' Betty interjected, 'I hope you are all looking forward to Sunday? Ivy's kitchen looks like a bakery at the moment. I'm sure there is enough cake to feed the entire British army.'

'It will be lovely,' Daisy said, who had been sat quietly as she listened to Hattie. She's always sensed something was bothering her, as she was quieter than most of the turners they worked with, but had just assumed she was missing her John, which must have only exacerbated how hard life felt. 'Is it still okay to bring my sisters along?'

'Absolutely!' Betty enthused. 'The more the merrier. The weather looks glorious, so I should imagine we will be overflowing into the garden. Ivy has insisted everyone brings their families. She just wants to have an end-of-summer get-together and use up the bumper crop of veggies we've had.'

'Is there anything we can do to help?' Dolly asked. 'I've got some free time tomorrow after I finish in the canteen. I can rustle up a couple of dishes if it would help?'

'That's ever so good of you, but I think she has it all under control. She's recruited her friend, Winnie, and a couple of others. They have been chopping veg, making pastries, cakes and buns all week. Every time I walk in the kitchen it's like a conveyor belt of cooking. Poor Frank has spent his evenings pulling up carrots, beetroot, and potatoes for Ivy to magically turn into one dish after another. So please, just come and relax, and don't forget to bring Millie and Lucy too. There will be plenty of little ones for them to play with.'

'We'll get Archie to entertain the kids again,' Patty said. 'He was like the Pied Piper at Linda's birthday party.'

'Gosh, he was, wasn't he?' Nancy laughed, taking a sip of her drink. 'Bert might not be much help to Archie, but he is really looking forward to meeting everyone.'

'I'm sure Archie will manage just fine!' Patty insisted.

'You just come and relax,' Betty added. 'Bert and Frank will no doubt have a good natter.'

'That's true and I know he's grateful to Patty's dad, Bill. He has been a godsend keeping him calm down the shelter every time those flamin' sirens start.'

'Let's keep everything crossed Hitler doesn't decide to send his chuffin' planes over on Sunday,' Patty exclaimed. 'It will just be my . . .' But she stopped herself mid-sentence, quickly remembering the promise she'd made less than five minutes ago to stop thinking about herself, and said instead, 'Everyone could do with a little celebration and after all the work Ivy has put in, Jerry best not appear.'

'Let him try!' Dolly warned. 'And he won't chuffin' know what's hit him!'

'I'll drink to that,' Patty enthused merrily, raising her glass of pale ale in the air. She was quickly joined by the rest of the group, and an enthusiastic chorus of 'cheers' was heard across The Welly as the women clinked glasses at the thought of the weekend ahead.

Chapter 30

'Come in. Come in.' Ivy smiled, welcoming her steady flow of guests through the front door of her Collinson Street home. For the last thirty minutes, friends had arrived in droves, the house and garden now awash with lively chatter.

'I'm so glad you could make it,' Ivy told Hattie as she ushered her onto the black and white tiles of the hallway.

'Thank you for inviting me. It's so kind of you.'

'Not at all. Now come on in. I think Patty is in the garden with Archie and the children, and Nancy is insisting on making everyone a cup of tea.'

'I don't think she knows how to stop!'

'You could be right there,' Ivy agreed.

'Hatts! You made it,' came Patty's familiar trill from the end of the hallway. 'Come and rescue me. I'm being surrounded by overexcited children. I've just managed to escape and left Archie heading up a game of hide-and-seek. Our Tom Tom is trying to hide in the hen's hutch and Nancy's Billy and his pal, Joe, were taking cover behind the blackberry bush. No doubt they will come out covered in purple blotches and stuffing their faces.'

'Poor Archie.' Hattie laughed as Patty led her into the kitchen, which was full to bursting with women from the factory, a handful of Ivy's friends and a whole host of dishes. Betty hadn't been exaggerating when she'd said her landlady had cooked enough to feed an entire army.

There were at least three quiches, countless plates of egg and cress sandwiches, a tantalizing tray of scones and several bowls of salad, boasting bright pink radishes, cherry red tomatoes and emerald green shelled broad beans.

'Hattie,' Dolly beamed, wrapping her arms around the younger woman, 'you got here, duck. I was getting worried you might not make it. Is everything okay at home?'

'Sorry. Nothing like that. My dad is actually still in bed. I tried to persuade Mum to come with me, but she was adamant she needed to stay at home and make Dad his Sunday dinner.'

'Are you okay, duck?'

'Actually, I really am.'

'Hey. Has something happened?' Patty asked, as it dawned on her that Hattie looked the happiest she had in months.

'It has actually.'

'What?' Patty shrilled, slightly louder than she'd intended.

'Give the lass a chance,' Dolly interjected. 'She's only just walked through the door.'

By now, everyone had turned around to face Hattie,

whose cheeks were turning as red as the bowls of beetroot Ivy had so meticulously sliced.

'Honestly, everything is fine. I just had some good news from John.'

'I'd say it's more than good news from the look on your face,' Patty teased. 'You look like that cat that's had all the cream.'

Patty's rather impatient remonstrations had gathered the attention of the men who had been outside but were now standing by the kitchen door that led out into the garden.

'I think you better tell us, duck,' Dolly gently encouraged. 'Before Patty, here, explodes!'

Hattie looked around the now very crowded room. Every pair of eyes was looking straight back at her expectantly. She hadn't meant to cause such a fuss, or inadvertently become the centre of attention. Hattie had simply intended to tell Patty her good news discreetly when they had a quiet moment together, but in her usual overexcited way, her exuberant best friend had put short shrift to that.

'I didn't mean to overtake the occasion. It's just that John has said he has got a weekend's leave next month and he's told me to book the register office.'

'You're getting married next month?' Patty shrieked.

'I think so.' Hattie giggled, reality dawning on her.

'That's amazing!' Patty said, jumping in the air, before throwing her arms around Hattie. 'And I'll be your maid of honour!'

'Patty!' Archie berated, in horror, yet again.

'Sorry. I'm just so excited.'

'Well, I definitely think that calls for a toast,' Ivy announced. 'Frank, there's some brandy and port in the cabinet in the front room. Would you mind bringing them through?'

'It would be my pleasure! It's about time we all had something to smile about.'

As drinks were poured and handed out, Hattie was surrounded by her friends, who all took delight in offering their congratulations.

'You deserve this, duck.' Dolly beamed, kissing Hattie on the cheek.

'You really do,' Betty enthused. 'I'm so happy for you.'

'After this summer. I couldn't be more delighted for you,' Nancy added. 'Enjoy every moment. It's a special time.'

'Thank you. I'll try to.' Hattie smiled. 'It really was a lovely surprise.'

'Right!' Frank said, clearing his throat, garnering everyone's attention. 'A toast. To Hattie.'

'To Hattie,' came the raucous and happy response, as arms were raised and glasses charged.

'Thank you.' Hattie cherished the moment, as she took in the sheer excitement and joy that was being so generously bestowed upon her. She'd never imagined how welcome she would be made to feel by Patty's friends at Vickers, but they had taken her under their wing when she'd needed it the most. *I really am very lucky*, she thought to herself, as the rounds of heartfelt congratulations and hugs continued.

'You are all so kind.' She blushed as once again she was enveloped in good wishes.

Nancy happily watched, recalling only too clearly how deliriously happy she had been on the day Bert had proposed.

'Penny for them.'

As Nancy turned round, Bert, leaning on his wooden walking stick for support, was facing her. 'I was just reminiscing.'

'Thought you might have been.'

'You know me too well.'

'Comes with the territory.'

'I suppose it does. Have you got a drink?'

'I wondered if we could have a little chat first. Just you and me.'

Nancy looked at her husband, his pale face tinged with emotion. 'I think the front room is empty.'

As the rest of the guests chatted to one another, Nancy and Bert quietly made their way through the kitchen, and down the hallway.

Bert carefully lowered himself onto the polished brown Chesterfield couch and gestured to Nancy. 'Come and sit next to me.'

She didn't hesitate, the much-missed affection in Bert's voice acting as a magnet.

'I'm sorry,' Bert said, taking his wife's hand in his.

'What's brought this on?'

'Oh, lots of things. Hearing Hattie announce she is

getting married. Remembering when I proposed to you. Thinking of how you have held our family together while I've been away. Your infallible patience since I got home. So many things.'

'As I've said a million times, I just want you to be happy,' Nancy said.

'I know,' Bert whispered, gently pulling his wife into his chest.

'I have one more request if that's okay?' Nancy asked tentatively.

'Tell me.'

'When you feel ready, will you try to talk to me about France? I hate the idea of you having so much trapped in your head.'

'I promise I'll do my best.' Bert nodded. 'I've wanted to talk to you but every time I try, a blackness comes over me and the words get stuck in my throat, and I can't get them out.'

'I want to say I understand, but I know I never really can, but I'm here for you when you feel able to talk.'

Before Bert had a chance to answer, the front-room door swung open. 'Mummy. Daddy. There you are. I've been looking for you everywhere,' Linda exclaimed. 'Ivy says we can have some dinner. Will you come and help me?'

'Of course, poppet,' Nancy and Bert said in unison, then turning to one another and laughing, the closest they had felt as a couple in months.

Each holding one of Linda's hands, Bert and Nancy

ushered their daughter into the kitchen, where an orderly queue had formed for the food, with an eager, and no doubt starving, Billy and Joe right at the front, their eyes nearly popping out of their heads.

As Nancy peered around at her friends, all of them happily chatting away, drinks in one hand and smiles adorning their faces, a sense of calm filled her. This war was far from over but she had her family by her side, and the promise of Bert staying on home ground filled her with untold joy. Patty and Archie were back to being love's young dream after his grand birthday gesture, and Betty, although concerned about her beloved William, was, as ever, throwing herself into one project after another. But the best news had to be that Hattie, who deserved every bit of happiness coming her way, was getting married to the man of her dreams. For today at least, Hitler had allowed them all to celebrate without any unwanted interruptions. There might be a rocky road ahead, but Nancy felt sure that somehow, they would get through whatever this senseless war threw at them together.

Author's Note

I started the Steel Girls series after spending two years researching the true-life stories of the women who worked in the factories which lined the River Don during World War Two. Their tales of hardship, strength and resilience left me humbled and in complete admiration of what this tremendous generation endured.

Many were mums or young girls, with no experience of what it was like to be employed in one of the ginormous windowless factories, which were described on more than one occasion as entering 'hell on earth.' The deafening, ear-splitting cacophony of noise mixed with the perilously dangerous but accepted working conditions, alongside the relentless and exhaustingly long shifts, was a huge culture shock for so many of the women who walked through those factory doors for the first time.

Those who had young children had no choice but to hand their precious sons and daughters over to grandparents or leave them in the care of older siblings, some of them only just out of school themselves, but who were expected to grow up fast and also do their bit to help.

What struck me in the course of my research, though, was how little resistance was offered to this new arduous, strangely unfamiliar and frequently quite terrifying way of life. 'We were just doing what was needed,' was an all-too-common answer when I asked the women I had the pleasure of talking to, why they so eagerly took on the somewhat risky roles they volunteered for. 'We had no choice. It was what was needed to keep the factories going.' This is true, the foundries desperately needed workers, with so many of the opposite sex signing up to begin a 'new adventure'.

It soon became clear to me that this band of formidable, proud and hardworking Yorkshire women were not going to just stand by and let Hitler and his troops reap havoc across Europe and beyond, without them doing what they could to aid their husbands, bothers, sons and uncles, who were off fighting someone else's war.

Over and over again, I was left in complete awe of how much the women of Sheffield sacrificed, day in and day out, for six long years. It's hard for most of us to comprehend now what a difficult and seemingly never-ending length of time this was. As well as working night and day as crane drivers, turners, making camouflage netting or working next to a red hot and at times fatal Bessemer Converter, they were also terrified by the very realistic fear they may never see their loved ones ever again.

One lady, Kathleen Roberts, told me whenever a shooting star was seen going over a factory, it was a sign another soldier had fallen and a telegram bearing the bad news would be delivered soon afterwards. To live with that level of sheer terror, let alone cope with the ominous air-raid sirens that indicated the Luftwaffe could be on their way, is truly unimaginable. But this is the harsh and constant reality which thousands of women lived with across Sheffield.

It wasn't all doom and gloom though. The one thing that struck a chord with me while talking to the women and their families was the way in which they counteracted the harshness life had thrown at them. They created unbreakable bonds with their new female fellow workmates and a camaraderie which even Hitler himself couldn't break. In a determined bid to 'keep up morale', our feisty factory sisters focused on safeguarding a warm community spirit to keep them all going when times got hard. Friendships were created in the most unlikely of circumstances, often among women who would never normally mix, lipsticks were snapped in half and divided between colleagues, and a single wedding dress could be worn a dozen times to ensure a Sheffield bride didn't walk down the aisle without looking her absolute best. It really was the era of sharing what you had with your neighbour and never letting someone in need go without.

Of course, it would be easy to romanticise this period, or hale it as 'the good old days', but the reality is it wasn't that either. It was simply a case of facing head-on the atrocities life dealt and getting on with it as best you could. Some had it easier than others but no matter what, all these women woke up in September 1939 to a new life and somehow managed to take it in their stride, but they really didn't have much choice. With no savings to fall back on to tide them over, or a welfare state to lighten the load, it was a case of 'cracking on' and doing what was needed.

In 2009, Kathleen Roberts rang the *Sheffield Star* and asked why she and others like her, who had sacrificed so much of their lives, had never been thanked, after watching a TV show on the Land Girls. What started as a frustrated phone call, developed into a campaign by the local paper to ensure the women of the city who had worked day and night in the steel works, were finally recognised. Kathleen, alongside Kit Sollitt, Dorothy Slingsby and Ruby Gascoigne, representing this whole generation of women, were whisked down to London to be personally thanked by the then Prime Minister, Gordon Brown. Afterwards a grassroots campaign was launched by the *Sheffield Star* to fundraise for a statue representing the female steelworkers to be commissioned and erected in Barker's Pool, in the city centre, directly outside the dance they would often visit on a Saturday, to escape the drudgery of their lives.

In June 2016, the larger-than-life bronze statue, paid for entirely by the people of Sheffield, was unveiled to the sheer and rapturous delight of the still surviving women of steel, their contribution to the war effort now eternally immortalised.

Although the characters in this book are entirely fictional, their experiences a result of my creative imagination having a bit of fun with itself, the truth is every page is based on the interviews I conducted, the factual books I've read from the period and the ongoing research I'm still undertaking. I hope within my books, I can also help keep this generation's memory alive. I interviewed women who flew up crane ladders, others who were scared witless and many who remember only too clearly what it was like to live in absolute poverty, the talisman a regular visitor to their door. So, despite the poetic creation of my feisty *Steel Girls*, I can envisage their real-life counterparts, hear their voices and recall their experiences – the reality of it is, I simply couldn't make the raw bones of some of these stories up. Only after hearing first-hand how terrifying it was to be hauled up to the dizzy heights of the factory heavens in a crane cab or listen to the raw heartbreak of not knowing if your husband was dead or alive in a faraway country, hundreds of miles from home, could I put pen to paper and serve our real women of steel, the justice they rightfully deserve.

Acknowledgements

Firstly, I would like to thank every female steelworker of the First and Second World Wars and their family members, who over the course of the last four years have so generously given up their time to talk to me, recalled memories and answered my endless questions. Without these women, the Steel Girls series would not be possible. Although the characters are fictional, they are created from the true-life stories that have been shared with me. I am also so grateful to the women and their relatives for their ongoing and tremendous support, which means so much. At every step of the way, they have been my biggest cheerleaders, and for that I will be forever grateful.

I am indebted to every author, historian, journalist and social commentator who enabled me to look at this period of time in extra detail, allowing me to understand the wider issues and feelings of the women who lived and worked through World War Two, creating a new way of life in the most troubled and hardest of times.

I must say a huge thank you to the fabulous Sylvia Jones, who's own 'little nannan', Ada Clarke, was a Woman of

Steel. Sylvia has become my 'go to' expert on anything Attercliffe-based. She never fails to come up with the details when I ask her something specific or something utterly random, at all hours of the day and night, about the area the women of these books worked, and so many lived in. Sylvia took me on a wonderful walking tour of the area, pointing out all the old shops, picture houses and pubs, so I could envisage all these landmarks, which was utterly invaluable.

I'd like to add my thanks to the late Dick Starkey, who recorded his wartime RAF memories in his book, *A Lancaster Pilot's Impression on Germany*, which I have read from cover to cover, after another reader, Sandra Kay, pointed me to it. My character, William, is also training to be a Lancaster pilot, and having a first-hand account to refer to has been invaluable. Reading Walter Lord's *The Miracle of Dunkirk* helped me to understand the profound, and longlasting, impact this period of the Second World War had on the Allied troops involved, as well as the complexities of the military operation. I am also very grateful to Margaret Drinkall, who penned *The Story of Sheffield At War, 1939 to 1945*, for his collection of accounts and historical notes, which I have referred to when writing this book.

I must also say how grateful I am to every book blogger who has been kind enough to support me.

Enormous thanks must be given to my agents at

Northbank Talent Management, who not only believed in me, but have continually supported me.

I must also offer the greatest of thanks to my extremely dedicated editor, Katie Seaman at HQ Stories, without whom the Steel Girls series would never have seen the light of day. Not only did Katie believe in me from the very start, when the Steel Girls was just an idea, but as I have said many times, has become the wisest and kindest of sounding boards whenever I need a little natter or a brainstorm. Katie's unfaltering and enthusiastic passion for the Steel Girls is infectious. I feel incredibly lucky to be blessed with such a dedicated editor. Our chats around character development and plots (or plot gaps!) never feel arduous or chore-like. When I can't see where a storyline is going, Katie is always there to talk it through. It's the epitome of a lovely chat over a cup of Yorkshire tea, while we bash out ideas until they come to life.

Alongside Katie at HQ Stories, I must offer my sincere thanks to my copyeditor Eldes Tran. A huge thanks to Anna Sikorska for designing the most fitting and beautiful of covers and I'd also like to extend my gratitude to Hanako Peace for her marketing skills and to Angela Thomson in sales, for getting this book on actual shelves.

I am so grateful to each and every one of my family members and truly amazing friends, who have offered unfaltering support in writing the book. My good friend and long-suffering running mate, Leanne Hawkes, who has very patiently lived every one of my books with me, listening to me three times a week as we pound the hills of Millhouse Green, and kept me sane throughout. I think at least two of my characters are named after members of her family – including Ivy (Leanne's lovely mum and now Betty's landlady), which we decided on during one very particular rainy and windy run. I must also thank Ann Cusack for offering relentless support and being the greatest friend anyone could ever wish for.

I would also like to say the biggest of thank yous to the truly amazing and quite frankly fabulous group of people I work with at The University of Sheffield, who aren't simply colleagues but the greatest of friends too.

I cannot end this passage of gratitude without saying thank you to my husband, Iain, who once again, has never once moaned about me turning my laptop on at least four evenings a week to make sure I reach my word count and is there with a ginormous and quite frankly much needed cup of coffee every morning – he knows I'm pretty grumpy without it. As for our two amazing children, Archie and Tilly, they are simply the best, even if my now teenage son rolls his eyes when I mention anything that doesn't relate to ice hockey. I sincerely hope I have instilled into them, that if you work hard enough for something, you can achieve your dreams, no matter how big or insurmountable they might feel.

Make sure you've read all the books in the heartwarming Steel Girls series

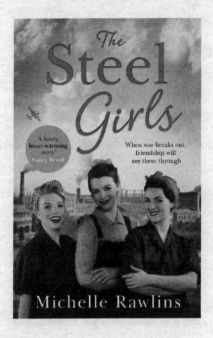

With war declared, these brave women will step up and do their bit for their county . . .

The Steel Girls start off as strangers but quickly forge an unbreakable bond of friendship as these feisty factory sisters vow to keep the foundry fires burning during wartime.

Don't miss this festive tale of courage and friendship on the Home Front

As the Steel Girls face their first Christmas at war, can they come together this winter?

In the harsh winter of 1939, our feisty factory sisters must rally around each other to find hope and comfort this Christmas season.

Catch up with the third heartwarming book in the Steel Girls series

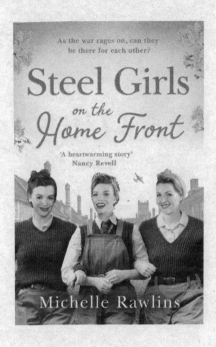

As the war rages on, can they be there for each other?

In spring 1940, the war is raging on but the Steel Girls find themselves fighting battles closer to home . . .